Praise for *USA TODAY* bestselling author

KASEY MICHAELS

"Kasey Michaels aims for the heart and never misses."
—#1 *New York Times* bestselling author Nora Roberts

"The historical elements…imbue the novel with powerful
realism that will keep readers coming back."
—*Publishers Weekly* on *A Midsummer Night's Sin*

"A poignant and highly satisfying read…
filled with simmering sensuality, subtle touches of repartee,
a hero out for revenge and a heroine ripe for adventure.
You'll enjoy the ride."
—*RT Book Reviews* on *How to Tame a Lady*

"Michaels's new Regency miniseries is a joy… You will
laugh and even shed a tear over this touching romance."
—*RT Book Reviews* on *How to Tempt a Duke*

"Michaels has done it again…
Witty dialogue peppers a plot full of delectable details
exposing the foibles and follies of the age."
—*Publishers Weekly* on *The Butler Did It* (starred review)

"Michaels can write everything
from a lighthearted romp to a far more serious-themed
romance. [She] has outdone herself."
—*RT Book Reviews* on *A Gentleman By Any Other Name*
(Top Pick)

"[A] hilarious spoof of society wedding rituals
wrapped around a sensual romance filled with crackling
dialogue reminiscent of *The Philadelphia Story*."
—*Publishers Weekly* on *Everything's Coming Up Rosie*

KASEY MICHAELS

MUCH ADO ABOUT ROGUES

Recycling programs
for this product may
not exist in your area.

ISBN-13: 978-0-373-77639-9

MUCH ADO ABOUT ROGUES

For questions and comments about the quality of this book
please contact us at Customer_eCare@Harlequin.ca.

® and TM are trademarks of the publisher. Trademarks indicated with
® are registered in the United States Patent and Trademark Office, the
Canadian Trade Marks Office and in other countries.

www.Harlequin.com

Printed in U.S.A.

Dear Reader,

It's always a bit sad for me when I have to say goodbye to beloved characters. But having been the one to set the Blackthorn brothers on their journeys in the first place, it was wonderful to watch them as they found their way to their destinations.

You see, with the Blackthorn brothers, as with any book I write, my "people" take over. They go where I never planned to send them, do things that surprise and even shock me, and say things that make me laugh and cry.

Jack Blackthorn and his Tess, for instance, kept me up nights worrying about them. These are two people who could very easily have become victims, were it not for their strong characters, their determination and the love they share…even when they're butting heads.

In all three books, *The Taming of the Rake* (Beau's book), *A Midsummer Night's Sin* (Puck's book) and *Much Ado About Rogues*, there are a lot of outside struggles, dangers to be met and defeated, problems to be solved. But the real stories between the covers are Beau and Puck and Jack, and the sort of men they are…the kind of men they become. And, most definitely, the women who dare to love them.

Happy reading!

Kasey Michaels

To Marcia Evanick,
one of the best friends a person could have,
a marvelous writer and truly the bravest lady I know.
I love you, Marci!

MUCH ADO ABOUT ROGUES

Speak low if you speak love.

—William Shakespeare
Much Ado About Nothing

PROLOGUE

DICKIE CARSTAIRS, pudgy of body and pleasantly vacant-eyed, stood a little too close to the yellow circle of lamplight across the street from the Duck and Wattle to remain undetected. That was Dickie's job, to be detected, and he performed this office with such brilliance that government clerk Miles Duncan was not only confident but smiling as he nipped out the back door of the inn whilst Dickie was so obviously watching the front.

The smile faded quickly as a firm hand clapped down on his shoulder even as a sharp tug on the satchel he carried relieved him of its burden. "Good evening, Mr. Duncan. Going somewhere? Mind if we join you?"

Miles Duncan did mind, but not for long, all his earthly cares forgotten as he slipped almost gracefully into the fetid puddle that had once been the contents of several chamber pots recently dumped from an upstairs window. Poor Miles Duncan, another victim of the violent crime rampant in certain quarters of London.

Will Browning calmly retrieved his knife from Duncan's mortal remains and wiped the blade on the deceased's coat. He then slid the weapon into the cuff of his boot before relieving the dead man of his purse and inferior garnet stickpin, to lend credence to the crime of robbery. "Jack? *Mind if we join you?* What a strange choice of words. Not where he just went if you don't mind, thank you."

Don John Blackthorn, best known as Black Jack, was already undoing the flap of the satchel, to assure himself the pilfered papers the prime minister had commissioned them to retrieve were inside. "Very well, Will. Next time you talk, and I'll wield the sticker."

"Ha! Isn't it just like you to want the fun for yourself."

Jack ignored the remark, knowing Will Browning employed his knife and sword without conscience or compunction. It was probably a good thing he'd found government service; otherwise, he'd have been hanged by now.

They were an odd trio of rogues. Dickie, third son of an earl, was socially inept, regarded as pleasant enough but rather dim, yet one of the bravest men Jack had ever met. Not just anyone would constantly set himself up as the most visible and vulnerable target. Dickie's was the public face that made it possible for the rest to work.

Will was the weapon. Handsome, wealthy, smooth, an impeccably dressed darling of the *ton,* and always ready with a pleasant word and a smile. His sense of right and wrong, however, was his own, and quite singular. There was a certain civilized *madness* about Will. If you knew you weren't quite a friend, you never wished to be his enemy.

And then there was Jack, the brains and nominal leader of the trio. Jack, who'd never quite felt at home anywhere. Bastard son of the Marquess of Blackthorn, he hadn't felt at home on the estate, with his brothers, or with the world in general. He was different, and he'd recognized that difference early in life. He had a fire deep inside him, a need that he couldn't articulate, let alone grasp. That had made him a wild, impulsive youth, and he'd learned life's lessons the hard way.

Finding work as one of the government's most trusted covert agents had fed the fire, for a time. Now he was growing tired of always being on the outside of life, the observer, never a real participant. Once, he'd thought he'd found the answer, a way to the unnameable acceptance he'd always been seeking, the one place where he knew he would fit. But then he'd lost his way, his purpose in living, and knew he could never get it back. Get her back. What he did now was merely exist from mission to mission.

"It's all there?" Will asked as Dickie joined them, both of them leaning in to see the contents Jack quickly began returning to the satchel.

"I wasn't made privy to an inventory, but there's enough here that Lord Liverpool should be satisfied," Jack answered noncommittally. "And more diligent about whom he trusts with the Crown's business in future. In any event, we'll be well recompensed for tonight's work, and that's what matters—correct, gentlemen?" He hesitated for a moment, and then pulled one of the pages back out of the packet when he saw a name he recognized. "Damn."

"Shouldn't be reading that, Jack," Dickie pointed out. "We know too much, we could end up like our friend here, and I don't much care for the neighborhood."

"He's not listening, Dickie," Will pointed out. "You're scowling more than usual, Jack. Is there a problem?"

Jack was still reading. "You could say that. It would seem the Marquis de Fontaine has gone missing."

"Really? Haven't heard that name in a while. Your mercenary mentor in the dark arts during the war, wasn't he? And then there was that business with you and his daughter. Tess, correct? You never said, but I'm assuming that ended badly."

"He doesn't talk about it, no," Dickie told Will quietly when Jack didn't answer, but only replaced the page and closed the satchel.

"Still, the war's over, more's the pity, or else we'd still be hunting adversaries more worthy of our time than overly ambitious clerks, and de Fontaine has been pensioned off, or whatever we do with mercenaries we no longer need. So what does Liverpool care if the fellow's taken a flit?"

Dickie carefully stepped over the late, overly ambitious Miles Duncan as Jack led the way out of the alley. "Old secrets or new, they're probably all the same to Liverpool, yes, Jack?"

"Governments never want to give up their secrets," Jack answered shortly. The mention of Tess, coming out of the blue along with seeing her father's name, had set off a cascade of memories he'd rather stay dammed up behind the stone wall he'd built for them in his brain.

"So what are they going to do about the missing marquis, Jack?" Will asked as they climbed into the unmarked coach waiting at the end of the alley.

"Find him," Jack said at last. "Liverpool's memorandum to his secretary concerns my next small project for the Crown. It has been decided that, since I know him best, I'm to be asked to find Sinjon."

"Liverpool wants to know what he might be up to since they set him out to pasture? That seems reasonable enough," Will said, settling back against the squabs.

"Yes, reasonable enough. Find him. Question him," Jack said, twisting the gold-and-onyx ring on his right index finger as the image of Tess's sad, beautiful face seemed to float in front of him inside the dark coach. "And then, for the good of king and country, eliminate him."

CHAPTER ONE

LADY THESSALY FONTENEAU sat perched on the window seat, her slim frame and riot of tumbling blond curls outlined by the sun shining through the windowpanes behind her.

Her long legs, encased in high, dark brown leather boots and tan buckskins, were bent at the knee, her heels pressed against a low stool shaped like a camel saddle. She was leaning slightly forward, her arms akimbo, her palms pressed against her thighs, her face in shadow. The white, full-sleeved lawn shirt she wore had been sewn for a larger frame, and rather billowed around her above the waistband, the deep V of the neck exposing the soft swell of breasts beneath the worn brown leather vest.

Just above her breasts hung the oval gold locket suspended from a thin golden chain. A pair of painted images were inside, one old, one newer, both painted by the marquis himself. The locket had hung from a black velvet ribbon until her father had pointed out that one should never wear a weapon in aid of the enemy: a thin chain will break, but a tightly knotted ribbon makes for a tolerable garrote.

She possessed the sort of classic beauty artists wept to paint. Aristocratic, finely boned. Gallic to the marrow. Yet with an air of sensuality about her, in those high cheekbones, that slim, straight nose, the wide, tempting mouth, those darkly lashed hazel eyes.

Those eyes, awash now with tears she refused to let fall.

"Where, Papa?" she breathed, surveying the shambles that was once the Marquis de Fontaine's neat study, now searched to within an inch of destroying it completely. Her anger, her frustration, her growing fear, it was all there in the aftermath of her latest search, evidence as damning to her as would be a bloody knife in her hand as she stood over a body. "There has to be something. You would have left me *something*."

Tess had instituted her search of the modest manor house a week ago, the day after her father's disappearance. She'd been slow, neat, methodical, as she'd been taught to be.

She'd begun with the servants, who either knew nothing or said nothing. You never knew with servants, where their loyalty truly stood, if anywhere. Her papa had never employed any of the staff for long, as familiarity invited a relaxation of one's guard; a paper carelessly left on the wrong side of a locked drawer, an unguarded word spoken at the table, with a servant still in the room. *Always assume you are among enemies,* he'd advised. *It's safer than relaxing with those you think friends.*

It had been a trusted servant who had betrayed her father all those long years ago, he'd told her, and the marquis's beloved Marie Louise who had paid the terrible price for her husband's indiscretion.

No, the servants knew nothing, save for the one who had immediately reported the marquis's absence to London. She'd known about that within days, having gone to the village to beg to be allowed more credit at the grocers until the end of the quarter, only to return home with a woefully inept government *tail* wagging behind her.

There had been no reason to dismiss the servants now, or to bother ferreting out the one who had tattled to Liverpool. Whomever she'd hire, one of them would be there expressly to spy on her. Save for Emilie, who had come with them when they'd escaped Paris all those years ago. Thank God for Emilie.

And no reason to hide the fact that she didn't know where her father had gone, or why he'd left, or if he'd ever be coming back. Indeed, it was imperative that she let everyone see her lack of knowledge as to what her father might be planning or doing at this very moment. Her safety depended on her ignorance. That's why she'd found no note, was given no warning. He'd been protecting her.

"But he would have left me *something,* something to assure me he's all right," Tess said aloud, pushing away the stool in a renewed burst of energy and getting to her feet. "I'm just not seeing it, that's all."

Pulling a key from her vest pocket, she approached the special cabinet the marquis had ordered built into the room, and inserted it in the lock. She pulled the glass doors open to reveal shelving holding various artifacts her father had bought or traded for over the past two decades. His treasures, he called them, some of them Roman, some Greek, most Egyptian. Bits of stone, chipped clay bowls, a small carved idol of some long-forgotten god, an ancient pipe with a broken stem. The prized possessions of a man who had traded in his love of things ancient and turned his mind, his talents, to revenge, a man at last left with nothing save these ancient, inferior relics of what had been. And a reminder of all this small family could afford, when the Marquis de Fontaine had once claimed one of the premier collections of ancient relics in all of France.

Tess hadn't touched any of these prized possessions during her earlier searches, but they were all that was left. Her last chance.

One by one, she lifted the items from the shelves. She looked at them from every angle before depositing each piece on the desktop, her frustration building until it took everything within her not to throw the very last item, the broken pipe, into the fireplace.

Because there'd been nothing. *Nothing.* She put her palms on the bottom shelf and leaned her head against the edge of another, her position one of abject defeat.

"Second shelf, the left end of it. Lift it...there's a button there. Push it, and then close the doors and step back."

Tess couldn't breathe. Every muscle in her body had turned to stone; heavy, immovable. Her mouth went dry, her heart stopped, then started again, each beat hurting. Hurting so bad. It was a voice she hadn't heard in nearly four years but would never forget, could never forget. She heard it nightly, in her dreams. *I love you, Tess. God help me, I love you. Let me love you...*

"You?" she asked, not moving. "They sent you? That's almost funny, Jack. The student, sent to find the master. And you came, you agreed, knowing what could be at the end of the day for the two of you." She turned around slowly, placing her hands on the edge of the sturdy shelf behind her, knowing that otherwise she might slip to her knees, sobbing. "You, of all people."

He remained where he stood, which was yards too close for her not to have heard him, sensed him, smelled him. *Jésus doux,* he still stole her breath away, just by looking at her. She knew every inch of him, had touched and tasted him, taken him in, given herself to him, even as he gave to her. A dark passion, too intense, too urgent and much too fleeting. The fire that blazed, but couldn't be sustained.

Her dark lover. Dark of hair, dark of soul and mind and heart. Even his green eyes were dark, intense beneath those black winged brows, and unreadable. He might have been chiseled from warm stone by a master of the art, his leanly muscled body perfection itself, and life breathed into that beautiful, sometimes cruel mouth by a goddess bent on mischief once he'd been placed on the earth with all the lesser mortals.

That sensual mouth opened now; Tess was mesmerized by his lips as they curled into a brief, almost amused smile. "Fetching outfit, Tess. I doubt those buckskins flattered their original owner half so well."

Tess snapped back to the moment, and took advantage of Jack's remark to throw out a barb of her own. "I wouldn't have noticed. They belonged to René."

At the mention of her brother's name, the winglike

brows lowered, the stare became unnervingly intense. "So now you've made yourself over into the son? You'd do anything to please him, wouldn't you? Have you ever succeeded?"

"Not as well as you did, no." Another barb that hit home. Those that didn't know him, hadn't all but been inside his skin, wouldn't notice. But she did. She'd hurt him. Good. They could both hurt.

Jack took a step forward. "I'm here to help, Tess, not go back over covered ground. Your brother's dead. You and I never were what we thought we were, nor had what we thought we had. That's the past. You don't know where Sinjon is, do you? He's left you here alone, to face me."

"He couldn't have known that you'd be the one to—" But then she stopped, shook her head. "No, he would have known that. I'm the fool who didn't realize you'd be the one. Nobody knows him better."

"But not well enough, apparently. I'd ask if you really don't know where he's gone, what he's up to, but it's obvious you don't. What were you looking for?"

Tess shoved her splayed fingers through her hair, curling her hands into fists at the back of her head, not caring that she was probably only making a tangled mess worse. "I don't know," she admitted. "How could he have done this to me, Jack? To…to leave me with nothing?"

"I'm here," he said, putting out his hand, but it was only to motion her aside so that he could approach the cabinet built into the wall. "He knew I'd come. He knew I'd be the one. That makes him either a genius or a fool, doesn't it? Let's see what he's up to, shall we?"

He reached into the cabinet, running a hand beneath the second shelf, lifting the left end of it slightly. She heard a slight click, and then Jack stood clear, closed the cabinet doors.

As they watched, the cabinet seemed to come toward them and then began to pivot until it stood sideways, allowing them access to whatever lay beyond the opening.

Jack lit a brace of candles as Tess could only stand there, staring.

"I never... He never told me about this. He told you, but not me. Not his daughter."

"We're keeping score now?" Jack asked as he stepped through the opening and then turned to extend his hand, this time clearly intending that she take it.

She shook her head. "I'm fine on my own."

Jack ran his gaze up and down her breeches-clad body. "Yes. Any fool could see that. Hug yourself close to you, Tess. Don't let anybody in."

"How dare you! It wasn't me who—"

But he was gone, seemingly disappearing below her line of sight, taking the candlelight with him. Stairs. There was a flight of stairs behind the cabinet. Tess looked toward the opened door to the hallway, knowing if she left the study, Jack would want to know why she hadn't followed him. She'd have to trust Emilie. Emilie would have learned by now that Jack had come to the manor house. She'd know what had to be done. *Please, God, just this one time, toss the dice in my favor.*

Tess quickly lit a candle and followed Jack down, into the depths.

WHEN HE'D GONE away, she'd still been more girl than woman.

No more.

Jack hadn't known what to expect when he saw her again, either from her, or from himself. Seeing her had turned out to be both better and worse than he'd imagined.

The hurt was still in her eyes, undoubtedly made more raw by her father's disappearance and his refusal to include her in his plans. This was an old pain for Tess. She'd told Jack she understood: Sinjon Fonteneau was not a demonstrative man, making him uncomfortable with any displays of emotion. He loved his daughter, yes, he did, but praise did not flow easily from his mouth. She understood, but understanding and acceptance are often strangers to each other, and Tess clearly was still trying to please her father, make him admit out loud that he was proud of her.

She was wearing René's breeches. Because she felt less constricted dressed that way while destroying rooms in her search? Or just because that's what she now wore? What the hell had gone on here these past four years?

With the familiarity of his former acquaintance with the underground room easing his way, Jack dipped the brace of candles again and again, lighting a dozen squat candles, illuminating the cool, dank-smelling room.

"Damn," he bit out as he turned in a full circle, seeing what was there, taking note of what was gone.

He heard the click of Tess's boots on the stone steps

and quickly rid his face of all expression as she joined him in the center of the room.

"I'd often wondered where he kept…" she said, but then her voice trailed off. "Did René know?"

Jack nodded, not wanting to discuss the fact that Tess's twin had been privy to this sanctum of sanctums, but she was not. Not then, not since René's death. "He kept everything," he said, still taking his mental inventory. "The disguises, the pots of paint and powder, the wigs." He walked over to pick up the crude wooden crutch leaning against one of the tables. "I remember when he used this. He'd even tied up his leg beneath his greatcoat to lend more credence to his role of crippled veteran. The French lieutenant actually pushed a sou into his hand before Sinjon slashed his throat. And all of it accomplished while balanced on one leg. I'd argued against the disguise, pointed out that a one-legged man was vulnerable. I should have known better."

"He only killed when necessary," Tess said firmly, her belief in her father's motives unshaken. "He only does what is necessary. Ever."

Jack replaced the crutch and turned to her. "Yes, of course, the sainted Marquis de Fontaine. And what is so necessary for him now, Tess? The war's over, he's been rewarded for his service to the Crown, cut loose, left to live out his life in peace and security. That's all he wanted, wasn't it, all he ever said he wanted for all of you?"

"Both of us," she corrected, wandering over to the large desk and opening the center drawer. "He never really wanted René to be like him."

"All right, Tess, let's do this now, get it over with," Jack said, walking over to slam the drawer shut. "Your brother was young, foolish. And wrong. Sinjon never favored me over his own son. René had nothing to prove that night. Nothing."

Her eyes flashed in the candlelight. "He had everything to prove. To our father—to *you.* He worshipped you. He wanted nothing more than to be like you. The so-brave and clever Jack. *See, René, how Jack does it. Observe and learn, René, Jack will show you how it is done. Jack, so fearless as he enters the wasp's nest. Jack, who is steel to the core, with the mind of a devil and the skills of an army. Watch him, even if you can never hope to equal him. He is one in a lifetime. Fearless.*"

"Christ," Jack bit out, putting the width of the desk between them. "Because I didn't *care.* Because I had nothing to lose but my life." *Until you,* he added silently.

"But it wasn't your life that was lost, was it, Jack?"

"And do you think you're the only one who grieves his loss? René was my friend."

"No, he was never your friend. You have no friends, you make sure of that. I knew him better than anyone. René was meant for books and beauty, never destined to bleed out his life's blood in that Whitechapel alley." Tess pounded her clenched fist against her chest. "*Me,* Jack. I should have been there."

"To die in his place?" Jack asked her, his voice hard, cold.

"None of you would have *been* in that alley if you'd allowed the original plan as my father and I drew it up, damn it, and you know it! René would never have been in any danger. We all knew he was too eager to please you and Papa, too eager to remember his lack of skill if the opportunity to…to…"

"To *show off* for us presented itself? Are you finally ready to admit that, Tess? Is Sinjon? Or am I still to take all the blame?"

"You convinced Papa to change the plan, to keep me out of it."

Jack felt the fabric of his composure split. He'd never wanted Tess involved in any of their missions; that had been Sinjon's choice to use his own children, Sinjon's mistake. "Because I loved you!" he all but shouted, his words echoing back to him from the stone walls. "Because I couldn't bear the thought of losing you." He pulled himself back together, not without effort, then ended quietly, "And lost you anyway…"

Tess said nothing, the silence lasting nearly to the breaking point, turning the physical space between them into a yawning chasm that stretched across the lost years.

"Wherever he is, he's well armed," Jack said at last, looking toward the glass-fronted cabinet usually filled with weapons both deadly and unique. Tools of the trade. The cabinet had been the first thing his eyes had gone to when he'd entered the room, for he knew it would tell the tale. A man didn't carry a dozen weapons into the woods with him if all he meant to do was blow out his own brains. Clearly it was destruction of some kind Sinjon had in mind when he'd done his flit, but not self-destruction.

He heard the drawer slide open once more. "There's this," Tess said, apparently just as eager as he was to put their recent confrontation behind them. "The Gypsy hasn't been active in England for several years, not since…since René. Why would he have kept this?"

Jack returned to the desk to pick up the calling card Tess had placed there.

"Cheap theatrics," he said coldly, looking at the card made of rich black stock and embossed with a golden eye with a bloodred pupil at its center. He passed it back to Tess. "I never agreed with Sinjon on that."

"Papa says the government believes the man is Romany, and the eye symbol is that of the *querret,* the seeker. That's why he was given that name. The seeker. As if he follows some higher purpose in what he does."

Jack shook his head. As the son of an actress, he believed he could recognize a flair for the melodramatic when he saw one. "He seeks lining his pockets, and always has. Working for the French, working for anyone who will pay him, and filling the rest of his time working for himself. Whoever he is or once was, now he's a thief and a murderer, and leaving these cards behind is his way of tipping his cap at those bent on stopping him. He's an actor playing a part, and we who pursue him are his audience. Each time he places that card on another body, on the cushion where some treasure had been resting moments earlier, he's taking his bow. We'd actually begun to believe him dead. But we found one of these cards a month or more ago, left behind after several very good pieces were removed from the Royal British Museum."

Tess looked at him for long moments. "So he's back. And you're hunting him, aren't you? Because of René. Because...because of everything." Then her eyes went wide. "You...you don't think...?"

"I don't know, Tess. He'd have to be mad to try to find him on his own. Has he spoken of the Gypsy often?"

She sat down on the chair behind her, her long fingers tightly clasping and unclasping around the ends of the chair arms. She was nervous, a highly strung filly ready to bolt at any moment. Why? She should be searching the room, eager to see what was there. Was it him? Was it that difficult to be in the same room with him?

"Never. Not since René died. It was all over then, just as you said. The war, the assignments, the reason for the fight. Mama was still dead, and all the revenges he'd exacted for twenty years hadn't changed that. He was given a small pension and told his services were no longer required. He still taught me things, although obviously he never trusted me, not if I wasn't allowed to see this room." She looked up at him. "But you know that. He's never been quite the same since René died. Since you left. Suddenly old, and defeated."

"I had no reason to stay, you'd made that plain enough. And it's clear nothing's changed there, either."

"Not for you, certainly. You're still working for the Crown, still doing their bidding. Which brings us back to why you're here. You've as good as said Papa summoned you by disappearing. I think I know what the Crown would ask you to do once you found him. But what does Papa want from you?"

"When I find him, I'll be sure to ask," Jack said shortly, suddenly needing to be out of this room, out in the fresh air, away from Tess and her incisive questions.

"I won't help you, you know. I'm not a fool. I know I can't stop you. But I won't help you." She got to her feet. "In other words, Jack—for us, it ends here. I've seen your party trick with the cabinet and I thank you for it. But now I'm telling you to leave. You're not welcome beneath this roof."

He looked at her as she stood there. Magnificent. Frightened, but hiding it so well, the way she'd always done. He wanted her so badly he ached with it.

When she made to sweep past him, he grabbed her wrist and pulled her around, chest to chest with him in the flickering candlelight, her wrist still in his possession, their bent arms pressed between them. She raised her chin, stared at him in defiance, didn't flinch, didn't fight him, didn't blink.

He needed her to blink.

"I know about this room, Tess. If you think there's only one way in here, you're not as intelligent as I gave you credit for being. I know every secret in this house, which clearly you don't. If I want to be here, I'll be here, with or without your permission. I will go where I want, when I want. Take what I want."

He captured her mouth, grinding her tight against him by cupping the back of her head, holding her still as he plunged his tongue between her lips, pressed his leg between her thighs. Four years of longing, of needing, of pent-up frustration combined in that kiss, stripped him of his hard-won ability to mask his every emotion.

Her free hand snaked up his arm to his shoulder, clasping it firmly, lovingly, her fingertips lightly pressing against him. For a moment, she gave. For that moment, she let him in. For a moment, they were fire again.

And then the moment was over. She dug her fingers into him, pushing down hard on his shoulder with her hand as her knee came up swiftly, taking him and his arousal unawares. His knees buckled, his hold on her relaxed, and she was gone, leaving him to bend over where he stood, his hands on his thighs, forcing himself not to black out, or throw up.

"I taught her that," Black Jack Blackthorn managed at last, speaking to the uncaring stone walls. And then, unbelievably, he smiled. "God, was I even alive these past four years?"

He looked at the far wall and then walked toward it, his hand out to push on one certain stone. It was time he saw what else Sinjon might be up to, what else might be missing.

CHAPTER TWO

TESS DIDN'T GO where she most longed to go, because Jack might follow her. She couldn't risk that. Not that she was safe anywhere.

He'd said there was more than one way into her father's secret room. But even if she managed to find the other entrance somewhere in the cellars or a third on the other side of the manor walls and block them, it would do her no good.

Jack was right. He knew the house better than she did, she who had grown up here. He knew her father better than she did.

The way he'd kissed her, perhaps he even knew her better than she did. Because she'd been a heartbeat away from surrender, from tearing at his clothes, biting him, urging him to press her down on the desktop as she wrapped her legs high around his hips, let him fill up all the empty places inside her as she took, and took, and took…

She heard Jack's boot heels on the stone steps and quickly exited the study for the hallway, but only to press her back against the outside wall, taking herself out of sight but not earshot. If he was going to search the room now, she couldn't stop him. But that didn't mean she'd go off to tend to her knitting, or whatever it was she might be doing if she'd been born in a different time, to different parents, had grown to womanhood in a different, less dangerous world.

But, although Jack didn't immediately exit the study, she heard nothing during the long minutes she stood guard. If he was searching the room, he was doing it with a stealth she could admire, if not at this moment.

Maddening! What was he doing in there? Were there more secret places her father had hidden from her? She wanted to peer around the doorjamb and see what Jack was up to. Desperately. But that would be as good as admitting her father hadn't trusted her with his closest-held secrets, and that she needed Jack's help. Damn him. *Damn both of them.*

"Boo!"

Tess nearly jumped out of her skin as Jack's head and shoulders appeared around the doorjamb. "You're not amusing," she managed, trying to catch her breath.

"And you shouldn't wear that lovely scent if you're attempting to stay hidden," he told her, walking into the hallway. "See that a room is made ready for me. My usual chamber…unless you want me to share yours? I'm fairly certain I could be talked round to that, if you ask prettily."

"Go to blazes, you *bastard*," she called out to his departing back, deliberately inflicting hurt where she knew it would cause the most pain.

His confident stride didn't falter, and then he was gone.

Tess walked back into her father's study and collapsed into his desk chair, dropping her head to her hands.

What was she going to do? She'd tried for a week—a full week!—to discover a single clue to her father's whereabouts, cudgeled her brain attempting to remember conversations she'd had with him, hoping to recall something he'd said that might lead her to understand why he had gone, where he had gone and what he planned to do when he got there.

And nothing. If it hadn't been that some of his clothing was missing from his clothespress, she could have thought he'd walked out into the trees and become lost, or was lying somewhere with a broken ankle, or worse. He'd been taking more and more long walks as of late, disappearing for entire afternoons. As it was, she'd spent half a day telling herself he had gone into the village and lost track of time, and half the night searching the nearby countryside before it had occurred to her that he'd simply gone. Left. Without a word to her. And without leaving behind enough of the ready to last them until the end of the quarter and the receipt of his pension.

He knew I'd come.

Jack was right. Her father had to know he was still being watched, the Crown never quite trusting the Frenchman, even though he had proven invaluable to them time and time again. He had to know that if he took a flit, the Crown would soon know of it. He had to know that the obvious choice to be assigned the job of finding their lost mercenary would be the man who knew him best.

But to expose her like this? How could her father do

something so cruel? He knew how she felt about Jack, about everything else. Didn't he, too, put most of the blame for René's death at Jack's door?

"Papa trained him. He knows what Jack can do. He needs him for something, but he's too proud to ask for help. That has to be it. He's trusting Jack to find him and then help him. What does it matter about his own flesh and blood, when the mission is all? At the end of the day, we're all his pawns, and always have been. Nobody has mattered to Papa, not really, not since Mama. When will I ever accept that?" Tess exploded as she opened and slammed shut desk drawers for at least the tenth time, somehow still hoping she would see something she had missed in the last nine searches.

Instead, in the center drawer, she encountered an empty space where she'd seen something every other time she'd searched. She pushed back the chair, looked down at the floor, in case her last angry foray into the drawers had ended with her throwing something down…but no, there was nothing there.

She looked at the empty space again. What was it? What was missing? She squeezed her eyes shut, forced herself to breathe slowly, concentrate. In her mind's eye she saw the contents of the drawer. The daily receipts book. A small knife to trim pens. Sealing wax. The funeral ring made up after René's death, the one Papa couldn't wear these past months because his fingers were becoming increasingly crippled by old age and hard use.

The newspaper. That was it, a folded copy of the

London Times. It was gone. Why would Jack have taken it, a newspaper more than a month out of date?

A month?

I last saw one of these cards a month or more ago, left behind after several very good pieces were removed from the Royal British Museum.

That was it. That had to be it! The newspaper had carried a report of the theft. She hadn't read the article. The Gypsy had been responsible for the theft? Yes, that's what Jack had said. He must have regretted saying it, and wanted any reminder of his slip removed before she could see the newspaper and remember.

His mistake. She had made a shambles of most of the room's contents during this last search, causing him to believe she was sloppy and inept. The amateur he insisted upon seeing her as, if only to ease his conscience. But, even in her ever-increasing frustration, she'd been very careful to record everything in her memory, what it was, where it was, as she'd been trained to do.

Had a black calling card with the imprint of a golden eye with a red center been mentioned in the article? It must have been; otherwise, why would her father have saved it?

She heard footsteps and quickly closed the drawer.

"Lady Thessaly? You are requested upstairs."

Tess smiled at her old nurse, easily falling into French along with her, as the woman may have reluctantly learned enough English in two decades of living on this damp island to get along, but she thought the language vile and "without music," and avoided it whenever she could. "Yes, thank you, Emilie, I imagine I am."

"But no more with the breeches the marquis so fool-
ishly allows when you go riding on that devil's spawn
you favor. Master Jack has no need of such a show of
immodesty."

"It's far too late for any modesty when it comes to
Master Jack, Emilie," Tess pointed out as she got to her
feet, suddenly feeling as old as time, decades beyond her
five and twenty years. "If you could have Arnette order
up the tub for an hour from now and lay out my white
watered silk gown, as I do believe Master Jack will be
joining me for dinner."

"The white, my lady? You haven't worn that one in
years. It will need to be freshened." Emilie's careworn
face assembled itself into a knowing smile. "Ah, now I
remember. As do you, as will he. It will be done as you
say."

"Yes, thank you, Emilie." Tess sat back down after
the servant left, the memory of the last time she'd worn
that gown washing over her.

*Look at you. So beautiful. Light to my dark, blessed
day to my lonely night. I love you, Tess. God help me, I
love you. Let me love you...*

Tess closed her eyes, hugging her arms close about
her. She could feel Jack's hot, hungry gaze reaching out
to her across the empty years, began to blossom again at
the memory of his touch as he'd instigated increasingly
bold forays that had sent flames of awakening desire
licking along her every nerve. She could still savor the
terror and thrill inside her as the white silk gown had
whispered down her body to puddle at her feet before

he'd lifted her, carried her to the bed, joined her on the cool satin coverlet.

What had followed had been an initiation of the senses, a tutorial of such precise, intimate detail that there could no longer be any question as to why God had formed her the way she was, Jack how he was, and for what purpose they'd been brought together.

He'd taught her all her own secrets, and then encouraged her to explore his. They'd touched, tasted. He'd taken her to the brink, again and again, with his mouth, with his clever hands probing her, taking her hand and introducing her to the pleasures of her body, teaching her what she liked so she could tell him, so he could follow her movements with his own.

Together, they discovered just the right rhythms to turn her limbs to water, to coax soft whispers and whimpers from her throat, to make her so ready for him she never noticed the pain that came and went in an instant, to be replaced with a fullness that had her grinding her hips against him, begging him to finish it, to let her fly free of this glorious torment.

She put a hand to her breast now, felt her rapid heartbeat. Allowed her other hand to drift down to the juncture of her thighs, to press her fingers against the ache growing there, the longing that threatened to destroy her. Release, that sweet, sweet explosion. She needed it, craved it, knew how to find temporary respite in the dark of a lonely night when the memories and the hunger became too much. But never how to truly satisfy it. Not across the long years, not now. Only Jack could do that.

But she needed more than that temporary release;

she needed parts of Jack he'd never given her, and never would. She needed to be *first* to somebody. Before Crown, before duty, before revenge or hate or the thrill of the fight. She needed a man who wouldn't walk away, even when she ordered him to go.

So not again, never again. They'd destroyed each other once, and once had been more than enough. She was a woman now, with responsibilities and no room in her life for what might have been. She knew that when it came to Jack she had few weapons in her arsenal. But that gown should serve her as well as any suit of armor. Jack would remember, as she remembered, and he wasn't the sort to knowingly make the same mistake twice.

Disgusted with her temporary weakness, she stood up and quit the room. She had much to arrange before Jack returned.

JACK SETTLED INTO the chair in the private room of the Castle Inn, nodding his greetings to Will and Dickie as the latter filled a glass with wine from a decanter and pushed it across the tabletop to him.

"Learn anything today?" Will asked, using the point of his dagger to skewer a small bit of cheese and pop it into his mouth.

"Yes. There are times your table manners can be execrable." Jack took a sip of wine. He wanted first to hear what they'd managed to unearth while he was at the manor house. "Dickie?"

"I agree, and we didn't just learn that today," Dickie Carstairs said, grinning at Will. "Oh, you want to know what we've managed to ferret out, don't you? Very well. Your mentor departed this benighted village eight days ago on the public coach heading north. He carried with him a fairly large trunk, purchased just that morning, and a rather cumbersome cloth bag he declined to place in the boot but actually put down the blunt for its own seat, so that he could keep it with him inside the coach. Although he is well-known here, the bumpkins I spoke with didn't know they were seeing the marquis board the coach."

"How so?" Jack asked, if only to keep Dickie talking. He already recognized where this story was leading. After all, hadn't a part of his training been to pass unnoticed under the eyes of the villagers who had been seeing him almost daily for a year?

"Oh, that. Yes, well, it would seem that the passenger they saw was described as looking much like a member of the clergy. One of those queer, foreign autem bawlers, you know? Wearing skirts, and with a rope of beads with a whacking great cross hanging at the end of it tied around his waist, a hat as flat and big as a platter pushed down over the cowl on his head. Kept trying to trace his blessings on everybody who came close, so the good citizens rather kept their gazes down as they steered around him, trying to avoid gaining his attention. A costume, of course."

"And a good one if you're walking where you would otherwise be recognized," Jack said, nodding. The monk disguise had been among those missing from the collection in the hidden room. There were others. "Go on."

Jack contemplated his wineglass as Dickie went on to

explain that the stranger had taken a private room at this very inn two weeks earlier, appearing and disappearing with no regularity, probably going out and about, saving souls. But always generous with his tips as he asked that his privacy be maintained so that he wasn't disturbed while at his prayers. He may have slept in his bed, he may not have, no one was certain. Overall, he was quiet and no trouble, coming in and out, always carrying something with him, the same cloth bag already mentioned.

"He was slowly bringing what he needed from the manor, both in the bag and beneath his monk's robes," Dickie concluded, stating the obvious. "He couldn't be seen leaving the place with a traveling trunk, he couldn't make anyone at the manor suspicious. So he did it piecemeal, and in secret. And no one suspected. Clever."

Will stabbed another bit of cheese. "Clever enough to disembark at the very next village and hire a wagon for his luggage, then head out again, this time going west. And, before Dickie drags the business out too far, an old lady driving a farm wagon entered the next village, only to ride away in the southbound Royal Mail coach, her traveling trunk on the roof, a large cloth bag beside her. He had to pay for an extra seat again, which is why he was remembered. He's for London, Jack. He's *in* London."

"May as well be on the far side of the moon, for all we'll be able to ferret him out in town. He could be anywhere. Anybody." Dickie raised his wineglass. "And clearly up to mischief. Liverpool isn't going to like it when we tell him we've lost him."

"We haven't lost him," Jack corrected. "We simply haven't found him yet. We already knew a man like Sinjon wouldn't make our job easy for us. Tess says she knows nothing. And, from the way he sneaked out of the manor piece by piece, I tend to believe her."

Will got to his feet, the dagger having already disappeared into his boot. "All right then, we're for London. I wasn't much enamored with the idea of passing the night in this benighted spot, not with the delights of the Season and a dozen invitations awaiting us in Mayfair. Except for you, Jack. A thousand apologies."

"All of which are accepted," Jack said, also getting to his feet. "Bastards aren't often invited into Society. I won't be riding with you, however. We'll meet in Half Moon Street in two days' time. Watch for the usual signal that shows I'm in residence."

"Some people just have the knocker put back on the door, you know," Dickie pointed out. "All this business about opening drapes, closing drapes. A man could get confused."

"He don't advertise his whereabouts the way you do, not our Black Jack," Will said, giving the pudgy Dickie a slight shove in the direction of the hallway. "You're going to take another run at the daughter, Jack? Going to bed her for the good of the Crown, or just for the bleeding hell of it? Either way, good on you."

"Sorry, Jack," Dickie apologized for Will. "He's pretty enough, but more than his table manners are execrable. Come on, Will, before Jack bloodies that too-inquisitive nose of yours."

Jack had already discounted both of Will's sly comments. He'd learned to ignore a lot of things over the course of his eight and twenty years, or he would have been forced to spend half of that life just knocking people down. As it was, by the time he'd reached his majority he'd gotten himself into trouble often enough to eventually bring him to the attention of the Marquis de Fontaine, who'd shown him an alternative outlet for both his quick mind and his aggressive nature...which had probably saved Jack's life.

"I don't have to tell you to begin at the Bull and Mouth. Sinjon's major problem is his lack of funds, which meant he had to bring his tools with him, not purchase them at his destination. Adding to his problems, his other weakness is physical, not mental. Someone at the Bull and Mouth helped him with that trunk—he clearly couldn't move it across London on his own. He's left us a trail, gentlemen, one I'm sure he's already eradicated, employing the same piecemeal tactics in London to shift his belongings sans trunk. He's well and truly gone to ground by now. But start with the trunk. Find that, and we're back in the hunt."

"Fair enough, Jack. And if we find him while you're still playing about with the dau—" Will quickly corrected himself "—while you're still searching for clues here? Do we approach, or wait for you? I rather fancy having the man sitting in your drawing room with a lovely big bow tied around his neck when you arrive. Lady Sefton's ball is this Friday, you know, and with one thing and another, I've damned well missed half the parties already. Liverpool and his missing marquis be damned, I say. We'd been promised some respite after our last brilliant success."

Jack was used to Will's grumbles, knowing the man loved a fight more than anything. It was the hunt that fatigued him, the necessary ins and outs of intrigue, especially when, at the end of the day, there'd be no fight. Just an old man, captured and put back out to pasture, or easily dispatched to hell. Where was the fun in that?

"Just find him, gentlemen, or at least a trace of him, and you can safely leave the rest to me," Jack said, walking with them to the inn yard, and waiting with them after they'd called for their mounts. "After all, the ladies must be pining for both of you."

"Only Will," Dickie said, sighing. "Not much use for a pudgy, penniless peer, I'm afraid."

"Just stay close by me, Dickie, my friend. I'll toss you my castoffs," Will joked.

The banter continued until the horses were saddled and brought out, and Jack remained where he was until the two men had mounted them and turned toward the roadway.

He'd been impatient for them to be on their way, although he hadn't let them see that. They'd been a true quartet of rogues for the past four years, now sadly a trio of rogues, with Jack as their acknowledged leader. That had been fine, at the beginning. Will had been content to let Jack do most of the thinking as, to hear Will tell it, thinking fatigued him. But lately he'd sensed a growing disenchantment with the arrangement in Will, and a burgeoning need for violence, a void left by the cessation of hostilities in France.

With Henry dead, Jack, too, was growing more restless. The Baron Henry Sutton had been the closest thing to a true friend Jack had allowed, and his death had left a void he wasn't eager to fill. With Henry, Jack was never the bastard son of the Marquess of Blackthorn; he'd simply been a man, the equal of any other man. Dickie was affable enough, but not the sort you sat with until the dawn, speaking of everything from literature, to religion, to the never-ending search to understand how they had come to be here, in this place, in this time and for what purpose.

Henry had known things about Jack's years with Sinjon, with Tess, that no other man had known. Jack missed that companionship, that quiet understanding, even as he'd been amazed to lately discover there were bonds between his brothers Beau and Puck he'd never suspected, indeed, had always gone out of his way to discourage.

And now Sinjon. And Tess. Both of them, without warning, come back into his life. The mentor. The lover.

Jack felt unbalanced, unsure. He was beginning to question what he'd made of his life, and wonder about the future. He'd never before thought of the future. Only the now. He'd never cared. That's what had made him so good at his job.

But he had cared, with Beau. He'd cared, with Puck. After promising himself that his mistake with Tess had taught him never to mix his feelings with his mission, he'd let his brothers in, and he'd nearly lost one of them. He had lost Henry.

It was time for this to be over. All of it. He wasn't

suited to the job anymore. Dickie enjoyed the thrill nearly as much as he needed the money the Crown offered for his services. Will relished testing his skills—the sharp, swift justice of the knife—maybe too much. But to Jack, with the war over, he increasingly saw his small band of rogues as nothing more than hired killers, meant to rid the Crown of potential embarrassments. Embarrassments like Sinjon, who knew entirely too much for Liverpool or any highly placed government official to sleep easily at night while the man was on the move.

Yes. Jack wanted out, as had Henry. They'd discussed the subject many times, and each time concluded that once you belong to the Crown, as they did, there was no such thing as simply walking away. Sinjon had proved that, as well. He'd been all but a prisoner on his small estate, his every move monitored and reported. Only an old man, broken in spirit and no longer of any use to them, but still a marquis, a fellow peer, so they hadn't killed him. There'd be no such reticence in eliminating a bastard son barely anyone knew and only a few might mourn if he attempted to cut free.

And Jack felt reasonably certain he knew the tool the Crown would employ for the job, should that time come. He took one last look toward the now empty road, and headed back into the inn for another glass of wine and time alone, to think.

CHAPTER THREE

TESS PACED THE drawing room, twisting the wineglass between her fingers. He was late. Jack was never late. He was doing this deliberately, delaying his arrival, drawing her nerves taut, making it clear to her that he had the advantage over her in every way.

Which he did. More than he could possibly know.

She'd never forgotten him, saw his face every day; he was always with her.

When he'd gone, she'd believed it would be forever. Black Jack Blackthorn didn't grovel, didn't bend. Would never beg. She'd handed him back his ring, the one she'd worn on a thin ribbon around her neck, hidden away from her father's eyes until this one last assignment was over, and exchanged it with the locket closed over the miniatures of her mother and brother. She'd replaced one lost dream with two lost souls.

He'd been wearing the ring today; she'd seen it on the index finger of his right hand. Heavy gold, with a large, flat onyx stone engraved with a *B*. For Blackthorn. For bastard. He'd said he had never known which, as the gift had been from his mother. But, although she'd encouraged him to enlarge on that strange statement, he had instead diverted her with his kisses, and he'd never mentioned his mother again. There hadn't been time.

There had been their argument when he'd told her of the change in tactics that would put her in the background, away from any possible danger. There had been the mission.

And after that, there had been nothing left but the funeral.

And goodbye.

If only there was some way to go back, to change the past. But there wasn't, and that meant the future couldn't be changed, either. There was only the now, the mission—finding her father before he did something else that couldn't be changed, fixed, mended. And this time, she wouldn't be left behind, to wait, to worry…to mourn.

How she missed René. They'd shared their mother's womb, they'd shared their lives, always together, living in one another's pockets, clinging to each other through their papa's frequent absences, vying for his attention when he was in residence.

Though Emilie spoke only French, their papa insisted his children speak only English in his presence. They were confined to the manor grounds, their only companionship each other and Rupert, their English tutor, who brought home his lessons with a birch rod. He'd most often wielded it on René, until the day Tess had jumped onto the man's back and nearly bitten off his ear before he could shake her loose.

She'd been ten at the time. When her father heard of the incident it had been the very first time he'd ever complimented her.

But then he'd scolded René in that quietly destroying way he had, for having submitted to the rod so that his sister had been forced to defend him, taking all of the joy out of Tess's victory. He'd then employed another tutor who was twice the disciplinarian as Rupert, and Tess's education was turned over to a succession of English governesses.

Rupert's replacement was discharged the day René had twisted the man's rod-wielding arm behind his back and run him headfirst into the solid oak door of the schoolroom. He'd been fifteen, and it had taken all of those five long years for him to find the courage his sister had displayed at ten—which their father had been quick to point out.

There was no winning with the marquis. Fail him, and face his quiet disapproval that was ten times worse than any possible beating. Do something right, and hear nothing, or wait for the flaw to be pointed out to you as the stinging hook at the end of the faint praise.

Yet all Tess and René wanted out of life was to please the man. René pretended an interest in the lessons their father began with him after the tutor was sent packing, but it was Tess who showed the most aptitude when René would share what he'd learned with her. Her twin would rather read poetry; Tess would rather hold a book on military tactics up to a mirror, to practice reading backward. René enjoyed playing the flute; Tess practiced for hours with the slim tools René loaned her, until she could easily open every locked door in the manor house. After every hour spent at lessons with his father, René would spend two with Tess, teaching her everything he'd learned until she'd not only mastered each lesson, but outshone her teacher.

The marquis finally found her out the day René accidentally pinked her as they practiced with the foils and the button had come off the tip of his weapon without either of them noticing.

That was the second time the marquis had looked at her with something close to approval in his eyes, as he'd tied his handkerchief around her forearm and ordered her to borrow a shirt and breeches from René and report to him in the gardens. Then he'd tossed her back her weapon and grabbed one for himself.

She'd excelled; she knew it, even if her father never acknowledged any new skill she mastered over the next years. But she'd lost a part of her brother to her success, and to their shared strong desire to please the marquis. René never complained, never said anything, but Tess knew.

He tried, so very hard, but he had not been born to experience the thrill of clearing a five-barred fence, or find the center of the target with a thrown knife. And there was nothing of stealth about him, either in action or in his mind. He was his mother's son, kind and gentle. She was her father's daughter, quick of mind, fascinated by intrigue and all that went with it.

But it was more than a simple love of the game, or even striving to please their father. René could never know it, but Tess felt it her responsibility to protect him, just as she had done years before with Rupert. More and more, she took his place on the marquis's more minor missions, even being included in the planning of those missions that included all three of them, invariably casting René in a minor role, safely in the background.

Until Jack. His inclusion had changed everything. The marquis at last had the perfect pupil—talented, and male. Tess had hated him for his intrusion into their lives. She'd watched in disgust as he mastered in months what it had taken her years to learn, and then gone on to do as she had done with René: outpace the teacher with his ingenuity and skills. She'd envied the trust the marquis placed in him, suffered in silence as René seemed to turn their successor into some sort of hero to be admired, emulated.

She'd fought Jack for well over a year, until her fascination with this singular man overcame her resentment at being usurped in her father's affection. She'd then begun to watch him, not with jealousy any longer, but with growing interest in Jack, the man. So darkly mysterious, so compellingly handsome, his rare smiles doing strange, delicious things to her insides. And, increasingly, he'd been watching her. For months more, they'd danced around each other, both of them knowing there was something unsettled between them, a growing hunger that sooner or later had to be fed.

And dear God, how they had feasted...

Tess took another sip of wine, hoping it would somehow settle her. The afternoon had dragged on seemingly forever, and over the hours she'd changed her mind about the white silk gown. Punishing Jack, punishing herself, made no sense. She stood in front of the glass over the side table and inspected her reflection as it was directed back to her in the candlelight.

Her gown was simplicity itself, even modest, save for the fact that the pale, unadorned orchid silk rather cunningly outlined her breasts and rib cage and slid smoothly over her buttocks when she walked, making it clear she wore no undergarments. Even the modest cap sleeves were fashioned of all but transparent veiling. She was more covered than she was in most of her gowns, and yet she might as well be naked to the discerning eye.

Jack had a discerning eye.

A triple strand of crystals hugged her neck, and she wore her blond hair loose, floating down over her shoulders. He had always liked burying his head in her hair, or fisting its length tightly as he tipped her head back, to nibble at the base of her throat. And lower.

She was making it easy for him, all but offering him a written invitation.

She couldn't push Jack away and at the same time convince him that he needed her with him when he set off to find her father. No, what she needed even more than finding her father was to get Jack moving, get him gone, get the two of them as far away from the manor as possible, as quickly as possible.

She had her priorities straight now, and fighting Jack couldn't figure into the mix, not when it was so important her father was found, that she was with Jack when her father was found. She couldn't know how much her lover had changed in four years, if he would actually execute his old mentor on orders from the Crown.

What had shocked her most when she'd realized it

was that she didn't know what she would do if he tried. She no longer knew how she felt about her father.

Tess only knew that Jack couldn't be left to his own devices. Where he went, she would go, or she would follow. He had to know that as well, so it only made sense that they travel together.

She'd make it worth his while. He wanted her; that was one thing that hadn't changed in four years. She'd give him what he wanted tonight, and he'd give her what she wanted tomorrow when they rode away from the manor house.

The meagerness of his government pension had long ago caused the marquis to forgo the costly services of a butler, and since Jack never knocked, and moved with the stealth of a cat intent on bringing down a rabbit, she did her best not to flinch when he suddenly appeared in the room.

She'd expected his usual, impeccable London tailoring, but he had not bothered with the formality of town clothes. No, tonight Jack was the dark and dangerous pirate she'd seen many times before, all in black, his shirt collarless and discreetly ruffled, full-sleeved and open at the neck, his breeches showing the narrowness of waist and hip, the smooth muscles of his long, straight legs.

"Planning on breaking into the squire's house tonight to recover Crown secrets, Jack?" she asked, indicating his attire with a sweep of her arm. "Or perhaps relieving some travelers of their prized belongings out on the highway as you were doing when Papa first found you, just to keep your skills sharp?"

He approached her without a word, walking in a full circle around her before coming to a halt, their bodies only inches apart. She could feel her nipples begin to harden under his hot gaze, pushing against the thin fabric of her gown. He didn't touch her, but she could already feel his hands on her. "And you, Tess? You also look ready for a nocturnal ride. Are we dispensing with dinner?"

She longed to slap his handsome, grinning face. But she couldn't blame him for attempting to get some of his own back after the way she'd treated him when he'd kissed her. She reached out boldly, cupped his sex. "Ah, yes, I suppose we are. You know the way."

She watched as his eyes darkened and then let her hand drift across his lower belly and hip as she walked past him, heading for the stairs, her mouth dry, her heart pounding. He'd never forgive her if he found out what she was up to…but he'd never find out. It was imperative he leave here and never return. And when she cut him, dismissed him a second time after they found her father, faced him down and told him she'd been using him, he never would return. Jack was more proud than he would allow anyone to know. When this was over, they would be over, done. Again.

That's the way it would happen. That was the way it had to happen. She wasn't going to lose anyone else to Black Jack Blackthorn. Only herself.

Tess left the door to her bedchamber open behind her and went to stand in the middle of the room, waiting for Jack to come to her, take what he wanted.

What she wanted. She couldn't lie to herself. Not as

her breathing had already turned ragged, as her body tingled with the anticipation of his touch. He'd made her this way, showing her delights she'd never dreamed of, taking her places she'd never gone since, and longed to visit again.

She drew her breath in sharply as the door to her chambers slammed shut.

He came up behind her, took hold of her shoulders, and roughly whirled her about to face him. "You think I've grown stupid, Tess? That I'm some raw youth, to be happily blinded by lust? Come with me, lie with me, fall under my spell, do my bidding. Is that all we had between us, all that you remember of me? Jesus, woman, or are you that desperate?"

Tess raised her chin in defiance. "I thought you made it abundantly clear this afternoon what you wanted from me. And consider it a trade, Jack, not capitulation for either of us. I give you what you want, and you give me what I want."

He dropped his hands to his sides. "And what do you want, Tess? What do you consider worth the trade?"

"I go with you," she said, searching his eyes for his reaction. "I can help."

"Help? Why do I doubt that, Tess? I haven't forgotten that you were Sinjon's tolerably efficient trained monkey. It's your father I'm hunting, and I don't intend to spend half of my time watching my own back, not even for the pleasure of putting you on yours."

She ignored his deliberate crudity. "You wouldn't kill him, not even on orders from your masters."

"Wouldn't I? Are you sure? Good, then stay here, and I'll bring him to you."

Tess backed away from him and walked over to lean against the side of the tester bed. She'd try another argument. "Let's do this with gloves off, Jack, all right? I remember what was printed in the newspaper you took with you this afternoon. He's after the Gypsy, and so are you. But you two aren't the only ones with a score to settle with that monster. He killed my brother."

Jack's eyes went dark. "Really? I thought you and Sinjon had hung René's death around my neck. Am I now absolved? How you ease my mind. Goodbye, Tess. Thank you for your kind offer, and curse you for your lies."

She took a single step toward him. If he was on the road before she could follow, she might never be able to find him, or her father. She needed him gone, yes, but not alone. "That's it, Jack, leave. It's the one thing you're good at!"

He'd already turned for the door, but her words stopped him, even as they backed her up against the bed, because she instantly knew she'd gone too far.

"I *left,* Tess, because you made it clear there was nothing for me here any longer. I *left* because you pushed me away. I left because you expected me to go."

"I *expected*—? What do you mean by that?"

He was standing in front of her once again, effectively holding her in place without touching her. "You never thought there was a future for us, did you, Tess? That's why you insisted we not tell Sinjon or René about us. I would leave you at some point, find a fault somewhere, become disappointed with you in some way. When René died you finally had your excuse to send me away, before I left on my own. You, and maybe your father as well, although God knows he had his own reasons. I couldn't be allowed to stay because I'd failed, hadn't I? Failed in our best chance to capture the Gypsy, failed to protect René. It fell on me, all of it, and I had to go. Admit it, Tess, if only to yourself."

"That...that's not true. I loved you."

"And I loved you," Jack said, his voice calmer now, almost gentle. "But it wasn't my love you needed then, was it? You were still trying to win Sinjon's approval, still needing him to be proud of you. Until you could gain his love, you weren't really ready to accept mine, believe in mine. And that hasn't changed, has it, Tess? Still hoping for that pat on the head, a word of praise, some acknowledgment of your achievements. But he didn't trust you with his secrets, even after René died. He didn't trust you with this damn *mission* he's taken on. You were good, but never quite good enough. That's how you see it, isn't it?"

Tess didn't answer him. She didn't need to say a word in order to agree with him.

He tipped up her chin. "Look at me, Tess. *Look at me.* Sinjon's a hard man, there's no denying that. Demanding, difficult to please, impossible to fully understand. I know you and René suffered for that. But you're a grown woman now. How long are you going to punish yourself for his failings? Because that's what they are, his failings. Not yours."

"He left me nothing, Jack," Tess said quietly. "Knowing what he knows, he left us with nothing. How could he do that?"

"I told you, Tess. He knew I'd come."

"You don't understand..." she said, and then let her voice trail off. She'd left it too late, years too late. And she'd done what she'd done because her father had said it was for the best, and she'd been too devastated to think clearly. "Take me with you, Jack. Don't leave me behind again. I have to see him, I have to talk to him, I have to know *why*."

He looked at her for a long time, and then nodded. "Maybe it's time you learned who Sinjon Fonteneau really is. Let's go downstairs. There's something I need to show you."

Tess nearly threw her arms around him, but held back in time. "Thank you, Jack."

"Don't thank me, Tess. You're not going to like it. I'm about to turn your shining knight into a rogue."

JACK LED THE way back downstairs to Sinjon's study. He'd shown Tess the hidden room, but had not disclosed all of its secrets to her.

He handed Tess the brace of candles and opened the glass doors of the cabinet holding the few pitiful ancient relics the marquis kept on display; the collection of a man who couldn't afford to indulge his love the way he had years ago, in France. Or so it would seem to the world. The Marquis de Fontaine had never shown his real face to the world.

Jack had heard the story only a few weeks before René died. He'd found Sinjon in his study after midnight one night, sloppily drunk and embarrassingly maudlin on what he said was the twentieth anniversary of the death of his wife. He'd been both intrigued and flattered when the man motioned him to a chair and began to speak—and, in the end, he was appalled.

He doubted Tess and René had ever been privy to what had really happened, who their father was and had been, why their mother had died, what had brought them to England, what drove Sinjon to offer his services to the Crown against France.

The Marquis de Fontaine was a man of varied background and myriad talents. He'd prided himself on his knowledge of Greek, Roman and Egyptian antiquities; indeed, he'd devoted the first nearly fifty years of his life to amassing his collection, traveling the continent in order to add to it. Until he'd met his Marie Louise. He'd been amazed at the birth of the twins, slightly bemused as to what the fuss was all about, but they seemed to please Marie Louise, and he was free to go back to what he called his studies.

And his other pursuits.

Then came 1797, and suddenly Sinjon, whose facile use of a loyalty that seemed to bend with the prevailing wind had miraculously kept him safe in Lyon, was faced with the possible loss of his way of life. The worst of the Terror might be behind them, but the Revolutionary Army was becoming too powerful, thanks to the success of General Louis Hoche and some upstart Corsican named Bonaparte. Of the three, the *Directorie,* Hoche and Bonaparte, he feared the Corsican most, recognizing a lean and hungry ambition when he encountered it. Sinjon began working in secret with other Royalists to bring back the *Ancien Régime* and all the privileges of rank that went with it before it was too late for any of them.

But it had already been too late. He should have seen the signs, made a decision as to what was most important to him, and taken his wife and children to safety. Instead, he and his band of compatriots goaded and pushed the *Directorie* at every turn. Employing a plan devised by Sinjon, they nearly succeeded in an attempt to assassinate several of its leaders.

And that, to Sinjon, had been his single biggest mistake. The *Directorie* retaliated with all the might still at its disposal, hunting down and disseminating their opposition. While Sinjon and his men hid in cellars, not knowing what was happening, his adored Marie Louise had become one of the casualties of his folly.

He'd cried then, great blubbering drunken sobs. Jack sat silent, as there were no words that could comfort the man, heal his guilt and his loss. At that moment, no matter what Sinjon asked of him, Jack would do it. Because he was looking at a beaten old man who had lost everything; his wife, his country, his fortune. Here in England he lived in genteel poverty in a run-down manor house, employed by the Crown but never quite trusted.

Genteel poverty. Forced to plot and often kill, not only to exact justice for all he'd lost and rid the world of that upstart Bonaparte, but also to save a prime minister from scandal, find a way to disgrace those whose voices in Parliament didn't agree with the Crown, employ his skills to clean up the many messes those in power made with regularity. He'd no choice.

Except that he did. He'd always had a choice. The man had been grieving? How much? Drowning his guilt and sorrows? Really? Jack knew he'd never know exactly where Sinjon's clever mix of truth and fiction had merged that night, but only the reality of what he had seen. He had been the man's audience, drawn in, made sympathetic to a supposedly sad and disillusioned wreck of a man. What had come next, his introduction to the second secret room, to the marquis's secret life, would forever color his opinion of his mentor.

Now he would show Tess her real father, the damning part of the man that could readily be seen. A dose of truth couldn't hurt her any more than the fiction she'd built up around the man, the fiction Sinjon had so cleverly encouraged.

"Give me the candles, Tess, and follow me," Jack said, and then led the way down the steps and across the room to the stone he'd located earlier.

"There's more to see?" Tess asked as he pushed on the stone and it pivoted easily.

Jack held the brace of candles at shoulder level as the cabinet holding Sinjon's inspired arsenal slid aside. "Look at what's there, Tess, and at what isn't. As one important piece is missing."

He stood back and allowed her to walk into the small chamber lined with shelves from floor to low ceiling on three sides. The only furniture in the room was a single chair placed directly in its center; where Sinjon would sit to admire his genius.

"To your left, the Greek. To your right, the Roman. Straight ahead, and most interesting of all for what isn't there, the Egyptian. Your father's treasures. Or should I say, your competition. What Sinjon loves most in this world. What he risked his family for, lost his wife for, sacrificed his children's childhoods for, I suppose some may think. I know I do."

Tess turned in a slow circle, the candlelight casting strange shadows on the rows and rows of artifacts, shining back to her from Roman shields and breastplates, dancing along gem-encrusted bowls, illuminating ancient busts, helmets, bracelets, necklaces...and reflected in the tears in her eyes.

Selling only a few small pieces would have provided more than enough to pay the village shopkeepers, repair the manor house, educate his son at the best schools in England, purchase a mansion in Mayfair, launch his daughter into Society.

If Sinjon could part with any of his treasures. If selling them on the open market wouldn't mean the end of him.

"I don't... I can't... How, Jack? *Why?*"

"Let's go back upstairs," Jack said, taking the brace of candles from her and leading the way, holding on to her hand as they went. Her suddenly very cold hand.

He poured her a glass of wine and took it to her as she sat with exaggerated erectness on the leather couch, staring at nothing. She shook her head slightly in refusal so he downed it himself, and then positioned himself at the front of the desk, resting against its edge.

Jack would have spared her this if he could, but she'd

made it impossible. Sinjon had made it impossible. The man she so admired, so longed to please, her so wonderful, perfect and heroic father. He wondered how long it would take her to understand the implications of what she'd just seen.

It didn't take half as long as he'd thought. She'd always been very bright.

"He's a thief, isn't he?" she said finally. "My father is a thief."

"I made that mistake myself, and was quickly corrected. He sees himself more as a private collector. A thief, you see, steals for profit. Sinjon was always most discerning, taking only the best and keeping it for his own private enjoyment. Your competition, Tess, the true loves of his life."

Tess bent her head and began rubbing hard at her temples. "God. Oh, sweet Jesus…"

Jack pushed himself away from the desk and sat down beside her, taking her hands in his and lowering them to her lap, not letting them go. "It was easy in France," he told her. "He had his title to protect him. Nobody suspected that the treasures he brought home with him from his travels were anything but the purchases of a wealthy man. He could display many of them openly, keeping only the most easily recognizable safely hidden away, where he could appreciate them. He was admired, sought after to speak about antiquities. An acknowledged expert, the so-fascinating Marquis de Fontaine. Nobody knew, Tess, not even your mother. That's what he was trying to protect when he sided with the other Royalists. His way of life. His treasures. In the end, the new French government got most of them, so he came here, and started over."

"Started over..." she repeated softly. "But...but he was working with the Crown."

"What better excuse to travel where he wanted, make use of secret channels of transportation, have access to ships, to the plans of the mansions of the wealthy, museums...palaces. There was a war going on, treasures were disappearing everywhere, for many reasons. Some say Bonaparte brought half of Egypt back to France with him. I think Sinjon hated him most for that, and that the Emperor had the treasures and he didn't. But your father also did his job, Tess, and very well, to give the man the credit due him. And then, when the mission was complete, he'd reward himself by adding to his collection. But Sinjon isn't a young man anymore. He could still choose the prize, formulate the plans, but it soon became apparent to him that he needed someone else to execute them."

Tess had been breathing rapidly, but now she took a deep, openmouthed breath that was nearly a gasp. She was attempting to get herself under control. "René?" she asked at last. "Did he...?"

"I don't think he knew, no. In any case, he hadn't proved as talented as Sinjon had hoped. You, however, exceeded his expectations, and he'd every intention of introducing you to that room down there. Until I came along. You want praise from the man, Tess? I'll tell you something he told me. You should have been born the son."

Tess smiled ruefully. "How very like him. Every

compliment has a hook on the end, one that digs straight into the flesh. Praise for me, at the expense of my brother. We were in a competition, weren't we? One of my father's deliberate making. The winner gets to *collect* for him. I think I'm going to be sick." But then she rallied, as another question struck her. "Did you…did you steal with him?"

Tess knew what he'd done before coming to the manor house. How he'd played at cards, played at high-wayman, played at most anything, running wild and angry, always searching for something, never knowing what that something was. Never knowing if he was running toward something, or away from himself. The bastard who belonged nowhere.

Sinjon must have thought the gods had personally delivered Jack Blackthorn to him.

Jack shook his head. "He said I wasn't quite ready, and that robbing a few coaches for a lark wasn't the same as what he needed from me. He said I'd never experienced joy of the sort I'd know when the prize was much more than some silly matron's gaudy diamond necklace. The prize was one thing, and worth any danger, but the *joy* of the acquisition itself, knowing what you had in your hand was now yours and yours alone, was worth more than anything else. But first I had to learn a few rudimentary things about antiquities, gain an appreciation for them so that I'd treat them with the care they deserved as I was…acquiring them."

He'd told her most of it now, but there was more. "I thought I'd found a home, Tess, a real purpose in government service. Sinjon had saved me from myself, and you'd given me a reason to believe I didn't have to be alone. Once he'd told me his secret, I knew my duty was to turn Sinjon over to the Crown. Yet how could I do that, knowing it would destroy you and René? Selfishly, I put off making my decision until we'd completed the Whitechapel mission. I shouldn't have waited, and I'll never forgive myself for that."

"Whitechapel. Where René died. And I sent you away anyway. But you never reported Papa to the Crown. Why?"

"Sinjon was already seventy or more, or at least that's the most he would admit to—definitely past climbing through windows or outrunning any pursuit. Without me, or someone like me, his *collecting* days were over. He'd lost. He'd lost his youth, his son and, when I walked away, his last chance at revenge. Because of you, I promised him I wouldn't turn him over to the Crown, but that if he went back to his old ways I wouldn't be held to that promise. And if he tried to recruit you, I'd know, and I'd kill him. He knew I meant what I said."

"And he believed you," Tess said quietly. "I would have."

"He was a broken man when I left, Tess. I'd like to think the errors of his ways, and what those errors had cost him, had finally come home to him. Instead, the need for revenge must have been eating at him ever since."

Tess shook her head. "Revenge? You mean on France, for what happened to my mother. But that was all so long ago."

And here it was, the moment he'd been dreading more

than any of the others. He'd never wanted her to know this particular truth.

"No, Tess. What I'm speaking of now has nothing to do with France or the war or any attempt to restore the monarchy. I doubt it ever was really about any of that, not for Sinjon. It was always about enlarging his collection. And remember this—he was already more than fifty years old when he came to England. I wasn't the first *pupil* he trained to do his bidding. There was another, before me. An exceedingly apt and eager pupil, and quite ambitious. They worked together for years. Until the student, who saw profit where Sinjon saw beauty, eventually betrayed the mentor, striking out on his own, hiring out his unique talents for most any venture, any government, and taking his own *rewards*. You don't know him, Tess, although you may have seen him here years ago. But you have seen his calling card. I've been hunting him for four years, ever since Sinjon told me exactly who he is."

Her eyes were wide and shocked when she turned toward him on the couch. "The Gypsy. That's who you mean, don't you? The Gypsy. The man who murdered René. Papa *trained* him? And now he's gone after him…"

CHAPTER FOUR

TESS SPENT THE next few hours alternately crying and cursing, pacing her bedchamber in her old nightrail and dressing gown, flinging herself into the chair in front of the fire, collapsing to her knees in the center of the room, wrapping her arms tight around herself, rocking in her grief and pain.

Jack had told her all of it. She'd pushed him until she'd heard it all.

A lie. Her father's life was a lie; everything she'd thought about him, believed about him, was a lie. Her life was a lie. René's death had been for a lie, and her mother's, as well. For greed. For *things*.

She and René had always thought they weren't worthy, weren't good enough, had not been smart or clever or, yes, lovable enough. That somehow they had failed their wonderfully heroic father, had been a source of grave disappointment to him. But that hadn't been it at all.

Things. People meant nothing to him. They were only the tools he needed to get him *things.* Her mother may have been the exception, but even she hadn't been able to divert him from his first love, his true delight. *Things,* locked up underground in a cold stone room. *Things,* the hunt for them, the taking of them, the knowledge that now they were his, seen only by him, touched only by him.

She and her brother had thought their father a hero, dedicated to the service of his adopted country, doing his best to help rid France of the hated Bonaparte and set the monarchy back on the throne. They'd wanted only to help him, make him proud of them.

While he'd seen them as two more tools. Inferior tools at that.

And for this man, this unnatural man, she had turned her back on her one true chance of happiness? She'd cut Jack out of her life so effectively that even if he still believed he loved her, he could never forgive what she'd done.

What she'd done because the Marquis de Fontaine had told her it would be best for everyone if Jack never knew. That had been his punishment.

Now it was hers.

"Tess?"

She was sitting on the hearth rug, staring into the dying fire, and didn't turn her head at the sound of his voice.

"I'm all right, Jack," she said quietly.

He sat down beside her, wrapped his arms around his bent knees. Was that to keep himself from touching her? Could he still want her, after all he'd told her? "It's all right if you aren't, you know. None of what you've heard tonight could have been easy to hear. If there had been another way…"

"No, I'm glad you told me. I only wish I'd known years ago, when René was alive. We could have gone, left him to his *collection*. After all, we were never really necessary to him, were we? And our mother? Do you think she knew, Jack? Did she die knowing how unimportant she'd been to his happiness?"

"He may have lived long enough now to regret how he's lived his life. All he's lost. I know you've already considered this. Sinjon trained the man in the skills he then eventually employed to kill René. An old man, no longer seen as being useful to anyone, put out to pasture as it were, while the evil he spawned thrives? A man like that has a lot of time to think, to look back across the years, and try to make at least one thing right."

"You think he's somehow *repented* or some such ridiculousness? You want me to forgive him, is that it? You think I'm that generous?" Tess asked, still looking into the fire. "I can't do that."

"No, I suppose you can't, at least not just yet. Sinjon has to know that, too. But you're his legacy, Tess, all he has left. Everyone else is gone. Those things he spent his life collecting mean nothing compared to a child's love, how he'll be remembered when he's dead."

Tess turned to look at him at last, knowing something Jack didn't know. "Do you really believe that? That he cares how—how I remember him?"

"The closer to death, the more a person realizes the need to be remembered, even mourned. He'd have to know that once I'd heard of his death that room downstairs would have to be emptied, his collection returned to the rightful owners, or at least turned over to the Crown. I lied to you this afternoon. There's only one way into the cellar rooms. You were going to know the truth about him one day, one way or another. And one thing more, Tess. Sinjon has unfinished business."

"The Gypsy," she said her hands tightening into white-knuckled fists.

"Have you read *Frankenstein,* Tess?" When she shook her head he explained. "You should, it's quite the talk of London right now, nearly the equal to the attention Byron received for his *Don Juan.*"

"Jack, I don't see what a book has to do with—"

He held up his hand. "No, let me finish. *Frankenstein* is rather a cautionary tale. In attempting to create perfection, Dr. Frankenstein instead managed to breathe life into a monster. The Gypsy is your father's creation and, right now, his legacy. I think he's decided it's his duty to destroy the monster. No, let me correct that. He plans to lead me to the Gypsy, so I can destroy the monster for him while he watches. While you watch."

A single tear escaped Tess's eyes. "Everything he does has a hook in it somewhere, doesn't it?"

She leaned her head against his shoulder. He put his arm around her. It felt like coming home. The feeling wouldn't last. It couldn't. There were things that could be explained, forgiven. What she'd done to Jack wasn't one of them. She'd chosen her father over him, believed her father's version of what had happened that night in Whitechapel rather than his, sent him away even before he could offer his own version of that last night. Yet, if only that had been the end of it there might still be a way to mend what she'd broken. But there had been more, so much more. Impossible to forgive.

"I want you, Tess," Jack said quietly. "I know we

can't have what we had before—what we thought we had before. But what we did have was good while we had it, wasn't it? I can help you make the world go away, at least for tonight. I know what you need, because I need it, too."

Release. He was offering her release. That was all, no more than that. Anything else they'd thought they'd had never really existed. If it had been real, the past four years wouldn't have been spent apart.

He stood up, reached down his hand to her. Dare she take what he offered? If her life had been empty before, how could she bear it when he left again? But it wasn't forever that he was offering her. Only tonight. Was one night not nearly enough…or too much?

She hesitated.

He was Black Jack Blackthorn. A proud, complex man. He wouldn't offer twice.

She looked up into his dark, handsome face and put her hand in his.

SHE WASN'T AS he remembered her. He'd initiated a girl four years ago, but a woman filled his arms tonight. Her body still slim, but more lush, the sweep of her hips somehow more welcoming. Her breasts heavier, even her nipples not those of a girl, but a more dusky pink than he remembered, and even more receptive to his touch, quick to pucker, to stiffen with her desire.

He took her first with his hand, pushing into her as she ground against him, calling out her pleasure as he found her center and exploited it with his stroking, pinching fingers. He bent over her, urging her on, watching her face as the tension rapidly built to a fever pitch, drawing her body taut as a bowstring before the pleasure washed over her, wave after wave, until there was nothing but sweet, boneless release.

Only then did he kiss her, only then did she wrap her arms around him, returning his kiss, burrowing into him, skin to skin, heartbeat to heartbeat. Only then did he dare to love her as he wanted; slowly, with infinite care, learning her again even though he'd never truly forgotten.

There had been other women since her. Four years was a long time, and he'd had needs. But that's all they had been. Never Tess, never what he'd found with Tess. Never this need to know, this never-ending journey of discovery that made each time feel like the first time. Her soft sighs. Her low cries of pleasure. The way she touched him, knew him, stirred him. How his heart could feel close to bursting when he knew he'd pleased her, how his pleasure intensified because he had pleasured her. The way she breathed his name just as he took her over the top…took him with her.

He kissed every soft, fragrant inch of her, soothing her, rousing her, taking her mind away from everything but the pleasure he was giving her, taking from her. Long strokes along her rib cage, trailing over the flare of her hips. Dipping between her thighs, raising her up to him, opening her, capturing her essence.

Only then did he move to cover her, bracing his upper body on his arms, watching her face as he slowly sank inside her. She slid her arms and legs up and around his back and held on tight, her chest rising and falling rapidly as she looked up at him, her eyes gone dark in just the way he remembered. *Now,* those eyes signaled to him. *Yours, Jack. All yours. Take me now. Take everything I have as you give me all you have. Now.*

He knew her rhythms, as she knew his. He knew that everything else had served to build to the next few moments, this most intimate melding of mind and body.

He began to move. Watching her, as she watched him. While inside his head, a part of him was chanting *I love you, I love you, I love, love, love...*

She slept in his arms as he watched the dawn beyond the windowpanes, reliving the past few hours. His silent words haunting him, keeping him from sleep.

He'd thought it was love all those years ago, believed it was love. Her smile, the way she had of biting on her full bottom lip when pondering a problem, her scent, which had never failed to move him. The way just thinking about her had made the world around him seem new and clean and hopeful. The way she looked at him, which made him believe he was a better man.

Their months together had been the best of times.

He hadn't known anything was missing, that they'd lacked some certain elemental piece that would hold them together in the worst of times.

Jack had been alone all of his life, even as a child, never feeling that he belonged, that he *fit* anywhere. The bastard, yet somehow more the bastard than his brothers, *different* from his brothers. But he'd never known what it meant to be really alone until Tess was lost to him.

Now she was in his arms again, and he would have savored the completeness of it if not for the realization that the feeling could only be fleeting, that the dawn had come, the glory of the night was over and nothing had really changed. Nothing could change until and unless Sinjon was found, until and unless Tess found some sort of needed peace in her feelings about her father.

As his mother's bastard son, Jack could understand that need for understanding better than Tess could know. But now was not the time to travel that well-worn ground again. His mother was a complex woman, in her way perhaps even more complex than Sinjon, and her motives doubly obscure. Like Tess, all he could do was learn to live the life he'd been given, play the cards he'd been dealt.

Careful not to wake her, Jack slipped from the tester bed and pulled on his clothing, his shirttail untucked, carrying his shoes with him as he slipped out of the room, his mind already engaged in the next step—his and Tess's removal to London.

With any luck, Will and Dickie had picked up the man's trail, making the mission easier. But Jack didn't put much faith in luck.

Leaning against the wall, he pulled on his shoes, deciding he'd first visit Sinjon's secret room. The man had taken much with him, but there was still much Jack might find useful.

The sounds of delighted laughter and running footsteps had him turning around in time to see the small, dark-haired child emerge on the second-floor landing just ahead of Emilie, the old woman's face flushed from the exertion of racing down the narrow stairs.

"Jacques! Vous coquin, reviens ici! Jacques, viens à moi cet instant. Jacques— Oh, Jésus, Mary et Joseph, c'est toi!"

The boy stopped in his headlong flight to look up at the tall man standing in the middle of the hallway, blocking his way.

"Maman?" he inquired, his huge green eyes wide in his cherubic face. His curls were thick and black as night, his cheeks flushed from the excitement of his escape from his nurse. And then his face lit in a smile and he was off again, his sturdy legs taking him past Jack. *"Maman!"*

Jack turned to see Tess drop to her knees on the carpet as the boy ran into her open arms. She held the child tightly against her, her hand cradling the back of his head against her as she looked up at Jack, her eyes pleading with him for— God, who knew what she was thinking?

"Jack," she began, his name a plea for understanding, he supposed. He didn't wait around to find out. With one last disbelieving look at the child, he whirled about and bounded down the stairs, through the foyer, all but wresting the door from its hinges and leaving it swinging open as he blindly made his way down to the gravel drive.

He didn't know where he was going. Just away. He had to get away. Where she couldn't follow, where she couldn't find him, couldn't see what she'd done to him. *His son.* He had a son. Goddamn her—he had a son!

CHAPTER FIVE

TESS RUSHED THROUGH her toilette as Jacques chattered and danced about the bedchamber all unawares. Emilie stood by wringing her hands, blaming herself for turning her back on the boy when he was so determined to visit his *Maman*'s bedchamber as he was accustomed to doing each morning.

The appearance of the tall man hadn't made any impression on the child, except to remind him to ask Tess yet again for the whereabouts of his beloved *grand-père*. *Grand-père*. Jacques was the light of her father's life, and had been since the day he'd been born. The man who had mostly ignored his own motherless children while they were in the nursery was now this stranger who would stand at Jacques's bedside, watching him sleep. His smiles were all for Jacques, and he'd bring him treats, bounce him on his knee and tell him silly stories when he thought no one else could hear.

It was Jacques who felt the hugs, received the kisses. Jacques who could so easily slip his hand into his grandfather's and go on adventures in the gardens. Jacques who had somehow, at last, been more important than *things*.

Jack had been right, and he'd been wrong. Jacques was to be the keeper of her father's legacy, the one he wished to guard, the one who must remember him with love, mourn him. He would live or die the hero, as the man who had at last put a stop to the Gypsy. Not for René, not for her, but for Jacques. And for himself... with Sinjon Fonteneau, there was always a hook.

"It's all right, Emilie," Tess assured the woman yet again, even as she struggled to do up the front-closing buttons of her morning gown with trembling fingers. "And probably for the best. We were wrong to hide Jacques from him. We've been wrong about too many things, and for far too long."

The nurse only sniffled into her handkerchief.

"Come along, my love," Tess said then, holding out her hand to her son. "Running is for outside, in the sunshine."

"Jacques's ball?" the boy asked eagerly as they made their way downstairs, bravely jumping down the last two steps and turning for the kitchens and the box near the door to the gardens, the one holding his prized striped ball.

Tess followed, waving away the muffin Cook held out to her, knowing she was too nervous to be hungry. Her world had turned upside down yesterday, and inside out this morning. Life would never be the same. This morning ritual might never be the same. But, for now, for Jacques, she would pretend nothing had changed.

"The path, Jacques," she called after him as he eagerly ran for the expanse of lawn beyond the kitchen garden. "Parsley is for eating, not for stomping, remember?"

He turned and grinned at her, the picture of his father

when Jack was warm from bed and in a mood to tease her, and kept running, throwing the ball ahead of him and then racing to catch up to it. He repeated the action a half dozen more times, until the ball rolled to a stop in front of a pair of shiny black Hessians.

Tess believed she could actually feel her heart stop.

Jack bent to pick up the ball and, still crouching down, handed it to his son. Jacques hesitated, but then reached out and put his hand on the ball, even while Jack still held it. For a moment, the two were a frozen tableau set out expressly to squeeze Tess's heart, green eyes looking into green, dark heads close together.

"Merci, monsieur," Jacques said, and then performed his much-practiced bow and added, "Thank you, sir," just as he'd been taught.

She watched as Jack raised his other hand as if to touch his son's cheek. But then the moment was gone and Jacques was off again, throwing the ball ahead of him and then chasing after it.

Jack stood up once more and approached Tess.

"Jack, I can— No, that's not true. I can't explain. I can't even ask for your forgiveness."

"No, you can't," he said shortly, his eyes on Jacques. "The boy should have a dog. That's what thrown balls are for. There are plenty at Blackthorn, but we can get him his own. A puppy. Nothing too large to start with, or it will just knock him down."

A dog? He was talking to her about dogs? "What?" she asked him, so nervous she was sure she must have misunderstood.

"Never mind," he told her, still looking at Jacques.

"I'll see to it. Emilie is packing his things now and I've ordered the horses put to the coach. They leave in an hour, and should arrive at Blackthorn tomorrow afternoon."

Tess shot a panicked look at her son. "You can't do that. You can't take him. He's *my* son."

At last he looked at her, but only for a moment before he returned to watching his son, following the boy's every move hungrily, greedily. "You and I are for London this morning, correct?"

She hid her surprise that he was still agreeing to take her. Warily, she nodded.

"Leaving my son here, with only Emilie to watch over him. That's not possible."

"Why not?" Tess was fighting to keep from running to Jacques and scooping him up in her arms.

"Sinjon showed me his treasure room. We can't be sure he did the same with the Gypsy, but the man knows of the collection. The sight of those treasures makes for a fairly impressive argument to fall in with his plans."

"No. I don't understand." How could she think? Jack was taking her son from her. All she had, all she'd ever had.

"Haven't you yet wondered why the Gypsy has never attempted to relieve your father of his treasures? He knows they're here. He helped acquire many of them. And with only one old man standing between him and a fortune? Yet he's never tried. Now why do you suppose that is, Tess?"

She watched as Jacques held the ball straight out in front of him with both hands and turned around and around in circles until he fell, giggling, to the grass. How strange. The sun still shone, a child still laughed. And yet her world was crumbling around her. She had to concentrate. Jack still spoke matter-of-factly, a man of no emotion. She'd always marveled at the way his mind worked. So coolly analytical. He'd figured something out in his head, and he had a plan. A plan that included removing Jacques from the manor house. Not from her, please God, but the house itself. "I...I don't know. It doesn't make sense, does it?"

"No, it doesn't. But they worked together for well over a decade, remember. There may have been some bond between student and pupil, some honor among thieves. Either that, or the Gypsy promised to never come after the collection while Sinjon still lived, and in return, Sinjon promised to never come after the Gypsy. Only the two of them know how or why they came to the arrangement, and why they abide by it."

"Papa always has a reason with a hook in it," Tess agreed, wondering where Jack's deductions had led him. "There's a hook somewhere that's kept the Gypsy away."

"True enough. There could be many reasons. Of the two possibilities I've been able to come up with so far, I think the latter makes more sense. There is no honor among thieves. But your father didn't like the terms anymore, not once he'd found me, once he felt sure I'd fall in with his plans to begin enlarging his collection again. So he tried to eliminate the Gypsy in Whitechapel. For that error in judgment, he paid with his son's life."

"Oh, God," Tess said quietly.

"I don't think God enters anywhere into this particular equation. Your father's monster left his card on René's chest. Sinjon somehow acknowledged the punishment, and they went back to their original agreement. Except that after a four-year absence, the Gypsy's calling cards are back in England, announcing his return, and your father's gone after him again. If he fails this time, the Gypsy might decide to come after the collection now, or to teach Sinjon another lesson. Either way, my son is not to be involved, because he's not going to be here. He goes to Blackthorn today."

"*Our* son, and his name is Jacques." Tess felt her hands drawing up into fists. "Besides, this is all simply assumption on your part. Everything you've said since you came here has been conjecture, assumption. Everything you've told me could be a lie. Everything!"

She was like a drowning seaman clasping at bits of floating straw, and she knew it. But he was using what *he* knew to take her son from her.

"You're right, Tess. Everything I said could be a lie. Or I could be wrong, straight down the line, and your father's a damn saint and is simply having himself a lark in London for no apparent reason." He looked to Jacques once more. "But are you willing to risk *our* son's life on that? I'm not."

"Then he goes to London, with us." As Tess heard her own words she marveled at what she'd just admitted. Her father was a thief. Her father, if he failed, could be risking the life of his grandson. And her life…but she couldn't be sure her father had considered her. Had she sunk that far, did she now think so little of her own father? Yes. God help her, yes. She had one objective now, one concern, and that was for Jacques. She'd risk everything, dare anything, to keep him safe, even if at the end of the day that meant losing him to Jack. Her father had sent Jack to them, hadn't he, simply by disappearing...

Jacques took that moment to approach Jack with the ball held out between his hands. "Frow?"

It was fate. It was the hand of God. It was the dice, just this once, being thrown in her favor. Did it matter what it was, as long as Jack was now looking down at his son with his heart in his eyes?

"Throw, Jacques, not frow. Please throw the ball with me. *Veuillez jeter la boule avec moi.*" She would risk everything, dare anything. "Please throw the ball with me, Papa."

OF COURSE THE reports to the Crown had contained no mention of a child. The child wasn't important, but only the man. Those assigned to watch Sinjon over the years had not been chosen from the top ranks of those employed by the Crown. They would have seen no reason to mention that a child was now in residence at the manor house.

But that didn't mean he shouldn't have known. He should have hired his own watchers. He should have made periodic checks of his own over the past four years.

Except that he hadn't been able to trust himself to see Tess again. He might have been inflamed by the impossible thought that she may have changed her mind, may welcome him back. He may have made a fool of himself again, ripped the scabs off a deep, slowly healing wound.

So he'd settled for the reports.

Coward. He'd been a coward. Selfishly protecting himself, falling into his old ways, as he'd done after his mother's cruel admission. *Run away, run away. You're not wanted here. You don't belong.*

Jack rode ahead of the coach, leaving the Crown's assigned watcher to tag along behind, not that the man would be much good if he hadn't the independent judgment to report that there was a child at the manor house, or to inform his superiors that the marquis was acting strangely, disappearing for hours at a time over the past month.

He shouldn't be doing this. Jacques should be on his way to Blackthorn, and Tess along with him. But, he'd told himself, Beau might be off on one of his inspections of the marquess's other holdings, and God only knew what Puck was up to now that he'd an estate of his own. The last letter he'd received from his younger brother had been full of ecstatic exclamations about the calf he'd personally helped bring into the world. He'd named the thing Black Jack, he'd written, because it was both black and stubborn.

That left the marquess, and possibly Adelaide, if she had deigned to visit the estate. His mother would probably be appalled at the thought she'd been made a grandmother, and it wouldn't do for the marquess to begin making grandiose plans for yet another bastard child.

Therefore, rationally, it was probably better that Jacques accompany his parents to London.

It was amazing how a man could rationalize selfishness until it suited his purpose. *Papa.* Jacques had called him Papa...

Jack eased back on the reins and allowed the coach to pull forward, and then paced his horse so that he was now riding just beside the door. He leaned down a bit to look inside. Emilie was dozing on the back-facing seat while Tess held Jacques close beside her, reading to him from some rather worn-looking book.

His heart squeezed at the sight, but even more so when Jacques spotted him and pushed away from his mother to press his palms against the side glass, smiling broadly as he mouthed something Jack couldn't hear.

He motioned for Tess to lower the window but she shook her head.

"Now," he mouthed silently, challenging her with his eyes. If he wanted to know what his son was saying, he'd damn well know, and she'd damn well not try to stop him. He held the cards, and she knew it. She also knew he wouldn't be all that reluctant to play them. She'd kept his son from him for nearly four years, and that was a debt that wouldn't be paid so easily.

Tess lowered the window while holding tightly to the squirming Jacques. "I was attempting to get him to sleep, you know," she said accusingly. "Clearly you've never traveled with a young child for long hours inside a poorly sprung coach. He's already been sick, twice. Not that it seems to bother him."

"Horse! Horse!" Jacques was shouting overtop his mother's complaints.

Jack looked at Tess. She did look a bit...disheveled.

Beautiful, but perhaps a little worn about the edges four hours into their ride to London, her bonnet lying partially crushed on the seat, a few locks of blond hair escaping their pins. His son was obviously a handful.

Jack smiled at the thought. *His son.* Of course he'd be a handful!

He called out to the coachman to stop the coach, and then leaned down and depressed the latch to the door. "Hand him up to me," he said to Tess. "What he needs is some fresh air."

Tess looked ready to object, but then a slow smile curved her mouth. Some might have called it an evil smile. "Of course. But I warn you, he doesn't smell all that fresh, not since the last time he was sick. How long until we're in London?"

"No more than another hour. I'll keep him with me until we're actually in the city. Then I want him inside with you, and the curtains drawn. Agreed?"

"Oh, yes. Happily agreed," Tess said, handing Jacques up to Jack. *"Jacques, essayez ne pas cracher sur Papa's bottes."*

Try not to spit on Papa's boots? "Very amusing, Tess. Why don't you take a hint from Emilie, and try to nap. You look as if you could use some rest. But then, you didn't get much sleep last night, did you?"

Insults exchanged, Jack lifted Jacques and placed him in front of him on the saddle. Tess pulled the door shut with decided force, signaling the coachman to proceed.

It was like old days come back again. The teasing, the sparring, and quite often, the competition. Except with the child now between them. And so much more.

With his left arm wrapped securely about his son's middle, Jack leaned down to kiss the child's soft curls, not yet used to the swift fierce feelings just being near his son engendered in him. *Mine.* What a curious thing to think. *Mine.*

He'd had no future. Now he did. He'd had no hope. Yet now he was hopeful. There were no happy endings. But maybe there could be.

All that lay between him and Tess now was the past, in the forms of Sinjon and the Gypsy...and René. But was it him that she couldn't forgive for what happened to René, or herself?

Jacques was now holding tight to the stallion's mane and bouncing up and down in front of Jack. "Horse! Horse! *Plus rapidement!* Faster! Faster!"

"Oh, really? Faster is it? I should have known this couldn't be your first time in the saddle, not with Tess for your *maman.* Very well, *mon enfant,* faster!"

CHAPTER SIX

"Good evening, sir," the Grosvenor Square butler said as he personally held open the rear door that led in from the mews, just as if Jack had been expected. The man was unflappable, even if he'd had to run down three flights of stairs when alerted that Mr. Blackthorn had arrived at the stables behind the Blackthorn mansion.

"Good evening, Wadsworth," Jack responded, and then passed him the soundly sleeping Jacques. "Any harm comes to this child and I'll have your liver for lunch while you watch. Understood?" he added in the same pleasant tone.

"I would expect no less, sir. Good evening, miss," he then said as Tess walked into the warm kitchens, looking about her as if to get her bearings.

"Lady Thessaly Fonteneau, Wadsworth. See that her belongings are taken upstairs."

Wadsworth, soldier turned butler, had never quite mastered the intricacies of proper butlering. However, thanks to Masters Beau and Puck, he did have fairly recent experience in these matters to bring to the subject the disposition of milady's portmanteaus. He wasn't blind, after all, and Mr. Blackthorn couldn't deny this dark-haired child any more than Wadsworth could stop the sun from rising come morning. "Yes, Mr. Black-thorn, it will be just as you wish."

Jack almost thought he'd detected a wink from the man, but discounted it as Emilie swept into the kitchens with a rapid stream of authoritative French, relieved Wadsworth of his burden and demanded to be shown the nursery.

Tess put out a hand as if to stop the butler and nursemaid as they took her son away from her, but dropped her arm to her side at Jack's slight shake of his head.

"I've been told the Blackthorn butler once knocked down ten of Bonaparte's elite private guard just by blowing on them. I imagine there was more to it than that, but I'd trust him with my son, and you should do the same. Come along. We'll go to the drawing room and the wine decanter I'm sure is already there, waiting for us."

"Come along? I'd rather you didn't order me about, Jack. It only serves to make me feel rebellious, and as I'm extremely thirsty, that would only be cutting off my nose to spite my face."

"And such a pretty nose, too. All right." He offered her his bent arm. "An it pleases you, milady, I would suggest we adjourn to the drawing room for refreshments. Lemonade, perhaps?"

She looked him up and down, as if inspecting him for vulnerable spots she might attack. "Arrogant *and* condescending, and both displayed within the space of a minute. Two of your less attractive traits, Jack, as I recall. Just lead the way, all right? I want to get the taste of road dust out of my mouth."

Signaling to the sleepy-eyed cook who'd just ap-

peared in the kitchens that food would be welcome, Jack
led the way through the mansion to the drawing room.
While Tess collapsed rather inelegantly on one of the
satin couches, he poured them each full glasses of wine
and offered one to her. Only Tess could act so rough and
ready and still be the most beautiful, feminine woman
he'd ever seen.

She downed it in one go. Ah, the French, weaned on
wine from the cradle. He sometimes wondered if she
could drink him under the table.

"That's better," she said, holding out the empty glass
to him to be refilled. "Now, I've had an idea."

"Not tonight, Tess. Sinjon's been in London for more
than a week. One more night won't matter. Either we're
in time, or we're already too late. We've other things to
discuss."

She shifted slightly in her seat. "True, but I don't
want to discuss them."

"And yet that's just what we're going to do." Jack took
up a position in front of the fireplace, one arm resting
on the mantelpiece below a portrait of the Marquess of
Blackthorn.

It proved a bad choice.

"That's your father?" Tess put down her wineglass
and stood up, walking closer to inspect the portrait of
a younger marquess, handsome, blond, fair of skin and
blue of eye, the portrait probably commissioned when
he was much the same age Jack was now. "You don't
favor him. Is your mother dark?"

"No," Jack answered shortly.

"No?" Tess looked at the portrait again, at Jack again. "Your mother's fair, then? Like me?"

"Adelaide is nothing like you, and you're nothing like her. If you were, that child upstairs would never have happened. We're here to discuss Jacques, and why you kept him from me."

He shouldn't have bothered to attempt to divert her. Tess, presented with a puzzle, was like a dog with a bone. She clamped on, and wouldn't let go. "Your brothers. Oliver LeBeau and Robin Goodfellow to your Don John. All named for Shakespearean characters, courtesy of your actress mother. Don John was a bastard, Jack. I've never much cared for Shakespeare, I'll admit, but I did learn that. Are the other two characters also bastards?"

"No, they're not. And my brothers prefer to be known as Beau and Puck. Just as I prefer Jack. Why didn't you tell me? My son, Tess. *My son.*"

He may as well not have spoken.

"Are they also dark? Beau and Puck?"

Jack deserted the mantelpiece for the drinks table, pouring himself another glass of wine. He never should have brought her here. He could have taken her to his house in Half Moon Street, but he preferred the mansion as being safer for Jacques. "They favor their parents," he said, and then turned to challenge Tess with his eyes. "You're not going to stop, are you?"

"Would you?" she asked him, standing her ground. "You once told me you didn't belong anywhere. I thought you were referring to your bastard birth. It had to be difficult, must still be difficult, to be the bastard son of a marquess. Neither fish nor fowl, as it were, I suppose, not knowing precisely where you fit, if anywhere. But we're in your father's mansion, and you clearly not for the first time. The marquess seems to be generous to his bastards."

She was working it through, piece by piece, and Jack allowed it, mostly because he knew he couldn't stop her.

"Is he similarly generous to your mother?"

"I suppose you'd have to ask her. He ordered a cottage built on the estate for her, and she stays there when she isn't traveling with the acting troupe he's bought her. It has a thatched roof. The cottage, that is. She enjoys playing the country maiden. There are a few sheep, and she dresses up like a shepherdess and carries a crook with a large pink bow on— Yes, I suppose she's content."

"You don't like her, do you? Your mother. It's not her fault you're a bastard, Jack. That's unfair."

Jack laughed shortly. "True. Poor Adelaide. Clearly you sympathize with her, one bastard's mother to another."

Tess crossed the room swiftly and slapped him hard across the cheek. "Don't call our son a bastard!"

Jack didn't flinch. "Pardon me. I seem to have forgotten our marriage ceremony."

She rubbed her hands together. Her palm probably stung; God knew his cheek felt as if it was on fire. "That's not what I meant. It's not what you said. It's the way you said it. As if…as if it mattered."

"It *does* matter, Tess. Christ, if nobody else knows that, I do. My brothers do. We were raised on the estate. In that sprawling country house. Raised to be better than we were. Given everything save the one thing we needed. Legitimacy. That's not how it's going to be for my son. I've already sent a message to Blackthorn. The banns are being read in the village church, and one way or another—if I have to carry you to the altar over my shoulder and drugged stupid—you and I will be married in four weeks' time. *That's* what we're discussing tonight."

Now he'd succeeded in diverting her.

"You don't want to marry me, Jack," she said quietly.

"You're right. I don't. I wanted to marry the Tess I knew. I don't know you. The Tess I knew wouldn't have kept my son from me."

"You've grown hard, Jack. Cold. You were never like that with me. You're not the man I remember, either."

"Four years is a long time," he agreed. "A lifetime, when you're carrying what I've carried with me, knowing what I know."

"René," she said quietly.

It was time they had this out. "Yes, René, he's a major part of it. I changed the plan, altering it to include you and include your brother. For that I am guilty, and I'll never forgive myself for not excluding both of you, which is what I should have done. I knew he was hot to please Sinjon, hot to impress him, prove himself."

"Not just Papa. He wanted you to be proud of him. He worshipped you."

"Then he was a fool. But still, there should have been another way, and I should have found it. That's my sin, Tess, and I admit to it. But there was more, and you know that now."

"Papa risked René to get the Gypsy."

Jack laughed ruefully. "That's it? That's all you think can be put at Sinjon's door? My God, you're still blind, aren't you?"

Tess's expression closed. "I'd like to be shown to my chamber now."

"What was the plan?" Jack shouted to her departing back. "Think, Tess. What was the plan!"

Her shoulders slumped and she turned to him, tears standing in her eyes. "I was to be the stalking horse, the decoy, the distraction," she said quietly. "I was to stand in the glow of the streetlamp outside Covent Garden, clutching the satchel supposedly holding the money to be exchanged for Bonaparte's next battle plan. Reveal myself, draw the man's attention, divert him, make him in turn reveal himself so that you and Papa could take him down once he'd taken possession of the satchel."

"Thank you," Jack said, his voice dripping venom. "You, not René. Out in the open, not in a Whitechapel alleyway. With only Sinjon knowing that the mission was not what we thought it was, with only Sinjon knowing we weren't going up against some inferior French traitor, but drawing out the Gypsy, the monster he'd taught every trick he ever knew."

Tess wet her lips as she nodded. "He would have known, yes. Papa's used the same ploy before."

Jack gave a quick thought to Dickie Carstairs. "And I've used it since, to great effect, I admit that. Making it easy for the Gypsy to recognize it and form a counter-plan of his own," he told her, approaching her slowly so that possibly she wouldn't bolt, run away from the truth. He spoke quietly now. "So why not put one of my children—it didn't matter which one—out there as a decoy, and then I'd wait for the Gypsy to ignore the obvious ploy. I'd wait for him to come out of the shadows just where he knew I'd be hiding, ready to strike. Except that didn't happen, did it? Sinjon wasn't even looking in René's direction when the monster cut him down."

Tess was standing with her arms tightly wrapped around her middle, rocking back and forth as tears rolled down her cheeks. She hadn't been there, she hadn't seen it, the quick savagery.

But Jack had been watching. He'd been in place, ready to move, when a blur of black, hooded cloak moved across the alleyway, barely hesitating in front of René before disappearing through a narrow door previously unnoticed by anyone. René hadn't even hit the cobblestones before the door had closed, the hooded figure gone.

Jack had run to the boy, not even remembering how he had leapt over the barrels that had concealed his position, arriving long seconds before Sinjon, who promptly knelt down, his ear close to his son's mouth. René grabbed his father's arm, said something Jack couldn't make out, and then his hand fell away. He was dead, the knife in his chest to the hilt, a strange black calling card with a golden eye at its center half-tucked into his waistcoat pocket.

The Gypsy had come to that alley not to sell French secrets to the Crown, as Jack had been told, but expressly to kill. But not to kill Sinjon. René's murder was a warning. Tess's death would have delivered that same warning had she been the one standing in the alley.

"He thought I'd—he thought René would be safely out of it."

"Which is where you both should have been, damn it. This wasn't for Crown and country, Tess. This was private, one man against the other. And for what, Tess? For that damn *collection*."

"You should have told me then—the secret room, the collection, all of it. You shouldn't have let me blame you. Papa said—"

"I know what he told you. That I froze. That I didn't move fast enough. I was closer, I should have been able to stop it. My most important mission, and I'd botched it. And I had, Tess. I should have put a stop to it all before we ever went into that alley."

"You didn't know then that our quarry was the Gypsy." She put her hand on his arm. "René's dead. We can't either of us change that. I wish you had told me. I wish I could believe I'd have been ready to listen. Everything would have been so...different."

Jack slipped his arms around her, pulling her close against his chest. "This time he dies, Tess. I promise you that."

She stepped back to look at him, to watch his reaction to her next words, he was sure. "And this time I'll be there to see him die."

All right. Now it was his turn to look at her, watch her. "And Sinjon? What about him?"

"I don't know, Jack. I just don't know."

TESS THANKED THE maid who'd helped her into her night-rail and dismissed her, already looking longingly at the turned-down bed across the large chamber. She'd been upstairs to see that Jacques was sound asleep, tucked up in a cot shaped like a swan, of all things, and that Emilie was snoring loudly in the next room, the door open between them.

Only a little more than a single day and night, and everything in Tess's life had changed. For the first time in her life she knew what it meant to not know if one was on her head or her heels.

She'd felt so good downstairs, wrapped in Jack's strong arms. It was a feeling she had to fight, because it could only lead to weakness when she could least afford to be weak.

He wanted the Tess he'd known four years ago, and she couldn't be that person again. She didn't believe she wanted to be that person again. Too young. Too trusting. All unknowing.

She'd adored her father. Worshipped him unreasonably, considering the life they'd led, a life of lies. It was one thing to think she had been young, vulnerable, easily manipulated by a master of manipulation. But that was not a real excuse. Unlike René, she'd questioned, she'd wondered. But she'd never taken that one real step, that of going to the marquis and putting her questions directly to him.

Instead, she had done as her father told her. *Let him go, Thessaly. He isn't worthy of you. Because of him, René is dead. René wasn't ready. I should have listened to you. We must both live with that pain, but we should not also have to look in that man's face every day. It's over, all of it. From now on, it will be just the two of us, the way it should have been all along.*

Oh, he was good, her father. He'd known just what to say, just how to handle her. Complete with the hook: *just the two of us, the way it should have been all along.*

And then there was Jacques, and her father had become this benevolent stranger who doted on his grandson. *Jack must never know. Jack would take the child. My son, your brother, lost to us. We cannot lose the child. Think with your head, Thessaly. You know he'd take the child.*

And yet now her father had gone after the Gypsy again and he'd done it knowing that Jack would be the one who came to the manor house, Jack would be the one sent to find him...and find Jacques.

Why? *Why?*

"Oh, God. Oh, my God," she breathed as realization hit her. She had to find Jack. She had to tell him what she'd figured out.

She looked down at her comfortable old dressing gown and then shrugged. What did it matter how she was dressed? He'd seen her in every way she could be seen, touched her in every way she could be touched. Maidenly modesty was for maidens, not the mothers of their lovers' sons.

She was halfway to the door to the corridor when it opened and Jack stepped inside, stopped, and raised one expressive eyebrow in her direction.

"My, my. Wadsworth must have misunderstood," he said, advancing into the room. "This is my chamber when I'm in residence. However, you're certainly welcome, although that gown is nearly as good as a chastity belt. Still, I think we'll manage a way around it."

"For a man who says he all but detests me, you certainly seem hot to…to…"

"Rip off that gown, throw you down on that bed and bury myself between your legs, pounding into you until you scream my name as I take you over the edge? Is that what you were trying to say?"

She longed to slap him. She felt a ridiculous urge to burst into tears. In those few words, he'd taken what they had shared and turned it all wrong, base and self-serving. "Yes, I think that's it. Although the phrase *randy goat* probably belonged in there somewhere. Last night was a mistake, Jack. Mine. But I don't make the same mistake twice."

"How do you know? You could already be carrying my child. Again."

"I really could hate you. I think I do." Nearly as much as she hated herself for the need curling low in her belly at the image Jack's suggestive words had placed in her head, the ache his last words had started in her heart.

But she was French. She was practical. Continued trips to the bed with Jack were not practical.

"I know what my father's planning to do," she said, ignoring his last statement.

"Really?" Jack slipped off his neck cloth and tossed it in the general direction of a nearby chair before beginning to strip off his jacket.

"Yes, really. He is going to sacrifice himself so that you can kill the Gypsy."

Jack hesitated in the act of shrugging out of his jacket. "Interesting. How?"

"He's going to be the stalking horse. Like René. He's setting himself up to die, Jack, so the Gypsy exposes himself, and you do the rest. He doesn't plan to live through the experience. Again, like René. After all, somebody has to pay for the mistake that cost my brother his life. In his heart he must blame himself. Not you."

"Now why do I doubt that?" Jack said, tossing the jacket after the neck cloth.

"You haven't seen Papa these last years. Jacques was his only happiness. He's old, Jack. Tired. And... and defeated. You said the collection is all that matters to him, and I think you were right. Then. But not now. Jacques... I don't know. Jacques changed something in him. He was soft with your son, nearly unrecognizable even to me."

"Always defending him, aren't you? Even when it's clear he's indefensible. Dear, kindly old Sinjon, bouncing his grandson on his knee. That's rather like trying to imagine the devil handing out Gunther Ice's in Hell."

His comparison stung, and Tess did her best not to flinch. Jack was entitled to his opinion, but only as long as he remained open to hers. "I agree the man's no saint, even now. But it was your idea that he and the Gypsy had some understanding about the collection—and why do we keep calling it that? Papa's ill-gotten goods, his booty, his obsession, that's what those things really are."

Jack held up his hand to silence her. "Don't allow yourself to be distracted," he warned her. "What you're saying is that Sinjon's old, probably going to die soon, and he couldn't let that happen before he eliminated the Gypsy, who would surely then turn up to claim the collection. We're already in agreement there, Tess. That's why Jacques is here, remember?"

"Yes, but it's more than that. He's *leading* us to the Gypsy. Papa's not the pursuer. He's the goat staked in the clearing, tied there to draw the wolf. You're the executioner, the one who will kill the wolf as he stands over the goat's body. He's setting himself up to *die*, Jack. To save our son."

Jack sat down on top of his jacket and neck cloth and raised one booted foot to her, signaling that he needed her assistance. Making it clear without words just who he believed was in charge here, and who was not.

"So now he's part tethered goat, part sacrificial lamb. And then you and I, and our son, will have the collection, all the untold wealth that collection can bring us. We'll leave this damp island Sinjon has always hated, sail off to America or somewhere, and live out our lives. Always cognizant, of course, of the fact that his noble sacrifice made it all possible, his past forgiven, his name honored for generations. You really expect me to believe that, Tess?"

"Probably not, no, not when you say it that way," she admitted, hiking up her dressing gown so that she could straddle Jack's leg and begin edging off his boot. "I only want you to think about the possibility, and how we could stop him from doing anything that stupid. Put your other foot on me, and push."

He did as she said, placing his booted foot against

her buttocks. "If you insist. But Sinjon isn't going to simply stand there and let the Gypsy put a knife in his heart. Sacrifice is not in his nature." He pushed his foot against her, hard.

Tess nearly staggered when his foot slid free of the boot, but she managed to stay upright. "Use the jack for the other one," she told him, refusing to rub at her rump where his boot heel had been moments before. "We're compromising, I'm not capitulating. Papa would need bait, to draw the Gypsy in. You said I should look for what was missing from the collection, remember? What did he take?"

She watched as he made use of the jack in the corner, hoping the leather of his boot would be irreparably marred. Sometimes one had to be content with the small pleasures in life.

"He called it the Mask of Isis," Jack said as he joined her once more in the middle of the room, seeming to *fill* the room with just his presence. "She supposedly was some Egyptian goddess."

"I know who she was. She gave birth to both the heaven and the earth—and is allegedly responsible for several other things I can't remember." His shirt was gone now, and if she was going to tell him to leave she should say it now, and mean it. Since she wouldn't mean it, she satisfied herself with a ridiculously obvious question. "So then it's quite valuable?"

"Things fashioned of solid gold usually are, yes," Jack said, and she suddenly realized he was unbuttoning her dressing gown. "It's a face-size mask, not a bust, although I doubt it was made to actually be worn. Too heavy for that, by half. Her facial features were painted on the gold, although the paint is fairly worn off, but Sinjon assured me it was Isis depicted there. Something about a headdress in the form of a crown, or some hieroglyphic that stands for the word *crown?* I don't know, Tess. He let me hold it, probably hoping I'd feel what he did, the glory of possession. I just felt its weight, and knew it was worth a king's ransom. Maybe that's what he'd hoped I'd feel, since he planned on making me his thief."

She loved this. Joining with him, mind to mind, as they worked out a problem, a scenario, and agreed on a solution. There was an excitement in the process, yes, almost a sexual excitement, and the two of them had more than once made love while at the same time planning out the details of his and Sinjon's latest assignment from the Crown. They were so alike, she and Jack. They neither of them cared for simple things, easy answers. They went for results yes, but the real pleasure came from the twist, the unexpected, never doing the obvious.

She still kept his only present to her, an eight-sided rosewood box made up from dozens of smoothly interlocking pieces. It had taken her days to solve the puzzle and be rewarded with the small golden locket hidden in its center. A locket surely meant to carry their miniatures, but that now carried those of her mother and brother.

She'd loved the locket. She adored the rosewood box.

"Then that's clearly the bait he plans to use now, as he did with you. The Golden Mask of Isis."

"I thought you wanted to tell me things I hadn't already thought out on my own. Perhaps we're done talking." He slipped his hands inside the dressing gown to cup her breasts through the thin fabric of her nightrail, began stroking her taut nipples with the pads of his thumbs.

She took a deep breath. "That's…distracting."

"Really? I'd hoped for more than simple distraction. I like your breasts like this, Tess. Fuller, heavier. Did you suckle him? Did you put my son to your breast?"

"Emilie was rather past the duties of wet nurse," she said, closing her eyes as Jack's touch, Jack's words, performed their sweet seduction.

He began lightly pinching her nipples between thumb and forefinger. "Was he greedy? Like his father? Did you ever hold him to your breast, and think of me?"

She could barely breathe, couldn't swallow. "Emilie… she said that was natural. That…that I might…might *feel* things. That the suckling was meant to stir my womb, tighten it after…after the birth. But it wasn't like when you— Jack. Oh, Jack, don't…don't do this…"

But he was doing it. He had bent his dark head to her after exposing her breast and now he was sealed against her, hot and wet and drawing her nipple into his mouth even as his fingers continued to play and pinch her other breast through her nightrail.

But playing fair was for other people, not for them. If he saw an advantage, he took it. If she saw an opening, she exploited it. That's just the way they both were made, just as they'd seemed fashioned to fit together like the puzzle pieces of that rosewood box, until it would take a very discerning eye to see the seams where they might be split open, separated.

Her father had seen where the pieces were joined and taken them apart like the master he was.

Now, he had put them back together.

Why?

Jack didn't believe her thought that Sinjon Fonteneau was setting himself up as some sacrifice in order to protect and assure Jacques's future, or even as some twisted penance for putting René in danger for his own ends.

Maybe she didn't believe it herself. Maybe she still needed to see her father as good, a hero, a man to be admired, emulated. Not a man who would take his candles and sit in the middle of a damp room, admiring his collection, risking everything for things he found more important than his own family.

Maybe it was simply time she gave in…surrendered her will to Jack's. Believed what he believed. If just for tonight.

She arched her neck, pushing her upper body forward, her mind swimming with disjointed thoughts, her blood singing in her veins as Jack took and took from her.

Here there was complete agreement. When he touched her there were no questions, only answers. No regrets could stand between them when they wanted, when they needed so badly. When all there was in the world was the two of them, the two halves of that single most perfect whole in the entire world.

She ground her lower body against his arousal. "I want you," she told him. "Take me." It was a demand, a plea, a whisper, a shout to the heavens, all in one. "Take me now, Jack."

He picked her up and carried her to the bed, sitting her on the edge of it while he quickly rid himself of his clothing. Pushing her nightrail up over her thighs, he spread her knees and pulled her toward him, his eyes dark as he guided himself into her before capturing her mouth with his own.

She wrapped her arms and legs tightly around him, feeling him deep, deep inside of her, their tongues dueling, keeping time with his strong, hard thrusts.

Later, he would love her, as he'd loved her last night. Later, she would give him what he'd given her and thrill at his release, his temporary surrender to her hands and mouth. Later, when they were both too exposed, too vulnerable to hide from each other, at least not in the dark in the middle of the night.

He'd hurt her, yes. But she'd hurt him, as well. They were both very good at what they did, and they both knew where to aim to inflict the most damage to the other.

And the most pleasure.

At some point they had to find a way to stop hurting each other. At some point they had to forgive, and to trust.

But for now they would simply take what came most easily to them. Just as they had last night, the years stood between them now. So much time lost, so much need to make up for. This wasn't making love. This was mating. Pure and simple and primeval.

And good. Ah, so very— *"Jack."*

CHAPTER SEVEN

"GENTLEMEN," JACK SAID, slipping into the empty chair at the table Dickie Carstairs and Will Browning shared inside the anonymous-looking tavern at the bottom of Bond Street the first evening after his arrival in London. "How wonderful, if predictable, to find you together. Too early for the theater? No invitations tonight, Will? No, that couldn't be possible."

Dickie looked at him in surprise. "I've been haunting Half Moon Street all day. You didn't give the signal. Shade up, you're in residence. Shade down, you're not. Half up—or half down, I suppose—meet you here. No signal, but we came anyway. You're supposed to signal, Jack. It's what you said you would do."

"I didn't signal? How remiss of me. Will? Would you care to remonstrate with me, as well?"

"Another time, perhaps. You're at the mansion in Grosvenor Square, aren't you? Doing a bit of showing off for the lady, Jack? She's here with you, isn't she? Couldn't leave her where she belonged, not that I blame you, I suppose. A pretty piece."

"And here I thought you meant your apology of the other day," Jack said silkily, even as he raised a hand to signal the barmaid for another glass. "There was a complication."

Will looked at him levelly. "They're the very devil, aren't they? Complications."

Henry Sutton had always been the buffer between Jack and Will, two men with rather high opinions of themselves when it came to their unusual talents, and rather an aversion to being considered second behind anyone else. Dickie Carstairs was a poor substitute mediator, but he did try.

"See? There you go. Complications. I told you there had to be something," he said, turning to Will after pouring Jack a glass of wine. "Had to be a reason."

Jack nodded to Dickie. "There was a child at the manor house. Not knowing what Sinjon could be up to, and how it might impact the daughter and the child, I felt it best to remove both mother and son to London until we know what's going on. Half Moon Street wouldn't have served. Have you had any progress at this end?"

Will's knowing smile would have meant his death if he hadn't quickly turned it into a frown of concern. "Well done, Jack. It's the marquis we're after, not his family, correct? A child, though, and a male child at that. How wonderful…generally speaking. As for the rest of it? We know our elusive quarry alit just where we thought he would. We know he hired a man and a wagon to move a heavy trunk. We located the man and the wagon, visited the inn, and found the marquis gone when we searched the attic room he had leased for the space of one week. The trunk remained, but it was empty."

"He was still an old lady at the inn, although nobody there could remember seeing her leave that last time.

She—that is, *he* left a small purse in his room, to cover his lodgings, I suppose, and left the trunk behind as well, as Will just said. Empty. Very nice trunk if I must say so myself. Oh, and it was the monk that left the inn. That's twice with that disguise. He won't use that again, I think," Dickie supplied helpfully. "But that's all we know. We don't know what to do next, Jack. Does the daughter have any ideas?"

"A few," Jack said, thinking about Tess's insistence that Sinjon was planning to sacrifice his life in order that Jack would kill the Gypsy for him. Not arrest him. Silence him. And without the Crown being given the chance to question him and perhaps learn of his dual role as Sinjon's thief, along with the location of the collection. Otherwise, the Mask of Isis and the rest could not be bestowed on Jacques and thus assure the boy's future, could it? He doubted Tess had considered that part, but he had. "I don't put much credence in what she thinks. He fooled her as completely as he did the Crown's none-too-bright watchdog, slipping away out from directly below their noses, which doesn't say much to her powers of observation. She thinks her father summons the dawn, but we know better than that, don't we, gentlemen."

Will snorted. "We don't know anything you don't tell us, and I'd like to go on record now in saying I don't much care for your secretiveness. We work together, Jack. Moreover, we work for the Crown, not a daughter upset over misplacing her doddering old father."

"You're questioning my loyalty, Will?"

"Absolutely not. I'm questioning what hangs between your legs, and would very much appreciate hearing something from you that would alleviate my fears that your brain may be hanging there, too," the other man said softly. "You haven't done so yet, but I'm fairly certain your next line will have something to do with needles and haystacks, and that Dickie and I should just take ourselves off and you'll handle the whole of it. Admit it, Jack, we're no closer to our runaway than we were before, and I find myself totally out of charity with the man. And you."

"Sounds the same way to me. Needles and haystacks, I mean—not the rest of it. Well, that's that, then, isn't it? So what do we do now? It seems we've run out of options."

"Oh, ye of little faith. And, in your case, Will, lively imagination." Jack smiled as he saluted the two men with his full glass. "We agree the daughter's useless, or at least I do. You didn't ask me if *I* had any ideas."

Dickie sat forward in his chair, first looking about him as if he expected several wagging ears to be listening in on their conversation—which anyone who hadn't been might be inclined to do now, as he looked so very suspicious. "Well? Do you?"

"As it happens, yes, I do." He pulled a folded bit of the *London Times* from his waistcoat and placed it on the table. "This same advertisement, or notice if you will, has appeared daily for the past five days. I've already checked."

Will deftly snatched up the newspaper before Dickie could even half reach for it. He unfolded the scrap, checking first one side and finding only part of an article printed there, before turning it over. "The advertisements? Really?"

"A timeworn method of communicating with interested others. I thought Sinjon might trot it out for us. Or at least I thought he'd believe I'd think so."

"He'd think that, would he?" Will read the first item. "'Devonshire widower seeking chaste, moral female of exemplary health and numbering no more than five and twenty years; to whom he might bestow the honor of wife, and invest in her the pleasures of mother and educator to his eight young children.' And he names a solicitor for the dozens of eager, chaste and moral females to contact. I don't believe I foresee a feminine stampede in the direction of this Devonshire solicitor's office. At any rate, I suppose that's not what I was supposed to be noticing here?"

"I wouldn't think so," Dickie said, shaking his head. "Eight, you said? No wondering why the first wife died, is there? Probably just wanted some peace, poor thing. Probably couldn't chance turning corners in the house too close to the wall, or he'd grab her and put her up against it, trying for number nine."

"I beg your pardon, did you just say what I thought you said?" Jack asked, surprised that the man even imagined such things, let alone said them.

Dickie's face flushed red to the roots of his hair. "It's only what I heard my father say about my uncle Robert. Who hadn't a feather of his own to fly with, mind you, and was always sponging off us, moaning about all the mouths he had to feed. Don't breed 'em, don't have to feed 'em, that's what my father— And what do you find so funny, Will Browning?"

Will waved his hands in front of his face as if in apology. "Nothing, Dickie. You're a man of many parts, though, I'll say that for you. I think I found it, Jack, next up after the prolific widower. But what does it mean?"

As Dickie grabbed the newspaper to read the advertisement for himself, Jack explained.

"Someone is advertising the sale of *objets rares d'art,* Dickie, of Roman, Greek and Egyptian variety. Discerning buyers, once qualified, will be allowed to view this aforesaid private collection for the purpose of making offers of purchase. Those interested are to deliver their correspondence to Mr. St. John at Number 9 Cleveland Row precisely at noon, the fifteenth of June, outlining their qualifications. That's in three days' time. If deemed reputable, they will then be contacted by the seller and an appointment made to view the collection, at which time bids will be entertained."

"Yes, yes, I see all of that here. Seen dozens like it, for that matter, although none so precise about the time. Some impoverished peer or other is always trying to sell something without letting the world know his coffers are bare. Can't let your creditors know you're pockets-to-let, or they'll all pounce. Half the ladies in the *ton,* to hear my father tell it, are wearing paste instead of diamonds, and only half of that half even know it. But what does that have to do with—"

"St. John," Will interrupted. "Sinjon. Am I right?"

Jack nodded. "Rather more blatant than is usual for

Sinjon, but I suppose he may not have trusted me to understand anything more subtle."

Dickie threw down the paper. "It's too bloody subtle for me. What does it signify? He's inviting you to come see him, is that it? After all this skulking about as old ladies and monks? All this changing of lodgings? Why would he do that?"

Jack had his lies carefully prepared. "My guess is that he's decided the quiet country life doesn't suit him any longer, and he'd like to make some changes in his arrangement with the Crown. Either the Crown pays him much better than it has to remain silent about twenty years of not always flattering secrets, or he sells them to the highest bidder. You did catch that line about *entertaining bids,* yes? He knew Liverpool would set me to tracking him down if he disappeared, just as he knew he stood a good chance of *disappearing* if he sat at home once his request, we'll call it, landed on the prime minister's desk. I'm actually rather insulted."

"How so?" Will asked, reading over the advertisement a second time.

"Obviously, Will, that Sinjon would believe I'd be willing to meet with him, be his tame messenger, carry his demands to Liverpool—and how sure he feels he knows me, that I wouldn't simply follow orders and eliminate the threat by eliminating him. He's planning to pull me into his conspiracy. I'm damned if I do, gentlemen, and damned if I don't. Turn on Liverpool by helping Sinjon, or follow my orders and needlessly murder a delusional old man, because that's what it would be. He's years past defending himself. And no,

Will, before you say it, I would not care for Tess's reaction were I to do the latter. There are still some small remnants there of what I once felt for the woman."

"Very prettily put, if dangerously idiotic. But, Jack," Will said as he poured himself another measure of wine, "think about this a moment. You're more of a dupe in this thing than you've realized. That's why he left the daughter behind. Your lost love, if you'll allow a moment of theatrics. You show up, asking for the father's whereabouts, and she looks at you with large, soulful eyes, asks you to remember what you once had together, and begs your help. How could you do anything less? And damn, man, you did bring her and her brat toddling along with you to London, didn't you? Saving the man the trouble of fetching them from the country before they set sail to God knows where, his pockets filled with Liverpool's gold. I'd say you might be a tad ashamed, but not insulted. You're acting just as your old master expected. Dare I say his trained monkey?"

"Enjoying yourself?" Jack asked, glaring at Will to let him know he'd come within a hair of pushing too hard this time. Will would expect no less of a reaction from him; besides, Browning wanted a challenge, and sliding a knife between the ribs of an old man didn't qualify.

But now it was Jack's turn again. "Still, did he have to be so unsure I'd pick up on his clues? St. John was enough. He didn't have to throw in all this nonsense about selling his supposed rare art objects. True, the man may have once been famous for his collection, but that was in France, which is where the collection remains. God, according to the daughter, they're in debt to half the local village, as he must have taken all of his money with him to pay his passage, hire helpers, secure inn rooms."

Dickie looked at him blankly. "Then there's no collection? It's all a ruse? Now there's a pity. But it makes sense. A man with a fist full of ancient art and such shouldn't have to come after Liverpool, or not pay the local tradesmen."

"Very good, Dickie, we'll make a thinker of you yet. The point, however, is that the marquis was hitting Jack here over the head with clues because he didn't trust him to understand otherwise," Will said, smiling at the man. "So, Jack, what next? We're heading off to Cleveland Row? Somehow I don't think the doddering Sinjon will let it be that easy."

"He won't. Sinjon isn't there. He will, however, have made arrangements for any and all responses to his advertisement to be delivered to him wherever he's hiding. Sinjon always had a flaw, gentlemen. He has always considered himself the smarter man, in any situation. He took plans too far, made them too intricate, when simple would serve us better. We argued on that head, quite often. As we all know, for every unnecessary twist or turn, every extra person added to a plan, another opportunity to make a mistake rears its ugly head."

"True enough, Jack," Dickie agreed. "Look what happened when your brother added himself to our last venture. Cost us Henry."

"Henry's mistake cost us Henry, we're all agreed

with that," Will Browning said tightly. "Dig him up, and Henry would agree, as well."

"Thank you, Will. Just when I'm convinced I don't like you, you show a twisted bit of opinion that somehow comforts me." Jack turned to look at Dickie. "Do I have your permission to continue?"

"Oh, yes, sorry. It's as Will says, sometimes my tongue is hinged at both ends, and silliness comes out. You're going to send him some sort of note, yes? The marquis I mean." He rolled his eyes at Will. "And I only said *that* so you wouldn't ask me if I meant Henry."

"Of course he's going to send a note. And that's when you and I come in, Dickie, old friend, when we follow whoever retrieves the communications left at Cleveland Row, since Jack, even in disguise, might be somehow seen and recognized by our sly old fox," Will said, glaring at Jack. "How condescending of you to include us, even in such a menial way."

"Each man to the level of his talents," Jack said coolly.

"*Touché*—and done. We've managed enough verbal fencing for the evening, haven't we?"

Dickie held up his hand, as if hoping to be called upon. "So you will send a letter—we'll call it a letter—and so will several others? Maybe dozens of others? What happens to them? The prospective purchasers, that is? They're bound to be disappointed when they aren't invited to view the art objects."

Of all the people to ask the one question Jack didn't want to hear asked, how could Dickie have possibly been the one to come up with it?

"Our friend here has a point, Jack, even if he doesn't see it. Why not an advertisement that summons you, only you? Or is my level of talent too low to understand this complexity?"

As the only explanation that made any sense would be to suggest that Sinjon had hoped to attract more than one party via his advertisements—in point of fact, the Gypsy—Jack chose not to answer directly.

He got to his feet, the chair scraping back loudly against the wooden floor. "I think we're done here. He's, as you say, one old man. It's bad enough I have to deal with him, but I'll be damned if I'll go about it while saddled with two constantly questioning old women. We'll meet again once I've completed my mission." He looked down at the two of them, first one, then the other. Black Jack at his most quietly fierce. "Agreed?"

Dickie was confused, which was how Jack wanted him. Will was angry, which was how Jack needed him. Best of all, he'd avoided having to answer the question. For the rest, all he could do was pray Sinjon hadn't gone senile in the past four years, and hadn't carefully planned out how the person he sent to retrieve the communications at noon on the fifteenth would elude pursuit.

"All right, Jack, you've made your point. He was your mentor, you know him best," Will said, sighing. "Now for God's sakes, climb down off your high horse and tell us your plan."

"Dickie?" Jack asked the other man.

"I like it best when we get along," he said quietly. "But I do miss Henry. Can't help that. He used to tease that we were a dashing band of rogues. Now we're only a trio of rogues, and not half so dashing. Ever since the war's over, we're not much more than Runners, as I see it, China Street pigs but without the scarlet waistcoats, and with the dirtiest of jobs. Chasing after old men who should have been taken care of a long time ago. Not so much the rogues now, are we? Rather sad, I think."

"Have some more wine," Will said, all but pushing the full glass into Dickie's face. "We're ready, Jack. What comes next?"

"As always, we take the next step," Jack said, retrieving the chair. He sat down once more, this time straddling the chair and leaning in confidentially, drawing them in to the circle of his plan, the circle of his lies. He pulled another square of paper from his waistcoat, a map he'd drawn of Cleveland Row, unfolded it and smoothed it against the tabletop. "And you definitely guessed correctly, Will, when you said I'd want you and Dickie positioned outside Number 9. Here, Will…and you here, Dickie…"

If he had a conscience, he'd be ashamed of himself. But he had Tess and Jacques to consider, and he wouldn't only betray his country, he'd sell his very soul to protect them.

SHORTLY AFTER TUGGING on the bellpull, Tess heard voices in the hallway, followed by the sound of Jacques's childish giggles, which was followed on hard by the sight of the so large and fierce-looking Wadsworth prancing into the drawing room like one of the Prince Regent's finest carriage horses put to a trot, Jacques sitting on his shoulders, holding on to the man's hair and urging him to *"Gullup! Gullup!"*

"I'm sorry, miss," the butler said, "but everyone else is busy what with one thing and another, and I was closest. Mrs. Emilie is tired from the journey yesterday, and napping. Is there something you'd be wanting?"

Tess did her best to keep from smiling, but it was a wasted effort, especially when Jacques moved his hands down to cover Wadsworth's eyes. "Actually, you just provided me with the information I wanted—the whereabouts of my son. Jacques, move your hands, if you please. Poor Wadsworth can't see. I'm sorry, is he being so much a bother? Mr. Blackthorn won't allow him outside, and he's used to roaming at will."

Wadsworth spoke with his arms raised above his head, securely anchoring Jacques to his shoulder. "It's some time since any of us has had a young'un about, miss. We're all that delighted belowstairs. Cook wishes to know if you'd honor her by inspecting the menu for this evening. To see if there's anything special you might want for Master Jock here." The man pronounced Jacques's name in the English way, which made Tess smile again, knowing Emilie would soon correct him. Although how she'd manage to get the man to slip the sound of a *z* before the *j* might prove interesting.

"Really? Well, isn't that nice of her. Please relay my thanks, and tell her I'm sure we'll both be pleased with anything she decides." She didn't wish to become too involved with the workings of the mansion. For one, she wasn't in charge. For two, she was a barely tolerated guest. And for three, Jack would have something amusingly cutting to say about it if he came into the room while Tess was choosing between beans and green peas.

"As you wish, miss." Wadsworth made to bow, seemed to remember Jacques was riding him and held back, then turned to leave the room. Just as Jack was entering it.

"Papa! Papa!" Jacques crowed in delight, reaching out his arms for his father, the man who had taken him up on his massive black stallion the preceding day.

Tess spared a moment to panic, to worry that Jack wouldn't wish this acknowledgment of their son's parentage. But she shouldn't have worried. Jack was Jack, a law unto himself. And as far as she knew, didn't give a damn what anyone thought of him...perhaps liked it even better when people thought poorly of him. That way, they left him alone.

But her panic returned, and this time remained, as she watched Jack's reaction to seeing his son. The way he looked at Jacques was...possessive. Yes, that was the word. *Mine.* Far from attempting to deny the boy, he was claiming him. She could almost feel the ache of love in his heart for this small scrap who'd just called him Papa.

Demanding that the two of them marry had nothing to do with how Jack felt about her, but everything to do with taking possession of his son. And either she agreed to the marriage or she lost Jacques. *Oh, Papa, what have you done...is this really what you wanted?*

Jack kissed his son's outstretched hands and told him to go with Wadsworth, who seemed caught between embarrassment and delight. Then he turned his attention to Tess.

She could feel heat climbing into her cheeks as he looked at her, remembering the dark hours of the previous evening when they'd used each other so shamelessly. When he'd made love to her so intimately. When she'd returned the favor, slowly sliding down his body, kissing him, kissing him everywhere. Cupping him, taking him deep. *Yes...like that. God, Tess, yes, just like that. Woman, you're driving me out of my... Oh, God, Tess... Tess...*

Why couldn't she look at him without wanting him? Wanting him to touch her, wanting to please him. Wanting...wanting.

Jack stopped halfway to where she was sitting, and pressed his hands against his chest. "What? I've got a smut somewhere? Sprouted a second head?"

She shook herself mentally even as she redirected her gaze to her shoe tops. "I...I was wondering if it bothered you. That Jacques called you Papa. Now Wadsworth knows, and soon the entire household will know."

"If they don't know by now the marquess should have them all sacked for bloody stupidity while staring into the teeth of the obvious. The obvious being our faces. Oh, wait a moment. Are you thinking about your reputation, Tess? The fallen woman? No, let me correct that, since you're under this roof. The kept woman. The mistress."

"I like him better in the dark," she murmured quietly.

Jack laughed, and suddenly he was sitting beside her, his mouth close against her neck. "Many things are better in the dark. But not all of them. If I might demonstrate?"

She sat stock-still as he cleverly pushed down the bodice of her gown, freeing her left breast.

"Jack, for the love of—"

"I think we'll both agree that love has very little to do with this," he said. "Just watch, Tess. No, no, don't close your eyes. Watch."

Her breathing was already fairly ragged, even before—his back to the door, shielding her from view if someone might chance to enter—he began lightly pinching her nipple between his thumb and forefinger.

She felt her nipple harden. Saw it harden. Saw what her body was feeling.

Jack leaned down and licked the very tip of her, his slightly rough tongue sending a shot of desire straight to her groin.

"There. Now touch it," he whispered. Commanded. "Make it come alive."

"I can't do that..."

"Yes, you can. You've no inhibitions in the dark, Tess. You know how to please yourself. Do it, and let me watch. Let me help."

His touch, and even more, his words, combined with the fact that her body had come alive again in these past two days, had her aching to feel more, more. The thought of him watching her stirred her, so that she knew she was growing moist between her thighs.

He was a magician, a sorcerer. He was evil to do this to her, and she was weak and selfish and...he licked at her again, suckled for a moment, so that when he let go the air was cool against her damp skin. He pressed the heel of his palm against her lower belly, ground it against her, adding need to the mix of arousal and nervousness.

She pushed him away and stood up, glaring down at him as she readjusted her bodice.

He was so beautifully handsome, so perfect in every way. When she looked at him she could never believe he could want her. She'd never quite trusted the passion in his eyes, never quite believed it could be meant for her.

When he'd gone, he'd proved her right; what they'd had wasn't real, and certainly wasn't enough.

Yes, he'd told her he loved her. Whispered it to her the first night he took her to his bed. Shouted the words at her in anger that first day in her father's study.

But he couldn't deny that he'd left, and that he wouldn't have returned, they wouldn't be here now, if not for the fact that her father had disappeared.

So what was it that Jack was trying to rekindle here and now? The love that probably never really was…or just this, the way they shot sparks off each other that had the power to very nearly ignite the world? Was he telling her that's all they had, all they'd ever have?

"Tess?" he said as the silence between them grew too long to ignore. "Tess, I'm sorry. I'm a bastard, in every way possible. I don't know what in bloody hell happens inside my head anymore. Forgive me."

She shook her head. "It's all right, Jack. You're not the only guilty party here. When you first walked in the door I—well, never mind."

"No, Tess, damn it, it's not all right. I saw your face. I *knew*. And I wanted to hurt you. I wanted you to admit that you needed me as much as— Christ! What did we do wrong? What happened to us?" He lowered his head into his hands.

Tess walked over to the bellpull, and not thirty seconds later Wadsworth and Jacques *gulluped* into the drawing room.

"Wadsworth, Mr. Blackthorn will take his son now, please. And if you'd have someone fetch his ball?"

"Yes, miss, I'll see that it is brought," the butler said, carefully lowering Jacques to the floor and bowing his way out of the room.

Jack looked up at her even as he held his arms out to his son. "Tess?"

"It's as you said last night, Jack. My father has been in London for a week at the least. Either we're here in time, or we're already too late. Another few hours won't matter either way. There's a lovely walled kitchen garden, I've already checked. Jacques needs to be outside. And you need to be with him."

Jack picked up the boy as he stood up. Held him high against his chest as Jacques confidently laid his arm across his father's shoulder. A matched pair of dark devils, born to destroy feminine hearts. Jack looked at Tess for long moments.

"You'll join us?"

She shook her head, knowing she wouldn't be able to speak without crying. The sight of Jacques's head so close to Jack's nearly had her coming undone.

He nodded, and was halfway to the foyer before he turned around to look at her one last time. "Thank you, Tess," he said quietly. "Thank you."

She smiled, blinking back tears, and sat down once more, feeling it was the first really *right* thing she'd done in four years.

CHAPTER EIGHT

TESS STOOD BEHIND the chair and leaned in close. "That's probably too obvious, Jack. We can't insult him," she said, reading what he'd just written.

"I'd like to do more than insult him, if admitting to that doesn't break our recent truce," Jack said. But then he crumpled the paper and tossed it in the general direction of his first several efforts.

They'd been closeted together in the study for over two hours, working out the puzzle of how they would handle the next few days. And they hadn't gotten much done past finally agreeing to allow Wadsworth into their plans. Jack had already seen the man in action, and he had no worries there; the butler was more than competent. And, happily, more than willing. He'd pointed out that he hadn't had any excitement since Master Puck last came to town, unless one was to count the day a bat made its way down from the attics and he had somehow ended up beating it to death with a bust of Sophocles, which was the closest thing to hand and now had a decidedly shorter nose than formerly.

Jack laughed softly, remembering the statement.

Tess turned herself about and sat down on the edge of the desk, facing him. "Something's suddenly amusing?"

"Not really, no. My mind wandered, that's all."

"Jack? Are you sure this plan of yours will work? I mean, as it concerns your…cohorts."

"Will and Dickie." He put down the pen and sat back in his chair. "It will work as long as Sinjon has anticipated that whomever he sends to pick up the correspondence in Cleveland Row will be followed, yes. But he's gotten this far. I doubt he'd make such an elementary mistake now."

"And it's that important that your friends fail? I understand not wanting too many people involved. But it's more than that, isn't it?"

Jack shook his head. "A dog with a bone," he said in some admiration. "Yes, it is. They both know my orders."

"You've been ordered to silence him. Kill him."

"Twenty years of secrets, Tess. Twenty years of sweeping up behind some of the most spectacular blunders and indiscretions of what was and still is basically a corrupt government. Yes, they want him dead. Frankly, I don't know why they allowed him to continue to draw breath for a single day after the war, and his usefulness to them, ended."

"They think he's harmless," Tess told him, avoiding Jack's eyes. "There were some small assignments after you left, for a while, but then nothing for months. Papa felt certain he would soon be seen as a liability. So I wrote to Liverpool myself at his direction two years ago, to inform the man that Papa had suffered some sort of attack that left him unable to speak or grip a pen to write. I begged for an increase in his pension, to cover the cost of caring for him in his profoundly debilitated state. If the government didn't believe me, we were going to be forced to flee, but even if they did believe me, we knew—Papa assured me—he'd still always be watched."

"I never heard of this," Jack said, sitting forward once more.

Tess's shrug was purely Gallic and delightful. "Perhaps because the watchers were all very bad, and Papa is very good at what he does? If you were to ask any of our few servants, anyone in the village, they would tell you that the poor, dear marquis is but a shadow of his former self these past two years, leaning heavily on a walking stick and, well, mumbling and drooling. It's only in his bedchamber and in his study, always with the doors firmly locked, that he is the man you remember."

"And he's kept up this elaborate charade for *two years?*"

Another graceful shrug. "He said he was biding his time, but he never would tell me what biding that time was in aid of, as much as I asked. Now I suppose we know. He was waiting for the Gypsy to come back. Where do you suppose he went, Jack?"

"Where the pickings were best, I'd imagine. A man with his talents could turn a tidy profit in several countries on the continent. Not to mention the opportunities presented by the Congress of Vienna. Selling secrets, spying on one's friends and enemies, doesn't stop just because the battle has been won. All that does is start another quieter battle. Not to mention the ease of picking up bits and pieces of *treasure* while the world is still

reeling. What's interesting is that Sinjon obviously believed the man alive and sure to return to England."

"I suppose," Tess said, frowning. "Papa keeps up a
lively correspondence with several friends on the Continent. Or so he says. Perhaps those friends were more
in the form of informants? I remember him telling me
about the theft of some painting in Paris. I'd wondered
how he'd known about that. And then, last month, that
daring theft here in England. What Papa was waiting
to see. It's all so clear now I can't imagine why I never
realized…"

"We should get back to composing our application to
the good Mr. St. John," Jack prompted her, as she looked
as if she was about to blame herself yet again for not
seeing what Sinjon had so deliberately hidden from her.

"Yes, we should. But first—you've decided to dis-
obey your orders? That's why you want it to appear to
your friends that Papa has eluded you yet again?"

"A fruitless exercise, to your mind, as you think
Sinjon is setting himself up as some sort of sacrifice
so that the Gypsy reveals himself to my blade. But yes,
that's exactly what I'm doing. I need them to feel included, even as I make sure they're excluded. When we
finally do get the location of this supposed *sale* your
father is setting up, I'll give Will and Dickie the incorrect time, and hopefully have Sinjon safely out of there
before they arrive."

"And if either of them guesses what you've done?"

Now it was Jack's turn to shrug. "The Gypsy's body
should be enough for them. That, and the Mask of Isis,
your father's most prized possession. Liverpool will be

content with that. Sinjon has to pay, Tess. In some way, he has to pay."

She looked at him for long moments, and then nodded her head. "Yes. Yes, he does. For so many things." She pushed a clean sheet toward him. "Let's try again."

Jack reached once more for the pen, wondering what the Lord's penalty for sins of omission might be. It was true enough that Will and Dickie would expect Jack to eliminate Sinjon. They knew his orders. But he couldn't be sure he knew *theirs,* if it should happen that Jack didn't follow his.

Dickie was one thing; transparent as glass, but Will Browning was quite another. A random line from Shakespeare's *Julius Caesar* had been tickling at the back of Jack's brain ever since Henry died, every time he met with Will Browning. *Yond Cassius has a lean and hungry look.*

"Jack? You aren't listening to me."

He shook himself back to attention. "I'm sorry. I was just thinking about something Jacques said to me earlier in the garden."

"Oh, and what was that?"

"That's the problem. I couldn't quite make it out. Something about a—a *hugit?*"

Tess smiled softly, knowingly, and painters all over the world would weep with joy to paint her as a Madonna. "That's his rabbit. Emilie sewed it up out of his softest blanket. It's all silly and long-eared, and Jacques sleeps with it. *Hugging it.* You must have tired him out this afternoon. When he asks for his hug-it, it's time to put him down in his cot."

"Smart boy, my son."

Tess looked at him questioningly.

"To want something soft to take to bed with him."

Now the Madonna was a stern schoolmistress. "The letter, Jack. It has to be written, remember?"

"Yes, indeed," Jack said, smiling as he bent his head to the task. "My dear Mr. St. John... It was with great interest that I read your notice..."

This time they were both pleased with the results, and Tess held the wax stick over a small flame until it softened and then made a smear of red wax on the folded page. Jack took off his ring and used it to press a *B* into the wax before it hardened.

"After all of that, you're giving us away? I thought we weren't going to be obvious," Tess said, watching him.

"I owe him at least one small insult," Jack told her, getting to his feet. "Now, if you don't mind, I have to meet with my small band of rogues one more time, to make sure they see how dedicated I am to locating our quarry."

Tess pushed herself away from the desk. "I have no right to ask, but will you be very late?"

"That would depend. Will there be someone soft and *huggable* waiting for me here in my bed?"

She rolled her eyes and walked away from him. He sat down once more, leaned back in the chair, and watched her go, enjoying the view.

Life wasn't good. Not yet. But it was showing signs of getting better.

And then, out of the blue, it got worse...

"Well, hello, beautiful lady. Which one of us, do you suppose, has stumbled into the wrong residence?"

"Son of a— Puck?" Jack leapt to his feet and headed out to the corridor to rescue Tess from his brother's charms.

"What in bloody hell are you doing here?" he asked, glaring at his handsome, openly amused sibling. "Go away."

"Jack—" Tess began in a scolding voice, but Puck merely waved his hand to dismiss her dismay.

"Your easy display of affection, as usual, bids fair to unman me, brother. Let me hazard a guess here. I've come to town at an awkward time?"

"My letter arrived at Blackthorn, didn't it?"

"Letter?" Puck frowned, and not even a frown could mar his handsome face. "You've learned how to write now, have you? Beau and I have been reassuring our father that you never mastered the skill, or learned to find your way home once you'd left." He turned and inclined his head to Tess. "Just as he has never quite gotten around to acquiring even rudimentary social graces, so I will introduce myself. I am—"

"Robin Goodfellow Blackthorn," Tess interrupted. "You're nothing alike, are you, in either looks or temperament."

And she was off again, clamping back down on one of those damn bones of hers. She might ease off for the moment, with Puck here, but the questions would begin again later when they were alone. Sooner or later, he'd have to answer them.

"Although we all know he already knows, Lady Thessaly Fonteneau, allow me the dubious pleasure of introducing to you my younger brother, known best as Puck. Puck, make your bow to Tess, daughter of a good friend of mine, the Marquis de Fontaine."

Puck did as ordered, making an elegant leg before bowing his blond head over Tess's offered hand and launching into a torrent of flawless French, expressing his delight in his good fortune as to meet her when he'd been expecting only his dark, brooding dragon of a brother.

Tess looked delighted and answered him in French as he offered her his arm, and the two of them headed for the front of the mansion and the drawing room, leaving Jack to either follow or go back in the study and sulk.

Jack considered his options, and fell in behind them like some puppy hoping for a treat. Damn his brother. He didn't need this complication.

Puck was handsome in the way only those comfortable in their skin can be, his hair tied back severely at his nape, his tailoring the creation of a master, a twinkle always in his eye, a smile very nearly always on his face, and a tongue that naturally seemed to find just the perfect words for any occasion. And, beneath that carefully built facade of amiable silliness lay a mind as sharp if not sharper than Jack's own.

"Other than to annoy me," Jack said once Tess was arranging her skirts about her on one of the couches, "why are you here, Puck?"

"No other reason," Puck said, grinning as he poured wine, holding up the first to Tess as if to ask if she'd like some and being told yes, she would. "Our father asked Beau to arrange for the first banns to be read this Sunday. Chelsea is planning something magnificent—her word, magnificent—with flowers, and my own dearest Regina is already consulting with the Blackthorn chef on the menu for the wedding luncheon. Do you like pears? On fire, I mean? At any rate, my bride is a happy woman, and that's all that matters to me. Shall I tell you what Mama is doing?"

"Oh, God, she's there? I should have taken a page from Beau's book of idiocy and chosen a run for the border."

"What is your mother doing, Puck?" Tess asked, the two of them clearly having cried friends during the short walk from study to drawing room. Jack couldn't understand that ease of simple friendship. He'd spent his life avoiding close involvement with anyone. Until Tess.

Puck handed her a glass of wine. "Taken to her bed, actually. All three of her sons, married? And Beau and Chelsea to present her with a grandchild before Christmas, not that she knows that yet. Beau's conflicted, Jack. Should he tell her now, or wait until we see if she either recovers or expires? Not until she's chosen the perfect soliloquy, of course. When I left her she was poring over a copy of her script of *Macbeth*. A perfect choice, although I cravenly refrained from telling her that. In short, in long, Adelaide is, and I quote, *not best pleased*. I envision her draped all in black from top to toe at the wedding."

"Christ. Why is she at Blackthorn? Shouldn't she be trodding the boards in some provincial theater?" The suspicion that the upcoming nuptials were not the cause of Adelaide's sulk, but instead it was the fact that Jack actually was going to come back to Blackthorn, he didn't bother to share. She'd made it clear years ago that he was not welcome there.

Puck took a sip of wine before sitting down beside Tess, crossing one long leg over the other before smiling at her companionably. "We're unnatural children, if you haven't as yet deduced that on your own. Jack more than Beau and me. You may want to reconsider marriage to the man."

"I never consented to the marriage," Tess told him, but she was looking at Jack. "I was *informed*."

"Oh-ho! Is that the way of it, Jack? Being masterful, were you? Now this is a story I need to hear. But, alas, not now. I sent a note ahead to my tailor and meet with him in an hour. Jack? Would you wish to bear me company? I'd say it would be so that I might avail myself of your advice on a new waistcoat, but who'd believe such an obvious crammer? All you ever wear is black. So boring." He stood up and bowed over Tess's hand once more. "Until we meet again at dinner?"

"If Jack doesn't strangle you between now and then, yes, I'd be delighted," Tess told him.

"I can see you two need to be separated," Jack said, tight-lipped, even as he was pleased to see the two of them getting along so well. "All right, Puck. Let's go."

Jack all but grabbed his hat and gloves from Wadsworth, who was standing at the ready with them as the brothers headed for the flagway.

"Go home," he said once they were walking toward the end of the square.

"I could do that, yes. But then Beau would come. Or I could drop him a quick note, summoning him. He'd be here now if it weren't for some business about a problem on one of the farms at Blackthorn. I suppose I don't have to tell you the uproar your letter caused when it arrived. 'Post the banns, I marry in three weeks.' She's too good for you, by the way. Even short acquaintance tells me that. What's going on?"

As Puck was going to spend at least one night beneath the same roof, Jack saw no reason to pretend he didn't know what his brother meant. "I've a son."

Puck stopped dead on the flagway and made to turn around, head back to the mansion. "Here? Hers? Yours? Together, I mean. Let me see him."

Jack grabbed his arm, redirecting him along the flagway. "He's…napping."

"How domesticated of you to know that. An infant?"

"Jacques is a little past three, maybe closer to four."

"You don't *know?*"

That stung. "I only learned of his existence a few days ago."

"Really. And how do you know he's yours?"

"He'd be difficult to deny. He looks just like me."

"Ah, too bad. Poor tyke! Perhaps we can find a surgeon who could remove the horns."

Jack stopped walking. Looked at his brother. "God, I've missed you," he said with some feeling. "I didn't think it possible, but it's true. Let's hope you were lying about your tailor, because I've just had an idea. Let's go somewhere and talk, all right?"

"All right? I've already got enough questions to fill

an afternoon. Are you in some sort of trouble? I mean besides the obvious one, that of convincing that astoundingly beautiful woman to marry you?"

"Why would you ask that?"

"I don't know. My unfailingly accurate intuition? An ability to read minds? Or perhaps it was Wadsworth greeting me with the words *thank God you're here, Mr. Puck, he wants me to dress up like some foreign heathen.*"

Jack smiled. "He wasn't very enamored when I told him, no. Unfortunately for him, he remains integral to that part of my plan, along with the rest of it. You can't be involved. Not this time."

Puck spread his arms. "I'm fine—see? I didn't *die,* Jack. I only got a little damp."

"You damn near drowned. I'll never forgive you for that."

"For not being *completely* drowned?" Puck teased as they entered a tavern.

Jack put his arm around his brother's shoulder. It felt good, that sense of easy companionship. "No, you dolt. For making me realize I cared one way or the other. You can't be involved because you'd be too easily recognized by people who already know you. That's one thing. The other is more selfish. I want you to take my son to Blackthorn tomorrow. And Tess, as well."

They sat down across a table from each other, Puck looking curiously at his brother. "And have you asked her this, or told her? I'm just being curious."

"And I'm wishing on stars," Jack said, signaling for two bottles. "She won't go. But, having met your charming self, she might agree you can take Jacques with you. She still doesn't trust me, not completely, but she's sensible enough to know we need Jacques out of harm's way."

The barmaid slammed down two bottles and a pair of not quite clean glasses. "Two more, my darling, if you would. We're about thirsty work here," Puck told her, winning over even the jaded woman with his easy smile.

Then he turned back to Jack, who had ignored the glass and was drinking deep straight from the bottle. "From the beginning, Jack. What's going on?"

Jack, a man of many secrets, a man who didn't share easily, put down the bottle, wiped his mouth with the back of his hand, and began to talk. Starting at the beginning.

CHAPTER NINE

TESS SAT AT the dressing table twisting her hair into a single braid, a small smile on her face.

She couldn't remember a more interesting evening. Jack's brother was a marvel. He'd played the pianoforte for them, with Jacques turning in delighted circles until he was so dizzy he fell down, and then insisted on personally carrying his nephew upstairs to Emilie before rejoining Jack and her in the music room. He'd sat at the pianoforte once more, this time playing his own accompaniment as he sang French songs, looking pointedly at Tess until she gave up and joined in.

And Jack? Well, Jack was very good at keeping time with his foot, she'd give him that.

They'd laughed through dinner, with the brothers sharing incriminating stories about each other's childhood antics before the conversation turned more serious and she heard about Puck's wife, Regina, and a harrowing time not that long ago that had brought Puck and Jack back together, as brothers, as fellow conspirators.

Rather than retire, leaving them to their brandy and cigars, she had stepped outside with them on the dining room balcony to enjoy the freshness of the air after a sudden shower, the sort that was no stranger to London at this time of year. Not that she would know that. Her visits to London numbered two. Both of them taking her no further than to the point of rendezvous with a spy or turncoat destined for exposure and discreet elimination. There was supposed to be a third visit, but René had gone in her place.

When she thought about those strange days now, when she looked back on them, she found it difficult to believe her father had allowed her near such danger, such violence. She wondered even more why she had been so eager to be included in his plans, trusted with his plans.

She would never expose Jacques to such a life, risk him in any way. But, for her, it had all seemed so logical. It was what her father did, it was what she and René would do. They hadn't been unnatural children, they'd had an unnatural father. Sometimes it helped to believe that. Sometimes it didn't.

She knew she'd gone quiet out there on the balcony, and that Puck was looking at her strangely, as if realizing she should have reacted with more shock than she had shown when he'd told the story of the adventure he'd shared with Jack. Perhaps he'd thought he had shocked her, enough to stun her into silence.

"I'm so sorry, Tess," he'd said into the lengthening silence. "White slavery is not appropriate conversation at any time, but most especially in the company of ladies."

Tess smiled now as she remembered what she'd done. She'd walked over to Jack and neatly taken his cheroot from him, putting it to her mouth and drawing in its flavor, blowing out a thin stream of blue smoke before handing it back to him. It wasn't the first cheroot they'd shared. "This *lady*, Puck, would be happy to challenge you to a duel to settle the question of who between us can more quickly pick the lock to the front door of this mansion."

Puck had laughed. "Yes, I did hear that about you earlier today. So we both have an advantage over Jack here in that area."

"It's faster to simply kick in doors," Jack had told them, which had drawn a teasing comparison between Jack and a charging bull, which had led to another child-hood story...

Tess rose from the dressing table and walked over to the window, leaning her forehead against the cool pane. Was it terrible to think, if only for a moment, that she and Jack could just walk away? Leave Sinjon and the Gypsy to their strange, shared history and whatever it was that would happen, and just walk away?

She and Jack had a son. Together, they'd made many, many mistakes, but they had also made Jacques.

When had they both given enough to Sinjon's twisted ambitions? When was it time to say no? No more. To Sinjon. To men like Liverpool and his sort. To the thrill, the heart-pounding excitement that added something in-toxicating to the danger that had seemed so important, not just to her, but to Jack as well, and that now seemed not only reckless and self-serving, but even insane. And, strangely, no longer necessary.

They had a son.

It was time to stop.

At least for Jacques, it had to stop. Now.

She didn't move when she heard the soft click of the depressed latch, and Jack entered the bedchamber.

"Feeling sick?" he asked, walking up behind her. "You impressed Puck all hollow with your party trick, I'm sure, but as I recall it, each time you insisted on sharing my cheroot, your stomach put up a protest."

"Not every time," she said, turning to face him, refusing to admit that she had gotten rather light-headed after her reckless show of bravado on the balcony.

"True. You never seemed to have a problem with one after we'd satisfied each other into near exhaustion. In fact, it was clear you enjoyed it. Shall we try that again tonight?"

She put her hands flat against his chest and raised her face to his in the moonlight. He was a proud man. She was a stubborn woman. But one of them had to give.

"I was wrong, Jack. Jacques and Emilie should have gone to Blackthorn. To your family. He was very drawn to Puck, who was wonderfully silly with him tonight, wasn't he? Would it be terrible if we asked him to take Jacques and leave here, as early as tomorrow. I know he's just barely arrived, but—"

"I don't want him to go," Jack told her. "I just found him."

"I know that," she said placatingly. "I'm glad you found him, I really am. I've never been apart from him, Jack. This will hurt me, too. But what if everything goes wrong? What if we're found out, and the Gypsy dares to come here? Or he follows us somehow? Can either of us really say that we wouldn't be compromised if we had to think about Jacques when our attention should be on destroying the Gypsy?"

"And on saving your idiot father from whatever quixotic sacrifice you think he's going to make," he pointed out, covering her hands with his own.

She lowered her eyes. "I didn't think mentioning my father would help my argument," she admitted quietly. "I think he's lost his mind, no matter how clever all he's done so far may seem."

"Forgive me if I'm not similarly impressed with his genius. We could drive the king's royal coach through the flaws in the fabric of his plan. Beginning with the fact that he should have realized Liverpool wouldn't feel safe sending me out on my own to eliminate my beloved mentor. In fact, his entire plan, as I see it so far, depended on Liverpool being a fool and me being brought into any of this at all. I could be in Scotland right now, and you and Jacques unprotected in the country. Or hadn't you thought of that?"

She kept her head down. "We... He always knew where you were."

Jack dropped his hands away from hers. "How?"

She turned away to look out the window once more. "I don't know. He's always had his ways, you know that. Sometimes he'd say nothing about you for months. Never mention your name. But then he'd tell me you were just returned from France, or Spain, or wherever. The last time he mentioned your name was to tell me you were listed as one of the mourners at the funeral of your friend Baron Henry Sutton. He always knew, Jack."

"Christ. I wonder which one it is," he said, almost to himself.

"Excuse me?"

"Dickie or Will. It has to be one of them. They'd both have their reasons. Dickie's always in need of funds."

"And the other one? Will Browning?" Tess's heart was pounding now. Was it the puzzle, the excitement of solving it? Or was it fear that this time maybe Jack was the prey, not the Gypsy, not her father. That her father was using the Gypsy, using her, dear Lord, even Jacques, as a way to bring an unsuspecting Jack into his web?

"Ambition? Jealousy? The challenge I present? With Will, I doubt we'd ever know. No wonder now, is it, that you were always so short of funds. Sinjon was paying for information. About me, about God knows who else. The question, Tess, is how much does this particular informant know of Sinjon's plan?"

"I doubt we'll ever know that, either," Tess said, her mind whirling even as she ordered it to slow down, think clearly, the way she'd been taught. "What's important, Jack, is that you know now that you have no friends in this strange adventure. Except for me."

"Really? I'm beginning to even doubt my loyalty to myself."

"You're the father of my child. I've taken you to my bed. If you can't believe—"

His smile was positively evil.

"You're not amusing, you know. But I suppose we'll have no more arguments as to whether or not I'm to be a part of this, all the way to the end of it."

His smile turned rueful. "How did you know I was going to suggest that you accompany our son to Blackthorn?"

"I didn't. You never said you wanted Jacques to go to Blackthorn. *I* said it. *You* said you don't want him to go." Her eyes narrowed. "Jack?"

"I was being polite. Allowing you to think the entire thing was your idea. It seemed the gentlemanly thing to do. Not that a bastard is well-acquainted with gentlemanly things, which is probably why I botched it so badly."

"Humph."

He took a step toward her. "Are we going to argue now over something we're agreed on? And, might I point out, just about the *only* thing we agree on?"

She stuck her tongue against the inside of her cheek, trying not to smile. He was right. She was being petty. But, God, she felt alive, sparring with Jack. "What time do they leave?"

"I believe we settled on noon. Puck does actually have an appointment arranged with his tailor. Vain puppy," he said without heat. "He'd check his image in a mirror before going into battle, as if it mattered."

"Everyone wears their own sort of armor, Jack."

He looked at her in question for a moment, and then nodded. "You're right. And for bastards, even more so. Ways to protect ourselves, shield ourselves. For Beau, it was always the pretense that he didn't care, when I know he cares very much. He loves Blackthorn, and as the oldest, he would have been the marquess one day. And he deserved to be, damn it. Puck? He *uses* our station in life, and makes everyone love him *because* he's a bastard."

"And you, Jack? What armor do you wear?" Tess asked, hoping he'd be honest with her. "You don't care for Blackthorn. You couldn't, not if what Puck said is correct. You left a long time ago, and never went back." She summoned a smile. "And God knows you don't go out of your way to make anyone *like* you."

"No? You seem to like me well enough."

She looked up at him through her lashes. He was wearing *that* look. One she knew very well. She dropped her hand and stepped back a pace. She wanted him, yes. She always wanted him. But she also knew he was trying to divert her. She wasn't going to be diverted. Not this time. "Jack…"

He reached into his waistcoat. "I brought two. One for each of us."

She looked at the cheroots he was holding up. Looked into his dark, dangerous eyes. Allowed her gaze to run down his body, to see his obvious arousal straining against the fabric of his trousers.

No. Not this time.

"I don't think we should keep…keep doing this. I thought I knew you four years ago. But now I'm not sure. You give me part of you, but I don't think you've ever given me all of you. You know everything about me. There's a Jack I don't know. Is that fair?"

"Is it fair that you kept my son from me?"

She held up one hand impatiently. "No. Don't do that either, Jack. I'm not going to argue with you. This has nothing to do with our son. This has to do with who his father is, *why* his father is who he is. I'm attracted to what you are, God knows I am, but I don't know you. How you can bring me to this place. How you and your brother—and your mother—can live at Blackthorn as if you belong there. And why you *hate* it all so much. Puck doesn't. It would seem Beau doesn't. What was different for you, Jack? Is it what I think it is? Is that why you're still so *angry* with the world?"

The cheroots had long since been put back into his waistcoat pocket.

"All right, Tess, we've danced around this ever since you saw the portrait of the marquess downstairs. And it's worse now that you've seen Puck—who looks very much like Beau, if you were about to ask, and I'm sure you were."

"You're not his son, are you?" She bit her lips between her teeth and waited. Watched him.

A small tic began to work in his lean cheek.

"You're Adelaide's son, but you're not his. Beau and Puck are. But not you." She took a breath, and when she let it out, her chest actually hurt. For him. "But not you. Oh, Jack…"

"Good night, Tess," he said flatly. "There are many emotions I enjoy seeing in your beautiful eyes. Pity isn't one of them." Then he turned and headed for the door.

"Jack Blackthorn, don't you dare! Don't you dare leave me now! *I* didn't make you a bastard. And I don't care that you are. I only care that *you* care."

He stopped, and she watched as he bent his head, rubbed at his nape, his fingertips turning white as his hand stilled and he pushed against the cords of his neck.

He had nearly lost control, and he was forcing himself to regain his composure.

"All right," he said finally, as he dropped his hand and turned to face her. "I've only ever told this story once before, years ago, to Sinjon. The very night I first met him, actually. He has a way of ferreting out secrets you think you'd never tell. You don't quite have his subtlety, but you know how to make your point. Let's sit down, shall we?"

Tess longed to reach out to him, to hold him, cradle him against her the way she soothed Jacques when he fell and scraped his knee. But that would destroy any chance she'd ever have of hearing about the demons Jack carried with him.

She walked over to the wingback chairs flanking the fireplace and sat down, curling her legs up beside her. "Would you want me to ring for wine?"

"No. There isn't enough of it in the cellars for this story," he said as he sat down, turning his head to look into the fire. The devil, seeking his own. "Beau and Puck are bastards. I'm twice the bastard."

"You can't be twice the— I'm sorry. I think I know what you mean, though. You thought the marquess was your father, didn't you? Until you learned that he wasn't, of course. Your brothers are only your half brothers. Do they know?"

"I think so. I mean, they joke, call me the black sheep, Black Jack. We've never discussed it. No more questions, Tess, all right. Let me just tell you about Adelaide."

She bit her lip, nodded. He had to want to tell his

story as quickly as possible, without interruptions. Get it out, get it over and done. She couldn't blame him. So, for the next half hour, she simply let him talk.

What he told her seemed part fanciful fairy tale, part tragedy.

The Marquess of Blackthorn was still quite a young man when he met Adelaide and her sister, Abigail. Of the two, the eldest, Abigail, was the more beautiful, almost ethereally lovely. But she also was fragile, in both body and mind. The marquess, while captivated by them both, instantly tumbled into love with the lively, enchanting Adelaide, and asked her to marry him.

She refused.

Adelaide, as the story went, loved her marquess very much, but she had long since dedicated herself to the notion that one day she would be England's greatest actress, and it was a dream she could not deny, a desire that could not be quenched. She would be miserable in the role of marchioness, which would in time poison their love...

At this point, Jack actually smiled. It wasn't a particularly lovely smile.

Adelaide, in fact, would have long since run away from her squire father and his new bride, to join with a traveling troupe of players and begin her journey to the London stage, except for Abigail. Dear, beautiful, vulnerable Abigail. Their father's new wife wanted both stepdaughters gone, and had more than once threatened to have Abigail removed to "a place where she belongs, with other imbeciles like herself."

And that was cruel. Abigail wasn't an imbecile. She'd just never quite grown up.

Adelaide stayed, sacrificing her dream as long as she dared, to protect and care for her sister. She could, she supposed, marry the marquess and bring her sister to Blackthorn, but that would mean an end to what she wanted so much. A light inside her would go out, never to be rekindled. Oh, no, no, the marquess couldn't allow that, not his dearest Adelaide. He would do anything— anything!—to make her happy. And so a plan was formed. Adelaide's plan.

The most ridiculous, insane plan Tess had ever heard!

Adelaide and her darling, besotted Cyril would love each other, always and forever, but he would marry Abigail. Adelaide would be free to live her dream, financed by Cyril, and Abigail would be safe from the madhouse.

At last Tess could no longer hold her tongue. "And your fath—I mean, the marquess agreed?"

Jack shrugged. "He was young, desperate not to lose the woman he loved, and I don't think he was thinking any further than his crotch, frankly. You haven't met Adelaide, remember. I admit this sounds ridiculous, but the woman always seemed to have this *power* to bend people to her will and make them think what they'd just agreed to was all their idea in the first place."

"You don't like her."

"I adored her," he said shortly, and she could hear the pain in his voice, the pain of a little boy who'd grown into a sadly disillusioned man. "We all did. She swooped in and out of our lives just often enough to keep us wanting more of her. Her laugh, that flowery scent that

wrapped around you as she hugged you close and show-
ered you with kisses. The plays we'd put on for Cyril,
her cottage on the grounds. And, when she wasn't there,
all of Blackthorn at our fingertips. We were raised like
the sons of the house, in everything but name. And then
there was Abigail."

Jack's expression softened as he spoke of his aunt.
She was dead now, her frail health finally failing a little
more than a year past. Abigail had been like a beloved
younger sister, with all three boys being fiercely protective of her, something that seemed to endear them more
to their father.

Theirs had been a strange household, Jack had admitted that immediately, but it was all the three of them
knew. For them, their lives seemed nothing out of the
ordinary, not strange in any way. They were happy, content.

*As I thought René's and my lives were normal, if not
really happy,* Tess thought, believing she understood
what Jack was saying better than most.

"What happened?" she asked when it seemed Jack
had become lost in thought. "What changed?"

He looked surprised at the question. "Me? Yes, I
think that's probably the answer that makes the most
sense. I changed. I began to grow up. Notice things.
Notice how different I was. Dark to their light, in both
coloring and the way I felt, thought. Thoughts Adelaide
must have seen and encouraged. I realized that eventually. We…we were her creations, and she handed us
each roles in the never-ending play that is her life. Beau
was cast as the oldest son, the rock, the dependable one.

Puck was the petted child, delightful to behold. And I was the outsider, the one who never quite fit in. Restless, reckless. The troubled one."

"The marquess must have known," Tess said, considering the thing. "Did he treat you…differently?"

"No. There isn't a better man in the world, Tess. Or a weaker, sorrier one. In many ways, I despise him. When I don't pity him. The moment Adelaide returned from one of her extended absences with Beau in her arms, it must have finally come home to him what he'd done. And when she came home with me in her arms, he had to know he was now twice the fool."

"Yet Puck is younger than you. The marquess must have forgiven her."

"As I said, Tess, you haven't met Adelaide. But as time went on I think she knew her influence was slipping, that Cyril had more regrets than he could live with anymore. On my eighteenth birthday, the day she gave me this ring and told me she'd always loved me more than she did my brothers, that I held a special place in her heart. And then she told me what I'd long since suspected, that Cyril wasn't my father."

"She wanted you gone from the estate, didn't she? Needed you gone if, as you say, Cyril was older now and no longer quite the besotted fool, but more the shamed father who'd destroyed his sons' futures. You were a constant reminder of her betrayal of the love Cyril had for her. *I love you best, Jack, now please take yourself off somewhere, where the marquess doesn't have to see you anymore.*"

"Yes, she did mention that last part. How did you know?"

"I think it was a reasonable assumption," Tess said quietly, her hands drawing up into tight fists in her lap. "Like Papa, every praise has a hook in it. How could a mother do that to her son?"

"How could a father do that to his daughter?" Jack countered. "At any rate, she attempted to excite me, I suppose, telling me then that my true father was a highwayman, a dark and dashing creature she'd succumbed to while traveling with her acting troupe. He was wonderful, magnificent, daring, and I was very much my father's son. Her eyes shone as she talked about him, but she refused to tell me his name."

"Doubly cruel, but I suppose it would seem all the more dramatic that way. The beautiful actress, the dangerous highwayman. What did she suppose you'd do, Jack? Immediately go haring off to try to find the man?"

"That would have proven difficult in any case, as she told me he'd been caught up and hanged years earlier. But she saw in me the same wildness and thirst for adventure as she did in him, and knew it was *stifling* me to remain on the estate. She didn't order me to go. She did point out that to stay would be nothing but a slow death for me, for I was her son as well, and she knew I was a caged bird, longing to fly free. She couldn't continue to watch me suffer for her sin." Jack smiled. "And so forth, mixing praise with guilt and romance, laughter with tears—all while I probably had yet to be able to close my mouth or think of a single damn thing to say. I left the next morning. The only time I've been to Blackthorn in the decade since was to sneak into the estate chapel at midnight to put a rose on Abigail's coffin. I understand from my brothers that Adelaide wasn't best pleased to see it there the next morning. After all, it meant that I hadn't completely divorced myself from Blackthorn and those who lived there. Otherwise, how would I have known so quickly that Abigail had died?"

A log broke in the fireplace and Tess nearly jumped out of her skin.

Jack laughed. "My mother, no doubt—issuing a complaint. But she's right. I think we're done now."

"Not completely. Where did you go? When you left, that is."

"Everywhere and anywhere. Angry, yet still giddy with my freedom, I suppose. Living by my wits, for money soon became a problem, plus my abnormal desire to feed my belly at least twice a day. I've told you before, Tess, I probably would have been hanged by now, like my father before me, if Sinjon hadn't found me."

"And you never questioned that he found you?" she asked, wondering why the thought of her father seeing Jack and somehow recognizing him as someone who would fit his plans was suddenly so disturbing to her.

"I was down to my last few coppers, fairly drunk, and on the run from the local constable. Sinjon was manna from heaven to me at the time. No, I didn't ask too many questions. But now I'll ask you why you're asking."

"I don't know," she said, getting up from the chair to begin pacing the center of the large chamber. "I don't wish to be insulting, Jack, but you don't make it sound as if you were any great prize to him. Why would he bother?"

Jack joined her, stopping her as her nervous pacing brought her close to him. "Perhaps because we were in a dark alley and I was holding a pistol on him at the time. He never told you that? I wanted his purse, and he wanted to talk. He was very convincing."

"Oh, Jack," she said, sighing. "You were drunk and desperate and Papa allowed you to get the better of him, hold a pistol on him? Do you really believe that? Even now?"

CHAPTER TEN

JACK LAY BESIDE Tess as she slept, the last words they'd spoken on the subject of his first meeting with Sinjon repeating in his head. *Papa allowed you to get the better of him, hold a pistol on him? Do you really believe that? Even now?*

How old had he been? Twenty-three? On his own for nearly five years, and not doing all that well, having in the past six months stooped to occasional dips into other people's pockets in order to survive. He'd had several very good runs at the card tables, but they hadn't been frequent enough, and his angry attempts to be as bad a man as his father had been had ended when he could no longer afford to feed his horse and the role of occasional highwayman had been lowered to that of petty thief.

He'd been about to join the army as a foot soldier, knowing he was otherwise going to end very badly, very soon. At least he might then have the chance to die for a better reason than being shot or knifed by an unhappy loser after a successful night with the cards.

Sinjon had talked him into joining him in an enterprise more worthy of his talents, and Jack had believed him. God, what talents had he possessed? Educated above his station, proficient in three languages, tolerably presentable. He wasn't useless, but he was far from a prize any sane man would covet.

But he'd decided to listen, especially after the offer of dinner at the inn on the next corner. Sinjon had been sympathetic, nearly a Father Confessor, and by the time dawn had crept into their private dining room, Jack had told this smooth-talking Frenchman the sad tale of his sad life and was snoring at the table, his head in his plate.

He moved uncomfortably in the bed, embarrassed for his pathetic, gullible twenty-three-year-old self.

When he'd awakened, his head pounding thanks to the drink he'd consumed, it was to hear Sinjon issuing orders for a bath for the "gentleman," followed by a hearty breakfast.

"Delightful as your company has been, Jack, I'm afraid I must be on my way. There's a horse and saddle in the stable, already bought and paid for. Not the best, as nothing to be had here could be, but it will do," Sinjon had told him, placing a folded piece of paper and a small leather purse on the table, just beside Jack's head. "Do you remember the offer I made you last night? A nod is sufficient. Ah, good. I've written the directions to my home. Once you're clean and fed, your next move is up to you, my son. Choose wisely."

Jack had ridden his new horse five miles in the opposite direction before soundly cursing the man who had provided it. Then he'd pulled sharply on the reins and turned it around, thereby sealing his fate, someone like his mother would have said.

But he'd taken to his new life immediately, and

shown a natural proficiency for intrigue that amazed him. He was welcomed into the de Fontaine household as if he belonged there. He enjoyed sleeping on clean sheets again, having a full belly, feeling…civilized once more. Life had taken a lot of the rebellious youth out of him, even as it had made him hard, a man who didn't trust easily or feel the need for friendship.

Yet he was in awe of his mentor, a truly brilliant man. He'd found himself growing fond of René, fonder still of Tess. He fed on the adventure of it all, the danger of it all, the heady feeling that success brought with it.

He was doing something important. He was serving his government in a time of war. He was a bastard, yes, and that would never change. But he wasn't his father. At last, he was his own man, one with a reason, a direction. A purpose.

And Tess slowly became more dear to him. And then against all reason indispensable to him. She was fire to his fire.

Sinjon knew. Sinjon missed nothing, so he had to have known. He'd done nothing to stop it. He'd said nothing, tacitly allowing the bastard to bed his daughter.

And then he'd pounced.

He'd told his own sad, drunken tale, and showed Jack his *collection,* offered his proposition. His daughter's virginity in exchange for becoming Sinjon's new tool, specially trained, fashioned and even compromised into helping him once again begin adding to his damned collection.

It was all so clear now.

Of course he'd seen Jack and wanted him. He'd

wanted a thief, someone to replace the Gypsy. Not a common thug, he couldn't use a common thug. Educated, civilized, but not quite a gentleman. And desperate. He wanted him grateful and willing and well trained, as only Sinjon could train him. Perhaps Jack was also chosen because he was passably handsome, and his daughter would see that, be attracted to him, or perhaps that had been a happy coincidence Sinjon coldly exploited. All in the name of that bloody pile of treasures that meant more to him than his own wife, his own daughter, his own son.

"That sonofabitch…"

"Jack?" Tess shifted her position so that she could look up into his face in the light of the false dawn. "What's wrong?"

"Nothing," he said, pressing a kiss against her forehead. "I was just kicking myself for being an idiot. At least twice over."

"Oh, well, if that's all," she said, snuggling against him once more, "may I help? If we put our heads together I'm sure we could come up with an entire list of reasons why you're an idiot, not just a piddling two. I'll start."

"Oh, no, you don't!" Jack said, rolling her over onto her back so that he could leer down into her face.

She raised a hand to cup his cheek. "Are you all right now? I know it wasn't easy for you last night, talking about…things."

"It's never easy to face the truth. For either of us. We should have talked more, Tess. Back then."

"*Back then,* as you call it, we wouldn't have had so

much to say. We didn't know what we know now. You weren't ready, and I wouldn't have believed you if you'd said anything disparaging about my father."

"When did you grow up, Tess, grow so wise? I walked away from a girl, a beautiful, headstrong girl. I've come back to find a woman."

"You told me you wanted the girl back. Do you remember saying that? It was only a few days ago."

"I told you I'm an idiot," he said, leaning down to begin nibbling at the side of her throat. "You should most probably forget everything I said that first day."

She sighed as he curled his hand over her breast. "Are we starting over, Jack? Do you think that's possible?"

He raised his head to look into her face once more, saw the tears standing bright in her eyes. "We have a son. I think we need to at least try."

"And is this the way to start? Or does it just confuse the issue? Because we've always had this, and it wasn't enough."

Jack closed his eyes, knowing she was right. Wishing she was wrong. There was still too much to be settled for them to even discuss the future. There was still the fact that, unless Sinjon had one more brilliant coup left up his sleeve, she would soon see her father dead, marched off to the hangman, or banished from England and her life, forever. With Jack the one in control of which way it would all end.

He rolled over onto his back to stare up at the emerald-green velvet canopy.

"Our son is an early riser," Tess told him in a rush, turning back the covers. "I think I'll ring for Beatrice, get dressed, and go up to the nursery and have breakfast with him. He's accustomed to seeing me first thing every morning, as you'll remember. I also have to speak with Emilie about the remove to Blackthorn. She won't be pleased, but she'll understand. Would…would you care to join us at breakfast? I suppose I can free him from his nursery prison and allow him downstairs. He needs to see more of Puck, for one thing, before they—"

"Tess? Come here. Please?" Jack said, taking her into his arms. He kissed her, not with passion, not with need, but just because he wanted to tell her something, and this was the only way they'd ever really communicated. She went rigid for a moment, probably expecting something else from him than the chaste kiss he was offering, and then melted against him until he placed his hands on her shoulders and gently pushed her away. "It's all right. I understand. We start over."

She bit her bottom lip. Nodded. And then, surprising him, she pulled the edges of her nightrail closer over her breasts, suddenly the shy, modest maiden. Just as if he didn't know every inch of her, intimately.

"Now why don't you go do what you said you were going to do? And please inform young Master Jacques that his father, never a slave to protocol in any case, requests the pleasure of his company at table this morning."

Tess's smile hurt his heart. "I'll do that," she said.

And then she was gone, into the dressing room, and he was alone.

But not really alone. Perhaps for the first time since

he was old enough to look around and see the world as it was for him, he didn't feel alone.

THEY STOOD IN the mews, watching as the luxurious traveling coach bearing the gold-painted Marquess of Blackthorn's crest pulled away from the stables.

Tess suppressed a sigh. She'd never been apart from Jacques. Her son had been the only real constant in her life these past years, since René died.

Only when the pair of outriders following the coach had disappeared around the corner did she turn for the house, Jack beside her.

"What were you and Puck whispering about while I was saying goodbye to Jacques?" she asked him. "I couldn't hear you."

"Ah, good, then it worked. That was the purpose of the whispering," he said, and she was struck yet again with his good humor this morning. As if a weight he had been carrying for a long time had finally been lifted from his shoulders.

"Did the whispering have anything to do with Jacques? You don't expect any sort of trouble, do you? We didn't announce his departure, have him carried out to the square and waiting coach, but you were only being careful. You're not really concerned. Are you?"

"No, not at all. Although I may have been remiss in warning Puck about Jacques's tendency to express his opinion of coach travel via his stomach contents. Do you think I should have done that?"

Tess smiled, relaxing. "It's too late now. But he'll know soon enough, I imagine. Poor thing."

"Puck? Or Jacques?"

"I would think Puck. It doesn't seem to bother Jacques in the least. But then what were you whispering about?"

"The marquess," Jack told her as they entered the study, Jack heading for the chair behind the desk while she tucked herself up comfortably in one corner of a massive burgundy leather couch. "Puck was reminding me that Cyril is anxious to speak with me. With all three of us." He picked up a brass letter opener and balanced it between his fingers. "As if I could forget, as both Beau and Puck have been hounding me about it for over a year."

And, obviously, Jack had been avoiding that particular meeting.

"What do you think he wants to tell you?"

"I already know. He's doling out unentailed parcels of land to each of us. Beau and Puck have already been given minor estates, and I imagine I'm to receive one, as well. I never took his damn allowance. I don't know why he'd think I'd allow him to give me an entire estate."

"Allow him?" Tess shook her head, smiling sadly. "It would be a privilege for him to do so, you think?"

Jack put down the letter opener carefully, as if it had been fashioned of delicate crystal, or so that he wouldn't be tempted to throw it against the far wall. "I'm not his son, Tess."

"He might consider you his son. You told me you were raised alongside Beau and Puck. Did he ever treat you differently, give you any indication you weren't welcome?"

"That's not the point," Jack said, an edge to his voice.

"Then what is the point?"

She watched his face as he stared into the middle distance for some time, seeing things she couldn't see, thinking thoughts she couldn't know.

"Jack?" She waited. "Jack?"

He blinked, turned to look at her. "I'm sorry."

"I know," she told him, longing to go to him, pull his head against her breast in some effort to comfort him. "I've always wondered. Where do you go when you leave me like that? To Blackthorn?"

"I suppose," he said, getting to his feet. "I loved him once, a son's love for his father. Before I despised him for his weakness, his selfishness and stupidity. Puck has an interesting theory. He believes our mother hoodwinked Cyril into marrying Abigail because then he couldn't marry anyone else and Adelaide would never lose her generous protector. Free to roam, indulge her obsession with the stage, yet always with a safe haven to return to and a man obsessed with her, one with very deep pockets. My brothers and I could have been unhappy surprises, temporary burdens that interfered with her dream. Me, most especially, I'd imagine. Why he took us in, raised us as gentlemen, tolerated me, none of us will ever know."

Tess took a breath and asked what she believed to be the obvious, although clearly it hadn't occurred to any of the Blackthorn brothers. "Why don't you ask him?"

Jack stopped, looked down at her. "Well, of course. So simple. Ask the man. But no, thank you for the suggestion. We'd never do that."

"They may be only your half brothers, but you all seem to have one thing in common. Pride."

"Pride? Bastards aren't allowed pride. But we do owe the man something. *His* pride, if you will. If he wanted us to know anything, he would have told us."

Really, men were so...*thick*. She uncurled her legs and got to her feet, determined to continue this conversation face-to-face.

"Has it occurred to you that he might be attempting to do just that? You told me he wants to speak with the three of you. Together. There very well may be more to that request than the handing out of unentailed estates. Or is that why you've been avoiding a return to Blackthorn? Because you don't want to hear what he wants to say. Because you're afraid of what he's going to say?"

Jack shook his head. "You know, there's a lot to be said for a beautiful face with nothing behind it." And then he kissed her forehead. "Please take that in the spirit it's offered."

"I'd rather take it as an admission that I'm correct," she told him, her heart easing as some of the tightness seemed to leave his expression. She was going to meet Adelaide soon, and the marquess. She was trying very hard to not form definite opinions about either one of them, but at the moment, any sympathy she had was for the marquess. Adelaide sounded disturbingly like a woman whose mind worked in much the same way as did her father's. A woman devoid of conscience.

Jack gave her a playful tap on her derriere before sliding his arm around her waist, leading her to the doorway.

"I'll take that under consideration. Now I have to meet with Dickie and Will to finalize our plans for tomorrow, but I should return in an hour."

"Alone? I can't go with you?"

He was going to say no, that was obvious.

"He's my father, Jack. And I may be able to add something to the conversation if you're going to be leading them down the garden path, as you said you were." She tipped her head, looking at him quizzically when he smiled. "What is that smile in aid of? You don't think I can help?"

"No, actually, that may not be a bad idea. Considering what they think of you."

She definitely wasn't liking his smile. "And what do they think of me?"

"They rather think you're an idiot."

"They *what?* Why would they think that?"

"I imagine because I cleverly encouraged them to do so."

She considered this for a moment, and then said, "Oh. All right, I can understand that. Shall I cry and beg you all to be gentle with him, bring the poor, sick, deluded man home to his loving daughter? Or just sit there looking blank as a newly washed slate, wondering what all the fuss is about?"

"They know about us. Or at least they think they do."

"Really?" She nodded her thanks to Wadsworth, who had somehow come into possession of her pelisse, bonnet and gloves and was now offering them to her. "Which would mean they know about Jacques. I don't think I like that. Not if one of them was Papa's tattler."

"A word, sir, if I might?" Wadsworth interrupted as he handed over Jack's curly brimmed beaver and gloves.

"You wish to cry off, Wadsworth?"

The soldier-turned-butler drew himself up to attention, his chest puffed out smartly. "No such thing, sir!" His expression turned from hauteur to pleading. "But, sir—those foreign duds, sir?"

"Necessary to the assignment, Wadsworth," Jack said as Tess busied herself pulling on her gloves, her head down so that her smile was hidden.

"Yes, sir," the butler said, bowing. "Master Puck said you'd say as much. It will be as you say."

"You're a good man, Wadsworth." Jack clapped the butler on the shoulder and then offered Tess his arm, winking at her. "See that the closed carriage is waiting in the mews in fifteen minutes, if you will, please."

Tess held up her skirts as she descended the marble steps to the flagway, before she could no longer contain her laughter. "Poor Wadsworth. You couldn't have made him an English gentleman?"

"No. If Sinjon is planning on being able to take advantage of his advertisement to people the room with enough eager gentlemen to confuse the issue if it comes to violence, I want him to know immediately that the Indian Nabob is my man. I doubt there will be more than one."

"Hence the *B* pressed into the sealing wax," Tess said, nodding as they turned and walked down the flagway. "You really think my father is planning to use innocent people as possible shields?"

"There are no innocent people," Jack told her, appearing casual, even as she knew he had seen and catalogued every person sharing the square with them. "That's what Sinjon taught me. I'm sure he taught you the same."

"He did. Jack…" she began, not wishing to ruin what was so far a lively but friendly discussion. "There may be one thing you haven't thought of, I'm afraid. What if…what if Papa isn't after the Gypsy? What if we are only being made to think he is? What if this is all one huge hum? What if…what if *you're* his target? If that's the case, dressing poor Wadsworth up like a Nabob would only help him know who else he had to eliminate."

She felt his body stiffen for a moment, but he never broke stride as they headed toward whatever destination he had chosen for his meeting with his…no, she couldn't call them his friends, could she? Jack didn't have friends. Doing what he did, he couldn't afford to get too close to anyone.

"An interesting theory," he said calmly. "How did you arrive at it?"

"Jacques," she told him, sighing. "Papa adores him, nearly beyond all reason. What if you were to come back? See him? He told me, over and over again, that you'd take him. He's no match for you, physically, but he's always believed he can outmaneuver anyone. I know you believe he has no feelings for anyone in this world, and as his daughter, I have to agree with you. But he loves Jacques."

"One more theory and I think we'll have an even half dozen. All right, I'll consider it. Ah, and here we are."

She looked up to see a mansion not quite the size of

the one they'd just left, but certainly impressive. "Very pretty. Whose is it?"

"Cyril's. His nearly obnoxious wealth comes from both his parents. Much of it to be passed to some distant and very grateful relative upon his death. As a rule, he leases this pile for the Season, but it's undergoing some sort of renovations, and stands empty. Wadsworth unlocked the door earlier. Will and Dickie are undoubtedly waiting for us. Shall we?"

Tess looked at the imposing facade and nodded. "I'd be delighted, sir."

The handle depressed easily and moments later they were standing inside a large foyer, dust coverings draped over everything, including the massive crystal chandelier that hung above them.

"That you, Jack?"

"Dickie," Jack said quietly, and then raised his voice. "You were perhaps expecting Father Christmas? Will, you here, as well?"

A tall blond man stepped out from the double doors leading to what had to be the small ground-floor salon used to entertain those inferior souls who didn't merit an invitation up the winding staircase to the main drawing room.

Will Browning was quite a specimen. Slim, broad-shouldered, impeccably tailored and wearing a smile that didn't quite reach his eyes. "Ah, and not alone, I see, hmm, Jack? Lady Thessaly, I presume?" He executed an exquisite bow. *"Je suis enchanté, ma dame, votre domestique humble."*

"Vous êtes trop aimable, Monsieur Browning," Tess

responded, dropping into a curtsy that acknowledged his compliment but did not give the slightest hint that she wasn't aware that she outranked him, even if her title was no longer anything but one of courtesy. "And now you will be so kind as to offer me a seat in this strange place that looks as if it is populated by ghosts, yes?"

"Charming, utterly charming," Will told Jack as they all three made their way into the small salon, where Dickie Carstairs was slumped in a chair beside a small table, lazily tossing dice one hand against the other…and apparently currently losing to his left hand. He sprang to his feet, the dice scattering on the floor, and the introductions were completed.

Dickie Carstairs tugged the dust sheet from a small curved-back couch and bowed Tess to it while Will and Jack pulled out chairs from the table and waited for Dickie to join them.

And then Tess was ignored by all three of them as they discussed what had happened thus far and went over their plans for the following afternoon one last time.

She sat quietly, watching them as she assumed a blank expression meant to make her seem too vacant-brained even to be bored. She played with her gloves. She patted at her hair. She gazed, openmouthed, up at the smaller chandelier in its temporary shroud. She yawned delicately. Twice.

And then, just as Jack pushed back his chair, signaling that the brief meeting was completed, she spoke.

"You aren't going to kill him, are you?" she asked, her bottom lip trembling. "He's old, he's quite sick.

Infirm, you understand? *Une faiblesse dans son cerveau.* A weakness in his brain, yes?"

Jack sighed audibly, as if he'd heard this particular argument before, several times. "Lady Thessaly, we've discussed this. We only hope to find him and return him to you. He's dangerous on his own. You know my great affection for your father. Our government's respect for his important service over the years."

"So you say, so you say. Mr. Browning, do you agree? I have…reasons not to trust Mr. Blackthorn."

"Yes, I've heard about the boy—that is to say, I sympathize with your misgivings, my lady. Jack may be rough, I would term it, but he knows his orders, as do we. We'll not harm so much as a single hair on your father's aged head. But, if you wish it, I will give you my word as a gentleman to add to that statement, as will Mr. Carstairs, I'm sure. Does that satisfy you?"

Dickie Carstairs said nothing. The tips of his ears, however, turned a painful red.

Tess got to her feet, so that all three gentlemen were likewise forced to rise. "I suppose I must be mollified. Very well. Mr. Blackthorn? You promised me a trip to the shops. Good day, gentlemen."

"Remember," Jack said as they walked back to the foyer, "follow and watch, that's all. And then report to me, here, tomorrow at seven."

"That sounded disturbingly like an order, Jack," Will said, sighing. "We've all agreed to the plan. There's no need for orders."

"My apologies. I just want this over and her ladyship

returned to the country. We've got a mission waiting for us in Calais, and I'm anxious we be on with it."

"Another Channel crossing," Dickie said rather piteously. "I've barely recovered from the storm we encountered during the last one. Good day to you, my lady. It has been a pleasure."

Tess pouted prettily. "No, it hasn't. I'm an unwanted chore, as Mr. Blackthorn has made most clear to me. But thank you for that kind lie, Mr. Carstairs."

Another moment for another silken utterance of empty flattery from Will Browning, and they were back on the flagway, the two men having agreed to wait ten minutes before they, too, departed the mansion.

"It has to be Browning," she said matter-of-factly once they were heading back to the Blackthorn mansion…the larger of the Blackthorn mansions. Goodness, she hadn't realized one man could be that wealthy and still be so naive, even stupid.

"Your reasons for that conclusion?" Jack asked, turning her toward the alleyway that would lead them between two tall buildings, and into the mews.

"Carstairs can't lie worth a fig. Not by word or action. Papa would never give that sort of man knowledge he wished kept secret. Browning has to be your man. Carstairs appears to like you, even though he's nervous about that, certain it upsets Browning. Because Browning loathes you."

"Taking orders from a bastard," Jack concurred. "Congratulations on that bit of acting, by the way. You had me half-convinced your head is full of feathers, and that's being charitable. Will probably thinks your head is filled with air."

"Thank you. Now where are we going?"

"Since there's very little we can do until tomorrow, as far away from all of this as I could think of taking us," he said as they turned to their left to see the small town carriage standing in the mews, the horses already in the shafts, a coachman on the box. He helped her inside and then gave a quiet order to the coachman before joining her on the squabs.

"So we're going to be able to travel to the ends of the earth and back again before tomorrow at noon?"

"Pardon me? Oh, I see, you're making a joke. A faintly creditable one at that. No, Tess. We don't have to go quite that far. We're going to a fair in Spitalsfield. It won't rival Bartholomew Fair for notoriety, but it should prove a reasonable afternoon's diversion. But only if you promise Sinjon and the Gypsy won't be mentioned."

Tess looked at him in surprise and sudden delight, slipping her hand into his. He looked so young, and slightly apprehensive, which was difficult for her to interpret because she'd long thought he was never apprehensive. "I think I might be able to manage that. I might be able to manage that quite well."

CHAPTER ELEVEN

JACK WATCHED TESS as she watched the Punch and Judy show taking place inside a small stage constructed on the back of a farm wagon. He didn't believe Jacques could be any more enthralled.

She'd never attended a fair, a fact that shouldn't surprise him, for Sinjon would have had to think them very poor entertainment. In the hour they'd been on the grounds however, Tess had more than made up for the lapse in her youth.

She'd eaten a meat pie, laughing and licking her fingers as the juice ran down them, finally bending nearly in half to manage the last two bites so that the greasy juice didn't touch her gown.

He'd kissed away the drips that clung to her chin.

And she'd laughed. And he'd laughed.

It was all very…strange.

They'd always been so serious. Dedicated to their craft. The heat of their lovemaking intense, with little room for anything but the need, the passion.

He'd probably been responsible for most of that. Looking back, he'd decided he'd been a bit of a stick, actually. Keeping himself private, guarding his secrets, his—hell, yes—his shame at who he was before and since his mother's confidences upon the passing of his eighteenth birthday.

Tess was right. She'd told him to go and he'd gone. Because he wasn't ready to stay. He wasn't ready to face who he was and feel worthy of anything, most of all her love. But, please, God, the man he was four years ago was not the man he was now. He had been an angry and often reckless creature back then, hot for adventure, heady with it. He'd been young, rash. Even believed he'd been dedicated to a purpose higher than himself.

Tess had been a part of his life, but not all of it. He'd at last admitted that much to himself. But somehow, she'd always known.

Those days, and those ideals, were gone. They'd begun to die when René died, and they'd disappeared entirely the day Henry Sutton was buried. Henry never got away, never got to live out whatever dreams he may have dreamed that didn't include selling his life to the Crown.

Jack wasn't about to let that happen to him. Not now, not when he'd been handed this second chance to get it right.

Damn Sinjon for putting them all in the middle of this confusing, dangerous coil. And bless him, for unwittingly forcing his former student to learn one last lesson—it isn't weakness to open your heart.

The curtain closed on the wooden puppets who had all but beaten each other into flinders with small wooden bats, and Tess clapped enthusiastically as she nudged Jack with her elbow when a grubby-cheeked young boy came up to them, hat in hand, to solicit a more solid form of appreciation for the performance.

"Tuppence at the least," she urged him quietly. "They were very good, except for Punch's strings breaking when Judy attacked him that last time. And what shall we see next?"

He offered his arm and she slipped hers around his elbow. He looked about, knowing they'd already seen most of the fair's offerings, and spied something rising in the distance, just beyond a thin line of trees. "Come along, little girl."

"That sounds ominous," she said, but didn't hesitate as he led her across the grassy field. "Do you still have my whistle in your pocket? I should hate to lose it."

"Your whistle, your polished coal piece, the paper fan with the drawing of a cow's face on it—why did you want that, by the way?"

"It has soulful eyes, and will make Jacques laugh when I unfold it and fold it up again—see, the cow is here, and now poof, the cow is gone. And the whistle is for Jacques as well, although I may regret that at some point, I fear. Oh, what's that?"

She was looking up now, and then down. Her eyes went wide as she gaped at the large structure that looked much like an enormous, spoked wheel, with two plank seats dangling from it.

"It's an Up and Down," he told her, "as I believe your reaction clearly indicates. You sit on one of those plank seats, holding on very tightly to me, which I would consider a benefit worth any price, as we are lifted up high on that wheel, up and over the trees, and then back down again. As many times as you like. Squealing in delight is allowed, as long as you don't squeal in my ear."

"I never squeal!" Tess impatiently tugged on his arm. "Come along, Jack, this is going to be such fun!"

She did hold tight to him as the Up and Down jerkily began its vertical circuit, but when it stopped with them at the very top, the plank seat suspended from two hopefully stout ropes swaying, she twisted and turned, looking out over the landscape in every direction.

"Oh, look! There's St. Paul's. That is St. Paul's, isn't it? It was drawn on a pamphlet I once saw, describing the sites of London. Perhaps not." She removed one hand from its grip on his forearm and pointed in another direction, half turning about on the seat. "And there's the Thames. See it, Jack? Just a ribbon, but it's there. And the fields. How very neat and orderly they look. Oh, and there's—"

"You could at least *pretend* to be terrified, you know," he interrupted. "It's rather expected. In fact, it's probably the entire point of the exercise. Why else do you think country swains pay down their hard-earned shillings to take sweet young misses up on this contraption in the first place? *Hold me,* they squeal. And they are held, and a soft breast is pressed against an eager young chest. Etcetera."

She looked at him, feigned shock on her beautiful face. "Why, Mr. Blackthorn, I had no idea. How...self-serving of you."

"Not as self-serving as that fellow down there turning the wheel while doing his best to catch a glimpse of bare ankle, and perhaps more," Jack pointed out, laughing.

"Well, shame on him, and on you, as well. But it was worth it, to see the world this way," she said, her eyes shining. "I mean, one can look out one's window, but this is different, don't you agree? This is as if we're a part of the sky. Birds, flying free," she added, kicking her feet, setting the plank seat in motion, like a swing.

"You'd best hope our son doesn't take his delicate stomach from his father," Jack said as he held her tight, held the rope even tighter. "Stop that."

"Oh, no! Don't tell me you're feeling *sick?* Jack? Oh, look—over there. What is that?"

The Up and Down began its descent, but Jack had time to peer in the direction Tess was pointing to now before they descended below the treetops once more. "I think that might be a menagerie. Shall we return to the coach and go take a look?"

She looked at him as if to say *is there any thought in your head that I might say no,* and then they spent the next hour admiring, as the florid-faced man in the red-and-white-striped frock coat repeatedly called out from his perch on top of one of the animal cages, "London's most Grand Collection of the wild, the extraordinary, the rare and magnificent, the fierce and the deadly, ladies and gentlemen, all for your delight and perusal. Leo himself, a most magnificent he-lion, and Brutus, the he-leopard. For a penny, ladies and gentlemen, admire Ebon, the fierce black panther. Hear the terrifying laugh of the hyena. And over here—a cunning civet cat, and the most dangerous of all, the lowly jackal. Come see, come marvel…"

"Come *smell,*" Jack said as Tess was forced again to

cover her nose with the handkerchief he'd offered her earlier. "I think our friend Leo has two teeth, and I can count the ribs on that leopard."

"I know," Tess said, turning away. "It's so sad, isn't it? Such beautiful creatures, to be caged that way."

"There are many ways of being caged. Some very effective cages don't even have bars." Jack winced. "Sorry. I was the one who declared we wouldn't speak of anything remotely serious this afternoon."

"And I'm the one who thoroughly agrees that we shouldn't. I *am* enjoying myself, Jack. Immensely. Isn't it strange, though? I had to come all the way to London to see what you've told me is common entertainment in small towns and villages all across England. I believe I've led quite a narrow life, René and I very nearly cloistered on Papa's estate, I would say. I don't want that for Jacques."

"Beau and Puck and I rarely left Blackthorn, but we did have the run of the nearby villages. Still, in these past years I've seen more of the world than most, and more sides to that world, and I don't want Jacques seeing half of what I've seen."

"He would have liked the Punch and Judy show. I would have liked to see his face while he was watching."

"Then we'll be sure to have him see one," Jack said, and then pulled up short when Tess sighed. "I'm sorry. I said we were starting over, and now I'm speaking as if I've made foregone conclusions. But we will marry, Tess. No matter what else, we will marry. My son will carry my name with him, even if I have no real right to it myself."

They walked on in silence until Tess asked, "Why would you have kept the name if you…that is to say, once you'd learned the marquess is not your father? Not that Blackthorn doesn't seem a strange choice in any case. After all, it's a title, not a name."

"You'd have to ask Adelaide that one, but knowing her, she probably chose it for some private reason, or just because nobody told her she couldn't. It's not that anyone often tells her she can't do something."

And Tess sighed again. So much for keeping this afternoon safe from serious discussion.

"The Crown will take back Papa's estate, won't it? Jacques and I will have nowhere to go. We're dependent on you now, Jack. I don't think I have many choices in any of this. But you've already deduced as much, haven't you?"

Lying was not an option, not with Tess. "No, I don't think you do. Although I'm certain Sinjon has prepared something for that possibility. That eventuality, I should say. He knows he's crossed the line with Liverpool and his ilk. I thought about this last night. He may have taken the Mask of Isis because it's the single most important piece to him, as well as the most valuable. If all his intricate planning for whatever it is he's up to were to come to nothing, he'd still have the mask, and could use it to set the three of you up somewhere. Anywhere in the world. Tess? What's wrong?"

"He'd leave all of that behind? All that René died for, because my brother died protecting that damnable collection, no matter what other reason anyone might try to give it."

"He had to leave his collection behind in France, remember. That didn't stop him from beginning a new one
here in England. The man is nothing if not determined.
He'll just begin again."

Tess shook her head. "No, Jack. He's too old. He's
made a choice. A few more years looking at his hidden
treasures before he dies, or life somewhere else, with
Jacques. I told you, he loves him to distraction. Almost
as if our son is his new obsession."

That statement had Jack drawing his hands up into
fists. *Mine.*

Tess looked into the middle distance, clearly con-
centrating on something that was circling in her mind.
"But even Papa won't live forever. He knows that. He
probably won't live to see Jacques reach his majority.
So what to do, what to do…"

"Find a way to bring me back in, I suppose," Jack
said, his mind also whirling in an attempt to think like
the most confoundingly clever yet conscienceless man
he'd ever known. "He needs the Gypsy gone, no matter
what, that's clear. I'm the tool he picked for that. But
why else did he pick me? Certainly not to take one look
at Jacques and remove him beyond his reach, which is
what any sane man would expect me to do."

"Papa is incredibly sane."

Jack looked at her, his heart suddenly pounding, his
breath coming quickly. "Yes, he is, isn't he? Or so thoroughly insane that he appears sane." He grabbed Tess's
arm. "Come on."

He half dragged her across the grass until she picked
up her skirts and began to run with him. "What? What

are you thinking? Is this about Jacques? Jack! Answer me! *Is this about Jacques?*"

Jack handed her up into the closed carriage and barked an order to return to Grosvenor Square at all speed. "*Now,* man. Anyone gets in your way, run them down!" He then tumbled into the carriage even as the coachman lashed the whip out and over the horse's heads.

"Oh, my God, Jack. He's taken him. That's what you think, isn't it? *He's taken Jacques!*"

Jack took her hands in his. "Can you think of a better way for him to be assured of my cooperation—and that I make certain he stays alive? Otherwise, how will we ever find our son? But Puck won't make it easy for him, or whoever the hell he's hired. Christ! Did I send my brother off to be killed?"

TESS LEANED FORWARD on the squabs all the way back to Grosvenor Square, hanging on to the strap as the coachman weaved through the ever-increasing traffic of carts, drays and other equipages, as if she could physically make the wheels turn faster.

Jacques...Jacques...Jacques. Each hoofbeat pounded out his name. Each heartbeat.

Jack wasn't wrong. She knew he wasn't wrong, even as she wanted to argue that he couldn't be right. Her father wouldn't do such a thing. Do this to her, his own daughter.

Four hours. How would they ever catch up to them? Would her father have waited until they were deep into the countryside? Could Puck be counted on to put up much of a fight? He was pleasant enough, but he seemed a bit of a fribble, a little too lighthearted to be of much use, although Jack hadn't said so. Was there still time to catch them?

Jack hadn't said a word, not a single word, in the endless time it took for them to return to the mansion. She knew what he planned to do. Quickly change into riding clothes while the horses were saddled, and take off after the coach. He wouldn't fight her when she demanded to accompany him. No man could be that foolish. She could ride, better than most men. Breeches, her hair tucked up inside her hat so as to not draw too much attention, no sidesaddle to slow her down.

They'd ride together. They'd face what had to be faced. Together.

"Come on," he ordered as the carriage finally arrived in front of the Blackthorn mansion. He had the door open and the two of them on the flagway even as the wheels were still rocking back and forth, and up the steps to the front door a heartbeat later.

That door opened just as they reached it, and Wadsworth stood back to let them in. "I see you've figured the lay of it, Mr. Blackthorn. Good on you. Master Puck awaits you in the drawing room, and the doctor has just now left. Young Master Jock is with him, my lady, having his dear self a bit of a nibble."

Tess clapped both hands over her mouth to hold back the sobs she'd been fighting for what seemed like hours, and raced up the curved staircase, Jack close behind her.

"Jacques!" she called out as she ran into the drawing room. *"Mon petit! Viens à votre maman!"*

KASEY MICHAELS   183

"Maman!" the child called out cheerfully, putting
aside a small dish of sugar comfits before turning onto
his belly and then sliding down from the couch where
he had been perched before running straight into her
arms as she leaned down to him. "Uncle Puck played a
game!"

Holding the boy close, she stood up, looking to the
chaise where Puck Blackthorn reclined at his ease, his
right arm tucked into a black sling. His jacket lay beside
him, cut and dark with blood, dark red stains on his shirt
and buckskins. "Oh, God…" she said as Jack approached
his brother.

"You were attacked," Jack said quietly.

"No flies on you, are there, brother mine?" Puck returned amicably as he struggled to push himself upright,
aim his feet at the floor. "The question is, if you knew
this could happen, why wasn't I let in on the secret?
Rather poor sporting of you, I think."

As Tess watched, Jack's body seemed to relax. He
even smiled, which greatly surprised her. "I hope you
didn't hurt them all too badly."

"There were only five of them. Hardly a contest.
Who's after you, Jack? This time, I mean. I suppose
this is almost an everyday occurrence in your line of
work."

"They were after Jacques, not me," Jack told him,
motioning for him to move over so that Jack could sit
down beside him. He picked up the ruined jacket, contemplated it for a moment, and then set it aside. He
looked suddenly very tired.

Puck looked swiftly to the boy, still in his mother's

arms, and probably to remain there for hours, if Tess had anything to say on the matter. "The boy? That hadn't occurred to me. In God's name, Jack—why?"

"We'll discuss that later. Tell me what happened."

"You're demanding, brother? Without first offering me a glass of wine to ease the telling? Expressions of gratitude aren't your strongest suit, I've noticed."

"I'll apologize later, as well," Jack growled. "Now talk."

Emilie, who had been sitting unnoticed in a corner of the large room, came to extract Jacques from Tess's embrace, her stern look brooking no nonsense from her former charge as she wriggled her fingers in a manner that demanded the boy be handed over to her. She leaned in and said quietly in French, "He was very brave, the pretty blond one. But he should drink the laudanum the doctor said to drink. His pain is not trifling. Now give me the child before you squeeze him to death."

Tess reluctantly handed Jacques over to his nurse. She watched as they left the room, Wadsworth standing guard in the hallway and wearing the sort of expression that would make most well-armed men throw down their weapons as they ran for their lives, or their own nurses.

"Jack," she then said, turning back to see him in the process of handing Puck a full glass. "Emilie says the doctor wishes Puck be dosed with laudanum and put to bed."

Puck quickly grabbed the wineglass before Jack could withdraw it, and downed its contents in two gulps. "And Puck says the doctor is a horse's ass—your pardon, Tess—and wine is clearly the superior medicine. Besides, I've been ordered to speak, and I can't do that if I'm upstairs snoring, now can I?"

"What happened to your arm?" Jack asked, taking the empty glass and refilling it, then drinking down its contents himself.

"A slice, that's all. Damned bloody, but a bit of clever stitching by the good doctor has it all sewn up again nicely. Admirable work, really. Admirable. Wouldn't you rather I began at the beginning?"

"You've already had wine, haven't you?" Jack asked, sitting down once more, this time on a low stool he'd pulled up facing his brother. "A good quantity of it, at that."

Puck smiled, and then winked at Tess. "His intelligence is near to terrifying, isn't it? Of course I've had wine, Jack. Or have you never had anyone darning several inches of your forearm as if it was a bloody sock? My apologies again, Tess, for my crudity. Regina would have my liver if she heard me like this. She'll probably have my liver anyway, now that I think of it. I've promised her after the last time that I'd never do anything even remotely heroic again."

"But you were heroic, weren't you, Puck?" Tess said, longing to hug him. Clearly there were depths to Puck Blackthorn she hadn't noticed...or he'd kept well hidden. "Would you please tell me what happened? Jack can listen, but we won't allow him to ask any questions."

Puck grinned, rather lopsidedly. His blond hair had come free of its ribbon and was falling around his face, making him boyishly handsome. He wagged his finger at Tess as he looked at Jack. "I like this gel. Too good

for you by half. Have I said that before? Probably. It's
obvious enough, isn't it?"

Jack got to his feet. "Never mind, Puck. Let me help
you upstairs."

"No, no, I want to talk now. Not that there's a whacking great lot to tell." He screwed up his expression and
then seemed to settle on a starting point, because he
nodded, as if in agreement with something he'd just
thought, and then spoke.

"Let's see. Not even an hour outside of London. A
fair amount of traffic on the roadway, so that the attack
was even more of a surprise than it might have been.
Clever ploy, don't you think? Five riders appearing as
if out of nowhere. One going to the lead horse, two engaging the outriders behind us, the other two on either
side of the coach, pistols waving, shouting. You know
how that is, all that blustering, meant to shake a person
to his boots. In any case, I couldn't really make out what
they were shouting, but it was apparent they wished for
me to open the door to them, even as the coach was still
moving. I, of course, declined."

Tess was forming a picture in her mind of how it was.
The men were slowing the coach only enough that Puck
could pass Jacques out to one of them before they disappeared as quickly as they had appeared. How? How
could her father have planned to catch anything so dangerous *with her son?*

"Jacques said you played a game," she said, thinking
of the boy being jostled about as the coach was forced
to a halt.

"That's true enough. A simple matter of lifting the

seat on my side of the coach even before those two riders came fully abreast of us, and dumping him into the storage space below. I told him it was a game, and then had Emilie exchange seats with me and, well, sit on him. Plucky. That boy has real bottom, Tess. He didn't cry at all, and it must have been dark as pitch inside that space."

She resolved yet again that she was not going to cry. She refused to cry. But, oh, she had not promised not to become incensed!

"I won't bore you with details, except to say that the rider on my side of the coach became impatient and made to lean down and unlatch the door himself, pulling it open. At which point—not realizing that I'm left-handed—his knife made a dead set at my right side, while I employed my own sticker with my left. To considerably more effect than he, I might add. Emilie, bless her stout French heart, used one of her knitting needles to persuade the gentleman on her side of the coach to withdraw, howling. I gave her a smacking great kiss square on her mouth for that one, something else I suppose I'll have to tell Regina.

"At any rate, with the door already happily open, I then climbed rather inelegantly up onto the roof, availed myself of the blunderbuss the coachman hadn't been able to reach while still trying to keep the horses moving, dispatched the bugger holding the off-leader's harness—and that was that, and here we are, and yes, I really do think I'd like to go upstairs and lie down, if you don't mind. Oh, and you owe me a new jacket. And a new shirt. And new buckskins, now that I think of it.

Shall I simply have my tailor send you a bill? Yes, why don't I do that?"

Puck stood up then, and swayed where he stood, his complexion alarmingly pale. Jack swore under his breath as he reached out to catch his brother before he could fall.

"Wadsworth!"

The butler was there in an instant, and between them they managed to half walk, half carry Puck from the room. Puck was singing snatches of some faintly bawdy French ditty as they disappeared up the stairs.

Tess stood alone in the drawing room, her hands clutched tightly in front of her, her knuckles going white with the strain of holding back her feelings for the past hour, the past eternity.

And then she slowly followed them up the staircase, as the tears began to fall.

CHAPTER TWELVE

JACK LEANED AGAINST the brick wall in the alleyway, one foot bent-legged against it, watching Tess as he smoked his cheroot.

She was a woman on the edge. Of something. Murder? Mayhem? Collapse?

In the past few days she'd lost everything she'd ever believed about her father, her life, her brother's death. Yesterday, she—they—could have lost their son.

He'd barely spoken with her since their arrival back at Grosvenor Square the previous afternoon to find Puck drunk and bleeding and Jacques stuffing his cherubic mouth with sugar comfits. By the time he and Wadsworth had gotten the happily inebriated Puck settled, she'd climbed up to the third-floor nursery, and hadn't come down again until this morning. When Jack had knocked on the door, begging admittance, the so recently knitting needle–wielding Emilie had opened it a crack, shaken her head, and warned him to take himself off.

"Puisque que vous vous occupez d'elle, monsieur, laissez lui à ses larmes." As you care for her, sir, leave her to her tears.

And so he had, taking himself off to the study, grabbing up the decanter of brandy and slowly, steadily downing most of it, until he finally slept the last few hours of the night slumped in the desk chair.

Now, as he watched, she walked to the edge of the building and once more looked out and across the narrow street to Number 9 Cleveland Row before sighing, and then returning to the spot she seemed to have chosen to stand—completely on the other side of the alleyway from him.

She looked magnificent, something he had decided he wouldn't waste his breath telling her. Once again clad in her brother's clothing, she'd tied her hair up and shoved it beneath a low-crowned and wide-brimmed brown hat. Only a fool would believe her male if given a moment to consider the thing, but Jack was sure she hadn't chosen the rigout for its benefits as a disguise. No, she wanted to be ready to run, if it was running that was required of her.

He didn't ask her if she had a knife secreted in her boot top. He was certain he already knew the answer to that.

She walked to the edge of the alleyway again. Less than thirty seconds after her last reconnaissance.

"Dickie will give the signal," he reminded her. "In the meantime, best we stay out of sight."

"I know that," she returned rather testily, he thought. "What I don't know is why you trust either one of them."

"I don't. I've another man on the roof of the building just above us. If Dickie's alert comes even five seconds after Jeremy's, I'll have my answer as to which one of the two is riding in Sinjon's vest pocket, won't I?"

She shrugged one shoulder and returned to her self-assigned position. "You seem to have thought of everything."

"Not everything, Tess," he said, thinking about Jacques. They had to talk about this, sooner rather than later. "I'd first have had to lay myself down in a gutter for a week to think up what Sinjon tried yesterday."

She nodded, speaking quietly: "I don't know if I want to confront him, or if it would be better if I never saw him again. How is it possible to hate one's own father?" Her hands drew up into tight fists. "How did I live with such evil, and not know it? Not know it—God, Jack, I *worshipped* it, didn't I? His supposed brilliance. His never-ending heartache over the death of my mother. And he'll tell me he did it all for my own good, René's own good. For Jacques."

"Perhaps that's what he believes," Jack offered. "He duped me as well, Tess. We can't waste time on regrets, or let what he's done confuse us now. All that's left is to play out his little game until the end. He's had to change his plans now, remember, thanks to Puck…and Emilie. He wanted Jacques safely hidden in order to gain our cooperation. I wonder what was in the note that would have arrived in Grosvenor Square yesterday evening, don't you? *The boy for the Gypsy and my safe passage to—* Well, we won't know that now, either, will we?"

She lifted her chin and looked into Jack's eyes. "The boy? I told you, Jack. He loves Jacques. The way he'd stand at his bedside when he was sleeping, just staring at him. For hours. And Jacques adored him. He would have gone anywhere with— *Oh, my God...*"

He hated doing this to her. But he'd had all night

to think, to put himself in Sinjon's shoes. "Watching him, thinking, plotting. *How do I use this child to my best interests? Is it time? Is he old enough to be without his nurse? No, not yet. And no sign of the Gypsy. I still have time. I'm still safe. Thessaly must believe my devotion, feel safe allowing Jacques to leave the estate with me, think nothing of it. Jacques must come willingly. Is he old enough now? No, not yet. But look, here, in the newspaper. It's him. He's back. I've got to make my move soon or it will be too late. Too young, the boy's still too young. If only I had some way of assuring he'd be brought to London. Then I could take him. But of course! Jack. I should have seen it sooner. Jack will bring him to London when he comes to rid me of the Gypsy...*"

Tess wiped at her eyes with the backs of her hands. "Stop it, Jack. Stop it."

"I'm wrong?"

She shook her head. "I want you to stop because you're probably right. A man who could pretend infirmity for over two years could certainly feign grandfatherly love for three."

"One thing more, Tess," Jack said, pushing himself away from the wall to cross the alley to her. "Jeremy? My man on the rooftop? He returned from a rushed visit to the manor late yesterday, and I spoke with him early this morning, before you were awake. I probably don't need to tell you what he told me."

He watched her slim throat as she swallowed hard, her eyes closing for a moment before she shook her head. "No. You don't have to tell me. The rest is gone, isn't it? The *things*. He took the Mask of Isis to be sure that if all else failed, he had the best of it, but he was never planning to leave the rest behind. Just Jacques and me. And…and he had you to take us away from the manor, leaving it unprotected so that everything else could be safely removed. He has another Gypsy. Doesn't he?"

"I don't think so, no." Jack had thought long and hard about that possibility as well, and dismissed it. "He has hirelings now. Two less today than he had yesterday, thanks to Puck, but that's all he has. It would be interesting to hear how he thought he would manage to rid himself of them once their usefulness was over, but not interesting enough to make me care. Four years, Tess. He's had four years to plan this. That we're as close as we are, that we know or have guessed at as much as we have in just these few days, is a compliment to the way he trained us both. In the end, *we* will be his downfall. You and I, Tess, working together. He trained us, and yet he has underestimated us both. It's Sinjon's most damning fault—his absolute belief in his own superior brilliance."

The low whistle had them both turning their heads toward the end of the alleyway.

"Dickie. Ah, and there's Jeremy's alert, close behind him." Jack pulled out his watch and noted the time. Not quite eleven-thirty, with the deadline being noon. He wondered how many there would be. "Shall we?"

The signal was to come when the first person approached Number 9, presumably to deliver a written application to view the items to be displayed for purchase.

And while Dickie and Will watched each delivery, Jack and Tess would wait to see what happened at noon.

"And there's Jeremy now," Jack said as his man approached Number 9 shortly after the first messenger had departed, to slide the application Jack and Tess had written into the metal box nailed to the front door that was straight on level with the street. "He makes a tolerable Nabob's page, don't you think?"

"Do Nabob's page boys wear turbans?" Tess asked, watching as the agent retreated back down the steps and walked away.

"I have no idea, my education not stretching to that degree, I'm afraid."

"I doubt they're that tall, in any case," she added quietly. "Do you really think Papa's somewhere close, watching?"

Another messenger, and close on his heels, another. What was that now, four? And how many others could be in that box, from earlier today, even from yesterday from those too anxious to obey Sinjon's instructions to deposit their requests at noon today? If the box had even been there yesterday, which it hadn't been, at least not when Jack had checked.

"Would you be?"

"I don't think so, no. It would be too risky. Here comes another one, just stepping out of that hackney. And clearly another costume, unless anyone would be fool enough to send his own footman in full livery. Do you recognize it, Jack? I thought the entire idea of this sort of thing was anonymity for both buyer and seller. Jack? Jack, what's wrong?"

He watched the footman deposit a folded piece of paper in the metal box and then reenter the hackney coach he'd exited moments earlier and drive off immediately. He'd been tall, noticeably so. Well muscled. Red hair, tied back with a black ribbon, a short, full gray cape reminiscent of the French King Louis's musketeers of a bygone age. The brim of his slouch hat worn low, hiding his eyes. The process hadn't taken more than five seconds, start to finish, and the man, with a sweep of his short cape, was gone.

"Nothing," he said, preferring to keep his observations to himself. It was already too late to attempt to follow the hackney; they all had to remain in place until noon. Damn. "It's just that we've got an even half dozen now, with one of them our own Nabob and one quite possibly an agent of the Gypsy. If Sinjon includes them all when he sends out his *invitations,* we're going to have a more difficult time sorting through them, and keeping them out of harm's way, for that matter."

"There are no innocent people," Tess reminded him, sighing.

Church bells all over the city began pealing the hour of noon. All that was left now was to watch to see what happened to the box. Would the door open, the contents of the box snatched up? Would they wait an hour, five hours, before anything else happened? He should warn Tess to stop pacing back and forth and conserve her energy, but that would be a waste of his breath.

Before the final chime faded an urchin who had been busying himself kicking loose cobblestones at passersby suddenly turned and scampered to the door, grabbed the responses out of the box, and then ran straight out into the street just as a hackney pulled to a halt. Strong arms reached out to grab him up, and the hackney moved on.

Quickly followed by the small farm wagon driven by a disguised Dickie Carstairs, Will Browning appearing out of a nearby doorway and throwing himself up onto the plank seat beside him.

"'There's a special providence in the fall of a sparrow. If it be now, 'tis not to come; if it be not to come, it will be now; if it be not now yet it will come: the readiness is all.'"

Tess looked at him as if he'd inexplicably lost his mind. "What are you babbling about?"

"Nothing, just some small remembrance from *Hamlet*. What it comes down to, Tess, is this—timing is all. So far, Sinjon's timing is excellent, rather like a well-choreographed play. Shall we take the stage to play our part now?" Jack said, indicating that they should cross the street now. "And lend ourselves to our own small part in the performance?" He didn't put too much hope in the possibility they'd learn anything of consequence, no more than he put in the idea that Dickie and Will would discover anything by following the hackney. But they had to try. They had to play out their roles as Sinjon would expect them to do if they hoped to convince him they had no other choice. Which, unfortunately, they hadn't.

Puck had been a complication Sinjon had not expected. Puck was often unexpected, as he preferred people to view him as delightful, but harmless. That Sinjon had lost two of his hirelings to Puck, not to men-

tion Jacques, called for some alternation of the man's
plans. At the moment, that might be the only *edge* they
had over him.

"Come on, Tess, come on," he said moments later,
standing in front of her, blocking the view of any interested passersby as she bent over the lock to the front
door of Number 9. "You used to be good at this."

"I'm still good at this," she said as she worked to
undo the lock. "I simply don't usually have to do it with
someone *nagging* at me like an old washerwoman."

"My apologies," he said, and then turned and followed her as she pushed open the door. She wasn't
simply good, she was magnificent. "No doubt an inferior lock."

"Yes, no doubt," she said without rancor as they
stepped into the small, gloomy foyer, Jack putting himself between her and whatever they might find, whomever they might find.

There were no stairs, the building having been constructed with a separate entrance for the upstairs rooms,
so that it didn't take long to see that the place was devoid
of furniture as well as people. There was nothing. Not
so much as a scrap of paper on the— "Damn it!"

"What?" Tess asked, heading back into the small
foyer. "Oh, for the love of— He stuck it to the back of
the door?"

"With a knife obviously from his collection. How
dramatic," Jack said, removing the ancient, ornately jew-
eled knife and sliding it into his boot top. "Let's go."

"You don't want to read it now?"

"Tess, we're being watched. We've been watched ever

since we entered this house, and probably while we were in the alley. It's time to go."

She nodded her agreement and waited behind him as he opened the door, looked outside, scanned the windows of the buildings across the narrow street, and then stepped out into a drizzle that had begun while they were searching the flat.

"Should I wave?" she asked facetiously. "Or would that be tempting fate?"

"I'd rather we both look confused, and angry."

"That won't be too difficult," she said, and struck a pose with her hands on her hips, looking up at the sky as if for divine assistance. "There's someone on the roof directly across from us, Jack. He just ducked behind a chimney. Sloppy."

"I told you. Hirelings. Ah, and look who's coming back, clearly to report their lack of success. I'd hoped we'd be long gone if they happened to return. Stay here. Turn your back, if you please, and keep your head averted." He stepped out into the street as Dickie Carstairs set the brake on the wagon. "So?"

"A waste of our time," Will Browning told him, pulling up the collar of his jacket, as the rain was beginning to fall in earnest now. "The boy was set down only a block beyond here, with the hackney barely stopping to perform that service. He ran off, and that was that. We saw no need to follow him, but remained in pursuit of the hackney."

"As you'd be expected to do. And?"

"And there was suddenly a rain of hackneys, Jack. They seemed to come from everywhere. All black, all undoubtedly hired to confuse us, but Dickie here amazed me by noticing that *our* hackney had one brown wheel, so we were able to keep it in sight."

Jack rubbed at his mouth, deciding not to tell the two men that the brown wheel was no mistake, no accident. He and Sinjon had used a similar ploy years ago, in Brussels. The paint on the damn thing was probably not quite dry. "Go on. Don't drag this out, Will. You caught up with the brown-wheeled hackney, only to find it occupied by—?"

"Nobody," Dickie said, sighing soulfully as he climbed down from the bench seat and rubbed at his abused backside. "I don't know how, but the fellow must have been able to shift himself from one hackney to another when they were all bunched so close together. I'm that sorry, Jack."

"Don't be. It was the boy you should have followed in any case, I'm sure. He still had the letters," he said shortly. "Very well. No need to meet tonight, and no need to meet at all until we hear from Sinjon. I'll keep you alerted."

"So there was nothing in the building? No evidence that the marquis was ever there?" Will asked as he joined them on the flagway. Dickie was already turned and poised to walk away.

"No. Nothing. He's running us a merry chase, gentlemen. But we'll get him in the end. Dickie? Aren't you forgetting something?"

Dickie looked around him as if the action might jog his memory. "No, I don't think so."

"There's a wagon half-filled with cabbages behind

you," Jack pointed out as, behind him, Tess laughed into her fist, quickly turning it into a cough.

"Oh. *That*. No, not mine. I was only borrowing it, as it were." He turned to look at Will. "Think there's any hackneys left anywhere for us to hire? I could use a bird and bottle. And a roof," he added, pulling his jacket closer around him.

"In a moment, Dickie," Will said. "Jack? This old bastard's making us look the fools. I don't care for it."

"Shouldn't say that, Will," Dickie murmured as he kicked at a cobblestone, doing his best to speak without allowing his lips to move.

"It's all right, Dickie. I know what Will meant. And he's right. The old bastard's still ahead of us. But we'll catch up, even if it's only when he wants us to."

"And that sounds disturbingly like you admire the man," Will said quietly. "Perhaps it's time you handed over the reins on this assignment."

"To you, Will?" Jack returned just as quietly, even as Dickie took two prudent steps away from both of them. "Is that what you're suggesting?"

"I am, yes. You're too involved. Oh, and pardon my manners—good afternoon, my lady."

Jack took a half step toward Will, but then stopped. "All right, you've made your point. What do you propose?"

Will's smile was wide and nonthreatening. "And there's the rub, Jack. I don't know what to propose. This entire mission is already so bollixed up, we may as well simply wait at the docks in Dover to wave the man on his way to wherever he's going, taking twenty years of government secrets with him. If he hasn't already gone, and all of this is just some twisted revenge on you, meant to keep you busy while he makes good his escape. Have you thought of that, Jack?"

"Am I supposed to?" Jack asked him, watching as the smile left Will's face.

"You sonofabitch. Is that why I saw Jeremy Hopkins skulking around as if trying to avoid us? You've got somebody watching *us?* Why? What are you implying?"

"Nothing more than you, I would imagine. Because somebody is in Sinjon's employ, Will. Think about that. I know I am." He then turned to Tess, and the two of them walked off down the flagway, turning at the first available alley.

"Why did you do that?" she whispered urgently as they headed for the small town coach waiting for them two blocks away. "What did you think you were going to prove? Now they know you're onto them. One of them, whoever it is."

Jack swore under his breath. "I know, I know. It was stupid. I let my frustration get the better of me. Damn it! Let's just get back to Grosvenor Square and see what Sinjon has to say for himself."

The rest, the disguise he'd seen on the last man to deposit a request in the box tacked to the front door of Number 9? He'd keep that to himself for now. It could have been coincidence. It could mean nothing. It probably meant nothing.

Or it could mean more than even the most imaginative brain could conjure up without recourse to fiction.

TESS SAT ON the hearth rug in her dressing gown, brushing her damp hair after her bath, having dismissed Beatrice to return to the nursery.

It would seem that Emilie had abdicated her role as nurse to Jacques in order to spend a good part of the day fussing over Puck, who had seemed to enjoy the old woman's fussing. The nurse had actually blushed when Tess had complimented her on her concern for Jack's brother, before bustling back to the sickroom.

Yes, Tess had decided. There was something about the Blackthorn men. She would be interested in meeting Beau, the oldest.

The drizzle had turned to a downpour before they reached the town carriage, and while a bath hadn't been necessary, Tess had wanted some time to collect her wits before she and Jack read the communication from her father. She'd taken the letter from Jack, and it sat now on her dressing table, the wax seal intact, all but glaring at her malevolently, impossible to ignore much longer. The truth couldn't be avoided forever.

There was a knock at the door and she turned in time to see Jack enter, followed by Wadsworth, bearing a silver tray holding a teapot, cups and a plate of iced cakes. The butler deposited the tray on one of the tables, bowed to Tess, and withdrew.

"That's wonderfully thoughtful of you, Jack, but I don't think I could eat anything. Not even cake."

He looked...wonderful. Handsome in his dark breeches and white shirtsleeves. He was a physically beautiful man. He couldn't help that, could he? But he also looked competent. In charge. Dependable. A safe haven. *Her* safe haven.

She twisted her hair into a damp knot and walked over to join him at the table, stopping only to pick up the dreaded communication from Sinjon. Not her father. Not anymore. He was Sinjon now. He was the bastard Will Browning had termed him, not by birth, but by nature.

"I'd rather you read it to me," she said, handing it over to him as she sat down, both of them pretending her hand wasn't shaking slightly. When he took the letter and then sat down across the table from her, she performed the duty of hostess automatically, preparing dishes of tea for both of them. Jack liked sugar. Three cubes. She remembered that. Like Jacques, he liked sweet things. Wasn't it strange that he also liked her...

Jack broke the wax seal and unfolded the page, each small sound of breaking wax, unfolded paper resounding like gunshots in the quiet room.

"There's no salutation," he said, looking over the top of the page as he told her. "I imagine he knew who would find it and be doing the reading. All right, let's get on with this. I dislike the thought that he's sitting somewhere in his web, rubbing his hands together in delight at our frustration."

Tess sat with her hands in her lap, twisting the smooth linen of her serviette, as the mind of Sinjon Fonteneau, Marquis de Fontaine, was laid open for them, surely not wholly, certainly minus the candor of a deathbed confession. He would play the game until the end, and then try to confound St. Peter into opening the gates of Heaven for him rather than send him spiraling down to the depths of Hell.

"My congratulations are offered that you've gotten this far, save for the sad realization that you've proven no more than a mediocre imitation of the master. I'd hoped for better, more of a challenge. Even your one small triumph is not yours to claim, as you sent the boy off, all unawares. Luck is not laudable, it is only luck, and does not last. Neither bad luck nor good.

"You might inquire this of the Gypsy, and he could tell you of his incarceration in a quite unlovely prison in Spain these past few years, courtesy of my efforts, and of his escape not so long ago, a result of stupidity on the part of the Spanish authorities. With luck, he was meant to die there. But such is life. Luck is not constant. The intelligent man prepares.

"With you, Jack, I prepared. I found you because I wanted to find you. You came to me because you had nowhere else to go save, one day, the hangman. Now you will repay me for my generosity. You are the man I made you.

"The Gypsy is a man of many faces, and for the nonce, with a single intent. My destruction. He has had long years to reflect on where he took the first misstep that led to his arrest in Spain, and doubtless concluded he'd made a bargain with the devil. You see, after René's death, he'd agreed to leave my Collection to me while I lived, and I'd agreed to discontinue my pursuit of him and furnish continued information that would be helpful to his lucrative contacts inside Bonaparte's puffed-up regime. So convivial, so civilized a settlement of our small falling-out. Equals, the Gypsy and I, in mind and heart, or at least in his. He truly believed me, that one day the Collection would be his for the taking.

"Ah, but wars end, don't they, Jack, jumped up emperors are banished, and the possessions of one's mentor will be then looked to with greedy anticipation. Our friend the Gypsy failed to realize this inevitability, as stupid men often deny the obvious.

"I returned to my Collection, and the Gypsy, armed with what he believed to be vital information Bonaparte would pay quite heavily to have, sailed for Spain.

"So now you understand, yes? In my generosity, I felt you should know. The Gypsy is back, and he is angry. But fool that he is, he doesn't strike at once, but plans to first terrify me, make me suffer for his years in Spain. The flaw of the flamboyant, Jack. A cobra strikes, it does not just sit up and wave its hooded head about, hoping to incite fear.

"But think, Jack. Think how the Gypsy must think. Four years is a long time. Where has Sinjon's Collection gone? Is it still at the manor house, locked in secrets? Or is it moved, gone? He needs me alive. I insist he die.

"He announces his return with that amateurish theft in London, his taste for melodrama always distasteful to me. In return, I throw down my gauntlet as Mr. St. John. We two go to war. Exciting, for a time, after too many years of idleness and ennui, feigned infirmity, feigned affection. But where is the sport, Jack, in fooling fools?

"So now I end this comedy and disappear, begin again, sans the Gypsy, sans Liverpool and his ilk, sans encumbrances. I had long since planned my exit from this damp isle. There are always beginnings, for those who earn them with their wits.

"Why didn't I go sooner? Take myself and my Collection off, hide myself away? You're asking that, surely, even as you know the answer. The Marquis de Fontaine does not run away. He exits, triumphantly. In his own time.

"That time is now.

"The Gypsy dies, at your hand. You will indulge me by employing the knife I entrusted to you today. He will recognize it just before he breathes his last, as he sees it buried to the hilt in his chest. Ah, I grow poetic in my advancing years, do I not? For this great favor to your mentor, I give you what you believe you already possess, and much more you had no hope of knowing. But for you to know, the Gypsy must die, and I must live.

"In two days' time, at ten in the evening, in the one place a fool would never think to look for me.

Make your preparations, as I have made mine, and do strive to display more competence than you have thus far. Strike from the shadows when I say, 'You appear familiar, sir.' Simple, yes? After all of this, a simple ending.

"Strike true,

"Sinjon.

"One thing more, as I feel generous tonight. You had once asked me René's dying words to his papa. A curse on me, Jack. Much like the one you may be uttering now. This is irony. For once in his life a man, and then dead..."

Jack laid the tightly written page on the table and gave it a small push away from him, as if he felt even its presence offended him. "Fool, ignorant, incompetent, mediocre. We're all inferior, aren't we? All save him. The great Sinjon, master of all."

Tess used the serviette to dab quickly at her eyes, hating that tears pricked there. "The boy. He couldn't even bother to write Jacques's name. As for me, I'm an encumbrance. And a fool. So many times the fool..."

"But no longer. No longer." Jack picked up the letter once more. "All right," he said brusquely. "Let's go through this. I believe we can skip over his tainted compliment."

"Always the hook at the end. Good, yes, but not a patch on the master," Tess agreed, reaching for her teacup. She would be calm. She wouldn't succumb to emotion. There was work. She'd been trained to concentrate on the work, allowing no distractions. "After that, I believe we're to applaud Sinjon's genius at having tricked the Gypsy and sent him off to Spain, overlooking the fact that his plan only succeeded in part. The Gypsy didn't die."

Jack nodded. "Luck runs out, good or bad, and he is always prepared for either. Yes, Sinjon twists even his failures into triumphs. I agree. In any event, the man's back, even announces his return by leaving his card at the theft here in London. He was calling Sinjon out."

"Because he can't simply kill him. He doesn't know the location of the secret rooms. Or if he does, he doesn't know for certain that Sinjon hasn't moved the collection. He's drawing him out so that he might easily capture him and then convince him to give up its location. I should think the most efficient way to do that would be to come directly to the manor house and put a pistol to Sinjon's head, don't you? Why these games?"

"The Gypsy is flamboyant, remember, even melodramatic? We probably should remember that, since we're going up against him. What else is he? Ah, here it is. *The Gypsy is a man of many faces.* All right, so now we know to expect a disguise of some sort. That's not surprising." He continued scanning the letter. "This one might be important—*I had long since planned my exit from this damp isle.* How long, Tess? How long has he been planning this triumphant exit of his? I would think years. Probably even years before he and the Gypsy parted ways."

Again, Tess nodded. She wished Jack would stop speaking, because an idea had begun floating about in her brain, close, but had not yet circled near enough to catch. "What did he say about you?"

"Other than the fact that I'm his trained instrument, you mean? He's going to reward me, remember? *For this great favor to your mentor, I give you what you believe you already possess, and much more you had no hope of knowing.* Well, that's typically cryptic."

"I don't think so." The idea was taking on more definition. "The first part—that's Jacques and me. That's a threat."

Jack frowned at the page. "Damn. You're right. He must think he can turn you against me once more." He looked across the table at her, his dark gaze intent yet questioning. "Can he do that, Tess?"

"He tried to kidnap my son!" she exploded, banging the side of her fist against the table, so that the teacups rattled. "No matter how he attempts to twist that around to make it sound plausible, even necessary, I can never forgive him for that. *Never.*" Then she took a breath, tried to slow her pounding heart. "He doesn't understand, Jack, because he never loved René or me. He's never loved anybody. Only *things.* Only his own twisted genius. What you and I do is for us to decide. Sinjon is nothing to me now, he holds no power over me."

"All right," Jack said quietly. "For us to decide. Clearly a decision not yet made."

"Jack…"

"No, not now, Tess. If this were anything else, I'd press my advantage. I can't do that to you. Not even for Jacques."

"It isn't that I—"

"Hate me?" His smile twisted inside her, nearly making her clutch at her belly. "No, Tess, I don't believe you hate me. But I also don't believe you know what you're feeling. Let's just get this done, and take Jacques to Blackthorn. What happens after that, happens. Or doesn't."

At last she summoned her own smile. "You're so damn arrogant, Jack Blackthorn."

"Yes, I know. Sinjon would term that a flaw, in all but himself. For now, let's return to the matter at hand. The place of this meeting, where I'm to dispatch my enemy's enemy."

She held up her hand. "No, not yet. There's more to what you read me. Something about him telling you something you had little hope of knowing. It has to mean something. Sinjon may appear to waste words, but he doesn't. They all mean something."

"I was hoping you'd not notice that," he said, handing her the page. "It may be the hook? After all, he finishes it by reminding me that he can't tell me anything if he's dead."

Tess read the line again. "'...and much more you had no hope of knowing.'" Her mind reached out, finally able to grasp what had been eluding it. "Think back to your beginnings with Sinjon, Jack. You told him everything about you, everything that you knew. He listened, didn't he? Intently, as he would, making you believe what you said was so interesting, so important. You'd never told anyone, yet you told this stranger who'd somehow talked you out of robbing him in an alleyway he'd had no reason to be in at any event. Sinjon, who could overcome a drunken man with ease, even one holding a pistol at his chest. It never sounded right to me, Jack. Not when you told me, and not now. Where is it? It's here somewhere," she said, reading through the letter again. "It's what started me thinking that— Ah, here. *'With you, Jack, I prepared. I found you because I wanted to find you… You are the man I made you.'*"

She put down the letter. "Jack? Jack, don't look at me that way, as if you can deny what's on that page. He found you because he went looking for you. He found you, and then he built you into what he needed. Because he prepares. Sinjon doesn't just measure out his moves on a chessboard as us lesser mortals do. He builds the board itself even before the game begins. He's never cornered, never checkmated, because he always has another move already prepared, even years in advance, just in case he needs it."

"So what are you saying, Tess? Other than that I'm a dupe."

She looked at him levelly for some moments. "You already know what I'm going to say. He knows who you are, Jack. Doesn't he? He already knew that first night. He found you because he wanted to find you. You were always one of his chess pieces, like the rest of us."

He pushed back his chair and got to his feet. "Damn him," he said, and then his arm swept out and the contents of the table all went crashing to the floor.

She watched as he left the room, not calling after him that he always seemed to run away from his emotions, as if they couldn't follow him wherever he went. Because he'd be back. She'd learned that now, so she'd give him what he needed, time with himself and his own demons.

Tess bent down and picked up Sinjon's letter, his instructions to them, the ink blurring thanks to the tea spilled on the page. She read the lines concerning René, and somehow they brought her peace rather than pain. René had died a man, daring to curse the father he'd always feared, and he'd left Sinjon a memory clearly he couldn't shake. René's gentle nature was not Sinjon's failure, he'd never accept that, but his death was. If there was a God, he still heard his son's curse in his head.

What had Jack told her? That Sinjon had once mourned that his daughter should have been born the son? But still, he'd taught her, and he'd taught her well. She knew just where they would all meet in two days' time. She knew where no fool would think to look for him.

"You could afford to be cryptic because you *know* Jack and I aren't fools. We're not ignorant, nor incompetent, nor mediocre," she said aloud as she consigned the letter to the fire in the grate and then pulled the bell cord to summon someone to clean up Jack's mess. "That should worry you, *Papa*. It really should…"

CHAPTER THIRTEEN

SHE CAME TO him after midnight, seeking him out in the bedchamber he'd closeted himself in for the remainder of the day, licking his wounds, cursing himself for a fool, wondering how he would manage to contain his rage when he and Sinjon met in two days' time.

She'd come to him just when he'd decided he would go to her. Needed to go to her. Needed to be with her. Could not possibly make it through the long night without her.

The firelight made a halo of her unbound blond hair, and outlined her body beneath the thin white cotton of her dressing gown as she stood between the bed and the fireplace. He could smell her perfume.

She didn't say a word.

He didn't dare to.

Their first night together again had been for her, to comfort her, to remind her she was alive.

Tonight, without words, he knew she had come to return the favor.

The dressing gown slid from her slim shoulders.

Slowly, she loosened the ribbons of her nightrail.

Her eyes were on him, even as the shadows thrown from the fire obscured her features.

He wanted to reach for her, but he stayed where he was. Watching.

She crossed her arms, gathering up the material of the nightrail, and lifted the garment up and over her head. It drifted down to the floor, forgotten. Unnecessary.

She lifted her arms once more, this time sliding her hands behind her head, beneath her hair, as she tilted up her chin. She ran her hands upward, lifting her golden tresses, her perfect breasts rising with the movement.

The firelight caressed her bare skin, accented the tilt of those breasts, the long sweep to her small waist, the inviting swell of her hips. Her long, strong, straight legs.

She held the pose. Until he could hear himself breathing.

She dropped her arms and allowed her long hair to fall, a single shake of her head arranging its golden length to settle perfectly below her shoulders, curl provocatively against her breasts.

Tess reached out and slowly pulled back the covers, drawing them down past his knees, revealing him as he lay naked in the bed, half propped against the pillows.

Jack lay very still, his breath coming even more quickly, his manhood stirring, filling, rising. He knew he wasn't to move, wasn't to touch her.

No. She would do that. For him, she would do that.

She cupped her breasts, sliding her thumbs across her nipples, scraping them lightly with her nails, teasing them into hard peaks. She began delicately pinching them between thumb and forefinger before shifting her hands…the left going to her right breast, her right, her fingers spread, beginning its slow, sensuous slide down her flat midriff. And beyond.

Yes.

There was nothing in his mind save her. Watching her. Imagining himself buried deep inside her.

He was untouchable, unreachable. He'd built himself that way; the world had contributed the bricks with which he'd constructed the walls around him. Nothing and no one got through.

Except her.

She broke through his every defense just by being who she was. He felt her hands on him even as she readied herself for him. He felt her hot wet heat surrounding him, feeding needs he didn't know he had.

She was there, standing at his bedside. She was with him, flesh to flesh. She was deep inside his body, his mind. His soul. She imprinted herself everywhere… without even touching him.

He would never be without her, not if she were thousands of miles away.

"Tess…"

But she knew. Even as he spoke her name, his plea, she was straddling him, lowering herself onto the pulsing arousal that would soon destroy any last defense.

She leaned forward, her hands on his shoulders. And began to move.

She teased. She ground against him, sensing what he needed. She bent her head and put her open mouth against his neck, mimicking her movements with her tongue against his heated skin.

She gave.

Take it. Take what you need. There's nothing but this

now. No shadows, no room for anger, for fear. For re-grets. Just take. Take.

And he took. Just as she had taken when he'd come to her. He buried his anger in her, his pain. He let it go, let it all go. There was no room for it anymore in his heart, not when Tess filled that heart so fully.

His hands came up to up her head, his mouth sought hers, fusing them together completely as they went over the edge together. *Mine. Please...please. Mine...*

He felt her tears on his cheeks, mingling with his own, and squeezed his eyes firmly shut against them.

Her kiss turned gentle before she slid herself off him. When he opened his eyes it was to see her clothed in her nightrail and dressing gown once more.

"Tomorrow, we get to work," she said quietly as she pulled the covers back up over him, bent to kiss him one last time. She was tucking him up, as she would a child.

He reached up a hand to keep her, but then put it down. "Tess..."

"He can't keep anything from you, Jack, any more than he can give you anything. Only you can do that. What's between us will be settled between us. But first we get to work. Agreed?"

He nodded his head, and she smiled.

"I think I rather like this. Being in charge. It's quite a different feeling for me."

He pulled a pillow out from behind him and sent it winging at her laughing, retreating form. Moments later he was alone. Yet not alone.

"God, I love that woman," he breathed into the empty air.

"GOOD MORNING, BROTHER," Jack said as he slipped into the facing chair at the large table in the morning room. "Yes, coffee, Wadsworth," he said as the butler stepped forward to serve him. "Just what I need. Thank you. How are you, Puck?"

"You mean other than faintly mystified at the sight of your cheery face? I barely recognize you."

"I don't always scowl, you know," Jack said, and then ignored the amused look that passed between brother and butler. "Are you fit to travel?"

"Tossing me out, are you?" Puck asked as he attempted to apply jam to a slice of toasted bread that immediately half slid off his plate. "Damn! Ah, thank you."

"Don't thank me," Jack said as he snatched the plate and finished the job Puck had so messily begun. "You wouldn't be in that sling if it weren't for my stupidity."

"Well, yes, that's true enough. Not that I'd wish you to don sackcloth and ashes, but I could do with another slice of ham, you know. Bite-size pieces would be best."

Wadsworth jumped-to with alacrity, and Jack was presented with another small plate, this one holding a thick pink slice of ham.

"The two of you should consider forming a small traveling company, and performing for paying customers," he told them. "However, if you think I'm going to feed you, you'd best get used to an empty belly."

"Ah, there's the scowl we all know so well. I knew that cheery face wouldn't last. Rather glad of it, to tell you the truth. A smiling Black Jack is almost more intimidating than a cheery one. Wadsworth, my good fellow, I suggest you retire now, while it's still safe to turn your back on the fellow."

The butler bowed and took his leave. "A good man, Wadsworth," Jack remarked as he sliced the ham for his brother. "Beau chose well."

"You know Beau. He's always most comfortable with those whose loyalty can't be questioned. Wadsworth might be lacking in polish in some areas, but there's nothing like a former sergeant-major for dedication to duty. You were never in the army, were you? In uniform, I mean. I imagine you were there somewhere, doing whatever it is you do. Have done. Will continue to do?"

Jack smiled once more as he handed over the plate. "Not said with your usual subtlety, Puck. Is your arm still paining you?"

"Thank you. No, pretense is painful enough on its own. I suppose I should simply go straight to the heart of the matter. What happens for you now, Jack? You feel the need to go after the marquis, surely. But for the Crown, or for yourself?"

Jack immediately went on guard. His brother was after something. "Why do you ask?"

Puck held up one finger indicating that he'd answer once he had swallowed his bite of ham, and then said, "Because it makes a difference, obviously. One is a job, a mission, if you will. The other is just bloody stupid revenge and could make you sloppy. In other words, I'm worried about you, Jack. It is allowed of brothers, you know."

"Your concern fair bids to unman me, if it weren't for the insult. I know what I'm doing."

Puck put down his fork. "You don't make it easy, do you? Allowing anyone in. Why is that, Jack? Beau and I have a theory, you know. One that begins and ends with our dear mother."

"Not now, Puck. I've got more than enough on my plate as it is. Besides, that's all ancient history."

"Not as long as it colors your present, no it isn't. Oh, sit down," Puck added as Jack pushed back his chair and made to rise. "We dance around you, and we dance around you. All of us. All right, so the marquess isn't your father. There, I've said it. And so bloody well what? You're our brother, and we damn well need to stick together, the three of us. It's time for you to come home."

Jack sat down with a thump, his hands gripping the arms of the chair until his knuckles went white. "She told you?"

Puck rolled his eyes. "Adelaide? Hardly. Do give Beau and me some credit for insight. When Beau turned eighteen, she gave him the same sort of ring you're wearing. He asked her if the *B* stood for Blackthorn or bastard, but she didn't answer him. Well, she did, in a way. She slapped his face. The morning after your eighteenth birthday, you disappeared. Being an observant sort, and not much caring for what had happened to Beau, and even less for whatever had happened to you, when I reached the age of eighteen and she handed me my own ring, I thanked her prettily and she patted my cheek, told me I was her baby, her treasure. I think I'd rather she'd slapped me."

"But you gave her what she wanted."

"Yes," Puck said slowly. "My mother's gift to me…a

talent for toad-eating. Do you know, Jack, I am possibly the most pleasing person you'll ever meet."

Jack smiled. "You could charm the birds down from the trees," he agreed silkily. "I often longed to toss you into the pigsty."

Puck picked up a crusty roll and halfheartedly tossed it at him. "I just thank God I went to Paris and finally grew up. But that's not my point. Adelaide cast us all into roles, did you ever realize that?"

"I did, yes. She damn near ruined Beau, convincing him that he could overcome his bastard state, be anything and anyone he wished. It was good to finally see him so content in his own skin." Jack picked up the roll and began turning it in his hand. "So now we're up to me. And what, in your infinite wisdom, did Adelaide build when she built me?"

Puck sighed audibly. "She didn't build you, Jack. She did the unforgivable. She tore you down. But she paid a price for that, you know. Papa…Cyril never forgave her for sending you away."

Jack sat back in his chair, surprised at Puck's words. "How do you mean? She's still there when she wants to be. He's still the same besotted fool he always was."

Puck got to his feet. "Let's walk," he said, and then headed for the hallway, leaving Jack with nothing else to do but follow him. He'd turned his back on his life at Blackthorn, told himself a thousand times that he didn't care, that he was better alone. But the past year had taught him that his ties to his half brothers were stronger than he could have thought. If Puck wanted to talk, he owed him the courtesy of listening.

They were silent until they reached the tavern they'd visited just the other day, Puck barely settled into his chair before the barmaid bustled to the table with mugs of hot, rather rancid-smelling coffee, giggling like a girl when Puck thanked her with a wink.

"Born to please," Jack said, seating himself across from his brother.

"And costs me nothing. Life is to be enjoyed, Jack, not endured. Watch that boy of yours, if you don't believe me. We all were like Jacques, once upon a time. And then life…intrudes. But only to the point when we say stop, I've got it now, I'll take it from here, thank you very much. Beau learned that. I learned that. It's time you did, as well. It's *your* life, Jack, not her idea of what or who you are. Make the most of it. Lord knows you've got one hell of a start with Tess and that son of yours. Let the rest go. All of it—just let it go."

Puck's expression was so earnest Jack had to look away. "You were going to tell me about Cyril," he said, uncomfortable with his brother's concern for him.

Puck sighed, nodded. "All right. Just think about what I said. She isn't worth it. This marquis isn't worth it. God knows Prinney and Liverpool and the rest of them aren't worth it." He held up his hand as Jack scowled at him. "Yes, yes, back to Cyril," he said quickly. "First and only time Beau or I ever heard him raise his voice to her. God, what a row they had! Beau and I barely had to press our ears to the door to hear every word."

Jack smiled, as he knew he was supposed to do. Puck was doing this best to get over this heavy ground as lightly as possible. "You were eavesdropping?"

"All but scribbling notes so we could compare them later, yes. That's when we learned for certain that you're not Cyril's—not that he doesn't consider you his. Raised you from a pup, I think were his exact words, and damn well somebody had to, seeing as how she wasn't a fit mother to a flea, let alone three fine sons. There was more, much more. About Abigail, about our mother's selfish ways, about his own madness having already ruined his own sons, his sickness for her—that's the word he used, *sickness*. God. She cried, she pleaded, she accused him of every sin in creation. Horrible things, Jack, about Cyril and Abigail. Perverse, ugly accusations. Lies, of course. He'd never… Well, the upshot was that she left and didn't return for over a year. She's rarely there now, and never closer than the cottage."

Jack didn't say anything. He couldn't find any words.

"He still goes to the cottage when she's there," Puck continued after raising the mug to his lips and then obviously thinking better of the idea of actually drinking any of its contents. "She's still Adelaide, the aging enchantress, I suppose you could say. But now it's she who clings, who seems desperate, and not him. I'm surprised none of us grew up seeing love as a disease, a failing. Or perhaps worse, a trap. In any event, whatever spell she worked on him all those years ago has mostly worn off now. And it began to wear off in earnest the day she sent you away. Not for what she did to him, or to Beau, or to me, but what she did to you. *You,* Jack. So don't tell me that man doesn't think of you as his son."

Puck reached his hand across the tabletop, laid it on Jack's. "He needs his sons' forgiveness. If it takes the form of accepting the unentailed estates, then so be it. He's been waiting for over a decade for you to come back. You were going to send Jacques to him. You can't hate him and do that."

"I never said I hated him. I've no reason to hate him. I despise what he did to you and Beau, but I don't hate him. I actually feel sorry for him. We're all Adelaide's victims, one way or another."

Puck sat back once more. "Shelley translated Goethe's *Faust*. I read it in France and was struck most by a few lines in the Walpurgisnacht scene. Let me see if I have it right. Ah, yes, I remember. 'Beware of her fair hair, for she excels all women in the magic of her locks, and when she twines them round a young man's neck she will not ever set him free again.'"

"Yes, I've read that old legend. Faust made a bargain with the devil, as I recall the thing. So you're suggesting Cyril made a bargain with Adelaide, and like Faust, has lived to regret it? An interesting theory."

"More than a theory, Jack. I'm not saying Cyril is seeking absolution from us, but we do owe him something. All he's asking is that we listen."

"I already said I'd go, Puck."

"I know that. And I know you'll be fair." He smiled rather sheepishly. "I hope. Trusting him with Jacques would be a good beginning. You do still plan to send him to Blackthorn, don't you?"

"He'd see it that way? That I was sending Jacques to him, and not to you and Beau?"

Puck shrugged. "I can make him see it that way. If you let me."

There can be no new beginnings without endings. That's what Jack had thought when he considered Tess's need to close the door on her childhood, her brother's death, her father's duplicity. She needed answers, or so she told herself. But did she? Did he? Should they both insist on some proverbial pound of flesh from those who had wronged them before they could move on? Or was moving on what was really important?

"All right," he said at last. "If you feel well enough to travel, let's get you and Jacques to Blackthorn. I'll give you a note for Cyril, asking his kind indulgence in keeping...in keeping his grandson until Tess and I can join him. Is that enough?"

"More than enough. Good on you, brother mine, good on you!" Puck lifted his mug to toast Jack, took a large swallow of its bitter contents, and spent the next minute coughing and sputtering and spitting into his handkerchief while Jack laughed.

CHAPTER FOURTEEN

TESS STUDIED THE sketch Jack had made of the interior of Number 9 Cleveland Row. The setup was a very straightforward affair, the rooms all coming off a wide, central hallway except for the kitchen to the rear, and a butler's pantry tucked between the small drawing room and adjoining dining room. They'd reconnoitered the previous day, relying on their combined memories for the interior and not entering the building, but counting windows, noting doors, checking vantage points from the rooftop across the street.

There were several drawings in fact. The surrounding streets, blocked out and labeled. Drawings of the building showing each side, each elevation. They'd even counted out the times between patrols of the night watchman, who couldn't be relied upon to do more than get in the way, in any case.

Perhaps to her shame, she'd enjoyed it all very much.

Over the years, she'd planned hundreds of forays, tricks, ploys, scenarios and whatever in her head. She'd studied tactics the way other girls her age would have studied the fashion plates and formed a battle plan for storming the London Season on the hunt for a husband.

She'd reveled in the exercise of her mind, matching

wits with her father as he played the part of either quarry or pursuer.

She'd done it for practice, for the joy and satisfaction of the thing, and for the year before René's death, she'd not only helped form the plans but also often had been included in the implementation of those plans.

And she'd learned one thing. Her father never lost. She'd never once beaten him.

"Still studying those things?" Jack asked, walking into the room. He'd been gone for hours, not telling her where he was going. Perhaps she should have asked. Perhaps he should have offered.

They'd come so far. They still had so far to go…

The drawing shook in her hand and she laid the paper on the desktop, hoping she hadn't betrayed her nervousness to Jack, who rarely missed anything.

"I think we should include your friends," she said as he perched himself against the corner of the desk. "You won't let me go inside with you—and I understand that, I really do—and Wadsworth is certainly brave, I'm sure. But Mr. Browning and Mr. Carstairs are probably better prepared for…for this sort of thing."

"One of the two of them probably has been reporting to Sinjon about me, or have you forgotten that? I prefer knowing who has my back, not worrying about my back. I'm more than satisfied to have Wadsworth there. However, I've decided I was wrong about excluding them entirely, which is why I met with them this morning. Dickie will be here," he said, leaning in to put his finger on the drawing of the streets, "and Will, here. Jeremy will take up his position in the alleyway behind the building. And you," he ended, giving her a stern look, "will be here."

She bridled. She knew that look. He was going to be difficult. "You aren't pointing to the drawings."

"That's because your part in this ends with the planning. When I say *here,* I mean exactly what I say. You'll be in this house, awaiting my triumphant return. Or my return, at the least."

She'd probably known from the beginning that he'd attempt something like this. But not this time; she would not be left behind to go quietly insane while he was risking his life. "You can't do that, Jack. I said I wouldn't interfere, and I meant that. But don't you dare think you can cut me out of this. I won't allow it."

"You won't *allow* it?" He stepped away from the desk, and then turned his fiercest glare on her. "You wouldn't want to rephrase that, madam, by any chance?"

"You're going to play the bully now, Jack? Don't bother, as I'm not in the slightest impressed. That's never impressed me, actually, not when I know I'm right." Tess got to her feet, her hands pressed hard against the desktop. "He's *my* father. He attempted to kidnap *my* son. He got *my* brother killed because he didn't tell us we were going up against the Gypsy rather than just another bumbling Frenchman selling secrets that were probably already out of date. He did his best to ruin my life, my son's life. *Our* lives, Jack. Yours and mine. If he hasn't already succeeded in that, because if you tell me again that I have no right to be there tonight you and I are still poles apart in how we see each other. This is my fight as much as it's yours. Maybe more so."

.

"And you're prepared to see him die. At my hand? Because it could come to that, Tess."

She struggled to keep herself under control. "You won't do that. You won't kill him."

"Sinjon's counting on that," he told her coldly. "You shouldn't."

So they were back to that? Who he was, why he was here with her in the first place? Because he hadn't come to her on his own. She couldn't seem to forget that fact. On his own, they might never have met again. "Because you have your orders?"

He slammed his fist down on the desktop and she jumped back involuntarily at his vehemence. "No, damn it! Because I bloody well want the man dead. Your son? He's my son, too, the son he convinced you to hide from me until he found a use for him. That was my brother in that coach. Not only your brother, but my friend who died in that Whitechapel alley. My life he looked at as if I was some bug under a glass, and then manipulated me, *built* me into one of his tools. Now he *dangles* some knowledge he supposedly has of my life in front of me so I'll kill for him? He can go to hell, Tess, and that's exactly where I want to send him. So don't think I'll keep him alive just so that he can try to manipulate either one of us again, because I won't. There's a part of me that doesn't want to go there tonight at all, that wants to do instead the one thing he'd never expect—simply leave him to deal with the Gypsy on his own."

"Then why don't you?"

The anger seemed to slip away from him. "I don't know. I don't even know why I said that. Maybe it's something Puck said to me. I can't get it out of my head."

She walked out from behind the desk, daring to lift a hand, press it against his cheek. She was still so angry with him. She loved him so much. They were at war with Sinjon, but she was also at war with herself. And Jack was still fighting his demons. "And what was that?"

He turned his head to press a kiss against her palm, and then took both her hands in his. "That it's time to let it go. All of it. I've been…angry for a long time. But can I really end it if I don't finish it?"

"Are we talking about Sinjon here, Jack? Or more than that?"

He lifted his eyebrows, shook his head. "You know, for a man who's lived his life keeping his own secrets, for the last few days the entire world seems to know more about me than I do. I thought I could walk away. From anything. At any time. I've thought I was better off on my own."

Tess tried not to react. She knew what he was saying was true, but she didn't really want to hear it. "I see."

"Oh, I doubt that," he said with a one-sided smile, a self-mocking smile. "For a man with little to be proud of, it would seem I'm as prideful as the devil. Life on my own terms. I convinced myself I didn't need anyone. No one and nothing touching me, because I wouldn't let it." He squeezed her hands. "I was so bloody wrong."

How easily he slipped through her defenses…

"Jack, you don't have to—"

The pain in his voice was palpable. "Yes. Yes, I do, and now's as good a time as any. How…how the hell did

I walk away from you? Every time I look at you. Every time I touch you. This time, Tess, you'll have to walk away from me. And even then I'd come after you, on my knees if you asked. Do you know how that frightens me? To need anyone so much? To know I'd have nothing if you were gone? To know I could still lose you?"

A single tear escaped her eye, and he looked at it as it rolled down her cheek and then shook his head, probably cursing himself for having brought her to tears. She should tell him why she was crying, but she could only do that if she knew the reason herself. Perhaps it was for the lost years, and how different their lives would have been if only he'd said those words to her then rather than now. He'd said Puck had told him to *let it go*. She had some letting go of her own to do, hadn't she? Let the past be the past. But, oh, it hurt. She was still working her way past the hurt of those lonely years, much as she wished she could simply *let it go*.

He released her hands and walked over to the fireplace to stand beneath the portrait of the man who was not his father. "I'd never ask you to stay with me. I thought I could order you to, that I could use Jacques to help convince you if you left me with no other choice. I can't do that, either. I don't…I don't know what we really have, Tess, I don't think either of us do, or if it's enough to make up for the mistakes I've made. Sinjon only played on my weaknesses, it was up to me to overcome them."

"We've both made mistakes. I refused to listen to you," Tess reminded him, for she carried her own share of guilt. "If I'd been stronger, Sinjon couldn't have convinced me that you were responsible for what happened to René. Perhaps I could have told myself that I wasn't partly to blame, knowing that if you hadn't thought yourself in love with me, you never would have insisted the plan be changed. You aren't the only one with demons to put to rest. I think we can do that in time, for some things. But not Sinjon. That part of our past has to be settled if we ever hope to escape him. It's malevolent, and will otherwise destroy us."

"I know. And much as I'd like to believe Puck's right, that we should just walk away from what we can walk away from, and forget the rest? I can't do it. There has to be an ending before there can be a beginning. At least for me. I don't want to come to you and Jacques with shadows still between us."

Tess nodded, not trusting herself to speak. She'd seen Jack truly vulnerable only once before, the day he'd knelt in front of his son and hesitated as he lifted his hand to touch Jacques's hair. Her heart was breaking for him now as it had then, but he wouldn't want to know that, for her pity wasn't what he was asking her for, even if he still couldn't say the words.

Even if she might not yet be ready to hear them. She'd heard as much as he felt able to say, and it would be cruel to push him for more. Not now.

"All right, then, Jack, at least we're in agreement on this. We finish it. All of it, with Sinjon, the Gypsy, your family. Put everything else behind, no matter how we resolve what's between us. Starting tonight." She returned to the desk and sat down, picking up the diagram of the streets and forced herself back to the task at hand.

"With Browning at the head of the same alley we were in a few days ago, and Carstairs in the darkened doorway just opposite Number 9, I could very safely wait in your coach at this corner. Not in the middle of things, but not out of them, either. Close by, so that Wadsworth can come get me once you feel it's safe. I can't just wait here, Jack. I'd go mad."

"That's as good as saying you want to confront him."

"Want to, Jack? I never want to see him again, hear his voice, listen to his lies. But I need to. You of all people should understand that. Please?"

"There's another way," Jack said, rejoining her at the desk. "I can't believe I'm saying this, but you're right. Who am I to keep you from the end of things?"

He had her full attention. Tess relaxed, even as she still trembled inside at Jack's admission of his need for her. A need he wouldn't act on anywhere but in the dark of night unless she signaled that she was ready. Knowing she had unfinished business of her own with her father, their shared nemesis. "You'll let me go with you? Be inside with you when they all enter?"

"No, Tess. Since I never planned to take you along, I've been allowing you to think that, but it's impossible. I never planned to be inside. Too many eyes watching. And Sinjon would know that. We're destined for a street fight. Ugly and messy, and totally lacking in finesse. With Sinjon having a figurative front-row seat even as he's ready to bolt in the confusion if things don't go exactly as he planned."

Tess frowned at the pile of diagrams. "Out in the open? Really? I'll admit it has been bothering me, the location. The windows are barred, and there's only the one other door at the rear. It certainly isn't a position of strength. I wouldn't have chosen it, and I doubt the Gypsy would freely enter a place where he's unfamiliar and Sinjon had all the advantage on his side. But it's awfully risky, even slapdash. Sinjon plans better than this."

She looked up at Jack, who was wearing the far-off expression that had once annoyed her but now intrigued her. He was thinking. Deeply. As if no one else was in the room. "Jack? Did you hear me, or are you ahead of me?"

"I don't know why I didn't see it before. We're wrong, Tess," he said slowly. "And what you just said proves it."

She got to her feet and walked over to him, seeing the tension in his eyes. "What did I just say?"

"That Sinjon plans better than this. 'You look familiar, sir.' At which point I'm supposed to leap from the shadows and plunge a dagger into the Gypsy's black heart. Really? What a passel of melodramatic rubbish. What happens once I've dispatched the man, Tess? He tells me who I am and then magnanimously tosses us the Mask of Isis and gives us his blessing, hoping we'll have a lovely life while he and the remainder of his damn collection begin anew somewhere else? No. I don't believe it. I don't believe any of it, not when I take it all apart, piece by piece."

"Then what do you believe?"

His smile was rueful. "Unfortunately, I think Sinjon may have been too clever for his own good, and expected us to be smarter than we are."

"What? But we both agreed. The last place a fool would look for him obviously has to be someplace he's already been, and that leads us straight back to Cleveland Row. You can't be serious," Tess said, wishing none of what Jack had just said were even remotely plausible.

"Actually, I think I am. But let's go through this, all right?"

Tess glanced toward the mantel, and the clock that had already ticked away the hours until noon. If they'd been wrong, they had precious little time to figure out what was right. "All right. Start at the beginning which, I suppose, would be the Gypsy?"

"The Gypsy's *return,* you mean. We've already agreed that the man threw down the gauntlet with his robbery at the museum, leaving his card there so that Sinjon would have to know he was back. Because he respects his mentor's skills, he doesn't attack Sinjon in his own lair, preferring to draw him out into the open, goad him into making a mistake."

"But Sinjon doesn't make mistakes."

"No. He makes plans, at least two for any possibility, and he's got a lot to choose from. He knows the Gypsy expects him to come to London, go hunting for him. So he disappears instead, taking the Mask of Isis along with him on the slim chance everything goes sideways and he has to flee the country. If he even took the damned thing with him. He could just as easily have been carrying a load of bricks in that sack, with the mask hidden somewhere at the manor house. He didn't need it gone, Tess, he only needed me to believe it was gone. I needed to connect it with the advertisement in the *Times.*"

"He planned all along to include you in his plan to kill the Gypsy?"

"Absolutely. One way or another, he always meant for me to come back to him if he needed me. Telling me about Jacques was probably his trump card, but it turned out he didn't need to play it directly. Not when he knew Liverpool would hear of his disappearance soon enough and send me as the logical choice to find him."

Jack had her full attention now. "Putting the Gypsy directly in your path. Sinjon always meant for you to rid him of the man if he came back. Pitting his former students against each other, as he watched. As you said, Jack, like bugs under a glass."

"Exactly. He knew I'd go first to the manor house. He knew I'd find Jacques. He knew I'd be able to follow his trail to London. He knew I wouldn't leave you and our son unprotected in the country—and if I'm right, that's important, as it left him free to raid his treasure room. But then we got a little too close, I don't know how, but we did. So he sent his minions to kidnap Jacques, gain my cooperation in exchange for our son's release."

"But that didn't work." Tess was beginning to feel hopeful for the first time in days. "So now he has to change his plans yet again. If nothing else, Jack, we haven't been making it easy for him. He writes that letter, surely not the one he'd originally planned for us to read."

Jack poured them each a glass of wine, clearly taking some time to think through his suppositions. "Yes, that damned letter. Trading his supposed knowledge of my past for keeping him alive, for disposing of the Gypsy.

He knows how to place his needles, I'll give him that. Hinting that he knows my father's identity was the perfect way to intrigue me, cloud my judgment. And all a lie. He only knew what I'd told him that first night we met, nothing more. He was attempting to use my past to control me."

"Don't think about that, Jack. What we do have to think about is his plan for the Gypsy. At least we hope the Gypsy saw Sinjon's advertisement, or else there'd be no reason to go back to Number 9 in any case. You don't suppose the Gypsy never responded?"

"No, he saw the advertisement. The Gypsy delivered his letter in person. Do you remember the liveried servant? The red hair?"

Tess frowned. "Yes. Yes, I do. Or at least I remember you saying something I didn't quite understand. That was the Gypsy? How do you know?"

"Two reasons. One, I've seen costumes very much like it on the stage. And two, no footman is that tall and well fed. The man's as arrogant and flamboyant as Sinjon described him. And reckless."

"Yes, I can see that. But I still don't understand. If Sinjon isn't going to be in Cleveland Row tonight, where is he going to— Oh, my God."

"The place no fool would look for him, yes. On his own ground, his own carefully prepared ground, I'm sure, the place he knows best and is most comfortable. He always must have believed the man would come to the manor house, and made his plans accordingly. Instead, the Gypsy called him out, and now Sinjon is returning the favor, bringing the man to him, full circle.

It's going to be a close-run thing, Tess, and a total disaster if I'm wrong. But I don't think I am. Sinjon wasn't lying, not completely, in his letter to us. He told us where he'd be. We just didn't see it."

"And he's sitting in his web at the manor house, waiting for the Gypsy, waiting for you to kill the man for him—while we're here, in London. How very strange, Jack. He nearly outsmarted himself this time, didn't he?"

"If I'm right. I have to warn the others in any case, because, if I'm wrong, your father and the Gypsy will be at Number 9 tonight, don't forget, and only God knows what will happen. I'm not sure Will is up to the sort of fight the Gypsy might present."

"I know we're right," Tess said firmly, with a quick glance at the clock. "Write your note and have Wadsworth order the horses around while I change. I can be ready to ride in ten minutes."

"Eleven," Jack said, pulling her into his arms and bringing his mouth down hard on hers.

She held on tight, taking in his strength, fueling her own courage.

"Thank you," he said against her ear as he broke the kiss but still held her close. "For trusting me. For the first time since this all began, I really feel as if we're on the right path."

"Lord knows we've taken enough wrong ones," she said, pressing a kiss against his neck before he let her go. "Now to see where this particular path leads us."

FIVE OR MORE hours by coach, three on horseback. They had time, if the Gypsy kept to Sinjon's timetable and arrived at the manor house at ten. But why would he do that, play the game entirely by Sinjon's rules? Jack knew he was done dancing to the man's tune.

He looked at Tess, sitting quietly beside him in the coach in her shirt and breeches. Was she considering what they'd do if the manor house was empty, or if they found her father's body there? Was death going to cheat her out of the confrontation she believed due her?

Was it wrong of him to hope that was the case, relieving him of the job of disposing of the man? Because, one way or another, Sinjon Fonteneau was going to die tonight; Jack had made up his mind to that. The man had lived long enough.

They were nearly clear of the city now, where they'd meet up with Wadsworth and their mounts, and soon there'd be no time for talking.

"Wadsworth all but fell on my neck in gratitude when I told him there'd be no need to have him rigged out as a Nabob," he said, just to fill the tense silence. "Although I should probably warn you that he'd already applied the betel nut juice to his hands and face, in preparation. With luck, he'll be his pale self again within the week, which is a good thing, as I'd neglected to take in the fact of his blue eyes. He would have made a very unconvincing Nabob in any but a very dark room."

Tess smiled, probably because she thought he wanted her to, even as her gloved hands remained drawn up into tight fists in her lap.

Jack had decided it was too risky to have Tess seen mounted on her mare, and equally foolhardy to have their mounts tied up behind the coach, just in case the

Grosvenor Square mansion was being watched by Will or Dickie. He knew he was burning bridge after bridge by cutting his supposed partners out of his plan, and if he was wrong in his conclusion that Sinjon was at the manor house he could probably count the time he'd remain in government service in days, if not hours. And then what? Would he replace Sinjon as the man Liverpool wouldn't care to have walking about, carrying so many dangerous secrets?

Tess reached over and put her hand on his. "I've left you to your thoughts, hoping they're brilliant. Do you have a plan?"

Jack smiled, remembering something Puck had once said. "According to my brother, he's the brain, and I'm the brawn. Since Puck isn't here, I was hoping you'd come up with something wonderfully brilliant and hopefully foolproof."

"I'm afraid I've been sitting here being selfish, thinking up questions to ask him, even knowing he'll tell me nothing but lies."

"At least his lies would be more palatable than any truths, Tess," Jack said as the coach slowed to a halt, "even if he still knows the difference, which I doubt. You don't need to talk to him. You don't need his lies or his truths."

"And is that how you feel about your mother?" she asked, her eyes flashing in sudden anger. "I thought we'd settled this, Jack. It's why I'm here. You even said it. We're on the right path at last."

"I didn't say we'd agreed on what to do when we reached our destination. I can't promise you anything,

Tess. If it comes to a fight, I'm not going to put either of us in jeopardy in order to save Sinjon. He's not worth saving."

"I didn't mean that," she said angrily. "Just remember you aren't going there as executioner. Or is that what you want?"

"Tess—"

The coach door opened and Wadsworth's more red than brown, blue-eyed face appeared. "Permission to ride with you, sir!" he said in fine sergeant-major tones.

"Let him," Tess whispered. "We don't know that the Gypsy will come alone."

Jack looked to Tess's pinched face, and then nodded. "Permission granted with thanks, Wadsworth."

"Thank you, sir! I owes the bugger one for trying to take Master Jock, sir!"

"Indeed you do. We all do," Jack said as he helped Tess down from the coach. "Are you armed?"

"To the teeth, sir!" Wadsworth all but shouted, and then grinned, said teeth showing frighteningly white in his betel nut–stained face.

"In that case, why are you standing there? Let's ride."

"Yes, sir!"

"Will he know not to be quite so loud once we're in sight of the manor house?" Tess asked as Jack helped her mount. "We hardly want to announce our arrival."

"True." Jack averted his eyes, hoping Tess was so caught up in her own thoughts she wouldn't be able to read his. "I'll point that out to him. Don't worry about Wadsworth. He'll follow orders, without question."

"And I won't?"

"I'd like to think you would, in which case I'd order you to get back in that coach and return to London. But I'd be wasting my breath, wouldn't I?"

"I think you already are. You should probably spend the next few hours thinking up ways to capture two very dangerous men."

He looked at her levelly. "Capture? Again, Tess? Will you never give up until I say I won't harm a hair on their damn heads, for God's sake?"

"I suppose I really don't care what you have to do with the Gypsy, as long as he pays for René's death. The hangman's rope or a swift knife to the heart."

"So now I have your permission to kill the man. How wonderful. Clearly I have my uses."

Her shrug was eloquent and maddening. "Yes, but are you being used? There is the fact that Sinjon so clearly wants him dead. And not just dead, Jack. Dead at your hand. Why?"

"I hadn't thought of that, but frankly, I really don't give a bloody damn what Sinjon wants. My only intention right now is to keep the two of us alive," Jack said shortly, and turned to walk over to his own horse. Once mounted, he urged the stallion forward at a walk, until he was abreast of Tess's mare. "You wanted to be a part of this, and I was idiot enough to allow it. But don't get in my way, Tess, because I'm going to do what I have to do, and you've always known that."

"So now we finally hear the truth. You're going there to kill. That's all you can see, isn't it? You don't really care about answers. You say you do because you think that's what I want to hear, but you don't. You just want

it all to go away. That's always been your answer. Make
it go away or, failing that, taking yourself away. How
do you think that will settle anything? All it does is
make you a murderer—Liverpool's or Sinjon's, it doesn't
really matter, does it?—and perhaps a coward, as well.
Think about *that* as you ride, Jack Blackthorn. Think
about that!"

She then dug her heels into her mount's flanks and
took off down the road, leaving Jack and Wadsworth to
catch up.

CHAPTER FIFTEEN

SHE'D GONE TOO far, said too much. She'd known it the moment the words were out of her mouth, but how could she fix it? She couldn't take back what she'd said. Especially since she'd meant what she said.

Jack was the bravest man she'd ever met. In most ways. But when his mother had told him about his birth and told him to leave Blackthorn, he'd done it. When she'd told him to leave her after René's death, he'd done that, as well.

She could understand that. In part. She wanted to run away from the truth about her father. She'd probably been doing just that for more years than she cared to remember. But who else did she have? So she'd chosen to believe Sinjon was invincible. Brave. Still grief stricken from the loss of his wife. Sincere in his mission to fight Bonaparte and bring back the France he knew. She'd looked away from his faults, excused his coldness. She'd spent her life trying to please him, bring a smile to his sad-eyed face. Earn his praise. Be like him.

To learn that everything she'd believed had been a lie had nearly destroyed her, so she could imagine what it had been like for Jack when his mother had told him he wasn't the marquess's son. Just as she had always sensed that something was wrong, that her life wasn't real, Jack had been told what he'd always suspected.

He'd run from what he'd learned. She, in her turn, was running toward what she'd learned. Toward her father, to demand answers.

But maybe Jack had been right and there were no answers, at least not any that could change the facts.

The facts were that her father was cold, manipulative and thoroughly evil. What could she possibly ask him that would bring forth the truth rather than more lies? What could he possibly say to make things better? *I'm sorry, Tess?* If he admitted what he'd done, would that change anything? Was she still harboring some faint hope that he'd had a reason for what he'd done, one that made any sort of sense?

He tried to kidnap Jacques.

Yes, that was it. That's what she had to know. His own grandson. How could he have held that little boy's hand, read him stories, kissed his head, watched him as he slept…all while figuring ways to use him as just another pawn in one of his perverse chess games?

Just as Adelaide had kissed her son, told him she loved him and then sent him away.

Tess surreptitiously wiped at her damp cheeks. How could people be so cruel? How could they care so little for their own flesh and blood? They'd have to be without conscience, not really human at all. Monsters.

You didn't ask a lion why it roared. It just did. And you didn't look for explanations when confronted with one; you either killed or were killed.

You ended it, and then you found a way to live with

what you'd had to do. Jack hadn't been able to change the circumstances of his birth. Of course he'd gone. What else was there for him to do? What was wrong was that he was still running.

"Jack?"

He slid the collapsible spyglass closed and turned his dark stare on her. He'd been staring down at the manor house for over an hour, never moving, hardly breathing. The sun had set only moments ago, and soon it would be completely dark here under the cover of the trees save for the nearly full moon.

The manor house was situated in the flat bottom of a sort of bowl, surrounded on all sides by hills dense with trees. There was more than enough cover to hide an army in those trees, but the width of hill and scythed grass could be a killing field between those trees and the manor house itself. In other words, they were close now, but still dangerously far away, depending on what Sinjon may have planned for them.

"I'm sorry, Jack," she said, hugging her knees as she sat beneath a large oak tree, trying to make herself small, even invisible. "I think I understand now. What I said was hateful and wrong. I kept trying to make you feel what I feel, and didn't consider what you felt."

"Not now, Tess," he told her shortly, and lifted the spyglass again.

"Yes, now," she insisted, inching herself toward him. "You're not a coward. You didn't run away. You left. There's a difference. If anyone's a coward it's me. I didn't leave. I didn't want anything in my life to change, even when I knew that life wasn't real. It was one thing when René and I were children, but not once we'd grown. René was so unhappy. We should have gone, I should have made him go. He'd still be alive, I'd still have my brother."

"You can't look back like that, Tess," he told her, still keeping his gaze on the manor house below them. "What you should have seen, what you should have done. René's gone, but you aren't responsible for that. You didn't put him in harm's way. Sinjon did that."

She laid her cheek on her bent arms. "I miss him so much. He was so beautiful, so pure. To end like that. For months, I'd wake at night, screaming, just to think about it."

"Tess, what are you trying to say to me?"

She drew in a breath and let it out slowly, attempting to ease the pain in her chest. "I don't know, Jack. I'm frightened, more frightened than ever, now that we're here. I don't think Sinjon is done with us. I suppose that's it. I don't know why we're here, except that Sinjon wants us here, or at least wants you here. Don't kill the Gypsy for him, Jack. Don't kill either one of them. Please. If that's what Sinjon wants you to do, that should be reason enough not to do it. We've all danced to his tune long enough."

"The man killed your brother. As good as executed him."

"I know that. How could I forget that? If Sinjon cared at all for his son, he'd want to exact his revenge himself. You would. I would. He only plays at old and feeble, re-member. He doesn't really need us."

"He using me because he knew I'd be sent to find him when he disappeared. I'm only convenient."

She put her hand on his arm. Somehow, she had to make him understand what she still couldn't quite grasp. She only knew that if Sinjon wanted Jack to kill the Gypsy, it wasn't because her father couldn't have managed the man's death on his own. There was some other reason. "No. That's what's wrong. That's what's been wrong from the beginning. There were ways, other ways. There had to be. So why this elaborate plan? Sinjon's been the spider in the middle of his web from the beginning, drawing the Gypsy in, drawing you in. Everything he's done has been meant to keep us from thinking clearly."

Jack rubbed at his eyes for a moment and then lifted the spyglass once more. "Then we should congratulate him, because it worked. Do you think he also planned for the two of us to be at each other's throats half the time? Because that seems to be working, as well."

Tess managed a small smile. "Yes, let's do that. Let's blame Sinjon."

Jack lowered the spyglass and grinned at her. "Much preferable to feeling like a horse's ass. I'm sorry, Tess."

"Then you agree?" She felt she had the advantage now, and she dared to press it. "We're still dancing to Sinjon's tune?"

"A dog with a bone," Jack said, shaking his head. "How could I have forgotten that about you, even for a moment. Yes, all right, I agree. But now I'd like to hear how you expect me to capture the pair of them, because

I don't think they'll put up their hands if I just walk in on them and ask nicely."

"I know," Tess said quietly, and turned to look toward the manor house once more. They had positioned themselves where they could see the windows to Sinjon's study, with Wadsworth having taken up his position facing the front door, not that Tess believed the Gypsy would ride up and bang on the knocker. Her stomach did a small, sickening flip. "Jack. Look. There's a light at the window. Someone's lit candles. Sinjon doesn't allow the servants in his study, I've had the cleaning of it for years now, when he'd let me. It has to be him."

"He's being fairly obvious. That can only mean he summoned the Gypsy here to talk, perhaps even with an offer to share his treasures with him, to make up for nearly having the man killed in Spain. He had to have offered him something, and the Gypsy had to have been greedy enough to believe him or else he wouldn't come within ten miles of the manor house. More fool, him, I suppose. *But then, what ho! Here is my protégé, my dear Jack, appearing out of the shadows to slay the dragon for me.* Yes, I'm afraid our Gypsy is a fool, Tess. I'm surprised he's lived so long."

She felt herself becoming almost giddy, seeking some sort of relief from the unbearable tension. "Or it's all part of the same game. I'm sure he's only going to play at cooperating, until Sinjon reveals the hiding place of his collection. The two of them dancing around each other, playing at honorable thieves, each believing the other is a gullible fool, waiting for an opening in order to strike. Can you just imagine it, Jack? *So sorry about that small misunderstanding in Spain, old fellow. Just business, you understand.* And then the Gypsy saying, *Yes, the joke was on me there, wasn't it?*"

Jack put down the spyglass, chuckling in appreciation. "I'll say this for you, Tess. I never laughed while on a mission with Will and Dickie. It's all in how you look at the thing, isn't it? At the moment, I don't much care how this works out. It's difficult to remember that I once did. Right now I'd just like to be out of these weeds and on our way to a late dinner in the village."

There came a short whistle that probably was meant to be that of some country bird, and Jack instinctively reached toward one of the pistols stuck in his waistband. "It would appear the Gypsy has arrived. And via the front entrance. For once, we were right, Tess. Sinjon's somehow made the man believe he's safe. All right. Time to go."

Tess hastened to scramble to her feet. "Time to go where?" And then, her eyes narrowed, she looked at him in dawning realization and anger. "Do you mean to tell me you've had a plan all along?"

He took her hand as they made their way out of the cover of the trees and down the embankment. "No, not all along. Not until you went to change and I was penning my note to Will and Dickie. I don't want to boast, but I haven't survived this long on my luck, you know."

"And you've let me go on and on, make a fool of myself and say things that— Damn you, Jack!" she said as Wadsworth appeared on the gravel drive, still definitely armed to the teeth. Had that been a ruse, back at the coach? Was Wadsworth always to have been a part of this? "And this is your plan? To knock at the front door? We can't just walk in there. Answer me!"

"I think you already know the answer, Tess. I'm done playing games with the man." He released her hand and put two fingers at the corners of his mouth and gave two quick whistles, and then a third, longer one. It sounded no more like a bird than had Wadsworth's attempt. She was certain it wasn't meant to trick anyone, but more to alert them. He was announcing his presence, obviously marshaling some sort of troops. Sinjon could not have been expecting troops, an assault, any audience other than himself. No, he had to expect Jack to obey him, because Sinjon was always to be obeyed. If the man had a flaw, that was it—he believed he could make anyone do what he wanted him to do.

"And a good evening to you, my lady," Will Browning said moments later, appearing as if out of nowhere. "Jack? Dickie's already inside the kitchens, probably stuffing his face. It was a close-run thing, getting here in time, and he had to miss his dinner. Jeremy and his men are being bored to flinders in Cleveland Row, I suppose, just as you suspected. I saw our quarry enter. Nice to know we didn't make this journey for no good reason. What now?"

"You..." Tess glared at Jack, too angry to even form a complete sentence as she continued to attempt to wrap her mind around what he'd done. "You... And you never... You let me think you...that one of them was working for—"

"I can be seven kinds of fool from time to time, Tess, for many different reasons. But not fool enough to give

Sinjon what he wants, whatever the hell that is, or to expose you to danger. Will? At the count of fifty, as we'll need that much time to get into position. And with as much bumbling official noise as possible, please."

Will Browning bowed as if in a ballroom. "It will be my pleasure, although I will point out that Dickie has me beat all hollow when it comes to bumbling."

Tess wanted to scream in frustration. "What? What are you— Where are you going?"

"You want to confront him, Tess, remember? Then we do it on our own terms, or at least on mine," Jack said, taking her hand and leading her away from the house even as she looked back over her shoulder to see Will Browning and Wadsworth approaching the front door, carrying a small, efficient two-man battering ram between them, clearly intent on making a considerable noise.

Half dragged by Jack, he and Tess rounded the side of the house and cut across the dark lawn, heading up the long hill to a small outbuilding situated just at the tree line. "How ridiculous. The door couldn't be locked. Where are we going? The *buttery?* But why would we—"

"Any servants inside will run to hide themselves when they hear the noise. We want them out of harm's way. As to the rest of it, that will be clear soon enough. Come on, Tess—run!"

Behind her, she could hear the sound of the battering ram against the door, until it was banged back on its hinges, the heavy wood slamming against the wall even as Will Browning shouted: "In the king's name! Sinjon Fonteneau, present yourself for arrest!"

Instantly, Will's shouts were taken up by Dickie Carstairs, with Wadsworth letting loose a convincingly barbaric war cry that echoed inside the house and out.

"Here," Jack told her, pushing her against the wall to one side of the door to the buttery. "Be ready to catch at the door when it opens. When they come through, when you can see their backs, slam the door, and then for God's sake, get yourself out of the way."

She couldn't speak. She was caught between fear and an anger so deep she longed to box Jack's ears. He'd had a plan. All along, he'd had a plan. He'd let her think he was dancing to her father's tune, let her make a fool of herself, say things she never should have said. And he'd had a *plan*. Oh, he'd pay for this!

And then, damn him, Jack winked at her before putting his back against the wall on the opposite side of the door, a pistol in each hand, raised and cocked.

She didn't have to ask him what was happening. Clearly her father had some sort of bolt hole somewhere in the house, a tunnel that exited in the buttery. More than once he'd told her about vulnerabilities of geography, and how the scythed lawn of the hills could be both a benefit and a curse to those inside the manor house, unless provisions were made. Clearly, provisions had been made. The moment he'd heard the commotion at his front door, Sinjon had to have gone on the move, and the Gypsy with him. If the man was still alive.

But when the door opened, as it did only a few rapid heartbeats later, it was only Sinjon who appeared in the moonlight. He bent over, his hands on his knees, attempting to catch his breath. Tess counted to three, and then slammed the door, already on the run, not stopping until she was a good twenty feet away, out of her father's reach.

"Hold there, Sinjon, if you please," Jack said, stepping in front of the man, the brace of pistols aimed at the man's stomach.

Tess didn't know what she was expecting to happen next, but it certainly wasn't what did happen. For her father straightened, and actually smiled.

Oh, how well she knew that smile. It somehow put him in charge, even with a brace of pistols pointed in his direction.

"Jack. Ah, and Thessaly, as well. How very lovely to see you both. For a time I'd actually feared you'd be in Cleveland Row this evening, chasing mare's nests. My congratulations," Sinjon said smoothly.

Tess watched as her father controlled his breathing, neatly shot his cuffs and took up a pose that she also knew all too well, one of complete and utter indifference toward the lesser mortals around him. Tess shivered, as if a goose had just walked over her grave, she supposed. And maybe it had.

"Yes," Jack returned just as smoothly. "We just happened to be passing by. You'll raise your hands now, Sinjon, if you please. I know you'll excuse me, but I have this need to see where they are."

"Is that really necessary, Jack? Oh, very well, but only if you indulge an old man. When did you learn about my…alternate exit? I'm quite certain I never told you."

"No, you didn't. But René did. It would seem one of his tutors liked to lock him up in there as punishment, often enough that René began carrying a tinderbox with him, so he wouldn't be alone in the dark. That's when he noticed a draft, licking at the flame of the candle he kept hidden there. He never did figure out how to get from the tunnel into the house, nor did I ever have sufficient time alone to find the way out. Luckily for me, I didn't have to, did I?"

The marquis smiled. "Well, aren't you the clever one, Jack. But tell me, please, is there a problem? My house has just been invaded in error by that asinine Liverpool's minions, and I have in all prudence escaped them as best I could until I could explain my actions to the man… only to find myself standing here with my arms raised and your pistols pointed at me. Again, not that I'm not delighted to see you, as I know you'll listen to reason. And you as well, Thessaly, my dear. I was that worried when I returned home from my short trip to find you gone. And dearest Jacques, as well. How is the boy?"

"Don't you dare speak of my son as if you care about him!" Tess took a step toward Sinjon, her hands drawn up into fists, but stopped at Jack's quick warning to stay back. She'd nearly made a dangerous mistake, and she knew it. But, God, she wanted to strangle him! She wanted to clap her hands over her ears, hide her eyes. Why had she thought she needed to see him again? She felt as if she might be physically ill.

"Females. Too much with the emotion, yes? Alas,

it makes them ineligible for so many things. Jack? I'm going to put my hands down now, if you don't mind. Ah, yes, that's better. Now, although it will probably fatigue you—I know how obstinate you can be once you've got an idea in your head—have you given a moment to consider what's occurring here?"

"No, I don't believe I have," Jack said, lowering one of the pistols. "Why don't you enlighten me, Sinjon?"

Tess looked from one man to the other, not understanding what was happening. They were both being so bloody *civilized.*

"Gladly. You were sent to find me because I disappeared from my home, yes? This home. But I'm here, aren't I? In fact, our dear friend Lord Liverpool is in receipt of a letter from me—or he will be, tomorrow, once the post arrives—explaining that I had learned of the Gypsy's return and put it in front of me to at last capture the man who had murdered my only son in cold blood. Surely a father can understand another father's grief and his need for vengeance. In order for my plan to succeed, however, I was forced to disappear for a time, but I assured him that, my quest a success, I am once more in residence and, of course, his loyal servant. Tonight's *attack* will be excused. I'm a reasonable man."

"Really?" Jack said, shaking his head. "So you've got the Gypsy trussed up in your study? Or dead in your study? My congratulations. Very neat, as far as it goes. And everything else? How do you explain everything else?"

Sinjon frowned. "What else, Jack? Oh, I forgive you for absconding with my daughter and grandson. I'm sure

you meant well. I'll be certain to mention that to Lord
Liverpool, as well. After all, I hold no grudges."

Tess couldn't remain silent. "I don't believe this! Jack,
he's actually trying to talk his way out of what he's
done!" She took two steps closer to him, still careful to
remain out of reach. "And how do you explain the rest,
Papa? How do you explain your years of thievery. Your
collection?"

"My what?" Sinjon looked at her, real pity in his
eyes. "Jack? Do you know what my daughter's babbling
about?"

"It's gone, Tess, remember?" Jack said, lowering the
other pistol. "We've no proof it ever existed. Oh, very
good, Sinjon. And I suppose, were we to press you on
everything else that's happened these past days, you'd
assert that you couldn't trust me not to make a mess of
capturing the Gypsy, so sent me off chasing my tail instead."

"You were always reasonably competent, Jack, but
not a patch on the master, as they say, that's true. I didn't
want you in the way. Nor did I want my daughter and
grandson to be on the premises when I finally summoned the Gypsy here. So you were…useful. I thank
you for that."

"Can't you see what he's doing? He's making it up
as he goes along," Tess said, livid with frustration. "For
God's sake, Jack—don't help him!"

Her father spared a moment to smile at her, acknowledging her fury. "Just as you say, Jack. I am a poor
man, existing on a government pension, nothing more,
nothing less. I do compliment you on a valiant effort to

prove otherwise, although your failure is no testament to my mentoring skills, I'm afraid. Now, if you don't mind, I believe I'd like to return to the house. We can continue our discussion there, and you and my daughter can tender me your apologies, which I will magnanimously accept. The evening is turning chilly and, you'll notice, I'm wearing only my slippers. If you'd first kindly remove your motley band of rogues from the premises, of course? Don't worry, again, I'll be sure to inform his lordship that you were all quite impressive. Failed. But impressive."

And with that, just as if he had no expectation of being stopped, the marquis began walking down the hill toward the house.

Tess's head was spinning with impotent fury. "Jack? Can he do this? Can he actually think he'll get away with it?"

"That depends, I suppose. If he's got the Gypsy, Liverpool won't ask too many more questions. Let's go."

"No, Jack, let's not," Sinjon said silkily, already turned about, a small silver pistol in his hand, pointed at Tess. "I'm afraid my daughter's right. The story wouldn't hold up for long, not under close scrutiny. Besides, I've already made other plans."

"You wouldn't shoot me," Tess declared, wincing at the lack of conviction in her voice.

"Stand where you are, Tess," Jack ordered tersely.

"Sage advice. And now, Jack, drop your weapons. Andreas! Time for you to take the stage, my good man."

The door to the buttery opened once more and a tall, well-muscled man wearing a flamboyantly red satin-lined black cloak emerged, smiling broadly beneath a black half mask. "And more than time! Truly, I'd almost believe that bag of moonshine myself, were it not for the fact that I'm not, what was it the boy said—trussed up or dead? And just when we'd agreed to work together again. But we probably should be going now."

"For all your other talents, you always were a deplorably stupid man, Andreas. The story needs some refinement, I agree, but I believe I can manage the details sufficiently to convince that bumbling Liverpool. I am, after all, the Marquis de Fontaine, and it will be my word up against that of the bastard who defiled my daughter. Although," the marquis drawled turning the pistol on the Gypsy, "you do realize that, much as I would have delighted in watching Jack here as my instrument, you have to die now."

And then he fired, the ball sailing harmlessly into the door behind the Gypsy as Sinjon staggered slightly where he stood, his eyes grown wide in his aristocratic face.

"How…" He allowed the pistol to drop and pressed his hands to his chest. "How…unexpected." Slowly, almost gracefully, he dropped to his knees in the dirt.

Tess looked at her father, attempting to understand what had just happened. How it had just happened. But then her arm was caught in a wrenching grip and she was pulled in front of the Gypsy, his knife blade stretched across her throat.

Jack had already bent to pick up one of his pistols, but it was useless when put up against the Gypsy's knife.

Sinjon spoke from his knees, bubbles of blood collecting in the corners of his mouth. "Shoot him! You pathetic bastard, do as you're told! Shoot him!"

"Shoot me? His own father? Hardly," the Gypsy said triumphantly, and then roughly flung Tess at Jack and ran into the trees.

"I've got him!" Will Browning yelled as he reached them, Dickie Carstairs and Wadsworth lumbering up the hill behind him.

"No!" Tess cried out, pushing herself away from Jack, who was looking toward the darkness that had just swallowed up the Gypsy, his face gone white as death. "Let him go! Let him go!"

Will stopped, shrugged. "As the lady wishes. It's damn dark under those trees in any event, and me without my knife. Sorry we took so long. Every door was locked, and it took us much too long to realize our man had bolted. Well, at least we got the one we came for, didn't we, Jack? Jack? Are you all right?"

The marquis was lying on his side now, his eyes closed. He coughed wetly, and tried to wipe at his mouth. Tess could now see Will Browning's knife where it had embedded itself in her father's back.

It all hardly seemed real. Sinjon Fonteneau, defeated. And clearly not immortal. She'd once admired this man? Once had feared him?

No. He was only a man.

She went down on her haunches beside him. "Don't you die. Not yet. Is it true? Is that man Jack's father? Is that why you sought Jack out? In order to control his father, possibly use one against the other one day? Or

is this just another of your sick and twisted lies? Damn
you—answer me!"

His eyes opened and he looked up at her. His smile
was grotesque, mocking. And then Sinjon Fonteneau,
Marquis de Fontaine, was dead, taking his lies and his
truths to Hell with him.

Will Browning bent down, bracing one booted foot
against Sinjon's shoulder. He pushed him over onto his
belly and yanked the knife free of the marquis's back.
There was the quick, sickening sound of blade against
bone, and Tess bit back the bile that rose in her throat.
He wiped the knife on Sinjon's coat before sliding it
back into his boot top.

And that was it. Over. Over and done. The self-
proclaimed most brilliant man in the world, at last out
of wiles and tricks and self-serving lies, his pale eyes
open and staring, his bloody face in the dirt.

Tess looked up at Jack. He was still staring off into
the trees, as if witnessing Sinjon's death wasn't important to him. As if he wasn't even there. As if nobody was
there, not even her.

CHAPTER SIXTEEN

JACK SAT BEHIND the desk in the study of the manor house, watching the moving shadows cast by the flames in the fireplace. Not really seeing. Not really thinking. Simply sitting and staring.

So the man was dead. And not, thank God, by his hand, because no matter what Tess had said, that would have made a difference.

Dickie had done what Dickie was so good at doing, digging graves by moonlight, and the marquis was already underground in the small family plot that was also René's final resting place. Poor old man, gone to his heavenly reward while away from his small estate, and brought home for burial. That's what the world would think. It was better than to have questions, considering the answers. Not that many would care. The marquis had never been popular in the village, or with his servants.

Tess had understood the need for haste. She'd contented herself with politely asking Dickie to stop when that man had attempted to say a prayer over the canvas-wrapped body before it was rolled into the newly dug hole.

When the sun came up in the morning…and one way or another, it always did…Sinjon Fonteneau wouldn't be there to see it. Or any sunrise, ever again. That had to be enough for Jack.

The mantel clock chimed out the hour of two as Will Browning entered the room and headed straight for the decanter of wine sitting on a table near the windows.

"What now, Jack?" he asked, taking up his seat on the worn leather couch, crossing one long leg over the other at the knee and ankle. "Dickie pointed out to me that, rather than rush back to London, it might be entertaining to go on a hunt for the marquis's collection. Not that he isn't hot to present it to the Crown. Just, perhaps, not quite all of it. He can't help himself, I suppose, poor bugger. He's always purse-strapped, and it does seem a shame to simply hand it all over to the Georges. One wouldn't know what it was, and the other would sell it all in order to put another onion-topped minaret or two on that monstrosity he's building in Brighton."

"Are you convincing me, or yourself, Will?"

"Actually, I'm just passing the time. Would he have gotten away with it, you think? His word against ours, and all of that?"

Jack rubbed at his temples with both hands, as if trying to erase the ache that had been sitting just behind his eyes for hours. "He didn't think so. Otherwise, he wouldn't have pulled out his weapon. I just wonder what he told the Gypsy to have the man believing he was in no danger, coming here."

"Does it matter?"

"No," Jack said. Will and Dickie had been too far away to hear the Gypsy's declaration, and there was no reason to repeat it to them. "I suppose not. In any event, he got away, didn't he? Liverpool isn't going to be best pleased. And that's my fault. I didn't react quickly enough."

In truth, he hadn't reacted at all. He'd stood there like a stunned ox after hearing the Gypsy—*Andreas*—proclaim he was his father. His supposedly long-dead father, hanged as a highwayman. Why would Adelaide lie about something as basic as whether the man was dead or alive? But then, why did Adelaide do anything she did?

Will laughed shortly. "Another argument for some treasure hunting. That pretty gold mask you told us about would probably go a long way toward appeasing Liverpool and anyone else that might have questions. Besides, you had your hands full with her ladyship as the man was lopping off. Literally. Is she all right, do you know? Hell of a thing, Jack, putting a period to a man's existence while his daughter watches."

"Dickie helped me carry up buckets of hot water for her, as the place is devoid of servants, probably, Tess says, because they haven't been paid for the last two quarters. She said she may have to scrub for hours, until she feels clean. She's a strong woman. She understands you did the only thing you could."

"It wasn't easy," Will said, never reluctant to sing his own praises. "At a full run, uphill, no less. Had to sling it underhand, you understand. Almost a cricket pitch, now that I think of it. Oh, come on, Jack, smile. Yell. Do something. Anyone would think we lost tonight. We did what we came to do, man, damn it."

"Is that what it comes down to now, Will? Winning or losing?"

Will looked at him as if he'd just said something quite obvious. "What else can it do? Don't tell me you're going to spout some nonsense about king and country, because it hasn't been about that since the war ended. We're bloody policemen, Jack, well-paid assassins more often than not. Dickie does it for the money, I do it for— Well, never mind that, shall we? Why do you still do it, Jack?"

Jack got to his feet. "I don't know. I truly don't know. If you'll excuse me?"

"As long as you leave the decanter," Will said, shrugging. "This couch seems comfortable enough for one night. We'll see you in the morning?"

"In the morning, yes." Jack headed for the hallway, but then turned back to his companion of these past four years. "Henry hated it, you know, these last two years or more, since the war. But it isn't as if we haven't done some good."

"Your brother Puck certainly would think so. But I know what you mean, Jack. Rogues like us? What we need is a good war. Otherwise we'd soon be fighting with ourselves over some damn pecking order or some such nonsense. I didn't much mind when Henry was alive. But since he's gone? I don't much care for the order."

Jack smiled. "Taking orders from a bastard nobody."

Will laughed. "No. Knowing that bastard nobody is perhaps better than me somehow. That rankles. I admire you for it, though, this strange sense of fair play or whatever it is you have, that Henry had. Like tonight. You wouldn't have put a knife in the marquis's back, would you? That isn't *proper.* You would have called out a warning so that he'd turn to you before you threw the knife, even if that meant he could take a shot at you. Just as you were going to give that idiot clerk a chance to think better of his actions that night behind the Duck and Wattle. Both men were destined for the hangman in any case, so why put yourself in danger when it's so much neater to simply dispatch them? Kinder, in the long run. It's a strange sense of right and wrong you share with our friend Henry. It upsets me."

"Yes," Jack said, tongue-in-cheek, "I can see where it would. This is a new side of you. I never thought of you as being particularly *kind,* Will."

"No, most people don't," the man said, either oblivious to Jack's sarcasm or serious in his answer. "Dickie's aged great-aunt is one strong summer cold away from the grave, you know. He's her favorite, which he should be, seeing as how he's been toad-eating the woman for years in the hope of some inheritance. It'll soon be just the two of us, and I think that's one too many, don't you?"

Jack raised one eyebrow. "Liverpool will let him go?"

"Dickie? God, yes. He'll let us all go, and be happy to wave us on our way. I know Henry thought otherwise, but he was wrong. Our dear prime minster is stronger now than ever. We're nothing but flies in his soup, part of a past that includes a brilliant win against Bonaparte, remember. He has little to fear from us. The marquis? He was another matter. Too many secrets there, and very little loyalty. Present our PM with the news of the marquis's death, and be on your way, Jack. That is what you want to do, isn't it?"

"It's that obvious?"

"It is to me." He raised his eyes to the coffered ceiling. "You've got other pressing matters to occupy you. She's quite the woman, the Lady Thessaly, miles above you, God knows. Still, I suppose she could do worse."

"She could have taken a fancy to you, yes," Jack said, wondering what Henry would say if he could be present for this strange conversation. He'd confided in Jack that he'd always wondered if Will Browning was a fallen angel or a raised devil. If he heard this exchange, he'd still be wondering. "I have a son."

"Yes. Heard that. Did you ever hear of a man named Simon Bolivar, Jack?"

The question took Jack unawares. "I don't think so, no. Why?"

Will got to his feet, to retrieve the decanter. "He's making quite a nuisance of himself in this place called Venezuela. Giving the Spaniards fits, which always delights we English. There's a contingent of both British and Irish *volunteers* sailing from an undisclosed port next week, to lend him a hand. All very unofficial. I've been offered the lead of the Irish force. A good war, Jack. Or a bad one. And with very few rules. I've accepted. I don't suppose you'd like to come along."

It wasn't a question, or an offer.

"Were you reporting my comings and goings to the marquis, Will?" Jack asked instead.

Will hesitated with the decanter poised to refill his

glass. "Oh, my, so you figured that out, did you? In his defense, let me remind you of Dickie's constant need for funds. It wasn't until the other day that he finally realized he wasn't reporting to one of Liverpool's men. He's truly embarrassed."

"Then I won't mention it to him."

"That would probably be best. And let him treasure hunt for a day or two, before we return to London. With our small band of merry men about to retire from the lists, it may be the last bit of fun he has in some time. And Lord knows the man can dig like a badger. He'll enjoy himself."

"Agreed. I'll need a few days here to help Tess close up the manor house in any case. The Crown will be taking it back now. Is there anything else you may have neglected to tell me?"

"Just one thing more, yes. Henry loved you, and Henry's opinion always meant a lot to me. For a bastard, you're a damn moral man, Jack Blackthorn. Don't let anyone value you less than your worth. Most especially you. And now for God's sake leave me to my drink before we become maudlin."

Jack looked at Will Browning for a long moment, and then nodded his head. "Venezuela? Really?"

Will shrugged. *"Un hombre tiene que morir en algún sitio."*

Jack's knowledge of Spanish was limited, but he'd understood what Will had said. *A man has to die somewhere.*

Or he can choose to live, he thought as he climbed the stairs.

TESS FOLDED THE dressing gown carefully, being very precise about each fold, rigidly controlled, and then angrily pitched the thing in the general direction of the other garments she had removed from the clothespress.

She didn't want anything from this room, this house. She wanted to leave it all where it was and burn the building to the ground. But she didn't have that option. Still, she would take only what she needed, and nothing more, only enough to fit into a few small trunks. Jacques's clothing and his few toys. Emilie's belongings. The few possessions of René's she had kept.

The Crown could have the rest.

She walked over to the dressing table and sat down, opening the center drawer to remove the packet of poems her brother had written. She had read them when she'd discovered them in his room after his death. He'd hidden them from her, from everyone. Probably because Sinjon would have destroyed them. Or laughed at them.

They weren't very good poems. Even a doting, grieving sister knew that. But they represented René's dreams, and it had broken her heart to read about his envy of the birds that fly free and the rivers that flow beyond man-made borders. The poems would go with her, where she went, and one day she would read them to Jacques, and encourage him to dream his own dreams, and then to live them.

The packet tied in its blue satin ribbon went into the hatbox that would ride with her in the coach when she left this place for the last time. She'd go to Blackthorn, because Jacques was there. Because Jack wanted her to go. Because she had nowhere else to go.

Because she couldn't imagine herself anywhere Jack was not, no matter where that might be.

His knock, when it came, wasn't unexpected. But still she jumped involuntarily at the sound, and quickly dried her wet cheeks as she called out an invitation for him to enter her chamber. She replaced the lid on the hatbox and left it there on the bed.

He was clad in a simple black shirt and trousers, a man most comfortable with midnight. His collar had been opened at the throat, and his beard had begun to darken his cheeks. His eyes looked tired, his black hair mussed, as if he'd been running his fingers through it. She was sharply reminded of their son, and decided that he would one day grow up to break female hearts, just like his father.

He looked at her carefully, as if attempting to gauge her mood or, she thought, as if she might somehow shatter into pieces or some such thing. After all, she'd seen her father die and then watched as he was buried not two hours later. Or maybe he'd been wondering if she was heartless, as she hadn't cried. She couldn't be that hypocritical, not even if tears were expected of a daughter.

"I'm all right, Jack," she told him before he could ask. "How are you?"

He smiled and shook his head. "I imagine we've both been better than we are at the moment. You had your bath?"

She looked toward the tub that was still sitting in the corner. "Yes. Thank you. And Mr. Carstairs, as well. That was very kind of him. Of…of you both."

"He's a good man, Dickie. His great-aunt may die."

Tess blinked. "Excuse me?"

"No, I'm sorry. I was just downstairs with Will, and he tells me Dickie may soon come into a small inheritance. So he'll be leaving government service. Will... he's going off to find another war. Venezuela. The war, that is. It's in Venezuela. As they've both got other things to do, I suppose I'll be finding something else myself. I don't know what. I really don't know anything else."

"I see," Tess said. Not that she did. What was he saying to her? "And do you think Lord Liverpool will allow that? Perhaps he'll give you a pension and your own small prison, like this one?" She felt a hint of panic. "Maybe even this one?"

Jack shook his head. "Bastards don't merit manor houses. Sinjon's pension, this pile, were more to please the new French king than anything else. No, to hear Will tell it, I'm just a fly in Liverpool's soup, and he'll be happy to have someone spill it out and get him a fresh bowl. The house in Half Moon Street? That isn't mine, either. I really don't have much of anything to show for the years I've worked with Sinjon, with the Crown. And no skills beyond a minor aptitude for intrigue."

At last she realized where this strange conversation was heading. "Will you soon be reduced to sleeping under the hedgerows, do you think?"

His one-sided smile caused her breath to catch in her throat. "The possibility does present itself, yes. But not for some time."

"But you have nowhere to live, just as I have nowhere to live," she said, prompting him, because she felt fairly certain that was what she was supposed to do. "So, because we have a son, and a son must be considered, I suppose we'll now be traveling to Blackthorn, where we may hope to be taken in, at least for a time?"

"It would be, um, practical."

"Practical," Tess repeated. "I see. And nothing at all to do with that man declaring he's your father. Nothing to do with confronting your mother about the circumstances of your birth. Nothing to do with seeing the marquess and, as Puck termed it, letting the poor man talk. Of course. I understand."

"And nothing to do with the fact that our banns are about to be announced for the second time. No. Of course not. It's pure expediency, visiting Blackthorn once we're through here. I've told you, I'm not going to ask anything of you, Tess. I can't. Especially now."

"Now that you'll soon be sleeping beneath the hedgerows. Or especially because—what, Jack? How many other *especially now* problems do you see? Other than the most obvious one—the Gypsy could very possibly be your father. You weren't the one who put a period to Sinjon's existence, but your *father* may have killed my brother. As if any of that is true, which is highly unlikely." She looked toward the floor, then toward the ceiling, and then, finally, directly at him. "You really can be a stubborn blockhead, can't you?"

"Apparently," he said, walking over to the bed and lifting the top of the hatbox before she could stop him. "Packing?"

"We can leave in the morning, can't we? Unless you think we should stay until someone can roll a very large boulder over his grave, to make sure he doesn't get up again."

Jack looked at her over his shoulder at her sudden vehemence. "You don't have to prove to me that he's better dead. You once thought the sun rose with the man. And not all that long ago."

She took the lid from him, replaced it and placed the hatbox on the floor. "That changed when I saw why René died. I admit I found it difficult to believe your words, but it's impossible to argue with what's in that room. What was in that room. I suppose we'll never know where it all is now. For all we know, it could be aboard some ship, bound for anywhere."

Jack leaned his hip up against the side of the bed. "I don't think so. He would have wanted to keep it close. Especially the mask. Or do you think he'd really hire someone else to move the collection for him?"

"He'd trust hirelings to effect a dangerous kidnapping of his grandson, but not trust them to move his *treasures?* Yes, I suppose you're right. It's all a matter of seeing worth as measured through his eyes."

"He didn't have that much time to come sneaking back in here after we left, move everything. Which means it's all close. Dickie wants to go looking."

"I don't," Tess said shortly. "I saw it all once. That was enough. Let it rot, wherever it is." And then her eyes went wide. "You aren't suggesting that *we*— All this hand wringing about your straitened circumstances if you don't continue working for the Crown. Damn you, Jack, that's *indecent!*"

"Not to mention damned insulting," he said, pushing away from the bed. "I doubt there's any way for the Crown to learn where the pieces belong, not that I can see anyone trying, but at least we can take them out of the dark, the way Sinjon kept them, and let the world see them for what they are. Relics of the past, works of art. History. I was thinking they could be in the way of a gift to the Royal British Museum. Presented as a collection in the memory of René Louis Jean-Baptiste Fonteneau, Vicomte de Vaucluse. By the time the Crown hears of it, it will be accomplished fact, and Liverpool and everyone else will just have to smile graciously."

Tess's breath caught on a sob, and suddenly all the days, all the years, came together, collided in a dizzying kaleidoscope of pain, of memories, of lost dreams and shattered illusions. It all burst within her, all around her, and then the pieces reassembled themselves.

And there, against all odds, was the rainbow, lighting the way out of the darkness to, at last, make something *good*.

Her knees buckled. "Oh, Jack…"

He was beside her in a moment, holding her as she cried. Cleansing tears, healing tears. She clung to him, taking his strength. "Thank you. Thank you," she said, over and over.

"Shh, sweetings," he soothed her at last, sweeping her into his arms and carrying her over to the bed, laying her down gently, disentangling her arms from around his neck. "Sleep now. Sleep as long as you want. We'll think about tomorrow, tomorrow."

She reached up her hands, grasping tight to his forearms. "No, please. Don't leave me. Not tonight."

"Tess…" he leaned in and pressed a kiss against her forehead. "This isn't over. Andreas, whoever the bloody hell he is, didn't come here to have drinks and cakes with an old friend. He came for the collection. He'll be back, if we don't beat him to it and find it, get it into the right hands. Just as you know I have to find him. I can't leave things the way they ended tonight. I have to see Adelaide, confront her. I have to know, one way or the other."

"But that's tomorrow," she argued, pleaded up into his dark eyes. "So many things for tomorrow. You said so yourself. Tonight, can't it just be us? With no shadows, no questions, no future and no past. Just us? Just us, Jack…"

His eyes burned into her skin. She felt the deep, steady throb of his heart as his strong, masculine features softened in some emotion she all but dared to give a name. She touched her fingers to his cheek and he closed his eyes, swallowed.

She felt filled up, nearly overwhelmed. It was the first time. The only time. Everything was new, still to be discovered. Together.

His kiss was gentleness itself.

She wanted to weep again, with the joy of it.

When he raised his head it was to look into her eyes once more, as if attempting to understand what it was she wanted. *What you want, Jack,* she told him with her own eyes. *You. All of you.*

He took her hands and she sat up, aimed her feet toward the floor, bringing her close up against his body, his hands now at her waist. Moonlight shone in through the open windows, the soft sounds of a country night the only accompaniment to the slow, sensual dance of two people who very much needed to hear the music.

He kissed away her dressing gown and nightrail, sculpted her with his hands as he went to his knees, nuzzled at her belly. And beyond.

Tess swayed where she stood and then bent her head to watch him, her hands skimming his shoulders, threading through his dark curls. She fisted her hands in the linen of his shirt, tugging at it, drawing him back up to her.

The buttons fell open and she kissed his heated skin, traced the definition of his sleek muscles, his flat belly.

And the moonlight danced over the walls and floor as a breeze ruffled the tree branches just outside the windows, and more buttons were eased from their moorings, and she slipped to her knees, and Jack fisted her long hair in his hands and moaned low in his throat.

When he urged her to her feet once more the intensity of his expression, the rapid rise and fall of his chest fed into her own building passion, her need for him. Not his body. Her need for him. His arms around her. A need to hold him close, draw him into her, until they weren't two people at all, but one. One person, one heart, one mind.

He laid her on the bed and followed her down, holding himself above her open legs, his arms braced on either side of her head.

"We're going to make it right this time, Tess," he whispered as he sank into her. His words were a plea as much as a promise. "We have to make it right this time."

She closed her eyes against the rawness of emotion, this strong man's vulnerability, which he would only show her at moments like these. "We'll make it right," she promised him even as he took her over the edge. "Somehow, we'll make it right..."

CHAPTER SEVENTEEN

THE TUNNEL FROM the buttery had its beginnings behind a cabinet in the butler's pantry. This was interesting, but not particularly useful. The two stone chambers built into the cellars indeed shared the same single entry from the study.

Or so it seemed. But with no success after a long, frustrating day spent looking elsewhere, last night Tess had insisted they visit the rooms again. She'd gone from never wanting to see Sinjon's collection to being nearly obsessed with its discovery, and if she wished her father alive again for any reason, it would be so that she could hold a pistol to his head until he told her its location.

Now it was the morning of the second day, and she stood in the middle of the empty room that had held the collection, looking at the equally empty shelves. "Can you imagine it, Jack? Sinjon coming down here with a brace of candles, sitting there on that chair, in the damp, in the cold. Just...*looking*? What did he do here? Do you think he would relive each theft? How he'd selected the item he coveted, and then planned the theft, perhaps for weeks, perhaps for months, and then finally executed it? Was it possessing all of these things, or the game itself that he loved so much, do you think?"

Jack leaned his shoulder against the doorjamb. "Does it matter?"

Jack looked and sounded tired, and very near the end of his patience. They could argue, if she wasn't careful, just because there was no other way to relieve their frustration. "No, I suppose not. We don't understand because we don't think the way he did."

"And thank God for that."

"Not at the moment. At the moment, we need to think the way he did. You don't suppose he told Andreas, do you?"

"He may have told him something, but not the truth. Andreas could be chasing his tail right now, thinking he knows where it is...or he could be out there somewhere, close by, patiently waiting for us to find it, thus saving him the trouble. You have thought of that, haven't you?"

"More than once, yes," Tess said, holding up a small lantern as she traced her fingers over the stone wall nearest the shelves. "I'm glad Will and Dickie agreed to stay for a few more days, and Wadsworth seems to make an admirable watchdog. It's not as if we can leave here before we know whether or not we'd be leaving the collection behind. And we certainly can't call back any of the servants, not when we don't know if any of them are in Liverpool's employ. We *have* to find the collection before he hears of it, we just have to."

"Will leaves tomorrow, to get his affairs in order before he sails."

"He's really going, then? It sounds so dangerous."

"Bread and butter to Will, and probably necessary

for life. At least his life," Jack said, taking the lantern from her.

Oh, yes, he was tired. Perhaps more than tired. "Will you miss it?" she asked him, searching his face for some sort of reaction. "I know the excitement can be…heady."

"I don't know. I'll only be able to answer that once I'm out of it, and we're not there yet, nor will we be if all we do is stand around and talk about Sinjon and how he thinks."

"You don't have to snap my head off, you know," she shot back, and then bit her lip. "You're thinking about your mother now, aren't you? The questions you have for her. Many more questions than you had before."

"No, there's only the one. Who in bloody hell was or is my father. Only that one. I'm past caring why she did what she did."

"Do you think she'll tell you the truth? She may think she had a very good reason for lying to you."

"Adelaide doesn't need a reason to lie. She simply operates inside her own version of the truth. She lives a play written somewhere in her head, always casting herself in the leading role, be it a comedy or a tragedy." Then he rubbed at his forehead, whether to ease the pain of a headache or wipe away some quick memory of his mother, she decided not to ask.

"I'm sorry. Let's get back to it, all right?"

"Agreed, but let's do it somewhere else. We've been over both rooms now, twice. Dickie and Will stepped off the foundation and the cellars, and these are the only two chambers down here. There's no room for another one. We've checked all the outbuildings. I think we'll soon have to conclude Sinjon did send everything off somewhere. Some hideaway we don't know about. Or, yes, to be loaded on some ship and sent God knows where. I'm sorry."

Her shoulders slumped in defeat. "You're right. It's not here. I felt so sure he would have kept it close. He didn't have time to do more than that. Not unless—"

"Not unless he had everything carefully planned, yes. Which is what we know Sinjon would have done. A pity he never kept a journal and felt some need to write about his own brilliance."

Tess looked up at Jack in sudden excitement. "But he did," she said, taking his hand, half pulling him toward the steps leading back up to the study. "My God, he did!"

"I never saw one," Jack said as he placed the lantern on the desktop. "And Lord knows I heard the sermon from him on the stupidity of ever committing anything to paper. Where is it?"

Tess shrugged out of the shawl she'd worn while in the damp rooms. "Upstairs. In the nursery. It's not a journal. Not really. He wrote stories, for Jacques. They were more like small puzzles, really. Silly things, rhyming things sometimes. *Now where are my slippers*—and then the several logical steps one would employ to trace where one had been, and then find the slippers. *Are they in cook's stew pot? No, not there.* On and on. I…I thought it was lovely of him, except when I thought he considered the stories Jacques's first lessons in growing up to be…to be just like his grandfather."

"What we're looking for is considerably larger than

a pair of slippers, Tess," Jack reminded her as they climbed to the top of the house and Jacques's nursery.

Tess went directly to the cupboard beneath the dormer window and extracted two journals. He'd begun the second one about six months earlier, the first already filled with stories in his neat copperplate. "I was going to burn them. Here, you take this one. We'll read them together."

Jack looked around the nursery, a simple room, but Tess herself had painted one of the walls to look rather like a farmyard. "Is that a sheep?"

"You would pick the one I had most trouble with, wouldn't you? Yes, that's a sheep. Jacques loved it. Although the rooster was his favorite."

Jack walked over to bend down, peer at the painted fowl. "A rooster," he said flatly. "And you're certain of that?"

"If you're going to criticize…"

"No, not at all," Jack said quickly, his grin wicked. "But we've better roosters at Blackthorn. The problem may come in convincing Jacques that they're really roosters, now that he's seen this one."

Tess plunked herself down in the window seat. "Jacques likes blue. I knew I couldn't paint a *real* rooster, Jack. So I painted a…a fanciful rooster."

"Fancy that," Jack teased, so that she longed to toss the journal at his head. But then he joined her on the wide window seat, lifting up her legs and resting them on his lap as the two of them opened the journals. "I don't know what this is going to accomplish, but God knows we've tried everything else." He turned the pages until he found the first story. "'The Toy Soldier Lost His Drum.' All right, and where did he go to look for it?"

"Don't read out loud, Jack, I'm trying to concentrate."

"Yes, ma'am," he said, and settled back to read the story, surfacing not five minutes later to say, "Well, unless Sinjon hid everything in the linen cupboard, I doubt we've found the key to the collection. Interesting—and unbelievable—as I find this, seeing this heretofore unknown side of Sinjon, I think we're wasting our time."

"Are we? Think, Jack. Sinjon never did anything out of *kindness*. He had a reason for everything he did. You remember what he taught us. *Everything* is a rehearsal for what is to come."

"And the careful man plans," Jack added. "So what you're saying, or at least what I think you're saying, is that what we have here are, what, a dozen hiding places? We've been looking for the collection, in total. Another secret room, a hidden door in one of the outbuildings, a false bottom in a wagon…"

"Instead of looking for a dozen smaller hidey-holes, yes," Tess said, turning another page in the journal. "We've been searching for the haystack, when we should have been looking for needles." She turned on the window seat, put her feet on the floor once more and stood up. "Get up, Jack. We can test my theory by finding the maid's best apron."

"In the window seat?" He pulled the cushion from the seat and lifted the lid to expose the storage space beneath it. "No apron," he said as Tess bent over the opening.

"You enjoy being maddening, don't you? Did you expect some golden helmet to simply jump up and announce its presence?" she asked as she began removing the contents of the cubbyhole. There were blankets, and some of Jacques's outgrown clothing, and Emilie's winter cloak, and— "Jack?"

"What?" His head appeared beside hers. "Oh, wait. Yes, I see it. Move over, Tess, let me give it a try."

She moved away, but only marginally, as Jack reached in and lifted what appeared to be a loose board at the bottom of the compartment. "There!" she exclaimed, nearly giddy with the thrill of discovery. "What's in it, what's in it?" she exclaimed as he pulled out the oilskin bag.

Jack, with only one quick look of amazement shot in her direction, lowered the window seat and cushion once more and then upended the bag on it.

And there it all was, or at least some of it. They counted out a half dozen rings, a variety of bracelets, and dozen necklaces; some ancient, some perhaps only a few hundred years old, and all of them heavy with gold and jewels. One of the brooches carried the Bourbon royal crest.

"Is that all of it?" Tess asked, holding up a small golden collar that had to have been fashioned for a child, most probably an Egyptian princess. "I only saw the collection the one time, and I'm afraid I wasn't looking as much as I was cursing him as I looked."

"All of the jewelry? I don't know," Jack said, already replacing the rings. "Look at this one. I remember this one. A diamond the size of a pigeon egg, for God's sake."

The ring was enormous as she slipped it on her finger, fitting from knuckle to knuckle, and engraved with strange drawings that might have been some sort of primitive birds. Hers was perhaps the first finger that had been adorned by the thing in over a thousand years. "But it's yellow. Are diamonds yellow?"

"I imagine anything that large can be any color it wants to be," Jack told her. "There, that's the last of it. But we've got a long way to go, Tess. Let's find Will and Dickie. How damn many stories did Sinjon write for Jacques?"

"More than a dozen," Tess said, grabbing up the oilskin bag and holding its considerable weight against her chest. "Jack, you know what this means, don't you?"

"It means you're smarter than I am?" he teased, kissing her cheek.

"Well, yes, that, too," she quipped with a smile. "But what it really means is that Sinjon never planned to go anywhere. He was only hiding his treasures until he'd dealt with the—that is, with Andreas, and with you. He wasn't *moving* his collection, as we thought. He was only temporarily *hiding* it, and he'd worked out his hiding places in advance. He truly did plan to end his days here, surrounded by the proof of his brilliance."

"Well, he had it half right, didn't he? He certainly *ended his days* here. Come on, Tess. There are a lot more stories, and a lot more treasures to be found. With luck, we can leave here tomorrow."

Once Will and Dickie had been shown the contents

of the oilskin bag, two decisions were made. One, Will and Wadsworth would leave for London immediately; Will to prepare for his journey to Venezuela, and Wadsworth to return with Jeremy and a small contingent of troops, so that if Andreas had any notion of relieving them of the collection as it was being transported, he'd find that task damn difficult.

And two, Dickie, Tess and Jack would use the journals to continue the hunt.

Emilie's favorite bonnet ribbon—a pair of bronze busts—were unearthed in the scullery. Jacques's wooden top—three gem-encrusted brass bowls—were hidden inside an old butter churn. Round Roman shields of various sizes were tucked up inside folded sheets on the shelves of the linen cupboard, and Roman helmets were run to ground in the henhouse, Dickie having been sent there to find "Where, oh, where could *Maman's* pretty slippers have gone to roost?"

Not everything was found so simply. But once they realized they were looking for pieces, and not the entire collection, the large dining room table was soon piled high with the fruits of their search.

Small golden statues of Egyptian gods all nestled together beneath the hinged bottom stair of the flight leading up to the nursery floor. Heavy Roman breastplates wrapped in sailcloth and tucked up into the open beams in the attics. Intricate Greek mosaic medallions and plates nestled in with René's clothing in an old sea chest in his chamber.

"A good thing he didn't have some strange passion for golden thimbles or some such nonsense," Dickie

Carstairs said as they surveyed their findings several hours later, "or else we'd be poking about everywhere for weeks. Do you think that's it, Jack? We've exhausted the stories, you know."

Jack shook his head. "The stories, yes. And it's not as if I could say one way or the other if this is all of it. I do, however, know what's missing. The Mask of Isis." He turned to Tess. "There're no other journals?"

She shook her head. She was hot, and dusty, and longed for a bath, not to mention something to eat. They'd been at it for hours. "I suppose all we can do is search everywhere we haven't already searched." She looked toward the hallway. "Which is nearly everywhere, isn't it? I never realized how large this house is."

"Here's an idea," Dickie said, putting down the Egyptian lamp he'd been rubbing, as if expecting a genie to appear. "I'll just nip down to the village and fetch us something to eat from the tavern, and you two can put your heads together again. You've been doing well enough so far."

Tess pushed herself up from her chair after Dickie left. "I suppose we've been given our orders."

"Orders, yes. But no ideas. That first day, you were searching Sinjon's study. Fairly thoroughly, from the look of the room when I arrived."

"But unsuccessfully, you'll remember, if you're thinking the room has any more secrets."

"Then you found the compartment under the desk?"

Her eyes narrowed. "No, I didn't find the compartment under the desk," she said through gritted teeth. "Is that what you were doing that day?"

"While you were standing outside, trying to hear what I was doing, you mean?"

"You don't have to recount the entire series of events to me," she said. "What was in the compartment?"

"Nothing," Jack said, holding out his arm, encouraging her to precede him out of the dining room. "I haven't looked there since. There seemed no need. The compartment would be large enough to hold the mask."

They walked down the hallway and into the study, and Tess immediately went to the desk, walking behind it and sitting down in her father's chair. "Don't show me. Let me see if I can figure it out."

Jack folded his hands across his chest, as if prepared for a lengthy wait. "Be my guest. Just let me know when you give up."

"Oh, and smug, too. Remember who connected the stories to the collection," she grumbled, opening the center drawer. She ran her fingers carefully along the inside edges of the drawer. It was a large desk, made of rosewood; the possibilities for hidden compartments were considerable. "You think he did actually take it with him, just in case he was somehow forced to produce a sample of his wares, as it were?"

"It's possible. Where is my golden mask? It's not in the butter churn, that is for butter. It's not in the henhouse, that is for the chickens—and blue roosters. It's not in the attics, it's not in the cellars. Oh, where, oh, where is my golden mask?"

"Stubble it, Blackthorn," Tess warned tightly. She had already worked through the remainder of the drawers, and was now on her knees on the left side of the desk, brushing her unbound and fairly disheveled hair back behind her ears before running her fingertips around the rosette carvings just beneath the overhanging top of the thing.

No, the rosettes were too obvious. Besides, Jack was still looking insufferably smug. She got up and walked to the front of the desk, motioning for him to take himself somewhere else to stand, and went down on her knees once more.

"Tenacity. One of your more laudable traits, Tess, when not taken to extremes," Jack said as he walked over to the drinks table to pour himself a glass of wine. "Would you care for a hint?"

"No, I would not *care* for a hint, damn you," she ground out, walking on her knees to the third side of the desk and repeating her inspection. "And before you ask, no, I'm not open to barter, either."

"Ah, that's a pity. Seeing as how you're already on your knees— *Ow!* Damn it, Tess, you could do a man permanent injury like that."

"Really? I was only hoping to render you speechless for a few minutes," she said, returning to her inspection, a smile on her face. Their moods had turned lighter once they'd begun unearthing the collection, and there were moments when she still felt rather giddy. "And don't say you weren't trying to distract me. I'm close, aren't I?"

"I'd answer, save that I'm speechless."

And then she heard it, a slight *click* when she pressed on the third rosette from the end. But that's all she heard, that single sound. No compartment opened anywhere.

"Perhaps there are two locks," she said, getting to her feet. She returned to the other side of the desk, found the third rosette, and pressed. *Click*. Strange how she'd missed that the first time. "Maybe they have to be pressed in succession. First the one on the left, and then the one on the right. Yes, that's probably it."

"Closer. But not yet there. Come on, Tess, let me show you. Or don't you care if the mask is in there or not?"

"I care, of course I do. But I want to solve the puzzle."

"Life's a puzzle, all of it. Puzzle upon puzzle. We can't solve every one of them."

She depressed the rosette on the left. Then the one of the right. Nothing. She reversed her actions. Nothing. She tried again, moving from one end of the desk to the other. "Oh, and would you listen to the man? Turning philosopher now, Jack?"

"Perhaps. What is life? What is truth? Can there be wrong, if nothing is right? Will Tess ever realize she has to depress *both* rosettes at the same time?"

"Wretch!" She stepped behind the desk and bent over, stretching out her arms, her nose against the desktop, only to find that she couldn't quite reach both ends of the desk at the same time. "You knew it! My arms aren't long enough. You knew I could never figure it out on my own."

"Yes, but I was enjoying the show." He stepped to the left side of the desk and put his hand on the rosette trigger. "At the count of three?"

The base panel next to her foot dropped down, and Tess went to her knees to reach inside the opening. For a moment she thought they were to be disappointed, but then her fingertips encountered what had to be a cloth bag, and she tugged on it. "Heavy," she said as she tugged, until the bag slid free and she was able to pick it up. She reached into the bag to pull out something wrapped in softest cotton, and laid it on the desktop.

"Careful, Tess. It's gold, but the painting on it is fragile, as I remember it."

Hands trembling, she carefully unfolded the cloth, until the Mask of Isis was revealed. "Oh, God. It's... How could he have taken this!"

Jack relieved her of the thing and laid it on the protective cloth once more. "It was his coup, he told me that. He wasn't the first to steal it, by the way, because he told me he *acquired* it—he said that of all his treasures—in France. For all we know or will ever know, he stole it right out from under the nose of Bonaparte."

"Who brought half of Egypt back with him, yes, I remember. And now England will have it. You'd think Sinjon would have learned something from that. Things. Ancient treasures from past civilizations? They can't belong to you, not really. They certainly aren't worth dying for."

"Or killing for," Jack agreed. "Ah, and there's Dickie, back from the local tavern. What do you suppose it will be tonight? Country ham and cheese or cheese and country ham?"

Tess smiled, and then her entire body froze in place. Jack was standing with his back to the door to the hallway, where Sinjon had years earlier inconspicuously positioned a small mirror, high on the wall and tilted toward the front of the house. Anyone in the area of the desk could see who might be approaching down the hallway before that person was visible in the doorway. Sinjon had never cared for surprises.

"We have company coming this way, Jack," she said quietly and folded the soft cloth overtop the golden mask. "Andreas."

Jack acknowledged her words with the slightest nod of his head, motioning for her to drop down behind the desk.

And then he was on the move, silent as a cat, his knife drawn from his boot, his back pressed against the wall beside the doorway. His eyes widened as he saw that Tess hadn't moved. He motioned her down, again, this time with anger evident in the gesture.

Clearly he was planning to wait until Andreas entered the study and then jump out at him, press the knife to the man's rib cage. It wasn't much of a plan, there wasn't time for much of a plan, but it was good as far as it went. Except that Tess could see the pistol in the Gypsy's hand. If there was a struggle, and there surely would be, it couldn't end well for Jack. He could be shot, for one, or he could be forced to dispatch his own father, or at least the man who might be his father. Could he live with that possibility? Would that possibility make him hesitate when it was necessary to strike, which could prove fatal to him?

Tess wasn't about to simply stand back and find out. She'd come too far, *they'd* come too far. They had a son. They were working toward a future, together. She wasn't about to let the past color that future, not anymore, and most especially not in the form of the Gypsy. He'd taken enough from her. He would not take Jack.

Still, if she could lure the man into the room, dazzle him with the mask, perhaps, then Jack could possibly get the upper hand without bloodshed. But it worried her. She loathed her father, but her hand would probably have shaken if she had been the one who'd ended up holding a pistol on him, knowing she might be forced to fire. A parent was a parent.

What she really wished was that the man would simply go. Let somebody else have the capture of him. Not Jack. He shouldn't have to carry that burden.

All these thoughts raced through Tess's mind in the space of only a few heartbeats. And then she made up her mind.

She stayed where she was, watching the intruder's slow but steady progress. "Dickie? Is that you? Have you seen Jack? I'm here, in the study. Come see, I've found something!" she called out, forcing her voice to remain steady.

Jack mouthed something under his breath. She was sure it wasn't complimentary.

Andreas, the Gypsy, walked into view, but prudently remained in the hallway, more than twenty feet away, almost as if he knew what would happen if he stepped inside the room. He wore no cape or half mask today, and Tess could see his strong dark features. She did have a clear view on the pistol he was pointing in her direction. He might not hit her, not from this distance, but she also wasn't eager to find out if she was right.

"Good afternoon, my lady," he said, and she noticed

something she had not the first time. He spoke with a very faint accent. Something vague and European. It was quite lovely, actually. *The Gypsy.*

This man, who had killed her brother. All but executed her brother, in order to teach Sinjon a *lesson.*

This man, who could be Jack's father.

Jack was motioning to her. She knew what he wanted. Was the man close enough that he could turn and confront him? What were the odds? Should he make his move?

She almost imperceptibly shook her head. *Let me do this, Jack. Trust me to do this.* "Mr. Andreas, is the pistol really necessary?"

Jack's expression hardened.

"I had considered a bouquet for the so-lovely lady, but decided on the weapon. My apologies."

She grimaced at this ridiculousness. "So it's true. You are the flamboyant fool my father believed you to be."

The man's teeth flashed white against his sun-darkened skin. Was his smile anything like Jack's? He was tall, like Jack. Dark of hair. Well-muscled, like Jack, although certainly older. Not half so handsome. Rougher. Thicker. If they fought, the result was not Jack's obvious victory.

"Oh? And which of us looks at the grass from below it today, my lady," Andreas asked, "and who stands above it, about to take possession of all those lovely bits and baubles, hmm?"

"Bits and baubles?" Tess repeated, her arms tightening involuntarily around the cloth-wrapped mask. René's legacy, his name always and forever to be connected to its beauty. This man wouldn't have it. "I'm afraid you've been misinformed. We know now that Sinjon had it all crated and sent to Dover, to be shipped to Athens. It's not here. I can show you the bill of lading I just found in a secret compartment in his desk."

"Lying doesn't become beautiful women such as yourself. The fat one outside didn't bother to lie."

Dickie. He must have returned from the village. "You didn't hurt him," she said. "He's harmless."

"Harmlessly sleeping at the moment. I saw the other two ride off earlier. I followed, until it was clear they were on their way to London. Where's Jack?"

Close. Very close. But miles too far away to chance rushing at you, not while you hold that pistol.

"You mean your son?"

"Yes, yes, my so-troublesome son. Sinjon's small joke. Where is he? Nearby, clearly."

Oh, God. He'd just acknowledged Jack!

"Precisely where you so obviously think he is. Standing just inside the doorway, ready to pounce on you the moment you come in here to get this," she said, and then unwrapped the mask and held it up temptingly. "You hesitate, *Andreas.* Why? You don't believe me? I'm not lying now. This is what Sinjon always believed, that nothing and no one can be more important than the prize. And he gets his perverse revenge. For the father to kill the son, for the son to kill the father. How happy Sinjon will be, even looking up from beneath the grass. *Mais, puis, telle est la vie, oui?*"

But, then, such is life, yes?

The Gypsy remained where he was, his smile slowly

fading, his eyes intent on her, and not looking to the mask at all, as if it didn't matter.

And then he touched the barrel of the pistol to his forehead, as if in some silent salute, perhaps even a gesture of thanks, and took off at a run, back the way he'd come.

"Jack, no!"

But Jack was already moving, with Tess racing after the pair of them. She half slid across the marble of the foyer in time to see Andreas on horseback, his huge black stallion moving off in an immediate gallop, with Jack standing on the gravel drive, his knife quivering blade-down in the ground, his hands balled up into impotent fists.

He turned to her in complete fury. "Why? *Why,* Tess?"

"One of you could have died."

"He murdered your brother!"

Tess closed her eyes. "I know. But that, as Sinjon would point out, was business. You heard what he said. He acknowledged you. You could have knowingly put a knife into your own father. I couldn't allow that."

"You couldn't *allow?* Who in bloody hell are you to decide what you *allow?* I could have had him!"

"Then why is your knife in the dirt, rather than in his back? You're not as proficient as Will, is that it?"

Jack wheeled back to watch as horse and rider crested the hill and disappeared. "I could have had him…"

CHAPTER EIGHTEEN

THE VAUCLUSE COLLECTION, donated in memory of René Louis Jean-Baptiste Fonteneau, Vicomte de Vaucluse, would take pride of place in the Royal British Museum, hopefully by the following spring, after the Royal Curator, impressed, curious and only marginally skeptical, had thoroughly inspected its contents for authenticity.

What he did not inquire was how the Vaucluse Collection had, indeed, been *collected*. He was much too intelligent, and too ambitious, to ever ask that sort of question. Those most embarrassing and unfortunate Elgin Marbles to one side, after all, the museum would not exist were it not for the lack of that sort of question.

Lady Thessaly Fonteneau, clad in full mourning in honor of her recently deceased father, the marquis, had turned over his Deed of Gift to the curator, accompanied by a massively impressive-looking document adorned with no less than three Seals of Authenticity, written in formal French script: the Verification of Ownership personally signed by the martyred French King Louis XVI only one short year before his head had fallen into the basket.

In all, it was, Jack had complimented himself as he'd carefully affixed the final Royal Seal the previous evening in Grosvenor Square, some of his finest work. But it had been Tess, solemn, gracious, heartbreakingly lovely and exceedingly French, who had impressed on the Royal Curator her late father's love of both his collection and his son which, when combined with his great affection for the country that had taken him and his small family in twenty years previously, had prompted the gift.

No, there would be no inquiry as to the origins of the Vaucluse Collection, and no opportunity for Liverpool to challenge the right of Lady Thessaly to give it, or the Museum to accept it. There would be much unofficial questioning and gnashing of teeth in Whitehall, definitely, but in the end, no choice but to officially say nothing.

As they'd driven away from the museum Tess had put her hand on Jack's arm and thanked him for everything he had done. He'd looked down at her hand until she moved it, and then knocked on the roof of the coach with his cane, signaling the coachman to stop.

At which point, Jack had left the coach and walked the rest of the way back to Grosvenor Square.

The next morning they left for Blackthorn. This time, Jack eschewed the coach entirely, choosing instead to ride his horse ahead of the traveling coach.

It had been five days since Tess had warned Andreas and sent the man fleeing Jack's wrath, his questions, his *right* to confront his father. Long enough for Jack to realize that Tess had acted in what she believed was his best interests. Long enough for him to understand that she may have saved him from harm, or at least from making a mistake he could never hope to overcome.

Now he was faced with a dilemma as old as time in the never-ending unspoken war between the sexes: finding a way to get back to where they'd been without admitting he'd been an idiot, or even discussing the matter again, because women seemed to feel everything had to be discussed to death. Especially when they'd been right.

He wasn't used to answering to anybody but himself. He wasn't used to worrying about anybody save himself. He didn't take orders well. He made his own decisions.

Now he had a son. He had a woman in his life he knew he had to keep in his life, because without her there was no life, not even the one he'd had before... before Tess, before Jacques. Which had been no life at all.

He'd thought he'd loved her four years ago. That hadn't been love. Not like this. He'd wanted her, lusted after her, taken her because he'd needed to...but he'd been able to leave her, even told himself she'd be better off without him, as he'd be better off without her, without entanglements.

Now he could be so incensed with her he wanted to throttle her, for God's sake, but the idea of ever leaving her, any notion of a life without her, was too ludicrous to contemplate. Loving her, furious with her, obsessed with her; angry or wanting or laughing or hurting, arguing or frustrated or simply baffled by the way her mind worked—she was a part of him now, and he was a part of her.

He still should really be quite angry with the woman. She'd turned his life upside down, to the point where he was acting like a total horse's ass. He used to be reasonably intelligent, and no stranger to common sense. Now he was where he didn't want to be because to be where he wanted would be the same as saying she knew him better than he knew himself...and knew what was better *for* him than he knew himself.

The fact that she was *right* had nothing to do with it, either, he was sure of that. It was simply *wrong* for her to be...for her to *know* that...for her to— "Bloody hell, I'm an idiot!"

Jack turned his mount around and rode back to the coach, signaling for the driver to pull to the side of the road and stop. He then dismounted, turned the reins over to the groom, who could ride the stallion or be bucked off it if he hadn't the seat for such a strong animal—Jack really didn't care—and then climbed inside the coach while ordering the coachman to drive on.

"Madam," he announced as Tess looked at him. "I am through with you not speaking to me!"

"Me? Not speaking to you?" Tess's eyes went wide as saucers. She had lovely eyes, even when they went wide as saucers.

"Exactly!" he said, cutting her off. "I won't have it."

"Oh, well now, Jack Blackthorn, I don't think you have to worry about *that!* I could speak very large *volumes* of things to you, starting with the fact that it's not me not speaking to you, but you being a horse's ass and completely unreasonable in the face of what was very clearly a reasonable choice when faced with—"

"I knew it!" he said, collapsing back against the

squabs. "It's not enough to win, is it? You have to *grind* it into the dirt, pointing out the obvious."

Tess squeezed her eyes shut—indeed, her entire face squeezed shut for a moment, as if she was attempting to squeeze some logic out of his last statement. "I'm doing what?"

"It's all right. It's a womanly failing, I understand that. I forgive you," he said magnanimously.

"You forgive me," Tess repeated dully. "I beg your pardon?"

"But you don't have to," he went on, the corners of his mouth beginning to twitch slightly as he tried not to smile. Really, he should have thought of this sooner. Confound her with his very real insanity. It was a foolproof defense—with him playing the part of fool, of course. "I'm perfectly willing to move on as if it never happened."

"Really," Tess said, tipping her head to one side as she inspected him warily, as if he might suddenly begin foaming at the mouth or some such thing. "And more. You also forgive me for daring to attempt to mention it again."

"Exactly!"

"Even though you know I was right."

"Ah-ah!" He held up a finger in mock warning.

"Oh, yes, I forgot. That womanly failing. However, since I am a woman, perhaps you will forgive that, as well. Since men have no failings, correct?"

"None that I can think of, no," Jack said, wondering if it might be too obvious for him to begin pulling up the shades, blocking the view of any passersby along the roadway.

"Other than sheer pigheadedness, you mean," she said sweetly.

"Perhaps that," he agreed.

"Yes, perhaps. You're eyeing those shades as if you think they will shut themselves."

Jack actually felt the tips of his ears begin to burn. "You'd probably be amazed at how profusely I could apologize if you were straddling me and I was moving deep inside of you."

"Jack!"

"Oh, God, I'm sorry," he said, amazed at himself. "I can't believe I just said that."

"I can believe you said that more than I can believe anything else you've said in the past five minutes. Or the past five days, for that matter," she told him.

And then she grinned.

"Tess?"

"You take care of that side, and I'll do this one. And then don't say anything else, Jack, because right now you're a very lucky man, and lucky men don't talk themselves out of their good luck."

TESS WATCHED HER son as he all but danced about the enormous nursery, showing her this toy, and that toy, and of course his favorite thing of all, a rocking horse she was not quite sure she approved of, as it appeared to have been covered in real horsehide.

She'd been amazed at the size of the Blackthorn nursery, which consisted of no less than five rooms, including a lovely chamber Emilie had claimed for her own and filled with flowers from what must be an enormous greenhouse somewhere on the grounds. There were three other sleeping chambers, with Jacques occupying the same one his father had slept in when he was a child. Jacques had told her that quite proudly, and then giggled and motioned her over to the window to see where his father had scratched his name on the windowpane.

It was all so odd. The bastard sons, raised as if they were true heirs to the marquess, surrounded by all that they could never possess. How very cruel.

And now here was Jack's son, retracing his father's steps, and most certainly taking to this luxurious life as if to the manor born.

"*Maman!* Watch me gallop! Gallop and gallop and gallop!"

She turned about to see her son rocking with all of his might. *"Jacques, fais attention, ou tu galoperaz sur votre tête!"*

"Silly *Maman*," the boy said, laughing. "I cannot gallop on my head."

"And that's my point," she told him, lifting him out of the saddle and putting him on the floor. She dropped to her knees and hugged him fiercely to her. "I've missed you so much. Did you miss me, darling?"

Jacques squirmed in her embrace. "Yes, *Maman*. Will there be cakes? Isn't it time for cakes?"

Tess lightly poked his stomach. "Is that all you can think of, young man? Feeding your belly?"

"Grandfather says there is nothing more important

for a young gentleman to worry about," Jacques said in all seriousness, his eyes wide and innocent as he so casually spoke of the Marquess of Blackthorn. "And I'm a young gentleman, *Maman,* Grandfather said so. I think about my belly *a lot!*"

She took his hand and led him over to the window seat, just for a moment remembering another window seat and what had been found there. The past, which was not really that past, not yet, somehow seemed a world away from this light and sunny room. "You do not pester the…your grandfather, do you? You are polite, and make your bow, and are careful not to step on his feet?"

"Yes, *Maman.* I am all things wonderful. Grandfather said so."

"He's beyond wonderful, actually. He's delightful."

Tess turned to look at the young woman who had entered the nursery. She was slim and blonde, and with the most interesting gray-blue eyes, and her smile seemed to light up the already sunny room.

"I'm Chelsea Blackthorn," she said as Jacques slid down from his mother's lap and ran over to hug the woman's knees. "Beau's wife. And you're Lady Thessaly. Jack told us you came directly up here, which is what I would have done myself, were I you. Welcome to Blackthorn."

Tess got to her feet and took Chelsea's outstretched hand. "I'm Tess. Just Tess. Thank you so much for agreeing to house my son in my absence. Although I suppose you didn't agree. Jack simply sent him, didn't he?"

Chelsea's laugh was open and unaffected. "He came

into the house riding Puck's shoulders and captured all our hearts in an instant." And then she sobered. "Well, most all of our hearts. Has Jack spoken to you of Adelaide? His mother?"

Tess went instantly on her guard. "He's mentioned her, yes. Is she here?"

"In the cottage. She hasn't set foot in the house since Jacques arrived, I'm afraid. Or delighted, which I shouldn't say, but if Jack has spoken of his mother, then you know the arrangement?"

"Knowing and understanding are probably two different things," Tess said carefully.

"I agree." Chelsea bent down to speak to Jacques. "I passed Letty in the hallway, young man. She was bringing up your tea to Emilie's room. I saw small cakes with pretty pink flowers on them."

Jacques turned his head toward the door to the nurse's room, even took two steps in that direction before turning back to bow to Chelsea. "Thank you, Aunt Chelsea," he said politely, and then looked to Tess. *"Maman?"*

"I'm certain there's porridge on the tray as well, Jacques. You will of course eat that first?"

"Oui, Maman! Chaque dernière cuillerée—et puis les gâteaux!"

"I'll settle for half the porridge, and then the cakes. Now go on," Tess said, making shooing motions with her hands. She watched him *gullup* off on his sturdy legs, smiling as he called out to Emilie, scolding her for not telling him his tea had been brought up to him. "As arrogant as his father," she said, shaking her head, and then turned back to Chelsea. "I suppose I've hidden up here as long as I can. I should seek out his lordship and thank him for his generosity."

"Oh, don't worry about Cyril, or standing on ceremony at all, for that matter. We're rather an odd household. Actually, we're an exceptionally odd household."

When Tess only nodded, Chelsea rolled her eyes. "What? Is something wrong?" she asked, following the other woman out of the nursery.

"Nothing," Chelsea said, heading down the stairs. "I was hoping for a good gossip, I suppose, but if you're going to be so unfailingly polite as to ignore my bald hints, I suppose I'll have to introduce Regina to the mix. She could get the Sphinx to talking, I swear it." She stopped at the bottom of the stairs and turned to Tess. "Aren't you in the least curious? About Adelaide, I mean. About, well, about all of it? And Lord knows we're curious about you and Jack. Jack? With a son? We didn't even know for certain that he was *human!* Regina and I have decided you must be the bravest woman in the world. Oh, or hopelessly deranged, of course. There's always that."

Tess laughed as she continued to follow Chelsea through the wide corridors that had to be the private living quarters of the huge mansion. "Jack said I'd like you," she said as they walked into a curtained antechamber that opened into an enormous bedchamber currently peopled by a dark-haired young woman who was just then leaning over what appeared to be a priceless china bowl, very definitely being sick to her stomach.

Chelsea immediately ran to her side, putting a hand to her back. "It's all right, Regina. But I did warn you, didn't I? It doesn't matter how much you enjoy kippers, not that I can understand how anyone would. But for now at least, you really should confine yourself to things that have a better chance of remaining where you put them when you ate them."

The woman named Regina, by the process of elimination, Puck's wife, said something Tess couldn't quite hear, and Chelsea laughed.

"Oh, you will eat again, I promise. Just not for a few weeks. Look at me, for pity's sake. I can barely *stop* eating now, and you know that wasn't the case last month, not by a long chalk. Tess? Tess, tell her—it does get better, doesn't it?"

Tess watched as Regina Blackthorn set down the bowl and pushed back her dark hair that had been hanging in her face, and then turned to look at this clearly unexpected witness to her bout of nausea.

"I once ate an entire roasted chicken," Tess admitted. "In a single sitting. An *entire* chicken. With plum sauce. It was…heavenly."

Regina was already at the basin, pouring water she then splashed on her face and hands. "That's very encouraging, if slightly alarming. Thank you."

"You're quite welcome. Now, if you think you could manage a dish of tea, which I highly recommend at times like these, perhaps we can all sit here and get to know each other, and talk about Jack because I really adore talking about Jack, and then talk about Adelaide because I think I really need to know more than Jack has told me about his mother, and then talk about anything else Chelsea here can think of that she'd like to gossip about?"

The two young wives exchanged grins.

"Puck told me I'd like you," Regina said as Chelsea danced off to summon a maid to bring the tea tray. "We already did, Chelsea and I, because you've made Adelaide a grandmother before either of us had to tell her that we're also making her a grandmother." She sobered. "She's not taking it well."

"Yes, I already gathered that," Tess said as they adjourned to a lovely alcove set with striped slipper chairs and a view of a large ornamental pond. "Chelsea informed me that she's hiding in her cottage."

"Hiding? Oh, never say hiding. She has *retired* to the cottage, where she is replenishing her artistic soul even as she prepares for another hugely successful tour with her sterling band of traveling players. She leaves in two days, and good riddance. Poor Cyril. He's caught between wishing her gone and begging her to stay. It's… difficult to watch."

"Here, here, Regina, you're starting without me!" Chelsea remonstrated as she joined them. She sat herself down and grinned at Tess. "I just now saw Jack in the hallway, on his way up to the nursery, and told him we ladies are having ourselves a lovely coze before dinner, the three of us getting to know each other better. He looked positively terrified. Isn't that nice?"

Tess settled more comfortably into her own chair, and even dared to slip off her shoes and tuck her legs up under her. She'd been worried about meeting these women, worried about so many things connected with

Blackthorn, but most worried about these women. She'd never really had friends, only her brother for company, and these past four years she'd been terribly isolated at the manor house.

She hadn't known what to expect, or how she would be expected to comport herself—after all, she was Jack's mistress, really, and the unmarried mother of his son. But here she was, within an hour of her arrival, swept up into the very real welcome offered her, and wondering why on earth she'd ever been apprehensive.

"Jack, terrified? Oh, yes," Tess said as a maid entered the chamber, nearly staggering under the weight of a heavily laden tea tray, "I'd have to say I consider that to be very nice, indeed."

"Hello, Mother."

Jack had been standing under cover of the trees, watching as Adelaide posed in the gardens of her thatch-roofed *cottage,* which was the ridiculous name she had given to the equally ridiculous structure she'd coerced Cyril into having built for her on the estate grounds. It was a country cottage the way the Serpentine in Hyde Park was a lake—too perfect to be natural, real. It was more like somebody's ideal of what a cottage should be, but not a real cottage.

Rather as if it had been built for the stage.

Even as Adelaide had been built to trod that stage.

She was quite petite, nicely curved, but with bones so slender they could be bird bones, filled with air, as she was filled with air—light, fragile, but with enormous cornflower-blue eyes that seemed to fill her face.

She didn't walk. She floated. She didn't merely speak. Her voice sang a sweet song each time she deigned to open her rosebud mouth. Her skin was like cream, her smile brought out the sun, her laugh could make the angels weep in envy.

Jack had once thought her the most beautiful creature in the world. Now? Now he believed she was a creature. A quite strange, complicated creature, perfect in so many ways, save for the absence of a heart.

Adelaide didn't garden at the cottage. She would never dirty her hands or exert herself in any way. What she did was *pose* in the gardens cared for by someone else. She would carry a basket while someone else cut the blooms for her. She would sometimes be seen with a shepherdess's crook adorned with a large yellow bow, and watch as somebody else prodded at a lamb to make it scamper for her, as she supposed lambs should do. She would call her children to her, shower them with kisses, hug them to her scented bosom, proclaim her great love for them, and then shoo them away if they dared to actually *act* like healthy young boys.

All the world's a stage...

While he'd stood there, watching her, she'd untied her enormous straw sunbonnet and shook out her heavy, nearly waist-length blond hair. It had always been so blond it was nearly white, but now it seemed more white than blond. She would be wise not to go out with her head uncovered on a bright day, because the sunlight revealed the passage of time as it was marked on her face.

Still, she looked much as she'd done the last time Jack had seen her, a long decade ago.

She'd tilted her head to one side and begun combing through her hair with her fingers, smoothing it away from her heart-shaped face, perhaps trying to lighten it with the sun. She looked a portrait, one some artist would itch to capture on canvas.

Beware of her fair hair, for she excels all women in the magic of her locks, and when she twines them round a young man's neck she will not ever set him free again.

Jack twisted the ring on his index finger, wondering yet again why he still wore it. He didn't need it to remember who he was, what he was. She'd made that abundantly clear to him that last night, when she'd told him about his father. The highwayman who had been hanged years earlier. The Gypsy, who he'd last seen riding away from the manor house only a few short days ago.

"Jack!" Adelaide exclaimed now, turning on the intricately filigreed cast-iron bench, her hands already busy twisting her hair and securing it atop her head with a single long pin. "I see you've successfully banished any shreds of common decency since last we met. I believe I'd made it clear, dearest. You don't belong here. You demean yourself by crawling back to Cyril, who is too much the gentleman to turn you away. And I had thought you cared for him. Obviously you've grown hard over the years."

Jack opened the white picket gate and stepped into the garden, and then closed it behind him. "I'm my father's son," he said as he approached and then sat down beside her. "Thanks to you, I've grown into the role you assigned me. In fact, I'm damn lucky to be alive. It was a close-run thing for a few years, you know, as I endeavored to follow in my sire's footsteps."

Adelaide's eyes grew wide. "Never say you went for a highwayman! Oh, Jack, that wasn't my intention. Not at all! But you agreed you didn't belong here. You were always so vibrant, so hot for living! Not like that plodding, *responsible* Beau, or the so-silly Puck. You were meant for *adventure,* Jack! I couldn't bear to watch you *suffocate* here, not even a son of the house. You needed to fly, Jack, fly free!"

"I needed to be gone, so as not to be a constant reminder of your betrayal of a good if misguided man who had finally begun seeing you for what you are. I knew that then, I know that now. Can't we at least be honest with each other, Mother?"

His head snapped to the left as her palm made sharp contact with his cheek.

"How dare you! You insolent cur! You dare to speak to me that way? I. Am. Your *mother!*"

"No. You're a bloody whore, Adelaide, and your time has just run out. When all you have are your looks, it's inevitable." He stood up, glared down at her, wondering when he'd feel the outrage; he should be feeling the outrage. "No more sulking like some ignorant child. You will be at table, tonight. You will meet Tess, and you will be civil. To her. To me. And then, tomorrow, I want you gone."

"You dare to tell me to leave?"

"Would you rather I told Cyril who I just saw?" Jack leaned down to speak next to her ear. "I saw him, Adelaide. I saw Andreas. I saw my father."

"No! No, that's impossible! You're wrong, Jack. Listen to me!" She grabbed at his shoulders, her fingertips digging into him through his shirt. "He's dead. He was hanged. He's dead!"

"Oh, Mother, that was entirely the wrong answer. You should have looked at me blankly, in all your most lovely confusion. Andreas? Who is this Andreas you speak of? I do not know the name."

"Well, yes, of course. I didn't realize you had said a name. You...you took me by surprise. Your vehemence. You frightened me. I...I..."

Jack put his hands over hers and rather roughly removed them from his shoulders. "No wonder you never trod the boards within ten miles of Covent Garden, Adelaide. You're a terrible actress. Almost embarrassingly so. I suppose you must be very...inventive in bed. Not that Cyril seems to care about that anymore, does he, and Andreas a long time before that?"

"You're *filth,*" she ground out, looking truly ugly, as if her inside had just for that moment become her outside.

"And you've outstayed your welcome. By about ten years, as I've heard the thing. Dinner tonight, Adelaide, and you will be on your best behavior. You can politely retire to your cottage before the tea tray is brought, as you'll want to pack before departing tomorrow morning. Everyone will believe you've simply gone back with your acting troupe. But we'll know better, you and I. You will never return here again. You're no longer welcome. Yet, remarkably, and contrary to everything you always wanted me to believe, *I am.*"

"I should have drowned you when I saw you were his," she said as Jack turned his back. "Black bastard."

Jack kept on walking, wondering when she'd notice that he'd left the onyx ring on the bench beside her.

CHAPTER NINETEEN

TESS STOOD IN front of the pier glass, wishing her wardrobe were more extensive. Wishing her hair could be tamed, made sleek and sophisticated, or whatever it was that it clearly wasn't, for only five minutes after the maid had finished with it, several tendrils had worked their way out of their pins. Wishing she wasn't so tall. Wishing she had more curves, or at least more bosom.

Regina had a lovely bosom.

Chelsea had the most engaging smile.

All Tess had, she decided, was a fairly attractive nose. Possibly.

What would the marquess think of her? Indeed, what would she think of the marquess? What could she say to him? How would Jack introduce her? *Your lordship, may I present to you the mother of my child?*

She rolled her eyes. No, Jack wouldn't do that, would he? Not that it wasn't obvious. After all, Jacques was upstairs in the nursery, wasn't he? Jacques spoke of the man as his grandfather, for pity's sake. What sort of man was the marquess? He acknowledged his bastards, and his bastard's bastard.

It was just as Regina had said. This was a very odd household, indeed.

The afternoon had been wonderful, thanks to Chelsea and Regina. By turns hilariously funny and then incredibly sad, their conversation had run the gamut, from their own stories—which were also at times harrowing, at times delicious—and then on to what they knew of the complicated matter of the marquess's late wife, Abigail, and her sister, Adelaide.

Beau and Chelsea had their own estate not ten miles from Blackthorn, given to them by the marquess, just as he had deeded another unentailed estate to Puck, who was supposedly now dedicated to learning all about something he called animal husbandry. They were only here at Blackthorn because Jack had promised to meet with the marquess, a request the man had first made over a year ago, shortly before his wife died.

Her new friends were certain that Jack, too, would soon be a landowner, courtesy of his "father." But Tess doubted that. Jack was much too proud, and much too stubborn, to accept anything from the man who was not his father. He'd rather sleep beneath the hedgerows.

She'd like to think he'd unbend enough to allow the man to ease his conscience, or whatever it was the marquess felt the need to do, remembering that he now had a son to care for. But she didn't have much faith in that. She could only hope he'd somehow manage to be polite as he declined.

And then there was his mother. Nothing Chelsea or Regina had told her had served to make her hold Adelaide in less than complete contempt. She could only hope she'd somehow manage to be polite when she finally saw the woman.

No, Tess was not looking forward to going down to dinner.

There was a knock at the door leading to the dressing room connected to the chamber, and she turned about in time to see Jack enter, dressed in evening clothes. He looked so handsome, so very much the gentleman. Or he would, if he could have somehow managed to take the scowl from his face.

"Loins sufficiently girded?" he asked as he approached.

"Yours or mine?" she returned, nervously patting at her hair. "At least you're presentable. I look terrible."

"You do? Where?" He walked completely around her, and then put his hands on her shoulders and looked deeply into her face. "No. I don't see it. You're beautiful. And much too good for me, clearly. I always want to remove the pins from your hair, and then bury my face in its warmth. Why is that, do you suppose?"

She rolled her eyes and turned back to the mirror. "It looks as if you've already done that," she complained morosely. "My gown is three years old, and entirely the wrong color. It was supposed to match my eyes, but it doesn't, not at all." She raised a hand to her bare neck. "A king's ransom in ancient jewelry moldered in the cellars for years, and I haven't so much as a simple string of pearls. Small pearls."

"There is this," Jack said, taking her locket from his pocket.

"My locket! I thought I'd lost it. Where did you find it?"

He motioned for her to turn around as he lowered the chain over her head and fastened the clasp. "In the dirt in front of the buttery. The chain broke, no thanks to Andreas and his rough handling of you that night. I had the chain replaced while we were in London."

Her bottom lip trembled as she clasped the locket tightly in her hand and then let it go, looking at the way the longer chain caused it to hang just below the neckline of her gown. "Did...did you open it?"

"I did. Your mother was a beautiful woman. René favored her."

She lifted the locket to her mouth and kissed it. "I can't tell you what it means to me, to have this back. Your first gift to me, and now you've given it to me again. Thank you, Jack."

He ran his fingertip down her cheek, and her stomach seemed to do a small flip inside her. "Consider it your shield as you go into battle. That is how you feel, isn't it?"

She lowered her eyes. "It's that obvious?"

"As I've never heard you worry about your gown or your looks, yes, it is. They none of them bite, you know. Well, perhaps my mother, and we'd have to apply to Cyril to be really sure."

"Jack!"

Tess slapped at his chest to protest his silliness, and he gathered her close, tipping up her chin. "She leaves here tomorrow, on my order, and she won't be coming back."

"On *your* order? Why would she do that? Good God, Jack, what did you do? How much havoc can you wreak in a month, if you can do this much in one short afternoon? Does the marquess know?"

"No, and that was the point. I hinted that I would tell Cyril about Andreas unless she left. It was calling her bluff, if we'd been playing at cards, I'll admit that. I was chancing that she'd told him about her lover, but then begged his forgiveness, telling him Andreas was dead, for one. I doubt Cyril would continue to finance her damn acting troupe if he found out she'd lied to him yet again. And it worked."

"Clever. You look fairly smug. I don't think I like that."

"Then you'll probably like this even less. I'm going to follow her when she leaves. I'm convinced she'll be heading straight to Andreas to find out what happened. My mother is clever in her way, but no one has ever accused her of being overly intelligent. Now, before you tell me all the reasons why I shouldn't do this, let me remind you yet again that the Gypsy killed René. He's not my father. If I ever had a father, it's that man waiting for us downstairs, who I've treated very badly, I'm afraid. Andreas is nothing to me other than a criminal soon to be brought to the bar, and the king's justice. I can't just walk away, Tess. I can't. Some scores have to be settled, and this is one of them."

She fussed with his neck cloth, proprietarily, protectively, ridiculously protectively, as if she had any control over his personal safety. "I know. Sometimes we have to settle the past before...before there can be a future. I think I've always known that, even as I was stupidly trying to pretend we could just...forget."

"There's another reason, a selfish one. If I can—when I can hand over the Gypsy, Liverpool will know a chapter has at last been closed. Sinjon, gone. The Gypsy, hanging for his crimes. The war's over, and he has plenty of minions for his purposes now, he doesn't need me anymore. I can resign from his service, Tess, hoping I won't have to watch my own back. Will had me half-convinced we can walk away, but Henry never believed it. Even presenting Liverpool with the Gypsy might not do it. It would still probably be best if I were simply to disappear."

She pushed away from him. "And is that also what you plan to do when this is over? Disappear?"

"I won't know that until I've spoken with Liverpool. If he assures me my services were highly valued and thanks me for my service, wishes me success in my future endeavors?"

"Then you'll stay?"

Jack grinned. "Hell, no. I'll run like a rabbit, knowing he'd just handed me a bag of moonshine." But then he sobered. "I've lived by my wits for a lot of years, Tess. But it's no life for a woman, a child. You understand that, don't you? I can't ask that of either of you. I—"

"Yes, yes, I heard you. You can't," she said, cutting him off. "But some could. Just not you. You still don't understand, do you, Jack? That you're *worth* the trouble you cause? Because you do cause trouble, you know. You're arrogant, and prideful, and stubborn, all the while thinking you're worthless because your father is a thief and a murderer and probably a traitor, and your mother is—what is your mother, Jack? Let's go find out, shall we?"

"Oh, Christ. Tess, wait a minute, damn it. You don't understand. We have to talk."

"No," she said, snatching up her shawl, her heart pounding so hard it hurt. "Let's not. Oh, and when you follow her tomorrow, when you confront the Gypsy? Don't think you're going alone. I'm fighting for my future, too, and our son's—with or without you."

"You're the most stubborn woman I've ever met."

"At least I've got a good reason—I have to deal with *you*."

She all but ran for the staircase, Jack following behind her, where she was lucky enough to encounter the third Blackthorn son, Beau, who bowed and introduced himself, and then offered his arm as they descended the staircase, only looking back at Jack a single time, but then putting his hand on hers and giving it a reassuring pat, as if to say, *Don't worry, we're used to his black moods. I'll protect you from the ogre.*

Caught between anger and despair—with anger definitely winning—Tess forgot to be nervous as she was presented to the marquess, who excused himself for not rising when she entered the room, pointing to the walking stick propped next to him.

He was quite a handsome man, although something, some pain either physical or otherwise, had etched deep vertical lines on either side of his mouth. His hair was white but she could imagine it as blond as that of his two sons, who very much resembled him. Jack was so unlike the three of them that only a fool would believe him to be the man's offspring. She wondered if a young, confused Jack had ever spent time anxiously peering into a mirror, straining to find some resemblance to the man he'd called *Papa*. It was strange; even when she wanted to strangle Jack, her heart broke for him.

She curtsied as she offered her hand and the marquess bent his head ever so slightly as he took it, squeezed her fingers. "Your son is an angel, my dear. Thank you so much for entrusting him to my care, for however long as you desire. It is my delight and pleasure. Jack? Have you seen your mother? I'm certain she's anxious to meet this lovely young woman."

"We spoke at the cottage this afternoon, yes," Jack said, presenting Tess with a glass of wine, and indicating that she should sit down next to the marquess. "*I'm* certain she'll be with us this evening."

Did anyone else recognize Jack's answer for what it truly was? His tone smooth, his words innocuous enough, but with so much more there for anyone who dared to listen closely.

If the marquess heard anything more than the words, he gave no indication, instead apparently continuing a conversation already begun with Puck, one that apparently centered on someone named Jethro Tull and his publication concerning horse-hoeing husbandry, which seemed to concentrate on the benefits of some new principles of vegetation and tillage.

"Yes," Puck said, winking at Tess after the marquess had made his point, "but you will admit it has been more than a century since the man's horse-drawn seed drill— and, yes, his horse-drawn hoe. So why isn't it time for improvement, that's what I say. I can envision a steam-powered engine at work in the fields, much like those

James Watt is so famous for, including this idea I've had concerning his separate condenser, which is a truly—"

"Which is a subject more truly stultifying than I can tell you, husband," Regina Blackthorn said as she took him by the hand. "Come along, Farmer Puck, and give Chelsea your opinion on the subject of grosgrain versus satin for the new ribbons she's contemplating for her second-best bonnet. You do remember when such things interested you, don't you? Over and above the proper spreading of manure, I mean."

Puck hung back to say to Tess, "She exaggerates. I was never all that interested in bonnet ribbons. I could, however, wax poetic over the cut of a new waistcoat for hours, and still could, actually. I'm that ashamed, really."

Tess laughed, as she was sure she was supposed to do, but then, as if her mind was somehow tied to Jack's— which it might well be, she thought almost sadly—she found herself looking in his direction just as he seemed to draw himself up straighter, as if anticipating a physical blow.

"And will you just look at this scene of domestic bliss! All my loved ones, together again. Oh, my heart simply *swells* at the sight!"

Tess turned to look at the author of this nonsense, delivered in a marvelously throaty voice, as if emoting for spectators in some gallery.

Adelaide, for who else could this petite goddess be, posed just inside the doorway, one small hand held up just inches below her perfect chin, her fingers spread, her palm facing her audience—for what else could they be but her audience. Her head was tipped just so, her magnificent white-blond hair done up in intricate curls and threaded through with what could very possibly be diamonds.

Her gown was the exact shade of blue midnight and cut perilously low, one of the cap sleeves having slipped from her creamy white shoulder, whether by accident or design only another woman would know.

By design, definitely, Tess decided, feeling horribly dowdy and plain.

When it was obvious that all eyes were now on her, Adelaide unfurled the lace, ivory-sticked fan that had been dangling from her wrist and fluttered it beneath that same perfect chin, setting the fairy-light wispy curls that artfully escaped her coiffure dancing in the slight breeze.

She and her scent drifted into the room as her sons and the marquess all got to their feet, Puck hastening to bow over her hand and effusively complimenting her on her *practiced* entry. In French. Which, clearly, his mother did not understand. Otherwise, she would have slapped his face rather than simper like a young girl and tip up her cheek for his kiss.

She simpered quite well, Tess would have to hand the woman that, even as she decided, without need of further evidence, that she did not like the woman. Not one little bit.

Adelaide spied Cyril and exclaimed fretfully as she rushed to him, urging him to please seat himself and then dropping gracefully at his feet, and laying her cheek against his knees. "Cyril, my sweetest, dearest goose. How many times must I urge you not to exert yourself simply because I have entered the room? Is your leg paining you again tonight? You should have had that horse shot for throwing you that way." And then she looked up, her huge eyes deliberately innocent, blinked in supposed surprise, and said, "Well, hello. I didn't even notice, my goodness, that gown positively *blends* with the couch, doesn't it? You must be Tess, yes? Aren't you…sweet."

"Adelaide," the marquess warned quietly.

"Cyril?" she singsonged back to him, getting to her feet. "My stars, what have I said? Surely I haven't said anything. My dear? You took no offense, surely?" She blinked furiously, as if holding back tears. "I would never, *never* seek to offend. I simply speak what I think, before I can think twice. Isn't that what you always say, Cyril, darling? And her gown *is* much the same shade as the couch, you must admit it. Not that it isn't a very lovely couch."

"Wine, Mother?" Jack said, all but shoving the glass into the woman's face.

Adelaide's smile stayed where it was, actually seemed to freeze in place as she took the glass in self-defense. "Ah, and there he is, my dashing rogue. Thank you, Jack. You've developed manners. I'd always held out hope, you know."

"Jack tells me he stopped by the cottage this afternoon," the marquess said as mother and son exchanged and held looks.

Adelaide's creamy complexion seemed to go unhealthily pale. "Yes, he did stop by. How it warmed this mother's heart to see the prodigal again." She lifted her hand and pinched his chin. "But I forgive you for deserting us so cruelly. You were always a difficult child."

"And there's the dinner gong," Beau said just a little too brightly, helping his wife to her feet. "We slaughtered a fine fat pig for you, Jack, as there were no fatted calves. Tess, I believe my father would reserve the honor to escort you to the dining room. Jack, you'll take care of Mother?"

"I believe I can do that, yes," Jack said, he and his mother still staring at each other. He offered her his arm. "Our first and last dinner together in ten long years. Are you still so set on leaving tomorrow, Mother?"

"I am, sadly," she said as Tess waited for the marquess to struggle to his feet, leaning heavily on the cane. "I'm afraid it's unavoidable." She spoke over her shoulder to the marquess as the small parade headed for the dining room. "I know I promised to stay for a few more days, darling, and so happy to be here to welcome Jack home, just as you asked. But he convinced me that Stoke-on-Trent is much too distant to expect to make the journey in a single day, and we do perform there on Friday afternoon. I anticipate great success, thanks to the new costumes you so generously provided. We're performing the bard's *Much Ado About Nothing*. Oh, how coincidental, Jack. You were named for Don John, you know."

Don John. The bastard. Tess's spine went rigid. Really, the woman was a nasty piece of work.

"That's quite all right, Adelaide. I understand," the marquess said, and then he smiled at Tess. "Adelaide much favors Shakespeare's plays, you see. Indeed, Adelaide, you perform only the bard's works, don't you?"

"We are Shakespearean players, darling," Adelaide snapped rather harshly. But then she softened. "There is no one else who can hold a candle to him."

"Really?" Tess said as a footman hastened to hold out a chair for her, unable to restrain herself. "I never really cared for his works, which seem more obscure in their language than necessary. For a rousing tale, I much prefer Cervantes. And our French dramatists, *naturellement*. Molière. And, as he has always been my favorite in both his plays and his letters, Voltaire. Such a brilliant man. He once wrote, *'L'homme est libre au moment où il souhaite être.'* Ah, forgive me, madam," she said, looking down the table to Adelaide, whose cheeks had gone an unflattering red at her insult to the bard, "as you do not speak French, I will translate. He wrote, 'Man is free at the moment he wishes to be.' Jack, you agree with that sentiment, don't you?"

Seated directly across the table from her, Jack inclined his head slightly, acknowledging the double hit, the first to his mother, the second to him. "You were always well-read, my dear. And she paints, too," he added, smiling sweetly. "Puck, with your new interest in all things agricultural, I believe you'd be amazed by her work. It's quite singular."

Tess laughed in true delight. *"Touché, monsieur."*

"I sense that I'm missing something," Puck said. "However, as I consider it a crime to be silent when I can say something silly, I am reminded of another of Voltaire's comments. Let's see, how does it go? Ah, yes, I remember now. And remember, dearest, I am only quoting, not pronouncing. '*Le mariage est la seule aventure ouverte de lâche.*'"

"'Marriage is the only adventure open to the cowardly'? Robin Goodfellow, you're a very lucky man that your wife knows you only say things like that in order to be amusing. Which, by the way, you aren't. Not when I spend half my days with my head over—well, never mind." Regina shot a panicked look toward the bottom of the table, where Adelaide reigned as hostess, and then quickly returned her attention to her plate, pushing at its contents with her fork, but not really eating anything.

"I've another," Beau said into the silence. "I read the lines while serving in Spain, and they certainly colored my vision of the supposed glory of war. I'll dispense with the French, as I've only read it in translation. 'It is forbidden to kill; therefore all murderers are punished *unless they kill in large numbers and to the sound of trumpets.*'"

"Well now, Beau, that's fairly morbid," Puck protested. "But, to redeem myself in my wife's eyes, I'll attempt another of my favorites from the man. 'I have never made but one prayer to God, a very short one: O Lord, make my enemies ridiculous. And God granted it.'"

"Well, I think that's above everything *ridiculous,* Puck," Adelaide pronounced. "What does it even mean?"

Chelsea raised her hand rather timidly, as if reluctant

to volunteer her opinion. "I believe, Adelaide, it means that a stupid enemy is God's greatest gift."

"I'll drink to that," Jack said, raising his glass. "May all our enemies be ridiculous."

"You have enemies, Jack?" the marquess asked with concern evident in his voice.

"Never for long, sir, no."

Tess rolled her eyes, but then looked down the table once more and realized that Jack's *ridiculous* statement had served to wash the angry color from his mother's cheeks.

TESS THREW DOWN her shawl and turned on Jack, who had followed her into the bedchamber. "Granted, it's an enormous pile of rooms, but I could have found my way back here on my own. You can leave now. No, please allow me to rephrase that. Leave. *Now.*"

Jack walked across the room to lean against the bed as he removed one evening shoe. "And here I thought the evening went so well."

"The *evening* was wonderful, save for your mother. Both for her presence, and for her, I suspect. You're a cruel man, Jack. She knows you hate her."

"Not hate," he said, easing off the second shoe. "She isn't worthy of hate. In fact, I find her fairly pathetic. She's getting old, Tess. I don't think she ever imagined such a thing happening, and she doesn't know how to deal with it."

"We all grow old eventually, if we're lucky. Why did you take off your shoes? Because you're not welcome here, Jack."

"No, you misunderstand her dilemma. Adelaide can't grow old. Her beauty, her youth, those were always her weapons, her only charms. Her beloved bard? She speaks his lines like a parrot, not understanding anything she says, not really. I couldn't have been more than twelve when I had to explain Birnam Wood to her, for God's sake. From *Macbeth*."

"I know where it's from." She picked up his shoes and held them out to him.

Jack ignored the gesture, instead shrugging out of his jacket. "I thought you didn't like Shakespeare."

She pushed the shoes against his gut until he took them. Then he placed them on the bed.

"Who doesn't like Shakespeare, Jack? For pity's sake, I was only getting some of my own back, and you know it. My gown is not at all the same shade of blue as your father's *couch*. Oh, and then she apologized. So sweetly—while getting in yet another insult while she was at it. Adelaide is a horrible, horrible woman, and I'm so, so sorry she's your mother. I'm sorry she's anybody's mother, because she doesn't deserve to be, and nobody deserves to be her child." She picked up the shoes yet again. "*Now* get out."

He took the shoes.

They made two very satisfying thumps as they struck the door to the dressing room.

"How dramatic, yet stupid, because now you just have to go chase them. I mean it, Jack. We're going to have a very *large* argument if you think you can come in here and…and attempt to do what I can clearly see in your eyes that you think you're attempting. And how dare

you! I must go alone. I must disappear. Oh, woe to poor
Jack Blackthorn. He can't ask a woman and a child to—
Stop grinning! Are you insane? What are you grinning
at? You look like the village idiot!"

"God, I love you," Jack said, careful not to get too
close, because she was really angry; only the village
idiot wouldn't know that. "You talk too damn much,
but I do love you. Which I would have told you earlier,
except that you wouldn't let me, and Beau shot me a look
that told me he'd appointed himself your protector from
his ogre of a brother."

He watched as her gorgeous eyes shifted left to right,
as if somehow she could hunt down their earlier conversation and dissect it. And then she looked at him. "You
weren't done?"

"No, I wasn't *done*. Would you like me to take up
where I left off? Or do you want to yell at me some
more?"

"I…I suppose you could, um, take up where you left
off?"

"Thank you." He bowed to her and then dared to put
his hands on her waist. "I believe, to recap, that I'd explained what could very well become my rather perilous
situation as to my soon-to-be former occupation. I also
mentioned that I'd lived by my wits for over a decade,
so the notion of doing that again, while not particularly
palatable, was a very real possibility. Furthermore, again
attempting to quote myself, I pointed out that it's no life
for a woman or a child. Children."

"You didn't say children," she interrupted. "You said
child. Referring, I believed, to the one we share."

"For now. Neither of us can say for certain that... recent activity may have us already on the way to changing that number. And then, before you interrupted to say that you knew what I was saying, I pointed out that a life such as the one I very well might be facing is not something I can ask either of you to share with me."

As he hesitated, she leaned her head forward, as if to help him get out the words. "But? Were you going to say *but?*"

"*But,*" he said, not as confident as he hoped she believed he was, "I'm going to ask it anyway. Because I love you. Because I love my son. Because there is no life for me without either of you, and even though I know that's selfish of me, and could even be dangerous, I'm going to ask it anyway. I don't know where we'd go, or what we'd do when we got there. I only know I'm ready to go down on my knees and beg you to love me, to marry me, to join our lives together, now and forever. I've walked away from so much, Tess, thinking it was for the best each time I did. But right or wrong, I can't walk away from you. Not again, not ever again. Don't ask me to. Please."

She opened her mouth, but no words came out.

He attempted a smile. "You're not going to make this easy for me, are you? I suppose I deserve that. Very well." He went down on both knees, holding her hands in his as he looked up at her, sure his heart was in his eyes. "I'll do anything you ask, be anyone you believe you need, go anywhere, do anything. I know I'm not an easy man, but in all fairness, you aren't an easy woman. Yet there's not a doubt in my head, Tess, that we're better together. Right or wrong, rich or poor, as long as we have each other nothing and nobody can defeat us."

Her bottom lip trembled, and she sighed on a brief sob. "We're invincible. Because...because you love me. Because I love you. With all my heart. You stupid, stubborn man..."

"Tess," he said, daring to get to his feet, gather her into his arms. "That's the most wonderful thing you've ever said to me, except that you still haven't said yes. Will you let me share your life?"

She nodded, biting her lip, the tears that shone in her eyes now running down her cheeks. "Yes. Yes!"

Jack grinned. He knew it was an unholy grin. "Are you certain? Because I wouldn't be averse to hearing you say it again."

"Oh, Jack..."

He caught her mouth in a kiss that told her they'd used up enough words, that it was time for that part of the marriage vows that had contained the words *with my body I thee do worship*—or whatever they were, he'd find out soon enough. Their lips still fused together, he lifted her in his arms, following her down onto the bed.

They had all night, and he was going to love her through every minute of it. Slowly. Thoroughly. Kissing every inch of her, *worshipping* her with his mouth, his hands, with words of love he would make up as he went along. Because it all came easy for him now, the words, the giving, without fear that there would be an ending that would leave him alone once more, on the outside once more; undeserving.

Tess loved him, and that made him what she said they

were: invincible. And he was more than that. Humble. Willing to bend, to give, to forgive. No matter how he had come to be, through love or passion, in secret or in betrayal, he was here. He would be the man he made himself. Not the shameful rogue his mother had attempted to create, not the hired assassin the government considered him, not the tool Sinjon had used to his own benefit. No. He would be the man worthy of the love Tess had for him, worthy of the son she'd given him.

He'd kill for her, he'd die for her. But what he wanted, what she needed, was a future for them, one totally divorced from what either of them had lived. A new world, one they would build together, with no lingering shadows from the past.

Tonight, in her arms, he would be born again, into that new world. Clean, and bright, and filled with hope. If that made him vulnerable, then so be it. It was more than time he let go, smashed all his carefully built defenses. He didn't need them anymore. He had everything he needed.

"I love you, Tess," he said as he sank between her legs. Coming home. "With everything that's in me, now and forever, I love you."

She touched his tear-damp cheek, her own eyes wet, her smile enough to break his heart. "I know," she said softly. "And it's enough, Jack. It's everything I've ever wanted. All of you…"

He took her then, with passion, with reverence, giving her everything that was in him, glorying in all she offered in return.

It wasn't finished, there were still remnants of the old world to be dealt with, run down and put to rest. But those were shadows now, not the center of their existence. Never again would anyone else hold the power to destroy them.

"All my life," Jack whispered against her ear as they lay together, their arms around each other. "All my life, I've been waiting for this. I didn't know what it was I looking for, and certainly didn't recognize it when it finally arrived. Maybe…maybe I was afraid I wasn't worthy…deserving. Yet now…now I understand. We have to be willing to give in order to get, don't we?"

Tess snuggled closer. "Your heart for mine, and mine for yours. It is rather daunting, isn't it? Which isn't to say I'm going to give yours back to you."

"I wouldn't take it. You'd have to drop it in the dirt and leave it there, broken into small pieces as you ground your dainty heel into it." He rose up slightly, turning her onto her back against the pillows. "God, that sounds like some asinine thing Puck would spout, and have the ladies swooning when he said it. What have you done to me, woman?"

"Some might say I've produced a miracle," she teased, sliding her arms up and around his neck. "But I know you for who you are, Jack Blackthorn. You'd much rather make love to me than wax poetic."

"Do you know," he said, trailing his fingers down her belly, so that she lifted herself to him, "I do believe you're right…"

CHAPTER TWENTY

TESS PUSHED BACK the sheer summer draperies and leaned closer to the window. The sights from her bedchamber included the sweeping west lawn, an artfully planted stand of trees and, in the distance, a partial view of Adelaide's cottage. "Jack? There's a pair of what I think are some sort of caravans lined up outside the gate to the cottage." She turned to look at him as he lingered over the breakfast tray that had been sent to the room. "Clearly, she's leaving. We have to follow her."

"We will. But there's no rush," he told her, popping one last bit of toast into his mouth. "We know where she's headed."

"We do?" Tess asked, already hunting through her clothespress for her shirt and breeches. "How do we know that?"

"We know because, last night, while you were contemplating ways to insult her, she told us. Stoke-on-Trent. Her troupe of players perform there on Friday afternoon. If she's meeting with Andreas, he already knows that. And if not there, then the next town, or the next."

His level of calm infuriated her. "If she meets with him at all. How can you be so certain they're still, well, lovers?"

"They have to be. Otherwise, why would she be so adamant to make me believe he's dead? She was protecting him, Tess. As difficult as it is to believe, it may be possible that my mother is capable of real affection for someone other than herself and her ambitions."

Tess returned to her chair. "I agree, that's difficult to believe. But if that's true, she must have been devastated when he disappeared. When he was prison in Spain, thanks to Sinjon." And then she looked at Jack as another thought struck her. "Do you think she even knew he's back in England? Until you told her, that is. We don't know exactly when he escaped, do we? Weeks, months, or even just days before the robbery that alerted Sinjon to his return. You may have delivered her quite a shock, or made her very happy."

"Making Adelaide happy." He stood up, so she did, as well. Perhaps he was rethinking his decision not to follow after Adelaide immediately. "That hadn't occurred to me. She's been at Blackthorn for several weeks. God, he may even have come here one night, for some grand, clandestine reunion in that damned cottage. I wonder if he'll even dare to meet with her at Stoke-on-Trent, as he has to know I'm still hunting him."

"Don't say *hunting him*. You're in lawful pursuit in the name of the Crown. And with the intent of capture, not execution. Correct? Because you're the better man, and civilized. This isn't revenge. It's justice."

"Yes, ma'am," Jack said kissing her cheek. "You can explain that to my mother when she goes for my eyes."

"Oh, don't you worry about that, Jack Blackthorn. I'm more than capable of handling your mother."

"And you're looking forward to it, aren't you? My guardian and protector."

Tess looked at him carefully. "You object?"

His smile eased her fears. "Actually, I rather like it. I may be a very bad man."

She slipped into his embrace, lifting her mouth for his kiss. After all, if they didn't have to go haring off to follow Adelaide, there were other, more pleasant ways to occupy their time. "But so very good, at so many, many things. I'm thinking of one in particular just now but, alas, we're both wearing too many clothes."

He stilled her hands, as she was in the process of loosing his neck cloth, and lifted her fingers for his kiss. "I can't believe I'm saying this, but not now, Tess. There was a note from Cyril on the breakfast tray. He'd like to see us, all of us, in the music room at eleven. It would seem the discussion I've been avoiding for so long is no longer avoidable. What's interesting is that he's including you and Chelsea and Regina."

"Chelsea and Regina told me he's going to offer you an estate. But you know that, because he's deeded estates to Beau and Puck in this past year, while you kept avoiding him." She patted his neck cloth, attempting to smooth it where she'd begun opening it and said sweetly, "You aren't going to be an ass and refuse him now, are you, the way you've always refused his offer of an allowance?"

"Is there anything you women didn't talk about yesterday?"

"I don't think so, but how would I know that, if we didn't discuss it?" she countered as the clock on the mantelpiece began to chime out the hour. "I wasn't aware of the marquess's injury, so there is that. A riding accident?"

"Yes. It happened when he was out riding with Adelaide a few weeks ago. I asked Beau about it, and he said they were surprised by a rider who came plunging out of the trees and charged across the riding trail. Cyril's horse reared, and he was thrown. He was never a strong rider. Surprisingly, perhaps, Adelaide is."

Tess looked at Jack, wondering if he was testing her. "And you see nothing strange about this?"

"I didn't want to, no. Cyril was adamant that it was an accident. But Adelaide is here only because he summoned her after Puck told him I'd promised to come... home. That's getting easier to say. Home. I certainly took the long way, didn't I? In any case, I'm not looking forward to hearing whatever it is Cyril feels he needs to say to all of us, but riding accident or some sort of plot, I'm fairly certain Adelaide would rather he never get to say it. Whatever it is, he felt all three of his *sons* should hear it at the same time—which I made fairly impossible these past ten years. And now you and Chelsea and Regina are to be included, as well. I admit to being curious."

They were descending the staircase now, with the butler looking up at them rather reprovingly, as if they were extremely tardy. "The family awaits you in the music room."

The family. Just as if the butler knew, the world knew, that Jack was not really a part of the Blackthorn *family*. Tess slipped her hand into Jack's. "You'll let him speak without interruption? Without walking out if what he has to say doesn't suit you?"

"Yes, I will. I'm done with turning my back on unpalatable truths. They only run you to ground anyway, sooner or later."

"I love you."

He squeezed her hand as they walked into the music room to see that, indeed, everyone else was already there, waiting for them. Two footmen shut the doors behind them. "Then nothing else matters, does it? Do you see the portrait above the fireplace? That's Abigail, Cyril's wife."

Tess drew in her breath involuntarily. The portrait was huge, the woman captured there life-size. The marchioness had been painted as a fairy sprite, complete with flowing draperies and feathery wings, the innocent delight on her lovely face catching at Tess's heart. Hair flowing past her shoulders, nearly white it was so light, her small, heart-shaped face filled by her huge, soft eyes. So delicate, even ethereal. Forever beautiful, forever young.

Beau, who had been standing just below the portrait, walked over to them. Tess admired him greatly; he exuded responsibility, honesty, and encouraged trust, even on such short acquaintance; a true eldest son. He spoke quietly. "I don't like this, Jack. You'd think the man's on his way to the gallows. Even Puck can't get a smile out of him. I don't know that the women should be here, but he insisted."

"It's not my place to say this, Beau," Tess said quietly, "but his lordship must know what he wants to say, and

whom he wants to hear it. You might upset him more
than he is if you suggest otherwise."

"I agree," Jack said, looking past Beau to where Cyril
was sitting, quite stiffly, and looking unnaturally pale.
"But let's get this over with, and we should probably
only be grateful he didn't include Adelaide—or she refused him. I thought he wanted her here."

Beau shot a look over his shoulder at his father, who
was just then accepting a glass of wine from Puck.
"Wine before noon? Another disturbing sign. But in
any case, he stayed at the cottage for hours last night.
I'm willing to wager there was an argument. Yes, let's
get this over with."

Jack nodded his agreement and, still holding tight to
Tess's hand, approached his father. He inclined his head
respectfully. "Good morning, sir. I apologize for being
the last to arrive."

"By a decade, at my reckoning," Puck teased, earning
himself a quiet yet forceful verbal warning from Regina.

Tess curtsied and smiled at the marquess encourag-
ingly before Jack indicated she should sit between him
and Cyril on the couch, as Puck and the Blackthorn
brides already occupied the facing couch, while Beau
took up his former position once more, standing in front
of the fireplace.

They all looked to the marquess, and Tess found herself feeling protective of the man, and actually had to
restrain herself from reaching over to take his hand, to
lend him courage.

"Firstly," the marquess said, his voice rather waver-
ing, "I should like to apologize to the ladies. What I

am going to say, must say, is far from fit for feminine ears. But it must be said. I can only remind myself that Adelaide was correct in one thing. My sons, all three, have been blessed to know that you love them, truly love them. For who willingly takes on a bastard son without prospects for any other reason than love? You three ladies are to be commended, and cherished all the days of your lives."

"Here, here," Puck said raising his own glass of wine, this time earning himself a reproving jab in the ribs from his wife. "If this is how it's going to be, Regina, darling, I may go stand by Beau."

"No, Puck, stay here where, if necessary, I can remind you that you're here to listen, not speak. Please excuse him, sir. It seems ingrained in my husband to attempt to lighten any mood, an attribute usually pleasing." She looked sharply at Puck. "Just not right now, dearest."

"Oh, but it's fine for Beau to stand over there as if he's in charge of the proceedings, and Black Jack to sit over there, scowling?"

"Each to his talents," Chelsea said brightly as she leaned forward to grin at Puck.

Tess bit her lip, trying to hold back her smile. Even the marquess chuckled, proving Puck right. Some of the uncomfortable tension left the room. She looked to the portrait once more. It was calming, just to look at it. Abigail very much resembled her sister, but there was a purity there that Adelaide couldn't emulate, probably because she had no purity in her. That had all gone to Abigail.

"What I'm going to tell you all is difficult. The most difficult thing I may ever do," the marquess began quietly. "Your mother is dead-set against the telling, in part because it reflects badly on her and, or so she insists, because it reflects badly on me. In any case, she has steadfastly refused to be here this morning, and is in fact leaving shortly, vowing never to return, which I highly doubt, as she has threatened that for years. Although her visits to the estate have become much less frequent, she always returns.

"In any case, we disagree as to the details, the reasons, so let me say now that you may feel you are hearing only what I wish for you to hear. I hope that isn't true, for the fault is all mine, at the bottom of it. I've waited too long, decades too long, but not too late, I'm told, to attempt to make things right. However, I will need, we will need, Adelaide's cooperation, which I have thus far failed to win."

He looked from face to face and shook his head. "And now I've completely confused you all. Perhaps it would be best if I told you a story. You'll recognize some of it, for Adelaide impressed it on all of you when you were younger. With repetition comes belief, I think it is said, and Adelaide can be very convincing. You all adored her."

"I think I speak for all three of us when I say, yes, we did adore her. She drifted in and out of our lives like an angel," Puck agreed. "But children grow up, Papa, and what seemed logical to the child is less believable to the man. Tell us your story."

After that, the marquess spoke for nearly an hour, or

so it seemed. Uninterrupted, as there could be no words other than his, not until the telling was done.

He told them something they all knew, about the day his horse had come up lame and he'd stopped at a cottage miles from the estate, and first encountered Adelaide and her sister, Abigail. He had just turned twenty-one, and had come into the title only a few months earlier, when his father and mother had been cruelly snatched from him in a coaching accident. He was still grieving their loss, confined to the country until his year of mourning was past; he was frightened by and unprepared for the heavy responsibility suddenly thrust onto his shoulders. And then, like some sort of miracle, he was looking at the most beautiful creature in the world and instantly tumbling into love.

With Abigail. Sweet, innocent, wholly unsuitable Abigail; not Adelaide. And that was when any resemblance to Adelaide's romantic fairy tale her sons had heard a dozen times began to unravel.

Cyril's love for Abigail was pure, and he knew she loved him in return. As she loved her flowers, the lace on her gloves, the pretty colored leaves she pressed between the pages of a book of nursery rhymes…the chaste kisses, which were all he'd dared. Even in his besotted youth, he'd known a true marriage between them would be impossible, unconscionable, yet he could not bear to let her go. She was everything that was pure and gentle in the world. She'd healed his heart. He wanted her in his life, needed her in his life, longed to give her a beautiful life in return.

"And you succeeded," Puck interrupted. "I've never

known anyone so completely happy. There wasn't anyone who knew Abigail who didn't love her. I'll always miss her."

Regina leaned in to kiss her husband's cheek.

"Thank you for that, Puck. There was some good to be found in all of this, and I suppose that's it," the marquess said on a sigh. And then he continued his story.

He pretended to court Adelaide, just so that he might be near Abigail. But eventually Adelaide discovered his duplicity, and was incensed to think she could ever be overlooked in favor of her "half-wit sister." Abigail was a pretty doll, not real. Adelaide was fire and excitement, vibrant and alive. She was prettier, smarter and much more worthy of his affection.

She set out to prove this to Cyril, playing on her resemblance to Abigail, and for a while did succeed in turning his head. He could kiss Adelaide and pretend she was Abigail. He could do more than dream about her; he could touch her, take her, slake some of his abhorrent need in her, and lie to himself. He could believe he had been mistaken, that it was Adelaide that he loved.

For a time.

But at last he woke up to the insanity he was living, and dumbfounded Adelaide by asking for and receiving Abigail's hand in marriage. She would never be his wife in anything but name, but he needed her close, needed to see her every day, know that she was happy.

Adelaide angrily confronted him about what she called his "perversion of the soul" that had him wedding one sister while bedding the other. She would tell everyone, and he'd never be able to marry his *beloved*.

Why, he wouldn't even be allowed to see her again, Adelaide would make certain of that!

However, she proposed, in return for her silence, he could promise to finance her need to be an actress, her need to be free and unfettered. In addition, she would continue to *service* him when his lust for the flesh grew to be too much for him. After all, she never planned to marry and had need of a protector. Her body, anytime he wanted, any way he wanted; her silence, for his money.

The marquess was a man torn between his love for a woman who could never truly be his and his base and twisted obsession for a dangerous and unique woman he could desire, but not love.

Ashamed, and fearful of losing Abigail, the marquess agreed to the arrangement.

But the day of the wedding, when he'd lifted the heavy white veil back from his new bride's face just after they'd signed the church registry as man and wife, it was a highly amused Adelaide who was standing there, now the Marchioness of Blackthorn. She'd convinced Abigail to remain at home, hidden in Adelaide's room, with her father none the wiser and telling the guests that his daughter Adelaide had taken ill and would not be at the ceremony. Nervously waiting at the altar, the marquess had not even noticed Adelaide's absence.

She had written her own name in the marriage register. She'd tricked him to save him from himself, she told him, admitting that the substitution had been the inspiration of a moment just that morning and, she thought, rather fun—didn't he think it was a delicious joke?

No one else would ever know, she promised him, no one else could ever know, but *he* would, and he would always take care of her, grant her every wish, or else the world would know of his unnatural desires.

And no one else ever knew. The vicar had been silenced with a heavy purse. Adelaide's father hadn't even proved that difficult; it was enough that he was now rid of both his daughters, as his new and fairly horse-faced wife loathed the two beautiful young girls equally.

Adelaide had what she'd always wanted, that unfettered and extravagantly financed life she craved. Abigail was safe, petted, cosseted. And the marquess? God curse him, he admitted shamefacedly, he had what he wanted, as well. Abigail, all to himself, to love her and nourish his soul…and Adelaide, to quench his physical frustrations.

And then Beau had been born while Adelaide was off touring Scotland with her troupe, and everything had changed again. When the marquess saw his infant son, he at last woke from what he now called his "terrible dream," realizing the full consequences of the deception. He wanted to tell the truth at once, acknowledge his legitimate heir, but Adelaide countered that she would tell the world that he had raped her, and in her sister's presence; he would be exposed for the sick and twisted creature that he was. Why, he could be taken off to prison.

Society was already shunning him, she'd reminded him, making disgusting remarks about his reasons for taking on a beautiful but clearly simpleminded bride. What would happen to Abigail if the truth came out?

Would she be taken away from Blackthorn and put somewhere safe from his perversity? Somewhere such as an *asylum?* Is that what he wanted for the woman he supposedly loved? Because Lord knew Adelaide had spent enough years forced to watch over her sister; she had her freedom now and would not be shackled once more to a sickly half-wit.

And then she had left Beau with him and gone off yet again, not returning for more than two years, this time with a dark-haired infant she'd named Don John.

Clearly Jack was not the marquess's son, but he took the child, his son's half brother, and found himself bowing yet again to Adelaide's wishes. Her demands and, God curse him, his twisted desire for her. The cottage was built for her use, and she showed every sign of wanting to remain at Blackthorn. She doted on her sister, she played at loving mother to her adoring sons, and she once more found her way into the marquess's bed. Puck was the result of that long and bizarre summer, and by now it was too late to go back, change anything.

He still loved Abigail, but it was now the love of a brother for a sister, as it was Adelaide who lived in his mind, tormented his soul. He'd thought he'd wanted purity, when it was really Adelaide, with her many moods, her teasing ways, her clever passions that held him captive to his folly. She was his disease, and he had no cure.

"Next year," she would tell him. "I'll soon be too old for the stage, and then we will put things right," she would assure him. "When Abigail's health is better, dearest, we will correct our past mistakes when she is

well again. I fear for her life if we were to do it now."
And more than once, "I'll be invited to London, I know
I will. Once I've played at Covent Garden, I will ask no
more of life and will do as you say. Just one more year,
please!"

Excuse after excuse, year after year. If she didn't
agree, he knew he couldn't set things right. So he in-
dulged her, financed another summer spent touring the
countryside. And then another. Another.

Adelaide always seemed to know when she was in
danger of outstaying her welcome. She'd swoop in, and
then, just as Cyril prepared himself to speak of serious
matters, she was gone again. If he pushed too hard, she
would stay away for a year, driving him insane to see
her again. He soon learned not to push too hard.

He was trapped; all of them were trapped in lie after
lie after lie. And so it went on, until and after the boys
weren't boys anymore; they were well on their way to
becoming men. With each year that passed, it became
more difficult to consider revealing the truth. He'd left it
all too late; he couldn't possibly tell them now. His boys
were educated, they had generous allowances, there was
nothing he hadn't given to them, save his name. Knowing he was lying to himself as well as to his sons each
time Adelaide deigned to return to Blackthorn, the marquess grew to loathe her more, because he still desired
her so much.

Until, suddenly, one day, he didn't. She smiled, and
he did not succumb. She teased, and he found her tiresome. She came to his bed, and he felt physically sick-
ened. She threatened…and he found he could no longer

concern himself with her threats. He could even put his finger on the moment he awoke from the last of his dream, to know it had been his nightmare.

It had been the moment she'd sent Jack away, sacrificing her son in some twisted attempt to hold on to Cyril.

Abigail had been retreating more and more into a small world, to the point where she barely knew him; she could not be harmed if the truth came out, if he revealed the lie of his marriage to her, acknowledged his sons. And those sons, no longer powerless youths, would protect her. There would be more scandal, yes, and those who would never truly believe, who would continue to shun them as bastards. But the titles would be theirs. In Beau, Blackthorn would have its first good, solid steward since Cyril's father had been alive. The title, the line, would endure.

It was never too late to right a wrong.

At last, years too late, he'd found the courage he needed. But he would have to speak with Jack. That had to come first. He had to be made to understand that he was not only the child of his heart, proving the marriage would mean he, too, would be considered by law a son of the house. God only knew how many peers were the product of their mothers and somebody other than their husbands. The Harleian Miscellany was only one example. Jack must be made to understand this, but Jack refused to be found. And then there was the war, and his sons had scattered everywhere.

He'd first summoned his sons to the estate the previous spring, to at last tell them the truth. But then Abigail had died, and Adelaide had returned to Blackthorn for the funeral, slipping almost seamlessly back into his life as he grieved, nearly convincing him that revealing the truth at that time would only hurt Abigail's memory. Besides, who would believe him, even if Adelaide admitted the truth, as well? Her father and stepmother were dead, the vicar was dead. Marriage lines could be forged. It was all simply too convenient to speak up now, with Abigail just in her grave.

Still, he'd written his explanation of what had happened, given it and the marriage lines to his solicitor, and for the past year and more that man had been petitioning the government and the church to have Oliver LeBeau, Don John and Robin Goodfellow Blackthorn declared his legitimate heirs, with Beau immediately being named Viscount Oakley, Jack and Puck to be addressed as Lord Don John Woodeword and Lord Robin Goodfellow Woodeword.

What the marquess did not say, but Tess was certain they all knew, was if Beau were then to die without male issue, Jack, the true bastard, would come into the title, and not Puck. Jack would never allow that! If he was going to protest, quit the room, this would be the time. Tess could scarcely breathe, and did not dare to look at him. But he remained silent, and the marquess continued with his story.

"Unfortunately, all of this is far from settled fact," the marquess said wearily. "My solicitor has told me we will need to have your mother's sworn statement as to her part in the deception. As late as last evening, she continues to refuse."

And you, my lord, just very recently suffered what

could very well have been a fatal riding accident, Tess told him silently. *Why? Why won't she allow the truth to come out? It was one thing when she was young, and insisted on her freedom. But why not now? She could be the marchioness, with all that entailed—the greatest role of her life. It makes no sense.*

The marquess struggled to his feet and walked over to Beau, who had stood quietly throughout the long explanation, his lips so tightly pressed together the skin around his mouth had gone white.

"I remember the day you were beaten so horribly. Because of me, Beau, because of my weakness. I can't ask for your forgiveness, and I can't promise that you will ever bear the title you so clearly would serve better than I have done."

Beau nodded shortly. "I long ago made peace with who I am, sir. And it is only because I was one of Blackthorn's bastards that I am blessed with my wife, who is worth ten titles. There's nothing to forgive."

"Very prettily put, brother," Puck said, joining them beneath the portrait. "I can say the same. It would appear our mother was correct in one thing. I don't know that I would ever have been there for Regina when she so badly needed me, were it not for my bastard status. I wouldn't change a single day spent as *le beau bâtard anglais.* I might regret a few of the more silly ones, now that I am a happily wedded man, but I enjoyed them quite a little bit at the time. It would be lovely to be Lord Robin, more than wonderful to be officially recognized as your son, sir, but legitimacy in the eyes of the world means nothing compared to what I already have."

Tess searched in her pocket for her handkerchief, and wiped at her eyes. Beau and Puck had made touching, totally believable speeches. Bastardy had made strong, sensible men of them. Watching their wives join them, lovely and gracious and clearly deserving of their unexpected good fortune, was wonderful to see.

Jack, however, remained where he was, still saying nothing.

The marquess hugged his sons and then approached the son of his heart. Jack quickly got to his feet, and Tess as well, slipping her hand into his and squeezing it tightly. "Sir," he said quietly.

"Son, I'm so sorry. For everything. I have always been proud of you for who you are, what you've made of yourself. You have a spirit and fire and courage I envy, as I have lacked all three my entire life. I'll never know just what your mother told you to have you leave, or what it cost you to return here at last. Seeing your son, that fine boy you entrusted into my care, warmed my heart as it hasn't been warmed in a long time. For him, for this woman standing so protectively beside you, please let me attempt to make amends to you in some small measure for all the hurt you suffered thanks to your mother and me. Please."

Tess held her breath.

"Sir," Jack said at last, "you have nothing to make up for, not in any way. You opened your home to another man's child, opened your arms to me, opened your heart to me, when you had every reason to turn me away. I can only thank you. I owe *you,* sir. I thought I owed you my absence, but I was wrong. So very wrong. But you, sir, are wrong now. I have no right to legitimacy simply because Adelaide was marchioness when I was born. I won't accept that."

"Here we go. Aren't we all so lucky to be able to witness Jack being thick as a plank?" Puck said, sighing. "The law is the law, Jack, not to mention that I think it's a splendid idea, and I don't hear Beau here objecting, do you, does anyone? For the love of heaven, brother mine, even as I know you're unfamiliar with the action, *bend a little*."

Now Tess did dare to look at Jack, and what she saw in his face caused her to speak. Did nobody else see the pain in his dark eyes? "I see no sense in beginning an argument about something that may well not happen. If your mother successfully avoided the truth all these years, I find it difficult to believe she'll have a change of heart at this point."

"And there you're wrong, Tess, although I thank you for, yet again, springing to my defense. Adelaide will eagerly testify to the legitimacy of the marriage lines. I'll see to it."

Beau slung his arm around Jack's shoulders. "No, Jack, not on your own. That's up to all three of us, acting together. We'll make her see reason."

"Reason? You'll make a fine marquess someday, brother, upstanding gentleman that you are. But it's my particular talents that are needed now."

"Jack's right, Beau," the marquess said, sighing. "I've always believed your mother to be somewhat in awe of Jack. Or afraid of him. Do you have a plan in mind, son?"

"Most of it, yes, sir. I'll work out the rest, Tess and I will, on our way to confronting her."

Beau seemed to consider this and finally nodded his agreement. "Then you'd better plan quickly. I could see the drive from where I was standing. The caravans are gone, but not that long ago. You can probably catch up with them easily, although I'll be damned if I know how you think you can convince her to return to the estate."

"No," Jack said shortly, his tone hard. "We'll meet with her elsewhere. She never comes back here. Never again."

Tess immediately understood what he was saying. He was protecting the marquess. If she knew nothing else about this man she loved, she knew he would slay dragons for those he cared for, and he'd use every weapon in his arsenal to do so, fair or unfair. She was looking forward to helping him plan his mother's downfall, perhaps even more than she was about the prospect of capturing the Gypsy. At least Adelaide carried her knives in her mouth, and words never killed anyone. Although God knew they could cause great harm.

"Never return? Why? No, I suppose I'm not to inquire about that, either?" Beau asked. "At any rate, do we even know where she's heading?"

"Where she always goes, when she's not with me. To be with her lover," the marquess said quietly. "To be with your father, Jack. It was always him, even before I met her, which is a bit of bitter fact she flung at me one night when she particularly wanted to hurt me. Him, and their free and unfettered lives. The *excitement* she needs as the rest of us need air. I must say, I admire him in a way. He picks her up and he puts her down, sometimes for months on end. This last time, for over three years. Poor Adelaide, how she suffered. But he's back now, I'm certain of that. I can always see the difference in her when he's back. If I was a fool for her, she is a fool for him, always stepping to his tune. A smart man, her lover. Wiser than I ever was."

Puck cleared his throat. "In that case, even as I hesitate to point this out—Jack, are you prepared to meet the man who sired you?"

"We're already met, if only briefly," Jack said tightly. "And all I'll say beyond that is to agree that our mother is a fool."

CHAPTER TWENTY-ONE

"THEY'RE CALLED BOTTLE ovens," Jack said as he and Tess halted at the crest of the low hill and looked down at Stoke-on-Trent, also known simply as The Potteries. "Because needless to say, they resemble nothing more than the tops of enormous brick bottles. These, however, belch black smoke. When the kilns are all firing, it can be difficult to see the sun."

"How fascinating. They're *enormous*. There must be at least one hundred of them. It's as if they've created their own landscape. You've been here before?"

"A time or two, yes, for the Crown. I don't recall a theater, however. Unless that's changed, Adelaide will be taking some sort of makeshift stage in the town square. Adelaide, and the smoke. So much for her grand ambitions."

"It's difficult to understand, I'll grant you. But clearly it's what she lives for. After all, duplicitous or not, she is the Marchioness of Blackthorn. Even if she doesn't care enough for her sons to put things right, I should think she'd acknowledge that fact for her own benefit. There's something we're not seeing, Jack. There has to be. You don't think she— No, that's impossible."

"If you were about to suggest that she joined Andreas from time to time in his exploits, I've already thought of that. What Cyril said the other day is correct. Sometimes she'd be gone for over a year. She may have left the estate with her troupe, but do we really have any way of knowing that she stayed with them? She could have been anywhere, doing anything. She lives for excitement. She feeds on it."

"You said she's quite an accomplished horsewoman. I don't know why, but that surprised me."

"And she's fearless. She plays at the helpless damsel, but she has a will of iron. She's so many different women, Tess, and all of them fairly fascinating. I doubt she even knows who she really is, as her entire life has been one role after another. We were all under her spell, I suppose, but Cyril most of all."

"While she, according to his lordship, has been under the Gypsy's spell. Imagine Sinjon's delight when he met your father, and at some point learned the entire story from Andreas. Of course he'd find some way to use what he knew to keep the Gypsy under his control. *You.*"

Jack nodded his agreement. "Me, yes. There were so many ways he could have used the information he had. In the end, however, he chose only to please himself, watching as father and son confronted each other, me all unknowing."

"Always with another plan," Tess said as they urged their horses forward once more, this time at a walk. "And always the hook at the end of it all. Can you imagine his delight as he complimented you on ridding him of a dangerous enemy, and then announced that, *by the way, that's your father you just killed, Jack, the price you had to pay for leaving my employ.*"

"Christ. It's strange. We called ourselves rogues, Henry and Will and Dickie and I. We thought ourselves to be very bad men, but always for a good reason, always in a good cause. Because we saw evil, in many forms, and in our foolishness thought we knew the game and played it better than anyone else. We saw evil in the pursuit of power, in the name of greed. But never like this, never just evil for evil's sake, just to be *better* than your adversary. And God knows my mother's motives, because they make no sense at all to me. She'll probably tell us she did it all for *love*. Damn, Tess, I want this over."

"I'm simply hoping she's here, and the Gypsy with her. It's nearly noon, Jack. Let's go." Tess tapped her heel against the mare's flank, urging it into a canter.

Jack watched for a moment as she moved ahead of him on the roadway. She was clad in one of the Blackthorn maid's Sunday best, and he was clothed as a laborer, in smock and leggings and a worn slouch hat. They made quite the pair. There were a dozen reasons why he should have insisted she remain at Blackthorn, but it had taken only one to convince him he needed her with him.

At least he would know where she was, because unless he tied her to the bedpost, and even then, she would have found some way to follow him.

Smiling at the thought that she continually believed he needed her protection, he spurred his mount forward.

Ten minutes later he was cursing himself as he realized it must be market day in Stoke-on-Trent, for the center of the town was clogged with wagons, carts, food stalls and too many people to make it easy to locate Andreas if he was somewhere in the crowd gathered in front of a makeshift stage in the very center of the square. There were at least twenty rows of benches set in front of the stage, and the audience was shoulder to shoulder, without a single open spot on any of the benches. It was a far cry from Covent Garden, but Adelaide must be in her glory.

He and Tess left their horses at a small livery stable and continued on foot, keeping to the alleyways as they slowly made their way around the square. Not that Jack expected Andreas to be standing in the open, not if Adelaide had met with him, told him what she'd learned at Blackthorn.

If Cyril was right, she was at least a little bit afraid of her son, his capabilities. She'd feel she had to warn her lover that his son was searching for him. The man had avoided a confrontation at the manor house, would he likewise run from one now? Was he already on horseback and miles away? Would Jack have to content himself for now with convincing Adelaide that it would be in her best interests to tell the truth about her deception that day at the altar, and leave the hunt for Andreas for another day?

Or did Jack's father feel as he did, that the time for running was past now, and there had to be an end to what had begun so many years ago?

Jack slipped his hand inside his waistcoat, to feel the knife tucked there. Could he use it if it came to his life or his father's? Is that why Tess was with him, to take that decision out of his hands? Could she do it, would she dare it?

Andreas, to save himself if cornered, could very well strike at his own son.

The man had murdered her brother.

Yes, she could do it. Which was probably the only reason Jack knew he could do it. He'd killed before, too many times to count. He would not allow her to live out the remainder of her days carrying that sort of memory.

"Damn it," he said quietly as their circular approach at last brought them within earshot of the stage. "They must have begun early. They're already more than half-way through the last act."

Tess had been reading a printed broadsheet nailed to the wall of the tavern. "That's all right. We'll just wait for her to come down from the stage. She is there, isn't she?"

Lifting the slouch hat he'd worn to help conceal his identity, Jack dared to look up at the players. "Yes, she's there. She's taken the role of Beatrice. She looks… beautiful. Damn, she does love it, doesn't she?"

Tess squeezed his arm. "I know this is difficult."

"Difficult. Yes, that's one word to use, I suppose. Come along, Tess. We need to make our way to the side of the stage."

"In a moment. Jack? Aren't Gypsies sometimes called travelers? I'm sure I read that somewhere."

"Hmm?" He'd just noticed that there were a few empty spots on the first row of benches. There were only four people comfortably seated there; two couples, much more elegantly dressed than the majority of the audience. One of the men threw back his head, laughing at one of the lines spoken on stage, and Jack got a clear look at his face. Sir Edward Starkley. Interesting. That had to be his lady wife beside him, and…yes, their lovely blond-haired blue-eyed daughter and her very recently, almost unseemly recently, acquired husband. Rusticating in the country, taking in a play put on by a band of traveling players. Wasn't that lovely.

And interesting.

"Come along, Tess," he said, his mind whirling with possibilities.

"I *said,*" Tess complained, pulling on his arm as he attempted to move away, "aren't Gypsies sometimes called travelers? Because the role of Benedick, according to this broadsheet, is being performed by someone named John *Traveler.* Doesn't that make you wonder?"

"Sonofabitch." She had his attention now. First he read the broadsheet, and then he turned toward the stage. Damn, Benedick wasn't in this scene. But he'd be in the next one.

He took Tess's hand and pulled her into the alleyway.

"Do you think it's him? Do you think he's— Just think for a moment, Jack, he could travel all over the countryside, all over *any* country's countryside, with no one the wiser. Just another traveling troupe of actors. Who pays them any mind?"

"Sonofabitch," he said again. "Adelaide traveled with him, she had to have done. She *knew* what was going on, and probably reveled in it, if she didn't also help him. And Cyril, all unknowing, financed them. All these years…all these years."

"Jack, you can't do this. You can't be angry," Tess warned him as they finally made their way to a place closer to the rear of the stage, the crush of people concealing them. "He's here. That's what you have to think about. As…as for Adelaide? I'll keep her out of your way, don't even think about her, only Andreas. Jack. Do you hear me?"

Jack could barely think. Barely see for the red haze of anger in his eyes. Everything and everyone Adelaide touched was used, even compromised. Abigail, his brothers. Even Cyril. She was a damn pestilence!

"It's all right, Tess," he assured her, the plan he'd already half-formed in his mind when he'd seen Sir Edward and his daughter once more in the forefront of his thinking. It could work.

He'd make it work.

He put his hands on Tess's shoulders. "They're nearing the end of the play. I don't have time to explain, sweetheart. Just be ready to grab her if she attempts to run."

"I can do that. I'll *sit* on her if I have to," she said fervently.

Jack smiled at her fierce expression and then kissed her. Held her for a moment, his world steadying, and then left her to find her way to the opposite side of the stage.

He made his way to the rear of the stage and the caravan closest to it, where he felt certain those actors not needed onstage were congregated, slipping quickly behind a fat farmer holding a cage of chickens as Andreas stepped out of the caravan and stood on the topmost step, adjusting an ornate brocade cape around his shoulders.

"Ah, good sir," he said as he spied the farmer. "Those will do nicely. Ring their necks and deliver them to the innkeeper at The Fox. Tell him my lady and I will repair there in one hour and require a private dining room."

Jack quickly hunched over to disguise his height and turned his back as the farmer ran forward to catch the coins Andreas tossed in his direction before flourishing his cape and bounding toward the wooden steps leading up to the stage. Bare moments later he could hear him speaking his first line. What a flamboyant piece of work—it was very nearly embarrassing to watch him, although he'd probably make a passable Benedick.

Much Ado About Nothing was one of Shakespeare's comedies, involving wronged lovers, confused motives, mistaken identities and one villain, the bastard, Don John. As the villain, he would of course be vanquished at the end and taken off to jail as Beatrice and Benedick celebrated their love.

Jack had never cared for the play, for obvious reasons. He'd been named for the bastard villain. By his own mother. But more than that, as he'd told her when she cajoled him into helping her with her lines, he believed the ending to be less than satisfying, with the capture of Don John taking place off stage. He'd had more of a thirst for violence than Shakespeare's farce had allowed.

But that didn't matter, as he was about to change the ending.

"You," he said, clapping his hand on an actor who

stepped down from the caravan, clearly preparing for his own entrance. "You're the messenger, correct?"

"Unhand me, cur," the man demanded, but quietly, so that his voice wouldn't carry to the stage.

The pressure of Jack's fingers, digging into the man's shoulder, laid emphasis to his next words. "I asked you a question, my good man. Are you performing the role of the messenger?"

"And every other small, meaningless role. What of it? I should be Claudio, but Jeremy, that wretched sorry excuse for a thespian, stepped into the role when John returned."

"Yes, yes, you're sorely used, I can see that." Jack fished a coin from his pocket. "A crown for your hat, your cape and your silence, good sir?"

The actor eyed the coin, and then Jack, who certainly did not look like a man who'd ever seen a gold crown in his lifetime. "Are you mad?"

Voices could clearly be heard from the stage. Time was running short. "There's a strong possibility I am, yes. But I wish to play a small joke on my good friend John. There's no harm in that, is there? And you're richer by a crown."

The man pulled at the lacing holding his cloak around his neck even as Jack removed his hat and tossed it aside. "And my sword? You'll want my small sword."

Jack looked at the wooden sword and shook his head. "Thank you, but not necessary." He snatched the low-brimmed, feathered hat from the actor's head and slapped it on his own before swinging the cape up and over his shoulders. "And now, if you'll excuse me, I believe I'm soon to hear my cue."

The messenger's sole line in the play announced: "My lord, your brother John is taken in flight, and brought with armed men back to Messina." Jack remembered it fairly precisely because he'd waited through the entire reading of the lines for the sword battle that would end with Don John's capture. But then, he could have been no more than twelve, and bloodletting was of great interest to him at that age.

Jack took up his position just at the curtain, concealed from the audience but with a clear sight of the actors on the stage. Beatrice and Benedick stood face-to-face, their hands joined as they declared their love for each other. Jack's stomach turned as he saw the naked adoration in Adelaide's eyes as she recited her lines. It was painful to watch.

"'Peace!'" Andreas interrupted. "'I will stop your mouth.'"

And then he kissed her, and Jack looked away.

There followed a few brief exchanges between Benedick and his fellows, Benedick's final speech, and then at last Andreas declared, "'First, of my word; therefore play, music. Prince, thou art sad; get thee a wife, get thee a wife: there is no staff more reverend than one tipped with horn.'"

That was Jack's cue, but he waited as the silence grew uncomfortable and all the actors on the stage looked to the wings, clearly wondering what had become of the messenger.

"Hark! Did someone say there is a messenger? Enter

a *messenger!*" the actor playing the part of the prince prompted nervously.

Jack didn't move. Now the heretofore slightly bored audience, as well as the actors, were all craning their necks toward the wings. Every eye was open and watching, every ear strained eagerly to hear the next words, including, one could only hope, Sir Edward Starkley.

At last, Jack stepped onto the stage, his head lowered as he bowed and addressed the actor playing the prince. "My lord, I am come here to arrest this man, Benedick, for crimes against the Crown. And his harlot with him."

The prince, a rather portly man with a rapidly reddening face, whispered hoarsely, "What? That's not your line, Chester. Wait! Who…who are you?"

Jack removed his hat, flourishing it as he bowed to his father. But when he straightened, it was with his knife in hand. "You are surrounded. There's no escape. And no mercy, not this time. Understood?"

"Jack!" his mother cried, stepping in front of her lover, her arms widespread as if to protect him with her own body. "What are you doing? You've slipped your wits. You can't possibly—"

"Shut up, Adelaide," the Gypsy warned, swiftly securing her close to his body, the sharp tip of a stiletto pressed to her throat. "You said nothing, you told me. He didn't suspect a thing, you said. Stupid bitch! And yet here he is. More my son than yours, God help me. Pray, Adelaide, that he doesn't care as little for your tiresome self as I do. Jack? What's it to be? I leave with the cow, and then leave her somewhere for you—or you force me to a rash and surely fatal act?"

"Let her go," Jack said quietly. "It would be for nothing."

"Oh, untrue, untrue. Call off your men, Jack, and give me safe passage. You need her to tell the truth. Don't you? *Don't you?*"

A small trickle of blood slid down Adelaide's white throat, and the crowd gasped as one.

"An interesting dilemma. Will you give me a moment to consider the thing?" Jack asked smoothly, even as his heart pounded in his chest. He allowed the tension to build, and then finally shook his head. "No, you're the bigger prize. Do what you want with her."

Adelaide's eyes rolled back in her head as she swooned, to become dead weight in the Gypsy's arms. He staggered slightly, which was all Jack needed, and he was immediately on him, grabbing at his father's knife hand as they both tumbled to the stage.

TESS WATCHED AS Jack and the man she'd heard addressed as Sir Edward spoke quietly in a corner of the taproom of The Fox. The shakes she'd acquired thanks to Jack and his ridiculous act of bravado had finally stopped, and she was actually enjoying the sight of the Gypsy stoutly tied to a chair, a large knot just above his left eye. He and Jack had rolled off the stage as they'd struggled for possession of the knife, dropping directly in front of Sir Edward, who had neatly conked the Gypsy over the head with his gold-topped cane.

The crowd had cheered wildly, and Tess wondered how many of them had never witnessed a Shakespearean play, and believed the finale to be of a piece with the rest of it.

And while thinking of pieces, she mused meanly, looking over to where Adelaide sat, weeping into her handkerchief. Her throat had been bandaged and Jack had secured her a glass of wine she'd accepted gracefully. She'd then stood up and walked over to her lover, and dashed the entire contents of the glass in his face.

If Tess didn't despise the woman, she would have applauded her.

At the moment, however, she longed to know what Jack and Sir Edward were talking about so congenially, and was even more amazed when the two men shook hands before Jack approached her and sat down, winking at her.

"Did I ever mention that I dislike you smug? Almost as much as I dislike being left to do nothing more than watch while you risk your life. That was the most ridiculous thing I ever witnessed. Telling the man he could kill her if he wanted, as if she was of no matter to you."

"I thought it was a very good line. Shakespeare missed out on that one, didn't he? A much better ending to his farce, I'd say. By the way, when you and the ladies were having your coze, did Regina happen to mention her small adventure of few months ago?"

Tess frowned. "Are you talking about how her cousin was abducted by slavers? That was dreadful. But what does that have to do with what's happening now?"

"Blonde, blue-eyed virgins, young ladies of quality, as is Regina's cousin, were being abducted, to be taken abroad and sold, and it has everything to do with what's happening now. You did see his daughter before her mother and husband took her away, didn't you?"

Tess's eyes went wide. "She...she was one of those women?"

"I would never say that, and you would never have heard it. She's been married off to her second cousin, and is reportedly happy, at least her father believes so. Sir Edward was most grateful to me when his daughter was returned to him safely, and he's delighted to be of any assistance I might ever need. In thanks, you understand."

"Indeed," Tess said, attempting a discreet glance in Sir Edward's direction. "And did you suggest a way he could do that?"

"We've come up with an idea as to how that might be accomplished, yes," Jack said, and Tess was torn between wanting to hug him or boxing his ears for his clear delight in the moment. He, too, turned to look at Sir Edward, who was now standing halfway between Adelaide and Andreas. "Ah, and we begin. Now to pray this works."

Sir Edward resembled nothing less than a pouty pigeon as he stood on the rough boards of the taproom floor, his feet spread, his hands behind his back.

"Allow me to introduce myself," he intoned gravely, his deep voice not quite fitting his stature, but definitively forceful, authoritative. "I am Sir Edward Starkley, which means little to you, I'm sure, save to say that I was great chums with his royal highness the Duke of Norfolk while at school. A friendship that continues to this day. Indeed, his royal highness did my family the great honor of standing as godfather for my only daughter. In other words, and not to refine too much on the thing, I hold a certain *influence* in some quarters."

Tess coughed into her fist, fairly certain she already knew where this small speech might lead. Sir Edward didn't disappoint her.

"Now, this young rapscallion here has sung me quite a tale, one, for good reason, I am inclined to believe. You, sir, will be transported to London, to answer for your crimes, most likely via a rope or at the hands of a firing squad. No problem there, as far as I can see, if half of what this boy said is true. At the very least, you will be made to pay for the murder of one René Fonteneau, Vicomte de Vaucluse."

Andreas glared at the man and said nothing.

Sir Edward shifted his stance, and his attention, to Adelaide. "I don't propose to assert that I know all the ins and outs of current law, madam, but it may be possible to save you from the hangman if you cooperate with the authorities, which I highly suggest you do."

"What!" Adelaide leapt to her feet. *"Me? Hang?"*

Sir Edward cleared his throat. "This gentleman, an official of the Crown, asserts that you, er, acted in consort with the prisoner here, committing serious crimes against that same Crown. In varying degrees of seriousness, and over a lengthy period of time. Therefore, much as it pains me, you, with your companion, will be put in chains, and also transported to London, at least until everything is sorted out. I see no other choice."

Adelaide whirled about to face her son. "Jack! How could you do this?"

"Do you deny that you have traveled with this man?" Jack asked her. "Remembering before you speak that I am, that is, I have incontrovertible proof of that fact."

"Andreas?" she begged, turning to the Gypsy. "Tell them. For the love of heaven, tell them! I'm *innocent* of any wrongdoing."

Jack's father looked at her and smiled. "On the contrary, Adelaide. You've never been innocent. Of anything, save any claim of intelligence. You do realize that I would not be in my current dire straits were it not for you? You swore he wouldn't follow you, remember? My sin is to have believed you."

"But...but you love me!"

Andreas looked to Jack. "She *thinks* I love her. I always warned her. She has her attributes, God knows. Her interesting talents. But I told her, never think, Adelaide, it's not your forte."

There was a knock at the door, and the innkeeper entered, carrying a length of rope. "All I could find, Sir Edward," he said. "For the woman, right?"

"No!" Adelaide shouted as she ran to Jack, frantically pawing at his chest. "You can't do this. You can't let this happen. He says he has *influence.* You heard him. Tell him. *Tell him!*"

Jack took hold of her hands, removing them from his chest. "Tell him what, madam?" he said coldly.

Adelaide's breath caught on a sob. "Who I *am.* I can't be arrested. I can't hang. Tell him I'm innocent. Tell him who I am."

"No," Jack said as Tess held her breath, worrying that he may have gone too far, but quickly realizing that

Adelaide had to say the words, Sir Edward had to hear her admission from her own mouth. "If Sir Edward is to testify on your behalf, you have to tell him."

It was strange. Until that very moment, even while laboring under considerable duress, Adelaide had been a beautiful woman. But now, suddenly, she was ugly. "I know what you're doing," she gritted out in a harsh whisper. "You want that man over there as witness. For them. You'd sacrifice me for them. Your own mother, *for them.* I *held* him, all those years, I held him by refusing to give him what he wanted. He would have tossed me aside again, the way he did for my half-witted sister. How *dared* he choose her over me? Did he really think I'd give him anything he wanted? I loathe him, I've always loathed him. Let his sons be bastards, let him suffer, go to his grave knowing how he'd wronged them."

"You terrible, terrible woman," Tess told her. "They're your sons, as well."

Adelaide glared at Tess for a moment, clearly not understanding her vehemence, before turning back to Jack, her desperation obvious. "If I give you what you want, you'll tell them? Jack? Whatever I did with Andreas, it was innocent, I swear to you. A game of sorts. We traveled all over Europe. We never really harmed anyone, it was just for the money. They didn't need so many baubles, did they? I saw Napoleon, Jack. And the tsar. I *danced* with the tsar, and he told me I was beautiful. Can you imagine? I didn't know it could end like this. I never *killed* anyone. It was all just a lark, and so exciting. Cyril would never give me any of that, what I needed so much. You understand, don't you? I had to feel *alive*. You can't let me hang."

"I'll help you, Mother," Jack agreed, a small tic working in his cheek. "Now tell him."

Adelaide drew herself up, brushing at her costume, patting at her hair. She smiled, and suddenly she was beautiful again as she turned to Sir Edward. "I would ask a boon, good sir, that you contact his lordship, my husband, who I am sure will vouchsafe for my innocence and put an end to this ridiculous misunderstanding."

"His lordship, madam?" Sir Edward responded. "I don't understand. You're an actress, are you not?"

Adelaide looked anxiously over her shoulder to Jack, who only nodded.

"Indeed, sir, that is incorrect," she then told Sir Edward, dropping into an elegant curtsy. "You have the pleasure, my good man, of being in the presence of the Marchioness of Blackthorn."

EPILOGUE

"THANK YOU, ROBERTS," Jack said as the butler handed over the mail pouch. "Ah, heavy today."

"Yes, sir," Roberts answered, bowing. "Some of it all the way from England. Perhaps with good news, Mr. Blackthorn?"

"Perhaps." Jack refused to hope. Lately, the news from England had been encouraging, but it had been encouraging before, with little result. He pushed his chair back from the desk, taking up the pouch as he headed for the large French doors that looked out over the James River.

He stepped onto the brick terrace, taking a moment to admire the vista that unfolded in front of him. He never tired of the view, no matter the season. He was grateful for it, and for the home he and Tess had made here in Virginia. But it wasn't England.

Six years. A lifetime; a moment.

They were happy here, he and Tess. Their daughters, Lucie and Marianne, had been born here. He'd taken to gentleman farming with the enthusiasm Puck had promised him he'd feel, and the estate had shown a profit every year.

But it wasn't England.

He ran Tess to ground in the herb garden, down on

her knees, weeding. She was a tyrant when it came to her gardens. It wasn't for her to stand posing with a basket while a servant cut the blooms for her. Not his Tess. She'd never done anything by half measures.

"The mail pouch arrived. It would appear there's something from England," he announced, and then smiled as she quickly scrambled to her feet and reached for the pouch. "You might want to first remove those gloves, darling. Are you sure you don't come out here after a rain in order to make mud pies?"

She quickly stripped off her gloves and made a second, this time successful grab for the pouch. "I've told you, the weeds surrender to me much more easily when the ground is soft and moist." She then grinned. "But I do like mud pies. Come sit with me while we see what's in here. Unless you've already looked?"

He made himself comfortable beside her on the bench. "After you made me promise never to look at any letters from England unless we opened them together? I'm not so brave."

"Only because no one should receive bad news alone. Or good news, for that matter." She reached inside the pouch and pulled out a wrapped package that was suspiciously the size of a book. "Probably another learned tome from Puck about contoured plowing or the joys of calving, begging your permission to allow him to implement one or both on our estate in your absence," she said, and put it aside, unopened, before reaching into the pouch once more. "Oh, and this one is from Beau. It's not very thick, is it? He usually writes two sheets, and then Chelsea adds another." She thrust it toward Jack. "Here, you open it."

"First a kiss," he said, leaning toward her. "For luck."

She smelled of spring, and sun, and freshly turned earth. She tasted of honey, so that he knew she'd made a trip to the beekeeper's hut, to indulge herself with some honey fresh on the comb. Could she be with child again? She'd always craved sweet things when she was pregnant.

"I love you," she told him, resting her forehead against his shoulder for a moment after the kiss, before looking up into his eyes. "We've a good life here, Jack. We've got our son, our daughters, we have each other."

"I can think of nothing we lack. Although," he added, trying to ignore the letter in his hand, "the idea of adjourning to our bedchamber holds some appeal."

"It always does," she said, laughing. "But we've probably delayed the moment all that we can. Open Beau's letter. Regina's child should have been born by now. You remember what she told me in her last letter, that she so envies me our daughters. She feels totally outnumbered by Puck and those sons of hers, which is the same as to say she has *three* sons. I adore the way they tease each other."

"*They* adore the way they tease each other. Just as Beau and Chelsea enjoy arguing with each other, with both of them saying they let the other one win."

"So they can *apologize* to each other," Tess pointed out knowingly, and then sighed as she looked down at the letter. "Six years, Jack. It has been so long."

Lord Liverpool had expressed delight in the capture

of the Gypsy. He'd commended Jack on his success, and smiled broadly as he'd agreed to release him from any further service to the Crown. He'd shaken his hand, even patted him on the back as he'd walked with him to the doorway of his office, and only at the last moment casually inquired as to his plans for the future, where he would live, how he would support himself. Such kindly interest from a man who wasn't known for being kindly, but only *interested*. Fools might think the man bumbling and ineffectual, but Jack knew differently.

Jack and Tess had married in the estate chapel three days later; he'd gracefully—with Tess there to convince him that it would please the marquess—accepted the deed to an estate just east of Swanbourne and then sailed from Portsmouth without ever setting foot on that estate, Jack carrying a letter from the marquess, installing him as his representative concerning his lordship's property along the James River.

They hadn't been in England the day the Gypsy had gone to the hangman. They'd only heard through Beau's letter that the marquess had settled an allowance on Adelaide, dependent on her promise to leave England and never return, and only through Chelsea's letter that Jack's mother had died. They'd had no part in the marquess's continuing struggle to have his sons declared legitimate.

They were a world away, together, building their life together. But on days like today, when the letters arrived…

"I suppose you're right, we can't put this off any

longer," Jack said as he broke the seal, unfolded the single sheet. There was no salutation.

Chelsea said you wouldn't mind such brevity, as she insists I don't miss the post. Firstly, Regina was safely delivered of a son last week, a fine, healthy boy, although, sadly, much resembling Puck. Ah, excuse the ink blot, which is entirely the fault of my lady wife, who is peering over my shoulder, suggesting what I should write, and clearly having taken umbrage over what I have written.

And yes, I did write lady wife. She still giggles when she thinks of her family's reaction, knowing they will one day be forced to curtsy to her. Regina is much more subdued, but Puck has more than made up for her calm acceptance. I believe he thinks London society has been deprived of his delightful presence long enough, and is already planning a remove to Grosvenor Square next year for the Season, never doubting his acceptance by the *ton*. I don't doubt it, either.

At any rate, you must know by now that Papa's efforts have at long last borne fruit. Difficult as this is to believe, after so much time and so many disappointments, the last hurdle has been cleared. As you know, the Church accepted Papa's petition two years ago, but he was never able to successfully bring the matter before the government until now.

So my congratulations to you, and to all of us.

Miraculously, by the stroke of some official pen somewhere, we are no longer bastards, but declared Peers of the Realm. Jack, Liverpool can't touch you now, and he'd be a fool to try. He's mellowed, clearly, and his reshuffled Tory Cabinet has assured his power for years to come. Frankly, Jack, you're no longer worth his bother.

And now my dearest wife, in her always gracious way, is demanding I end this. Papa sends his best to you and Tess, and his hope you will know what he wishes.

As do we all,
Beau

Jack lowered the letter to his lap and looked at Tess. She was crying, huge tears running down her cheeks.

He put his arm around her, drew her close. There was so much he wanted to say to her. To thank her for her love, her belief in him when he couldn't believe in himself, her willingness to join her life with his. For his son, for his two precious daughters, for helping him realize the true meaning of *family*.

When he could finally speak, he said it all, everything that was in his heart, in three simple words. "We're going home."

* * * * *

REQUEST YOUR FREE BOOKS!

2 FREE NOVELS
FROM THE ROMANCE COLLECTION
PLUS 2 FREE GIFTS!

YES! Please send me 2 FREE novels from the Romance Collection and my 2 FREE gifts (gifts are worth about $10). After receiving them, if I don't wish to receive any more books, I can return the shipping statement marked "cancel." If I don't cancel, I will receive 4 brand-new novels every month and be billed just $5.99 per book in the U.S. or $6.49 per book in Canada. That's a saving of at least 25% off the cover price. It's quite a bargain! Shipping and handling is just 50¢ per book in the U.S. and 75¢ per book in Canada.* I understand that accepting the 2 free books and gifts places me under no obligation to buy anything. I can always return a shipment and cancel at any time. Even if I never buy another book, the two free books and gifts are mine to keep forever.

194/394 MDN FELQ

Name _____

(PLEASE PRINT)

Address _____ Apt. #

City _____ State/Prov. _____ Zip/Postal Code

Signature (if under 18, a parent or guardian must sign)

Mail to the **Reader Service**:
IN U.S.A.: P.O. Box 1867, Buffalo, NY 14240-1867
IN CANADA: P.O. Box 609, Fort Erie, Ontario L2A 5X3

Not valid for current subscribers to the Romance Collection
or the Romance/Suspense Collection.

Want to try two free books from another line?
Call 1-800-873-8635 or visit www.ReaderService.com.

* Terms and prices subject to change without notice. Prices do not include applicable taxes. Sales tax applicable in N.Y. Canadian residents will be charged applicable taxes. Offer not valid in Quebec. This offer is limited to one order per household. All orders subject to credit approval. Credit or debit balances in a customer's account(s) may be offset by any other outstanding balance owed by or to the customer. Please allow 4 to 6 weeks for delivery. Offer available while quantities last.

Your Privacy—The Reader Service is committed to protecting your privacy. Our Privacy Policy is available online at www.ReaderService.com or upon request from the Reader Service.

We make a portion of our mailing list available to reputable third parties that offer products we believe may interest you. If you prefer that we not exchange your name with third parties, or if you wish to clarify or modify your communication preferences, please visit us at www.ReaderService.com/consumerschoice or write to us at Reader Service Preference Service, P.O. Box 9062, Buffalo, NY 14269. Include your complete name and address.